The groom kissed her perfunctorily, and they moved on to sign the register. Having somehow contrived to write her name, Lisette heard a sudden muffled snort beside her. What was he doing now? Surely he did not mean to disgrace them all.

She glanced up in dismay. Strand took the quill from her hand, grinned, and winked at her. Bewildered, she looked down again and thought an appalled, My heaven! How could I have done so stupid a thing? But—there it was. Instead of "Lisette Hermoine" she had written "Lisette Heroine"! She could have sunk, and felt her face burn.

Strand pulled her hand possessively through his arm. "What a slip!" he chuckled. "Or did you mean it?"

Facing the assembled throng, she smiled sweetly and whispered, "But of course! I deserve a medal, do not you think?"

"A small one, perhaps," he quipped. "But—you will likely earn a large one . . . as we go along."

Fawcett Books
by Patricia Veryan

LOVE'S DUET
THE LORD AND THE GYPSY
MISTRESS OF WILLOWVALE
SOME BRIEF FOLLY

MARRIED PAST REDEMPTION

PATRICIA VERYAN

FAWCETT CREST • NEW YORK

A Fawcett Crest Book
Published by Ballantine Books

Library of Congress Catalog Card Number: 82-17019

ISBN 0-449-20336-0

This edition published by arrangement with St. Martin's Press

Manufactured in the United States of America

First Ballantine Books Edition: April 1984

For Gladys McC.

"I am to be married within these three days, married past redemption."

JOHN DRYDEN

Chapter 1

The front steps of the house on Portland Place were of marble and, whatever the vagaries of London's weather, were kept immaculate. The front door, very tall and topped by a pediment, was flanked by stained-glass windows and boasted a brass doorknob so highly polished it seemed to puff itself out with its own consequence and sneer at any hand presuming to encircle it. The windows sparkled, the lace curtains were like snow, the iron railings protecting the steps leading down to the areaway were black and glossy, and the entire exterior exuded quiet and well-mannered affluence. So, to a point, did the interior. The ground floor rooms were gracious and the main drawing room, located on the first floor, was large and most elegant. Nor could any fault be found with the music room and three guest bedrooms, all most nicely appointed. Only the parlour, wherein family gatherings took place, showed signs of becoming shabby, although it was still a quite comfortable room.

Deterioration was more noticeable on the second floor. The bedchambers and connecting private parlour of Mr. Humphrey Van Lindsay and his wife Philippa overlooked the street and were a very good size, but more than a suspicion of wear was manifested in fading bedcurtains and carpets inclining to the threadbare. Here also were the three bedrooms of the children. As thirteen years divided the sons of the house, Timothy had shared the bedchamber only on the occasions when he came down

• 1

from University. These past five years he had been building himself a fine record with his Regiment and was now in France with the Army of Occupation. Norman, aged sixteen, was thus left in sole possession of the room, a circumstance he extolled publicly and privately despised. From early childhood the eldest Van Lindsay daughter had required a private bedchamber (this demand resulting in a marked lack of opposition from her two sisters), but three years ago, in June of 1813, Beatrice had married Sir William Dwyer, whereby Lisette and Judith now also had rooms to themselves. In marked contrast to the elegance of the lower regions, however, these bedchambers were far from luxurious, the furniture being sadly past the stage at which reupholstering or repairs would have redeemed it, the carpets downright tattered, and the apartments spared from being dismal only by the inventive young minds of their occupants.

The top floor contained the schoolroom and the servants' quarters and was, to judge from the occasional pithy remarks of the housekeeper and cook, *decidedly* dismal.

On a rainy afternoon in early April, the large house was unusually quiet. Mr. Van Lindsay was in his study writing a speech to be delivered in the House of Commons, of which august body he was a Member of long standing; Mrs. Van Lindsay was laid down upon her bed, resting; Judith was at her dancing lesson, and a sulky Norman was exasperating his tutor by attempting to explain both his execrable failures in Latin and his conviction that not even when he reached the ripe old age of eighteen would he be able to pass Smalls. In the rear corner bedroom, Lisette Van Lindsay sat alone, head bowed as she ostensibly mended a lace tablecloth. Thick hair of a very dark brown, styled in one of the new shorter cuts, accentuated the beautiful shape of her head, which remained down-bent until a gust of wind drove raindrops in a busy pattering at the windowpanes. Lisette looked up then, revealing a heart-shaped face blessed with a clear, creamy complexion, a straight nose with just the suggestion of an upward tilt, and a full-lipped mouth, just now tragically drooping above a firm little chin. The grey skies outside were no greyer than the hue of Miss Van Lindsay's world; the raindrops no damper than the tears that fell with distressing frequency from great eyes, near-black, to wet her rather uneven stitches. At the advanced age of one and twenty her future stretched out bleak and hopeless; a spinster's existence. For she would, she thought grievously, never wed. Not now that she had been spurned, tossed aside like—

"Lisette! Lisette! Are you in there?"

An impatient scratching at the door accompanied that urgent enquiry, and the tablecloth was brought into play to dab hurriedly at the tearful eyes that then blinked down at the stitch to be set. "Come in," Lisette invited rather belatedly as the door burst open.

Judith Van Lindsay, a plump and tomboyish fourteen, exploded into the room, her long pigtails flying. "Only guess who I just saw!" she cried. "Only guess! You'll *never* guess!"

Bending to examine her stitchery—and conceal her somewhat reddened eyes—Lisette guessed dutifully, "The Duke of Wellington?"

Judith's round face sank. With a regretful sigh she admitted that her hero had not been the one observed, but then, her own dark eyes bright with importance, she divulged, "That dreadful Rachel Strand woman! She was with her brother—or at least Elinor *said* it was her brother. And I thought she was not so spectacular as everyone says. She's not near as pretty as you, and why that stupid Tristram Leith should have chose *her* is more than I—or Elinor either—could fathom! Oh, now I have made you prick your finger!"

"No, no," Lisette reassured. And thus provided with an excuse to look strained, as she knew she must, corrected, "The lady is now Mrs. Leith, Judith. Not Rachel Strand."

"And not a lady," Judith said pertly. Her sister's frown caused her to hurry on. "But do you not think her daring to venture into Town with her *shocking* reputation? I could scarce credit it. And you would never *think* her a notorious woman, for she is angelically fair—" She broke off to add loyally, "but nowhere *near* as pretty as you!" In need of sustenance after all this excitement, Judith then bounced onto the bed and produced from her reticule a sticky glob from which she began with great concentration to remove some much wrinkled and not too clean paper.

Such a procedure would normally have ensured her immediate banishment, but watching her ebullient sister unseeingly, Lisette murmured, "So she really *is* a beauty."

"In a blond way, I suppose." Judith licked her treasure happily and went on, whenever her tongue was not otherwise employed, "She must have all the looks . . . in the family, for I heard Mama telling Papa that her sister . . . Charity, is a plain little dab of a thing."

Attempting to be objective, Lisette set another stitch and remarked that she'd heard Charity Strand did not enjoy good health. "Have you seen her, also?"

"No. But I saw the brother, and *he* certainly could not be said to be even slightly handsome. Oh, he's a good pair of shoulders, were they not so bony, and straight legs, but—"

"Judith!"

The bold young miss giggled. "Well, he has. But he is so *thin*, Lisette! And his face is *brown*, which makes his eyes look positive weird!" She licked again, then paused, her mood changing as she observed, "Poor soul. I know how he must feel. Look at me. Fat and plain. And this hair!" She gave one thick rope a deprecatory tug, then pulled a face as her fingers adhered to the long strands.

Lisette groaned in exasperation and went to the washstand. Wetting a cloth, she returned and handed it to her sister. "If you would not eat so many sweets, Judith, you'd likely put off some of those extra inches. But it is just puppy fat, after all. I suppose by the time you reach fifteen you will be slim, if only you are a little more careful. Now give me that horrid stuff."

Relinquishing her prize with a martyred sigh, Judith dabbed at her fingers and mourned, "Even if I do manage to become thinner in the next year, I shall never have your looks, dearest. You could have wed any bachelor in London, and you know it, had you not set your cap for—"

"What fustian!" Lisette intervened hastily. "I shall never marry, because I do not wish to be wed." With a prideful tilt of the chin, she added a reinforcing, "I am much too modern to submit to a man's will! And—and as for Leith"—oh, how hard it was to say his name!—"only think what a narrow escape I had, for he must have very little sense of family obligation or pride to wed into so unacceptable a house. Indeed, my heart quite goes out to his poor father for—"

"Not—*marry?*" gasped Judith, who had been momentarily struck dumb. "But, Lisette, you *must* marry! Papa told Timothy we are pinning all our hopes on your making a brilliant match. And with *your* looks. . . . Only recall that fellow who kept writing those odes to your eyes.'' She gave a squeak of laughter. ''Remember the one that went: 'Great eyes that glow like dusky pansies . . .'?''

''Yes.'' Lisette sat on the bed and giggled. ''And as though that were not bad enough, he finished it with, 'Despair to every hope of man's is!' Dreadful!'' Briefly, they both succumbed to mirth. Still smiling, Lisette asked, ''How do you know that Papa told Timothy I was the hope of the family? Did Tim tell you?''

''No. It was in a letter Papa was writing. I saw it when I was sent to his study to be punished for putting water in the bottle with Norman's silly model ship.''

''Judith!'' gasped Lisette, much shocked. ''You never did?''

Judith's chin set mulishly. ''Well, he will never finish it, and it was all droopy on one side at all events!'' She brightened to a redeeming notion. ''Now he can say it sank!''

''I didn't mean that. You *read* Papa's letter? That is dishonourable!''

To receive such a scold from the sister she both adored and admired, and to realize the justification for that rebuke, was crushing. Her face reddening, Judith said defiantly, ''Well—well, look at what *you're* doing! Darning that old thing! Mama would be properly in the boughs did she see you.''

''I know, but someone must do the mending, and Mrs. Helm is always saying she has not the time because she is so short of maids. Poor Sandy has her hands full, trying to take care of Mama and me. So who else is to do it?''

''There would not be so much to be done if Mama did not persist in using lace tablecloths. Someday she will have to admit we are poor, instead of forever pretending we are better than everyone else.''

The criticism was well based, but stifling a sigh, Lisette said, ''You must not forget, dear, that we are of a very old house. Mama is proud of being a Bayes-Copeland. And Papa—''

''Papa is proud of Mama, and tells his cronies that 'Poor Norman' could not go to Eton because he is too frail. Frail! The great monster is sturdy as any bull, and had we the ready, would have been—'' She broke off with a guilty start as the door opened to admit her mother's regal figure.

Mrs. Van Lindsay swept into the room with a shushing of silks and a breath of expensive perfume. In her youth, Philippa Van Lindsay had been a great beauty. At seven and forty, she was still a handsome woman. She had long ago determined she would never allow herself to become a fat and indolent matron, with the result that she was, if anything, rather too angular, but she had a clear skin, the luxuriant dark hair that marked all her children, and the same big, dark eyes that enhanced Lisette's lovely face. "So you are back, Judith," she observed redundantly. "Did you get your feet wet?"

Judith, who had sprung up respectfully, now replied in the rather scared voice she invariably adopted towards her parent that she was perfectly dry, thank you.

"Well, I must say your lessons seem to become shorter and shorter. I would by far prefer that you go to Madame Coutrain. Your cousin Matthilde moves with such grace, and I am assured it is only thanks to the Coutrain woman, for her mama was of most indifferent upbringing. However, your grandmama *would* have Alexis is more the thing, so . . . Well, that is neither here nor there." She folded her hands, her eyes slightly frowning as she reflected that since her mother was paying for the lessons, there was little she could do about it. That vexed gaze came to rest on the lace tablecloth that Judith's plump form did not quite conceal. Her frown deepening, she demanded, "Lisette, whatever are you about?" and, seizing the tablecloth without waiting for a response, eyed the hanging thread and needle with disapprobation. "How many *times* have I told you, child? You are *not* a seamstress!"

Lisette, having also come to her feet, said anxiously, "No, but someone must mend them, Mama, and we do not have a seamstress or anyone who—"

She quailed into silence, for her mother's fine eyes held a formidable flash as they rested upon her. "We may not, just at the present," admitted Mrs. Van Lindsay in a voice of ice, "be enabled to procure such servants as we would wish. We are, nonetheless, of such consequence as would forbid us to engage in menial tasks. If you have no sense of your own pride, Lisette, you might do me the courtesy to consider mine!"

"Y-yours, Mama?"

"Mine! How bitterly humiliated I would be did the servants

spread the news that one for whom we had once entertained such brilliant hopes was reduced to spoiling her pretty fingers by hours of drudgery.''

Lisette lowered her lashes to conceal the tears that, these days, sprang to her eyes so readily. Judith saw the painful flush that stained her idol's cheeks and, with unprecedented courage, proclaimed, "Lisette *still* has brilliant hopes, Mama! She may be one and twenty, but she is quite the prettiest girl in all London, and has lots of beaux! You should only see how the gentlemen stare when we walk out. She'll likely find a far better catch than that old Tristram Leith! And who wants him, anyway, with his face all scarred as it is since Waterloo.''

For a moment there was an awful silence, Mrs. Van Lindsay regarding her youngest child in outraged disbelief; Lisette, pale and awestruck, gazing at her sister, and Judith, aghast at her own daring, now suddenly all great eyes and terror, so that for the first time her mama was brought to the realization that her youngest was beginning to show signs of the family looks. Slightly mollified by that hopeful thought, she demanded, "Open your mouth at once, Miss Insolence!''

Trembling, Judith obeyed.

Mrs. Van Lindsay peered inside and drew back with an exclamation of disgust. "Purple! Good God! Are you run quite mad? On top of having the temerity to address your mother with all the abandon of a *bourgeoisie,* you must stuff your stomach with rubbish! Do not *ever* let me discover you to have been so thoughtless again! If you start throwing out as many spots as a dog has fleas, your poor parents will very likely find themselves with *another* daughter they cannot fire off, year after year!''

At this dreadful denunciation, Judith burst into tears, and Lisette found it necessary to turn away, a hand pressed to her mouth. Mrs. Van Lindsay advised Judith to repair to her own room at once where she could entertain herself by writing, "I will not Curdle my Insides with Rubbish" two hundred times.

Judith fled, shattered. When the door closed behind her, Mrs. Van Lindsay crossed to put a consoling arm about Lisette's shoulders and draw her down beside her on the bed. Kindness was the one quality well calculated to break the floodgates, and Lisette's grief overflowed. Holding her through the storm and in her dignified fashion attempting to comfort her, Mrs. Van Lindsay at length drew a handkerchief from her pocket and began gently to dry the wet cheeks. "Hush now, child," she said. "I comprehend that your affections were deeply engaged. How wretched of Leith to jilt you! And of all people, for that disgusting Strand woman! Quite insupportable. I wonder if Timothy should come home and call him out."

"Oh, no—no, Mama!" quavered Lisette. "Truly, there was never anything between Colonel Leith and me, save . . . save friendship. Only—after Mia Buchanan married Hawkhurst, he seemed to—to turn to me. And I did hope"—A sob hiccuped again, and she could not go on.

"It was a sad disappointment, for I'll own I myself had fancied Leith's attentions fixed on you. Although, whatever he has done, he is very much the gentleman and he never did address your father in the matter, so I suppose— Had he not been recalled to active duty for that wretched Waterloo— Still, there are plenty more eligible bachelors in town, and you are an uncommonly fine-looking girl, you know."

Deeply grateful for so rare a display of affection, Lisette stammered out her thanks. "I cannot tell you, Mama, how—how sorry I am to have brought you such disappointment. D-does Papa hope—I mean—is it *vital* that I marry well?"

Mrs. Van Lindsay did not immediately answer. After her fashion she was fond of both her husband and her daughter and, despite a rather vexed feeling they both had failed her, had no wish to hurt either. "I am persuaded you must be aware, child," she said slowly, "that our finest families are not necessarily those blessed with great wealth."

"Oh, Mama! Are we *quite* in the basket?"

Shocked, her mother cried, "There is scarce the need for such crude expressions! If you mean to suggest that our financial situation is—er—not good"—she sighed, her shoulders drooped suddenly, and she muttered in distracted tones—"you would be quite correct. Our situation is near desperate—I'll not dissemble. Never in my youth did I dream that a Bayes-Copeland could come to such straits. How much longer we can continue to keep up this house and pay the servants, I dare not guess. Norman *must* go to University. And Timothy should have bought his promotion long ago. . . ."

Horrified by this display, Lisette was emboldened to clasp her mother's clawlike hand. "Oh, poor Mama! How dreadful for you. I do not wish to marry, but if anyone acceptable should offer, I hope I know my duty to my family."

"Good girl." Mrs. Van Lindsay squeezed her daughter's fingers briefly, pulled back her shoulders, and stood. "But we must not allow ourselves to be maudlin over the matter. We shall come about, I am assured. As a matter of fact, there is someone—" She closed her lips over the rest of that rather premature remark and turned to the door. "No more darning, child." With her hand on the doorknob she added, "If you feel you must sew, however, the flounce on my magenta silk evening gown is quite sadly torn, and—" She had opened the door and now stopped, one hand flung aloft, her head tilted, birdlike, as she listened intently. "Your papa is at his pacing again! He must have finished his speech and will be practicing it on Powers. Oh! My poor carpets!" and with a flash of skirts she was gone.

Lisette smiled faintly as she envisioned the scene in the drawing room when her volatile Papa was caught at his depredations once more. Her smile soon faded, however. "As a matter of fact, there is someone—" Whatever had Mama been about to say?

Lisette awoke to the sounds of strife. She pushed back the faded bedcurtains and was blinded by early morning sunlight. She thought, A nice day, thank goodness, and stepped into her furred slippers. Another rageful shriek, followed by shouts of boyish laughter, rent the air. Judith and Norman. Again! Lisette hurried into the hall casting a fearful glance towards the front of the house, but as yet the doors to the front bedchambers remained tightly closed.

His cherubic face alight with mirth and mischief, Norman shot past her and began to pound down the stairs. Lisette leaned over the railing and hissed, "What have you done?" then jumped aside, a shoe barely missing her as it hurtled after her brother's retreating form.

Judith, armed with another shoe and a slipper, launched them one after the other, while screaming animadversions upon her brother's character. Her zeal and indignation were dimmed only by the arrival on the scene of Mrs. Van Lindsay, clad in cap and wrapper, whose demands for an explanation of "this disgraceful behaviour'' were echoed by her life's companion, who hove into view wearing a bright red dressing gown and with his thinning brown hair all on end—as Judith later giggled to Lisette—''like the bristles of a worn brush.''

To be rudely awakened for any cause upset Humphrey Van Lindsay, and to be rudely awakened before nine o'clock in the morning had thrown him into a passion. He was a large man with a larger voice, given to making hasty judgments and adhering to them with bulldog tenacity, so that there were many who considered him to merit a brilliant future in politics. There were others, of course, who considered him to be a loud-mouthed idiot and an intolerable snob. The latter charge, at least, was justified. Humphrey was almost as conscious of social position as was his spouse and considered that in wedding Philippa Bayes-Copeland he had pulled off the coup of the century (an opinion she shared). She was the only person who could manoeuvre him, which she did with firmness and regularity, and being well suited they enjoyed a reasonably happy marriage, despite their precarious monetary situation. There was little evidence of connubial bliss at the moment, however, for between Mrs. Van Lindsay's strident demands for an explanation, Judith's decision that her safest course was to launch into hysterics, and Humphrey's bellowing rage, the scene more nearly resembled bedlam.

Experienced in such fiascos, Lisette said two magical words: ''The servants!'' At once, the elder Van Lindsays stifled their rancour. They all adjourned to Judith's bedroom and closed the door.

''Will you stop, Judith?'' Philippa enquired. ''Or must I slap you?''

Thus appealed to, Judith lowered her shrieks a few decibels to spasmodic sobs, between which she opined that her brother was a hideous brute, a sadistic savage, and the greatest beast in nature. ''Look,'' she wept, holding up a much folded piece of tissue paper. ''Only look what he d-did! It is a pattern of Ruth MacKay's new party dress. Elinor copied it for me, and—and Norman met her last evening and p-prom-promised to give it me. But—look! *Look!*''

Snorting his wrath, her sire opened the pattern. This took a few minutes and seemed to involve an inordinate amount of paper. ''Good . . . gad!'' he breathed, holding up what must only be a garment for a giant. "Surely, this is the wrong size, Judith?"

His daughter uttered a new shriek of rageful chagrin and cast herself on the bed. Over her recumbent form, the eyes of her sister and her mama met, alight with guilty laughter. Recovering herself, Philippa snatched the paper from her spouse's hands. "Of course it is not her size, Mr. Van Linsday!"

Humphrey had seen the twinkle in her eyes, and mirth crept into his own.

"Er—oh!" he said. "I see the light. Copied it, did he?"

"And enlarged it, Papa," Lisette nodded, stroking her sister's tangled hair comfortingly.

"Yes. I can—ah, tell he's spread it out a bit," he chortled.

"By a good four sizes!" said Mrs. Van Lindsay.

"Four!" howled the maligned Judith. "*Forty,* more like! I am *not* that fat, Papa! I am *not!*"

"Norman," said Mrs. Van Lindsay sternly, "must be spoken to, sir."

"Quite so. Yes, I'll—ah—see if I can find the lad. . . ." And Humphrey deserted the scene in favour of his bedchamber, whence soon emanated gales of laughter.

Mrs. Van Lindsay proceeded to make it clear to her stricken offspring that while she did not approve of Norman's teasing, Judith should perhaps consider that the model he had been attempting to construct in the bottle might well have meant as much to him as did the dress pattern to Judith. "One thing," she murmured to Lisette, as she walked to the door, "it has put your father into a very good humour, which is more than I'd hoped for when first I heard that uproar!"

Mr. Humphrey's good humour endured, and later that morning, when Lisette was summoned to the drawing room, she found him awaiting her, his broad features wreathed in smiles. "How pretty you look, child," he beamed. "Come and chat with your papa for a few moments."

Lisette sat obediently, but whatever he had in mind he evidently hesitated to broach, for during the next ten minutes he spoke only of commonplaces, asked her twice if she was happy, and commenting three times on the charm of "that pink gown." Refraining from pointing out that her muslin was peach-coloured, not pink, Lisette began to be uneasy. Papa was nervous, which must mean he had something unpleasant to say. She was mildly relieved when Powers appeared and announced that Mr. Garvey was belowstairs. Lisette prepared to leave, but her father requested that the caller be shown up, adding as the butler took his lugubrious countenance from sight, "This is a happy coincidence, m'dear. Mr. Garvey has been plaguing me for an introduction. Now's as good a time as any, eh?"

"Is the gentleman Mr. *James* Garvey, Papa? The Regent's friend?"

Humphrey chuckled. "Clever little puss. You know I do not usually cultivate the Carlton House set. You're right, but James is a good enough man. He can trace his house back almost as far as our own. Came into a considerable fortune some years ago, when his father went to his reward. James has been in Europe for several months, but I make no doubt you will recall having seen him at this or that occasion, for he is very—Ah, good morning, good morning, my dear fellow!" Humphrey rose and walked to extend a hand to his guest. "You chose a fortunate moment, James," he said heartily. "M'daughter and I were enjoying a cose. Lisette, I present Mr. James Garvey. James, this is my middle daughter. You know Beatrice, I believe. Don't think you've met our Lisette."

Lisette made her curtsey to a dapper gentleman of about five and thirty. He was not above average height, but well proportioned, and with a head of thickly curling dark hair that was gracefully bowed before her. She thought, as he straightened, that he was quite the dandy, for his shirt points were very high, his cravat a masterpiece, and his blue jacket extremely well cut. A green and blue brocaded waistcoat complemented the jacket neatly, and his pearl-grey inexpressibles were beyond reproach. Two fobs and a seal hung at his trim waist, and a large sapphire flashed on one hand. Unbidden, the recollection darted into her mind that Tristram Leith had never worn fobs or seals, the only jewellery she had ever seen him affect being his heavy gold signet ring. . . .

Her gaze drifting back to the visitor's face, she encountered a stunned look in his fine green eyes. He murmured in a bewildered manner, "Jove, sir! You said your daughter was lovely, but—I never dreamt—" He faltered into silence.

Lisette blushed and was both pleased and puzzled, for she had the distinct impression it was not at all what he had intended to say. She lowered her eyes, paying little heed to the polite pleasantry of her father's response. When she looked up, Mr. Garvey had recovered his air of sophisticated assurance. His admiration was obvious, but he displayed it now with a light-hearted effusiveness that was a balm to her bruised spirit. She was, he said, as pretty and sparkling as this beautiful morning. She would, did she venture outside, quite put the sunlight to shame with her radiance. Lisette was startled, and slanted a glance at her papa, who would have flown into a rage had she told him one of her beaux had made such bold remarks on first acquaintance, but Mr. Van Lindsay seemed no whit put out.

Mr. Garvey was aware of her reaction, however, and at once addressed himself to her parent. "My groom is walking my horses this very moment, sir. Have I your leave to ask that your daughter accompany me on a short drive?"

Mr. Van Lindsay never drove in the park save during the fashionable late afternoon, and up went his brows. "At this hour?"

"No time like the present," said Mr. Garvey with a smile. And receiving permission, begged that Miss Van Lindsay do him the honour of accompanying him. All the time, his eyes twinkled at her, and a dimple that came and went beside his mouth was quite attractive, she decided. Garvey's close friendship with the Regent made him a powerful man, and he was much admired by the ladies. It would be quite a feather in her cap to be seen with him. And if Colonel the Honourable Tristram Leith chanced to ride by, she would lift her nose at him and show the *ton* how little she cared that he had wed another! With a shy smile she accepted, and hurried upstairs for bonnet and shawl.

Judith, quite transformed from the howling banshee of two hours previously, danced around the upper landing in triumph. "Only *think!*" she cried, clinging to Lisette's hand, "James *Garvey!* Ruth MacKay is fairly gooseflesh whenever she mentions him! I *knew* you would make a recover, Lisette! I knew it! Oh, how proud—"

"Lisette!" hissed Mrs. Van Lindsay from the open bedchamber door. "Come here, child. Now, you must wear the bonnet with the cherry flowers."

"But, Mama, will it not clash with the peach?"

"No, no." Already, Philippa was arranging the dainty straw

upon her daughter's sleek head. "Ugh! Horrid! It clashes dreadfully. As I thought. Well, we must—Sandy? Where *is* the woman?''

Louise Sanders, who had been personal maid and dresser to the mistress of the house and her daughters, and "Sandy" for as long as any occupant of 359 Portland Place could recall, emerged from the wardrobe, her plain but pleasant face triumphant as she unwrapped silver paper from a wide-brimmed straw confection having a cluster of faded orange silk roses at one side, and long brown velvet ribbons that fell from the crown to tie under the chin, causing the brim to poke high. "I knew it was in there somewhere," she exulted. "You remember, missus, you wore it only once and stuck it away—must be three or four years since.''

"But—it is so faded," demurred Lisette.

"No, no—it don't look faded," her sister said eagerly. "Only dust it a little, Sandy, and when it is worn next to that peach gown, Lisette, everyone will suppose it made for it.''

As wild a tomboy as she was, Judith had an infallible eye for colour, and it did not err in this case. The bonnet that looked faded to those who remembered the bright orange of the original blooms seemed perfectly matched when worn with the peach muslin. Judith, who had been scrabbling frenziedly through a drawer of the chest, now produced a cream silk shawl with an intricately knotted fringe, which perfectly finished the ensemble, and when Sanders had provided a sunshade and long cream kid gloves, Lisette was ready.

"Remember, now," urged Mrs. Van Lindsay, "should you meet the Prince, have a care; he's a wicked fellow for the ladies. In point of fact, I'm not at all sure that James Garvey is all he should be. But, such a *fine* old family, love, and ten thousand a year, if he's a penny!''

There came a frantic scratching at the door. Sanders hurried to open it, and Norman, his boyish face flushed and excited, rushed in. "Hello, Mama! Lisette, d'you know who is downstairs with my father?''

"James Garvey," mocked Judith, curtseying. "Everyone knows who is downstairs, stupid boy!''

Mrs. Van Lindsay said a stern, "That will do, Judith. Mr. Garvey has come to take your sister out driving, Norman. I trust you behaved properly to the gentleman?''

''Garvey called for *Lisette?* But—he's a nonpareil! They say he and Prinny are thick as thieves. And besides, I thought Lisette had a *tendre* for—'' Here, catching Judith's enraged scowl and the flash of his mother's warning glance, he was dumb.

The sad light returned to Lisette's eyes. With her hand on the doorknob she turned back. ''*Tendre*—for whom, Norman?''

Mrs. Van Lindsay said an urgent, ''Pay no heed to the foolish child. Run along, do, or Mr. Garvey will be quite out of patience!''

Walking to the stairs, Lisette wondered ruefully if Mr. Garvey suspected the excitement his lineage and ten thousand a year had evoked in the Van Lindsay family.

''Oh, how beautiful she looks,'' sighed Sanders, as the door closed upon her favourite.

''The very essence of feminine charm,'' murmured Judith, her eyes dreaming.

''Like a side of beef to be sold,'' snorted Norman, revolted.

Judith gave a squeak of outrage. Sanders glanced apprehensively at her mistress. ''What . . . did you say?'' demanded Mrs. Van Lindsay, awfully.

Scarlet, Norman stammered, ''I said—er, one should hide grief, I—hold.''

Sanders smothered a grin and turned quickly away. Judith, glaring, met a mutely pleading gaze, pursed her lips, and was silent.

''Hmmnnn . . .'' said Mrs. Van Lindsay.

Chapter 2

Mr. Garvey owned a splendid team of matched bays and a well-sprung phaeton of a dusky blue, picked out with paler blue, and having pale blue squabs. Noting that the gentleman also wore those colours, Lisette felt somewhat at odds with the decor, and wondered if he changed his vehicles to match his attire, or vice versa. He assured himself that his fair charge was comfortably settled, took the reins from his groom, dismissed the man, and drove off, feathering the corner neatly.

It was a glorious morning, the air washed clean by the rain and the temperature beginning at last to feel like Spring. Many people were out, and it appeared that Mr. Garvey knew or was known by them all. He was an easy conversationalist, maintaining a pleasant flow of chatter even as he bowed, waved, or smiled upon this or that passing carriage. In Hyde Park they encountered Lady Jersey, enjoying an early drive with the Countess Lieven. Lady Jersey smiled warmly on Lisette and ordered her groom to pull up the horses, but her eyes then alighting on Garvey, the smile in them died. A tiny frown touching her brows, she glanced again at Lisette, lifted one gloved hand in polite salute and told the groom to drive on.

Garvey chuckled. "Pray do not feel that slight was on any account but my own, ma'am. 'The Silence' don't approve of your escort."

She looked at him uncertainly. "Surely you mistake it. I know she chatters, but she is the kindest person."

"To you, who could be otherwise? She considers me a bad influence on our beloved Regent." He shrugged and added whimsically, "One might suppose that Prinny, *au contraire*, corrupts *me!*"

"Were one to judge by rumour—" Lisette laughed—"your point would be well taken, sir."

"And do you judge by rumours, Miss Van Lindsay?"

"I try not to be influenced by idle gossip, but I confess that sometimes there is so much of it, one cannot help but wonder."

"I beg you will not allow my Lady Jersey to prejudice you against me." He smiled roguishly. "I really am not so very wicked, and—good God! What the deuce has poor Bolster got with him?"

Two gentlemen occupied the approaching curricle. The man driving was young, sturdily built, and having a pleasant, ruddy-complected countenance. Beside him sat one of the biggest and ugliest bulldogs Lisette had ever seen, and she watched the animal, fascinated.

Garvey called, "What have you there, Bolster?"

Both vehicles came to a halt. Lord Jeremy Bolster snatched off his hat, revealing straight hair gleaming pale yellow in the sunlight. "It's Br-Br-Brutus, Garvey," he stammered, his abashed gaze flickering to Lisette.

"An unlovely brute. 'Ware, Jeremy, lest it devour you!"

Bolster grinned, bowed jerkily to Lisette, and took up the reins once more. His companion had been turned away exchanging pleasantries with another rider. He now swung around, and Lisette encountered a pair of very blue eyes that stared at her from a gaunt face, the darkly bronzed skin seeming to accentuate that piercing regard. They were past then, and she looked straight ahead, wondering why she felt so shaken. Rather belatedly she became aware that Garvey was making a remark. To allow one's attention to wander whilst with a gentleman could be fatal, besides being most ill-mannered. "Oh, I do beg your pardon," she apologized. "I fear my thoughts were on that most unattractive creature."

"You're very frank, ma'am." He laughed. "Strand ain't a beauty, I'll own."

Strand! No wonder that searing scrutiny had made her so uneasy! Some part of her mind must have remembered what Judith had said of him. She had gone on to remark that he was not exactly a handsome man, or words to that effect. *Handsome!* That he most certainly was not! Did his notorious sister resemble him, one could only pity poor Tristram Leith for he must have lost all sense of good judgement and— The foolish incident had so discomposed her that she'd not taken heed of the balance of Mr. Garvey's remark, but now his words came back to her and, blushing, she exclaimed a dismayed, "Oh, no! You cannot think I referred to Mr. Strand? You must not—" She saw the teasing glint in his eyes then, and, with a little laugh scolded, "Ah, so you roast me, sir! You knew very well that I meant the bulldog."

He chuckled. "Forgive, dear lady. I certainly knew you could not refer to Bolster. One can but hope the brute may prove of comfort to the poor fellow, for he has taken his loss very hard. But I expect you know the story?"

Know the story? Of course she knew the story! Rachel Strand had stolen the man she loved, and now the wretched woman's sinister brother had dared to ogle her as if she were a common— but Garvey was speaking of Lord *Bolster*, not *Justin Strand*. She must be wits to let for her mind to wander so! Her cheeks hot, she confessed her ignorance and begged to be enlightened.

"Most gladly. I am sure you will remember the sensation last autumn when Lucian St. Clair came to grips with that revolting trafficker in White Slavery? He called himself the Dandy Lion, but was in fact a member of the Quality."

"Yes! Oh, yes, I do!" Her indignation forgotten, Lisette clasped her hands, her dark eyes sparkling as she recalled the dramatic events that had set all London agog. "Papa never did tell me the whole, but I know there was a dreadful fight, no? It was all very exciting!"

Glancing down at her, Garvey was enchanted both by her beauty and the swift change of mood. "Exciting, indeed," he breathed, and then as curiosity came into her eyes, added with a grin, "Nonetheless, had it not been for Bolster and a few others who went to his aid, St. Clair would be only a memory today."

"Oh, how splendid to be such a loyal friend!" Lisette turned to glance back, and at once wished she'd not been so impulsive. The curricle had halted, and the dark face of Justin Strand had also been turned. For the second time their eyes met and, despite the distance, Lisette was as though hypnotized by that brilliant gaze. She jerked around then, her heart thundering. She felt confused and frightened. Why the miserable creature should so upset her was more than she could guess, except that he stared so, and with such a stern, fixed look, not at all in a friendly or admiring fashion. A horrifying new suspicion brought with it a shudder of humiliation: Could it be that he knew of her secret regard for his brother-in-law? Was he contemptuous of the girl who had made such a hopeless little idiot of herself? The very notion was sickening. She was perfectly sure those hard blue eyes were still boring into her spine, and she began to feel so unnerved that she had to take herself sharply to task. It was all too nonsensical. She had concealed her heartbreak, surely? No one knew of it—save only her immediate family. Tristram Leith did not know; he could not know. Could he? Oh, Lord! Please, *please* let him not know!

Her unhappy introspection had caused the hot blush to recede from her cheeks, which was as well since Garvey was peering at her with some concern. Lisette Van Lindsay, she thought firmly, stop allowing that wretched Strand person to panic you into behaving like a silly widgeon! She clenched her fists and managed to say brightly, "So that is Lord Jeremy Bolster. I was trying to recall what I did know of the matter, and even to do that frightens me."

Garvey smiled and said with approval, "As any gently nurtured female *should* be frightened by such villainy, my dear lady."

Relieved that her small fib had been accepted, Lisette went on, "One would suppose his lordship would be proud, rather than distressed."

"His distress springs from another cause." Garvey flourished his whip but did not stop when that dashing young blade, Mr. Galen Hilby, reined in a spirited grey mare the better to bow to Miss Van Lindsay. "You may know," said Garvey, "that Bolster was betrothed."

Lisette smiled after Galen, one of her more ardent admirers, who was so wicked as to blow her a kiss. "Yes. In fact, I met her once. Amanda . . . Amanda—Oh, dear! I cannot think of her last name, but I do remember her."

"And did you approve?"

"Very much. She is the dearest girl, and has such pretty red hair. I recall that there was not an ounce of affectation about her."

"True. It's a pity, it really is. But you do remember the Dandy Lion?"

"Yes, indeed. Dreadful creature, how could one forget such wickedness? And he a member of the Quality. He was a highwayman, too, and a ruthless murderer of his victims. It makes me shudder! His name was Hersh, was it not? Winfield Hersh?" Her eyes widened. 'My heaven! *That* is Amanda's surname! Oh, never say they are related?"

He nodded. "Her half-brother. Beastly luck, because Hersh will hang—not a doubt of it, so there's no hope for her. She cannot wed Bolster."

"Oh, the poor girl. And she and Lord Bolster were deeply attached, I heard. How very sad."

"And how kind that you are so touched by their tragedy. But it would not serve, you must agree."

"No . . . it would not." She sighed regretfully. "Bolster is from a very fine house. Even were he willing to ignore his own obligations to his name, he could scarcely expect his family to consent. Indeed, it would be dishonourable to ask such a thing."

"If there's one thing Bolster ain't, it's dishonourable. I must ask your pardon for failing to introduce him, but—well, you saw how he is."

Perplexed, she said, "No. What do you mean?"

"Nothing to his detriment, I assure you. He was badly wounded at the Siege of Badajoz. He's the best of good fellows, but a little . . ." He tapped his temple significantly.

"Oh, my! How dreadful! And now, to have lost the girl he loves!"

"There are still some wagers on the books at the clubs, but she'll not wed him. If it were up to Jeremy . . ." He paused thoughtfully. "He's not the man to puff off his consequence. But I don't have to tell you that, for you saw who was with him." He met her enquiring gaze and said mischievously, "The—ah, unattractive creature."

Lisette stiffened. "I have already said, sir, that I intended no such implication. I should be most distressed did you hold me guilty of so unkind a remark."

"What—about a dog?" He looked at her askance. "You are very nice, ma'am, but I thought you spoke only truth. He is, indeed, unattractive."

"Good morning, Miss Van Lindsay! How do you do, Garvey?" The Duke of Vaille smiled on them from the driver's seat of a splendid high-perch phaeton. "Do not forget my waltz, dear lady!" he called, then swept past.

"Shall you attend the ball for his son's betrothal?" asked Garvey eagerly. "I implore—I *beg* to be allowed to escort you. *Do* say yes!"

Lisette thanked him but said she had not yet made up her mind as to which of several offers to accept, and beyond asking that she consider him also, he did not press her. During the balance of their drive he was all a lady could wish for on such an occasion, bringing her to laughter more than once with his recountings of humourous episodes concerning the Regent's Pavilion at Brighton and some of the dinners and entertainments he had attended there. He was charming, bright, witty, and poised; very much a man of the world. Lisette could not but be flattered by his very evident admiration, nor was she unaware of the many curious glances that followed them. She enjoyed herself as she had not done for weeks, and when Garvey returned her to Portland Place and escorted her to the front door, she was sincere in expressing her thanks for a delightful drive.

Once in the house, she was pounced upon by Judith and begged to recount all that had happened. To an extent she complied, amused by her sister's excitement, but when Mrs. Van Lindsay returned from an afternoon card party and joined them in the family parlour, she was obliged to tell her tale again. Her mother was ecstatic to learn of Garvey's request to escort Lisette to the Vaille ball. "You must have a new gown!" she decreed. "You have moped at home for too long, and nothing could be better than to return to Society with so consequential a gentleman as James Garvey as your partner. It will be all over Town by now that you are his new interest!"

"But, Mama, I only just met the man. Surely, I—"

"What has that to say to anything? Never say you have taken him in aversion?"

"Well, no, but I scarcely know him."

"You could do a deal worse, Lisette. He is a man of insinuating address to which you may add impeccable lineage, wealth, influence. . . . Only think of Timothy and the doors a word in the Regent's ear might open!"

At this point, Powers made his dignified way into the room, followed by the parlour-maid carrying a huge bunch of red roses, a small flower box, and two letters. Mrs. Van Lindsay accepted the letters and the small box. The red roses were from Garvey, the card reading "To London's fairest flower." Admiring the perfect blooms, Lisette heard her mother utter a derogatory snort. The small box held a bunch of lilies of the valley set in a filigreed container. Frowning at the card she held, Mrs. Van Lindsay said, "What impertinence!" and tossed the flowers into the wastebasket.

Lisette took the card she extended. There were no written words, only the printed name, Justin Derwent Strand. She experienced an odd little jolt of the heart, and could almost see those brilliant blue eyes scrutinizing her as they had in the park. She said nothing, but when she was alone, she rescued the posy. It was, she thought, quite dainty, and she was fond of the fragrant little flowers. No matter who had sent them.

She was tidying her hair when Mrs. Van Lindsay returned to advise that Miss Charlotte Hilby and her brother Galen had come to call, and that Sir Aubrey Suffield's chaise had just stopped outside.

"You see?" Philippa cried trimphantly. "It has begun! London believes you recovered from the 'slight indisposition' I had set about. You will likely become more popular than ever, my love!"

She was quite correct. It was the start of a flood, and even Cook, apprised at the last moment of the fact that they would sit down twelve to dinner, broke only two glasses and a chipped plate by way of protest. When the teatray was brought in at ten o'clock, a merry crowd of four and twenty, mostly bachelors, with a sprinkling of parents and sisters, had gathered in the drawing room.

"Thank God!" Mrs. Van Lindsay murmured in an aside to her spouse. "Lisette is in looks again. For a time I really feared she would go into a decline. Only think how mortifying *that* would have been!"

"Silly chit," grunted Humphrey. "She was sure all the *ton* thought her jilted. Was you t'ask me, not a soul so much as suspected she gave a button for Leith! She's too sensitive and flighty by half. An overabundance of pride has that daughter of yours, ma'am!"

"And as she should have—nor begrudge her it, sir! It is that very pride and knowledge of her position in Society will compel her to make the best match she may. How clever of Garvey to send those beautiful roses, but not call tonight. Much that wretched Strand girl may count her triumph. Lisette will eclipse her yet!"

Mr. Van Lindsay slanted an oblique glance at his wife, pursed his lips, and said a cautious, "Hmmnnn. . . ."

It said much for Philippa's excitement that she did not take heed of this warning signal, turning instead to chatter graciously with the beautiful Miss Hilby, although everyone knew *her* family tree could be traced only to the fifteenth century, and there was some suspicion her great-grandfather had been a wealthy merchant.

All in all, it was a triumphant evening and by the time she retired, Lisette was very weary. Sleep eluded her, however, and she lay reliving the events of the day. Her thoughts lingered on poor Amanda Hersh. How deeply she must love, and how unselfishly, since she had chosen to reject Lord Bolster sooner than disgrace him by her unworthiness. What a contrast was offered by Rachel Strand, who, for all her famed beauty, was the daughter of a man known to have cheated at cards and to have evaded debtors' prison only by his own death. As though that were not sufficiently shameful, Miss Strand had won even more notoriety by jilting the French nobleman to whom she had been betrothed and running off from her own engagement ball with some unknown. Utterly disgraceful conduct! There was no understanding why Tristram Leith, one of the most handsome and well-born young aristocrats in all England, should have wed the girl. One thing was sure, however, he was now just as much an outcast as his bride! Lisette tried to feel triumphant and, having failed, sighed miserably. How strange a thing was Fate. Rachel Strand had stolen the man she loved. And even now, Justin

Strand's flowers were adding their fragrance to her bedchamber. She sighed again, and went to sleep, to dream of mushrooms growing in a field of lilies of the valley.

The next five days raced by. The word that one of London's most spectacular beauties was recovered of an illness that had confined her to her home for several weeks swept the *ton* like a whirlwind, and quiet Portland Place became the target for more traffic than it had seen since before Miss Van Lindsay's "illness."

Lisette was showered with invitations. She was taken driving in the park by Galen Hilby and by Sir Aubrey Suffield; James Garvey escorted her to a rout party and a musicale and sent flowers every day; Jocelyn Vaughan, one of London's very popular bachelors, became a member of her court, which pleased her, since she found the handsome young man most charming. The morning callers meanwhile seemed to increase daily. Among these latter was Lady Jersey. That revered patroness of the mighty Almack's complimented Lisette upon her recovery and, taking Mrs. Van Lindsay aside, remarked that her daughter was again in great beauty. "It is certainly understandable she is so admired by the gentlemen," she observed, "for she looked ravishing when I saw her driving with James Garvey on Tuesday. You—er—approve, my dear Philippa?"

Mrs. Van Lindsay smiled rather smugly and acknowledged that Mr. Garvey had been added to the list of her daughter's admirers, which fact did not in the least surprise her.

"No, indeed," said my lady, with a lift of her thin eyebrows. "But it does surprise me, Philippa, that you and Van Lindsay would countenance it."

Astonished, Mrs. Van Lindsay drew herself to her full height and said at her most regal, "Countenance it? My dear ma'am, Garvey's lineage is second to none."

"His lineage, perhaps. But—his morals?"

"Good God! I'd heard only that he was of the Carlton House set, which I cannot quite like." Alarmed now, Mrs. Van Lindsay asked, "Is there more, Sally?"

"Too much smoke for there to be no fire. But—" my lady shrugged her shoulders—"perhaps I am prejudiced. I do not care for the man, which he well knows. Now, do I say more, I shall invite the criticism that *I* am the one who is vindictive and has a poisonous tongue. I will add only this: I should want no daughter of mine to associate with a man who whistled a fortune down the wind in only five years!''

Mrs. Van Lindsay paled.

Upon being apprised of this conversation in the privacy of his wife's bedchamber later that evening, Mr. Van Lindsay paled also, then uttered a shocked, ''By thunder! So it *is* truth! I had heard a whisper or two, but fancied it malicious gossip, merely.''

''Then he *is* ruined? Oh, lud! And I have given the wretch every encouragement! I even influenced Lisette to accept his escort to Vaille's ball! Why in the world does he pursue the girl? Does he suppose us to be wealthy?''

Humphrey frowned at his reflection in the mirror above the fireplace. ''Perhaps. More likely he has it in his mind that your mama is very well to pass. And a little stricken in years.''

''But—but whatever my dear mama has—which is very little— will all go to Tim!''

''True. But very few people know that, my love, and although many consider the old lady to be cheese-paring, there are more who believe her full of lettuce!''

Philippa's indignation that her mother should be spoken of in such a disparaging way might have bloomed into a full-scale attack upon her luckless spouse had not a greater outrage taken precedence. ''That villain!'' she exclaimed. ''I believed him to be a chivalrous gentleman, when in truth he is no more than an unprincipled fortune hunter!'' Having uttered this righteous complaint, she marred it by adding, ''What a disappointment! Well, we shall have to look elsewhere, and there are so few bachelors just at the moment who have satisfactory family and expectations. If *only* Leith had offered . . .'' She then proceeded to list the various wealthy and acceptable young men who had been snapped up by mediocre girls with not a tenth of her daughter's beauty. Humphrey paid little attention to this gloomy recital. Being far more harassed than his wife suspected, he had already taken inventory of London's possible candidates for Lisette's hand. Since Garvey had been the leading contender, the runner-up must now be considered the only logical choice. It was a choice that would, he knew, create considerable consternation in his household, and he was seeking for the least offensive way to nominate his man when Philippa asked, ''What do you think of young Hilby? Were he to attempt to fix his interest, it would be splendid, no? The boy's vastly wealthy, and if his lineage is not of the finest, it certainly is not contemptible.''

"True. But I doubt he's ready to be leg shackled. And there are some more likely gentlemen, my dear. Vaughan, for instance, Cossentine, Strand, Alastair, Den—''

"*Strand?*'' Philippa echoed, then went into a ripple of laughter. "You jest!''

With a fine nonchalance, her husband answered, "It might serve. The boy's come home from India a regular nabob. Paid off all his papa's debts, and I hear has dropped a mountain of blunt on that place of his in Sussex. The family's not ancient, I allow, but it ain't *totally* beyond the pale, and Strand can scarce be held accountable for his sister's manners—or lack of 'em.''

Astounded that her husband should stoop to consider Justin Strand a suitable prospective son-in-law, Philippa tightened her lips. But after a moment's thoughts, she said with a thin smile, "Lord! I can well imagine how Lisette would react did Strand offer. To have *Leith* for her brother-in-law. . .? And his odious wife for a sister? I declare she'd sooner wear the willow all her days!''

Mr. Humphrey said slowly, "I've no doubt she would, my dear.''

Lisette's new ball gown was as far from "wearing the willow'' as one could imagine. A cloud of net of the palest pink over deeper pink tulle, with tiny spangles here and there, it arrived the day before the ball that the Duke of Vaille held to honour the betrothal of his only son, the Marquis of Damon, to that lovely young widow, Lady Sophia Drayton. Lisette returned from walking with two of her cousins to find the large box on her bed, and Judith all agog to see it opened. The gown looked even lovelier than Lisette had remembered, and she was holding it up against her when an unusually firm scratching came at the door. In answer to her call, her brother burst in, impelled by the enthusiasm of an ugly and vaguely familiar dog.

"Did you hear him scratch at your door?'' Norman laughed, clinging to the leash. "' 'Pon my word, but he's the very cleverest brute.''

"Brutus!'' gasped Lisette, remembering.

Her utterance of the name was heard, and the response was as fervent as it was immediate. With a bark that shook the windows, Brutus hurled himself at the lady who had thus invited him. Lisette gave a shriek as two large paws were planted upon the dainty and pristine fabric of her new gown. Brutus very obviously did not count this a rebuff, for he continued to jump and bark, while Lisette shrieked and Judith berated and Norman shouted with laughter.

"Get him away! Get him away!" cried Lisette, dodging frantically.

Judith shrilled, "Horrid dog!" but ran behind the chair when Brutus turned eager eyes her way.

"He is not a horrid dog!" Norman protested. "I met Lord Bolster outside and he was kind enough to let me bring his puppy up to show you. I might have known you'd—"

"What in the name of creation is happening?" roared Mr. Van Lindsay, appearing in the doorway.

"It is my new ball gown, Papa," Lisette wailed, inspecting her sullied net with anxious eyes. "Norman brought that hideous creature upstairs—"

"And he jumped all over poor Lisette and chased me behind this chair," put in Judith indignantly, if not altogether accurately.

"Well, get the dirty hound out!" ordered the master of the house, advancing purposefully.

Brutus trundled a few interested paces towards him, and the master of the house retreated precipitately.

"Come on, poor fellow," said Norman, tugging on the leash.

Brutus began to growl at Mr. Van Lindsay, and took a few more paces towards him.

"Go away!" screamed Judith, taking one of Mr. Garvey's roses from a vase and waving it threateningly.

Brutus emitted a piercing yowl and shot under the bed, the leash whipping through Norman's hand.

"Now see what you've done!" Norman knelt by the bed, and called a cajoling, "Come out, poor frightened puppy."

"Puppy?" snorted Mr. Van Lindsay. "The brute's a behemoth, rather! Remove him, sir! At once!"

Norman proving singularly unwilling to reach under the bed and drag Brutus out by a paw, this adjuration was not immediately complied with, as a result of which Mr. Van Lindsay's temper worsened and his son was treated to some decidedly cutting remarks.

Not until Norman sacrificed a piece of toffee was the dog at last lured forth. Norman grudgingly voiced the apology his sire demanded but, on his way out, dimmed the effect by muttering, "Women! He didn't hurt your silly dress!"

Fortunately this appeared to be true. Lisette could find no rents, and the few snags were easily corrected. By this time, however, the afternoon was far spent and it was necessary to change for dinner. Their guests came early and stayed late, and it was not until the following morning that Lisette was able to try on the gown. With loving hands she took it from its protective covering, held it up, and uttered a shriek of horror. The gauze was torn and ripped; large, muddy pawprints defaced it, and several sections looked to have been well chewed. For a moment, recalling the frightful expense of that gown, Lisette was actually dizzied. With a choking sob she laid the victim on her bed, and only then saw that the damaged gauze was of a slightly different hue. Puzzled, she investigated. Several recent additions had been clumsily pinned onto her lovely (and mercifully unsullied) gown. Her first reaction was one of soaring relief, but a muffled chortle from the door brought her swinging around in time to see Norman's grinning face jerk from sight. Rage boiled through her. The *monster!* What a fright he had given her—her heart was still hammering!

It had been a long time since she had allowed herself to lose her temper, but this was too much! She snatched up the nearest thing to hand, which chanced to be her new parasol, and ran in hot pursuit.

Norman was leaning against the stair railing, laughing his triumph, but he straightened when he saw retribution at hand and tore down the stairs, Lisette close on his heels. He reached the ground floor a very short distance ahead and, turning to the right and the rear of the house, barely avoided two gentlemen leaving the study. Lisette, parasol upraised, was able to stop at the very last instant, halting all but under the chin of a tall, slender man clad in the height of quiet elegance, who regarded her with one mobile brow lifting. Staring into that bronzed face, Lisette thought that the skin seemed almost stretched over the high cheekbones, and that he was younger than she had supposed—somewhere in the neighbourhood of thirty. Her appraisal brought a smile creeping into the extremely blue eyes, but it did not touch his mouth.

"Lisette," said Mr. Van Lindsay, palpably annoyed, "I must make you known to Mr. Justin Strand. Mr. Strand—my second daughter."

Strand's bow was brief and remarkable for a lack of embellishment. Renowned for her serene grace, Lisette realized with a considerable shock that the parasol was still flung up over her head. For a horrified instant she could not decide what to do with it, and her arm wavered. The smile in Mr. Strand's eyes spread to a quiver beside his mouth. Scarlet with embarrassment, Lisette thrust the parasol behind her and favoured him with a dignified curtsey. The most graceful curtsey in the world, however, can only suffer when the *derrière* of the lady executing it suddenly comes into violent contact with the handle of a parasol. Lisette, in fact, was thrown so off balance that it was necessary for Strand to steady her,

"Lord's sake, girl!" expostulated Mr. Van Lindsay. "What are you about?"

Wishing the floor might open and swallow her, Lisette mumbled, "I—er—Norman—that is to say—Brutus—"

"Yes. Precisely why I came," said Strand, coming to her rescue. "I heard my dog had caused you some inconvenience, Miss Van Lindsay. My apologies. May I hope to make amends in some fashion?"

He had a brisk but pleasant voice. And he was Rachel Strand's brother. Recovering herself, Lisette said a cool, "*Your* dog, sir? I understood he was the property of Lord Bolster."

She had made an excellent recovery, thought Strand. How charmingly the thick dark hair waved about her face, and those great eyes were like dusky pansies . . . as he had heard. But her back was very straight now, and those same dusky eyes were tinged with ice. "I—ah—bestowed him upon Bolster," he explained. "So I feel responsible."

Lisette was in no mood to return that quirkish smile. Of all the people in this world, Justin Strand was the last to whom she would have wished to show a foolish front. Whatever must he have thought to see a lady of her station in life racing down the stairs, brandishing her parasol like some hobbledehoy? And as though that were not bad enough, she had all but thrown herself at his feet! Small wonder he smiled. One scarce could blame him did he laugh aloud! "I certainly do not hold you responsible, sir," she replied. "And I believe I have to thank you for some very pretty flowers."

"Have you?"

The twinkle in his eyes was even more pronounced and, disconcerted, she stared at him.

"I am flattered you remember who sent 'em," he went on with a shrug she could only find deliberately provoking. "I suspect you are fairly deluged with floral offerings, Miss Van Lindsay."

Lisette managed a smile, excused herself, and walked on in the manner of a queen moving towards her coronation. She knew that Papa was vexed with her and wondered why he should give this man house room, let alone expect her to be civil to the creature.

Wandering into the breakfast room, she came upon her erstwhile prey choosing from some fruit on the sideboard. He threw up one arm and begged for mercy. "I did not harm your gown, I swear. And I'd not intended to land you in the suds again—did Papa come the ugly?"

"Not with me. But I cannot guarantee he will not have a few words to say to you!"

"Oh, well. It was worth it. Truly, Lisette, the expression on your face when you fell off your parasol was priceless."

Strand had doubtless thought the same! "At least," she snapped, "no one has yet wished to pay to view it. Do you continue to gobble up every piece of food in sight, they will offer a pretty sum to see you at Astley's Amphitheatre!" The instant they were spoken, she would have given a good deal to have retracted those unkind words. The grin died from Norman's face. He flushed, and in silence replaced the apple, bowed with surprising dignity, and left her alone. She thought with a trace of shock, He's growing up! and felt confused and unhappy.

When she was sure the hall was clear, she hurried upstairs and was arraying herself in a gown that Papa favoured when a quiet scratch on the door announced the arrival of Norman and Judith. They both looked solemn, and the fact that they were side by side with no appearance of animosity told its own story. Lisette ushered them inside, allowing her hand to rest an extra minute on her brother's shoulder, and asked, "What's wrong?"

He saw the rather anxious smile in her eyes and grinned his forgiveness.

"Beatrice," he said succinctly.

"And poor Sir William," nodded Judith.

"Come for the Damon ball," Norman finished.

"Oh, dear," sighed Lisette.

Lady Beatrice Dwyer was, at four and twenty, a younger but slightly more waspish version of her mother. In a little less than three years, she had succeeded in so cowing her gentle husband that, when in her presence, he seldom spoke without first looking anxiously for her approval. Beatrice had her share of the Bayes-Copeland good looks, and it was those looks that had snared Sir William. He had neither an athletic build nor a handsome countenance to recommend him, being short and rather stocky, his colouring florid and his hair of an undistinguished brown. He was (besides being the possessor of a fine old name, a baronetcy, and a comfortable estate in Somerset) a kind-hearted soul whose interest in his fellow man had won him far more friends than he knew. He idolized his wife, humbly marvelling that he'd been able to win so pretty a prize, not realizing that more worldly-wise gentlemen had taken heed of Beatrice's tendency to shrewishness, and turned their attentions otherwhere.

At the luncheon table that day, Sir William was a little more spirited than usual. Lisette always went out of her way to be kind to him, being very aware of the burden under which he laboured. Taking their cue from her, Judith and Norman, who were both now allowed to join the family for luncheon, treated him with a deference he found gratifying. Beatrice was rattling on as usual, allowing him little chance to contribute to the conversation, but when Lisette found an opening and asked if he had been able to get in any hunting after the Christmas holidays, he answered joyfully that he had, by Jove! "Was invited to ride with the Melton men. Bought m'self a dashed fine hunter. Splendid beast. Sixteen hands, good shoulders, and a fine barrel. If I say so m'self—"

"Oh, pray do not, William," Beatrice interpolated with a tight smile. "The family don't want to hear all that hunting talk.

Now, Lisette, tell me what is all this we hear of your having been in queer stirrups? You look well enough to me. I hope you don't mean to become one of these sickly women, always ailing. It's high time you was wed. She needs a husband, Mama. She is getting to be a positive old maid, which will never do. We all expect you to at least *try* to make as good a match as did I, dear one.''

Judith looked daggers and opened her mouth for an impassioned defence, only to gasp as Norman's shoe connected hard with her shin, and a warning frown was levelled at her across the table.

"Lisette is much better now," said Mrs. Van Lindsay. "And is, in fact, being courted by several gentlemen."

"Well, I hope one amongst 'em has two groats to rub together. I vow I could have wept when I heard Colonel Leith was snapped up by that Strand woman! I was sure you'd catch him, Lisette—though you must have been his second choice at best, for everyone knows he was mad for Euphemia Buchanan. Lord knows why; *she's* nothing for looks, heaven only knows.''

Lisette kept her eyes on her plate and was silent. Norman and Judith looked at each other in a mutual fuming. Mr. Van Lindsay coughed and said grandly, "I'd allow your sister's admirers to be a fairly well-breeched lot. Young Hilby will never be able to spend the half of his fortune; Vaughan is wealthy in his own right, to say nothing of what Moulton will leave him; and Garvey—'' He exchanged a meaningful glance with his wife. Few people knew of Mr. Garvey's financial dilemma, and his prestige was such that Lisette's reputation could only be enhanced by his attentions. "Garvey," he finished, "is fairly crazy for her."

"Garvey?'' put in Sir William. "*James* Garvey? Jove! He's an out and outer if ever there was one! And as well breeched as he can stare! What d'you say to that, milady!"

His wife's eyes were very wide. "A most splendid catch," she said, with only a trace of hollowness.

"How regrettable that I have no intention of 'catching' him," averred Lisette, her cheeks flaming.

Norman murmured softly, "Just like a blasted butcher's shop!"

Fortunately, his withering comment did not carry past Lisette, and she did not betray him. She was, in fact, completely in agreement with him.

Chapter 3

Like everything else about the Duke of Vaille, his house was as close to perfection as was possible. This edifice was located in Bond Street, not far from the home of his good friend the Earl of Harland, and with its unusual red mansard roof, white exterior, and wide red steps was a spectacular sight. Inside, it was rather awesomely lovely, but the majestic proportions of the rooms did not detract from a sense of warmth and welcome. Tonight, those rooms were ablaze with colourful gowns, and music vied with the merry talk and laughter of the guests. Camille, Marquis of Damon, his betrothed, and his father were still receiving latecomers two hours after the first guests had arrived, but even then the house was not uncomfortably crowded, the Duke not holding with the popular notion that a party was not a success unless the guests were so jammed in they could scarcely move about.

The arrival of Lisette Van Lindsay, escorted by James Garvey, created quite a stir. Lisette's new gown admirably became her, and the small necklace of rubies and diamonds that she had borrowed from her mother (and which she suspected were paste) complemented it charmingly. Well aware of the admiring stares of the gentlemen, Garvey was also amused to notice the glares of several mamas having less spectacular daughters they hoped to fire off this season. He confided to his fair partner that he squired the loveliest lady at the ball. Lisette smiled and thanked him, but she was unimpressed by flattery. If anything, she thought the guest of honour the loveliest woman in the room, for Sophia, Lady Drayton, was a great beauty with her golden hair and long violet eyes. Those same eyes were bright indeed tonight, and having congratulated her handsome fiancé, Lisette embraced Sophia, happy for the joy of this good friend.

"Dearest," Sophia whispered in her ear, "would you keep an eye on Amanda for me? I bullied her into coming, but I fear she means to hide somewhere. It is all so ridiculous because—Oh, Admiral Peterson. How kind of you to come."

Lisette had, perforce, to move along, not having had time to apprise Sophia of the fact that she scarcely knew Amanda Hersh, and was not at all sure she wished so uncomfortable a task as to befriend a disgraced girl.

Once they had moved into the ballroom, however, she became such a centre of attraction that Sophia's request quite slipped her mind. The gentlemen crowded around, begging for a place on her dance card. Jocelyn Vaughan stole it and at once it was whisked away. Even as she started to demand it be returned, Captain Miles Cameron came up to present Lord Bolster, his lordship so obviously petrified with shyness that she put aside her vexation and was as gently kind as she knew how to be. Her reward was an incoherent mumble and a look of gratitude wherein she also thought to read such misery that her heart was touched. She was still looking after Bolster worriedly when Vaughan swept her a deep obeisance and proffered her dance card, completely filled.

Half laughing, half annoyed, she protested, "No, really, Vaughan! This will not do, gentlemen! I must have a new card."

"I fear they are not to be had, dear lady," chuckled James Garvey, offering his arm. "And since my own name heads the list and a waltz is about to begin, I claim my fair prize."

She slipped her hand onto his arm and walked with him onto the floor. "Well you may laugh, sir, *your* name was written in honestly. I likely do not even know half the gentlemen who signed my card!" She started to raise it, but the music began and she was whirled into the dance.

The next hour flew by. The happiness of the occasion was contagious, and Vaille's wisdom in holding the guest list to no more than two hundred and fifty resulted in the room staying fairly cool and allowed the dancers to move freely. The lilting music, the lovely ladies, the charming and elegant gentlemen, and the gracious house all combined to create a most enjoyable evening, and Lisette was almost sorry when Galen Hilby appeared to lead her in to supper. As always, this very eligible young bachelor was light-hearted and full of plans for her amusement. They would have a boat party, he proclaimed. They would go down the Thames to Richmond, where they would disembark at the home of Lisette's dear grandmama, who would be delighted to serve them all a five-course dinner to follow their picnic. The idea of her sharp-tongued and reclusive grandparent making such an offer sent Lisette into peals of laughter. Glancing up, she encountered from across the room the gaze of two intent blue eyes, and her laughter died. For a moment she returned Strand's gaze, then, her cheeks hot, she moved too hastily, overturned her glass, and sent ratafia cascading over the pink net. Mr. Hilby gave her his napkin. Chagrined, she thanked him, but excused herself and went in search of a maid.

She was returning to the ballroom ten minutes later, the stains removed, when she saw a lackey carrying a tray to a secluded ante-room. Sophia's request was brought to mind and, dismayed that it had been neglected, Lisette waited until the man left, then entered the room. Sure enough, a forlorn red-haired girl huddled at one end of a sofa, reaching for a macaroon.

"Good evening, Miss Hersh," said Lisette, at her most friendly.

Amanda Hersh jumped, the macaroon shot into the air, and she all but flipped the plate over as she turned a startled face towards the newcomer. It was a wan face, the freckles that dusted the bridge of the small upturned nose being very noticeable against the white skin, and the big blue eyes rather pink-rimmed. "Oh!" gasped Miss Hersh. "I thought you were my godmama!" And then floundered, "Not that I mean you sound that old—I didn't I meant to—"

Lisette gave a ripple of laughter and sat beside her. "May I join you? We have had little opportunity to chat, and I know Sophia Drayton holds you in very high regard."

"Yes," sighed Miss Hersh, her eyes wistful. "Sophia is all kindness but I have heard your family is—I mean—" She blinked and said unsteadily, "I should not be here you know for we—I am quite disgraced and you perhaps would not wish to be seen—"

Her heart won, Lisette touched the trembling little hand. "Why, I am perfectly sure you have done nothing even remotely dreadful."

"No," gulped Miss Hersh, her eyes filling with tears, "b-but my wretched brother did and—and J-Jeremy was almost killed as if it wasn't bad enough I'd drawn the wrong molar, I used a piece of string and the doorknob and it was dreadful I assure you and oh I wish Sophia had not been so consistent that I come although she means well of course but it makes it quite—quite decrepit for . . . for me!" She sank her face into her hands and sobbed.

Her ready sense of humour battling with her sympathy, Lisette took the weeping girl into her arms. "Poor Amanda. May I call you Amanda? Is it not dreadful to be heartbroken? I understand exactly how you feel."

Amanda raised her head from Lisette's damp shoulder and blinked at her. "You—do?" she said. "But—you are so very high—er—I mean—"

"High in the instep?" Lisette suggested, laughing. "Oh, never say so."

"I meant—highly born." Amanda accepted the handkerchief offered and attempted to dry her eyes with that tiny wisp of lace and fine cambric. "I cannot concede how you could know h-how I feel." And noting the curiosity touching the great dark eyes that watched her so sympathetically, she sighed. "Oh dear I must have said the wrong word again I always do it I try not to but somehow things get muddled up and Lucian my cousin Lucian St. Clair he's Jeremy's best friend next to Strand and Harry Redmond, Lucian is always quizzing me about it only I don't mind because he is the very dearest boy do not you think?"

The ingenuous gaze was lifted trustingly to hers. Astounded that so much had been said in one breath, Lisette smiled. "I know Lord St. Clair very slightly, but it would seem you've a most interesting story and I should so love to hear it. Would you call on me soon?"

"How very kind you are but—" The eager face became woeful again. "I doubt your mama would—"

"I have found you, I see."

Amanda gave a gasp, and Lisette turned, a horrible suspicion that she knew that brisk masculine voice confirmed when she saw who stood in the doorway. Justin Strand's ball clothes were very well cut and flattered him, she thought. The jacket was superb and the knee breeches revealed lean but surprisingly shapely legs. There was a suggestion of carelessness about the cravat, and his fair hair was neat but had certainly not been coaxed into one of the more modish styles. Yet Judith had spoken truly, and if he were only less gaunt he might be fairly attractive. A sense of repressed energy radiated from him, or perhaps that thin face made him look more intense than most men. Assuredly, he had his share of effrontery, for he had doubtless sought her out so as to beg her for a dance. Well, Mr. Justin Strand was in a fair way to being disappointed, for her card was quite full, as she would show him, did he dispute the matter! Why he should presume that she would condescend to dance with one of *his* revolting clan, was—

"I have come to beg you will dance the quadrille with me," he said predictably, coming into the room, a smile crinkling the corners of his eyes.

Lisette drew herself up, her brows arching quellingly. She began to lift her dance card, the better to emphasize her refusal.

"Good evening, Miss Van Lindsay," he said pleasantly, and walked past her, offering his arm to Amanda. "I do not mean to take no for an answer, Mandy."

Amanda voiced an inarticulate hodgepodge of protest. Strand bent, took both her hands, and pulled her to her feet. "Foolish child. Come now, or they will begin." And with a sideways grin at Lisette, he swept his reluctant partner from the room.

Lisette stared after them. "Well!" she said in a sort of gasp, and taking up a macaroon, sank her teeth into it with unnecessary ferocity.

When Lisette returned to the ballroom, an indignant Jocelyn Vaughan hurried to her and complained that the quadrille was almost over.

"And what has that to say to anything, young man?" demanded a querulous voice beside them.

Vaughan jumped, bowed deeply, and lifting the wrinkled hand of the old lady who viewed them with fierce dark eyes, kissed it.

"Had I known you were here, dear ma'am," he flirted, "I'd have spent the entire time at your side."

"I don't believe a word of it," snorted Lady Bayes-Copeland, not unkindly, rapping him with her fan. "Now, be off with you, Vaughan. I'd have words with my lady Toast, here!"

Still battling astonishment that her grandmama should have made one of her rare excursions into Society, Lisette was commanded to give her arm. She obeyed at once and, with the frail hand leaning on her quite heavily, led her ladyship to the side. No sooner had they found an empty sofa and sat down, than Camille Damon was before them, professing himself quite overwhelmed by the honour done them. "What may I bring you, ma'am?" he asked with a smile in his turquoise eyes. "A glass of ratafia . . . or negus . . . or . . .?"

"Rum, you wicked devil!" said my lady. "Nor tease an old woman when you've so lovely a girl of your own."

Damon bent over her. "God grant, ma'am, both I and my lady carry our years as well as do you!" And again, her hand was kissed.

"How many times tonight, Grandmama?" enquired Lisette, as he limped away.

"Well now, let me see . . . There was Vaille—lud, but you should have seen *him* in his youth! What a wild, wicked, handsome fellow! Camille has much of him, but not all—not all. And Ridgely, such a sweet, good soul. And Bolster, who has left, looking so sad, poor boy. And St. Clair, and Strand, and Vaughan, and—and what a'God's name is your sister about?"

"Judith?" asked Lisette, startled for more reasons than one.

"Beatrice. Has she run mad, the minx? I came upon her in an alcove with James Garvey! A good tongue-lashing I gave 'em both, I can tell you! I'm told you came with him. Why?"

Garvey and Beatrice? Taken aback, Lisette stammered, "Why—he asked me, ma'am. And why not? He is good *ton*, and from a fine old house."

"In my day, girl," her ladyship snarled, rapping her cane on the polished floor, "in my day, a woman could smell out a rake were he dustman or duke! Faith—*now* why must you blush and simper and peer around as though I'd filched the crown jewels? Because I said 'rake'? It's a prudish lot ye are these days and no denying! Now, what's to do with Beatrice and that milquetoast she's wed? Do they not deal well?''

"I think—that is to say . . . well, Beatrice is—is of a certain temperament, and William is—''

"Is a sorry fool. But a better man than she warrants, withal! 'Twould be like Madame Airy Contrary to cast aside the gold for the dross! And are you over your Leith megrims? It's time and past that you were looking elsewhere. Now why is your mouth at half-cock, miss? D'ye all think me blind?'' She gave a cackle of mirth. "Will ye look at the scarlet cheeks! You shall raise the temperature in this room, I don't doubt!'' She accepted the glass the Marquis returned to proffer, and bestowed a smile on that young man that gave one an inkling of what she must have been in her youth. "Thankee, Damon. And glad I am to see you limping so noticeably. You're not wearing that ridiculous boot you was used to fool us all with, eh?''

Damon had concealed his infirmity for years, and the colour of his own lean cheeks was somewhat heightened. He did not avoid those keen old eyes, however, and answered gravely, "No, ma'am. I am lame. There is a time for pride, and—''

"And a time for love?'' She cackled again. "Be off with you, then, back to your lady. And—no less than three, nor more than six, Camille! Hear me now!''

He threw a grin over his shoulder and was gone, leaving Lisette to gasp a shocked, "Grandmama!''

"Tush and a fiddlestick! He's more wits than you, child! Did you hear what he said? 'A time for pride . . .' '' She saw her granddaughter's pretty chin toss upward and sighed as though suddenly wearied. " 'Tis little I can set at your door, Lord knows. Your mama fairly bristles with the ugly vice, and that fool of a hus—er—ahem! Sufficient. Has Garvey offered?''

"Good gracious, no, ma'am! I have only known him a few days.'' Lisette's dark eyes grew troubled. "Mama and Papa think him very fine.''

"They would!'' The cane rapped angrily, causing the old lady to right her small but beautiful tiara which had become dislodged by the force of that movement. "It escapes me why I bother with the lot of you. What with your sister and her haughty ways, yet not above cuddling in alcoves! To say naught of that spoiled brat of a brother, and—''

"Your pardon, ma'am, but Norman has much to recommend him. He has a good mind, and always his nose is in a book."

"And his hands in the sweets! Is a fat little ill-mannered, sulky boy."

Despite the harsh words, Lady Bayes-Copeland was devoted to all of her grandchildren, knowing which, Lisette pointed out, "Had he but been sent to Eton or Harrow, they might have brought out the best in him. Only look at how well Timothy turned out."

"Aye." The old lady's eyes softened at this mention of her favourite. "But they'd have to dig deep to find aught of our Tim in Norman." She scowled and counter-attacked. "And do not evade the point, miss! What d'ye think of Garvey? Do you love him? Or is it too soon after Leith for you to know?"

Refusing to be flustered by these direct tactics, Lisette evaded, "He has been very kind and generous. He is a fine-looking man, well born, and with excellent prospects. He could only be a—a pleasant husband. And—if it would help my family . . ."

The old lady snorted. "A real love match! And with a lover at the side door before long, I'll wager! Well, perhaps 'tis the way of things for such as ourselves. Lord knows I'd my share of— Hum! Enough! Nor suppose your grandmama can be forever picking up bills. I've all I can do to keep my own tradesmen from the door. And besides, no good ever came from gifts. If that indolent do-nothing of a Humph—" She closed her lips and took a deep breath. "Your papa must raise his own lettuce. Not look to me. Or to you, gal! They've no right to push the burden onto your shoulders only because you're pretty as any picture. And I could wish you would look otherwhere than James Garvey. He ain't the man for you, Lisette. Had I to choose a mate for you, he'd be more after the style of—" She broke off, and asked sharply, "Well—and why must you be backing and filling, Strand?"

Lisette's head jerked around. Sure enough, there he stood. Bold as brass!

"I was merely waiting for you to finish your remarks, ma'am," he said courteously, but with his eyes twinkling at the old lady.

"And supposed it would be never, eh? Deny it, and you're a shifty rogue!"

"Either way you must think ill of me, so I'd best be dumb do I hope to win your favour."

Her lips quirked. She chuckled suddenly. "Neatly said. Rogue. Now, what are you about?"

"Merely claiming my dance with your granddaughter, ma'am."

Lisette stifled a gasp, her heart for some reason jumping into her throat.

Strand said calmly, "It *is* my waltz, I believe. . .?"

"You mistake, sir. You did not sign my card."

One eyebrow lifted. He said a cool, "No?"

She flung up the card and glared at it. His name seemed to leap out at her. "Oh!" she said, in such obvious dismay that the old lady frowned and shot an oblique glance at Strand's unreadable countenance. "If 'tis there, girl," she remarked, "you must honour your word."

"I did not give my word," Lisette fumed. "Someone must have written—" but she bit off that vexed accusation.

Strand asked, "Do I understand you to refuse me, Miss Van Lindsay?"

His eyes were cold, and he was perfectly right, of course. However slyly it had been accomplished, there was no graceful way to deny him, and undoubtedly many were watching to see how she rose to the occasion. With an effort, she controlled her indignation and got to her feet. "My apologies. I was surprised, merely. It is, as you said, your waltz, Mr. Strand."

He was not the best of dancers, but his clasp was firm, and at least he did not count aloud, which she had half expected. Not a few amused glances were directed at them as they whirled about the floor. Gritting her teeth, Lisette went out of her way to be charming. Strand vouchsafed scarcely a word in response to her efforts, but dreading lest she appear a spoilsport, she persevered. "I can see you have a kind heart, sir. It was good of you to dance with Miss Hersh."

"To the contrary. It was good of her to dance with me."

"Well, of course." She stiffened, unaccustomed to being taken up in such a way. "What I meant was—she was upset and shy, but she's not lacked for partners since."

"No reason she should. She's a deal more pleasant than many debutantes."

Enraged, Lisette murmured sweetly, "I stand corrected."

He flashed a swift glance at her set smile. "Am I being clumsy? I'm trying not to trample on your feet." Some of the ice went out of her eyes, and he added, "You also were kind. I overheard a little of what you told her." His sardonic grin flashed. "One might almost suppose you to be an expert in unrequited love."

Lisette caught her breath, and her hand trembled, so violently did she yearn to slap his mocking face. So he *did* know of her *tendre* for Leith! His horrid sister Rachel had boasted to him, no doubt! They had probably laughed over it. The vicious wretch, how *dare* he so taunt her? "I think," she said, struggling to conceal her loathing, "there is no question of unrequited love, sir. Lord Bolster's affections are deeply engaged, so I'm told. There is merely the matter of unfortunate family background."

"I'd thought Bolster quite presentable," he said nonchalantly. "And the Hershes are in some way related to the Raymonds, I believe, for I'm sure St. Clair's a distant cousin, and—oh, egad! You cannot mean because of Winfield Hersh? I was in India when it all came about, but surely Amanda is quite innocent. I'd scarce think his disgrace sufficient cause to break her engagement."

In view of his cruel gibe, Lisette would have died before admitting her agreement, and said crushingly, "Perhaps you would not, sir. But there are many who feel that *any* scandal would be sufficient cause—especially in the case of so ancient and unsullied a house as that of Lord Bolster."

If Mr. Strand was crushed, he gave no sign of it. "Tradition?" he shrugged. "I had hoped such antiquated and bacon-brained notions were in a fair way to being abandoned."

The waltz came to an end. Mr. Strand, a noticeable gleam in his eyes, bowed. Miss Van Lindsay, a noticeable spark in her eyes, curtsied. "Such a disappointment for you, sir," she murmured. "But I fear my sentiments are with those who revere tradition and place family and honour above all things."

"Bravo!" he said irrepressibly, ushering her from the floor. "Spoken like a true Whig, Miss Van Lindsay." He bent to her ear. "I was quite thrown in the close, wasn't I?"

Surprised, she looked up at him. The quirk beside his mouth was pronounced. Before she could restrain it, her own laugh rippled out. She managed to cut it short, but not before she had seen admiration change his expression.

*   *   *

"She is *detestable!"* Lady William Dwyer dabbed a tiny handkerchief angrily at her reddened eyes and, settling herself a little more comfortably into the old armchair in Lisette's bedchamber, sniffed, "She always has had an acid tongue, but to think of her—literally *pouncing* on us as though we had been engaged in—in a passionate embrace. The *look* she gave us! And the things she said! Oh! It quite makes me *shudder* for poor Mr. Garvey's sake!"

Since Beatrice was possessed of an acid tongue of her own, Lisette found it difficult to be deeply in sympathy with her remarks. "I'll admit Grandmama can be a trifle caustic sometimes," she began, "but, on the other hand—"

"Caustic indeed! And the frightful thing is she is sure to mention it to Mama, and if William hears of it, he will be *so* hurt."

She was closing the barn door when the horse had already bolted, thought Lisette. This tiresome interlude had lasted above half an hour, and she longed for her bed. "Grandmama mentioned William," she said, stifling a yawn. "She seems fond of him."

"And *I*—I suppose, am not? I, in fact, am a heartless wanton, conducting a torrid *affaire* behind my poor husband's back! With—with a man I scarcely—*know!*" The last word was a martyred wail, and the tears began to flow again.

"If you scarcely know him, dear," Lisette pointed out, striving for patience, "surely it was unwise to be alone with him in the alcove?"

"Oh—*base!*" flashed Beatrice, sitting bolt upright and fixing her sister with an indignant, if watery, eye. "A *fine* thanks for my efforts in your behalf! I risk my marriage; my reputation is . . . dragged in the mud! And all for a sister who only berates me for—for my sacrifice!"

Suddenly wide awake, Lisette exclaimed, "In *my* behalf? Whatever do you mean?"

"Well you may ask." Beatrice dabbed her at her eyes and, watching her sister from under her lashes, murmured, "Truth to tell, some rather odd rumours came to my ears. Rumours concerning you and—a certain gentleman. When I learned Mr.

Garvey was courting you—well, I know how splendid is *his* repute, so I made so bold as to ask his advice.''

Apprehensive, Lisette said, ''I wonder you did not take this tale to Papa and allow *him* to deal with it, rather than seeking counsel of a comparative stranger.''

''Much good that would have done! Papa is hand in glove with the man in question—besides being deep in his debt! You may be sure I would have got my ears boxed for interfering.''

Suddenly very cold, Lisette stood. She faced her sister, chin high, and with a bleak look in her eyes that reminded Beatrice of her grandmother. ''Very well,'' she said. ''Have done with the drama, or let us go to Papa together.'' Raising one hand to quiet her sister's frightened squeal, she demanded, ''Name this gentleman who speaks ill of me.''

''Not ill,'' Beatrice grumbled sulkily. ''Only confidently.''

''*What?* Then Timothy must come home and deal with the cur! His name!''

Her dark eyes blazed with passion; her gentle mouth was tightly compressed, and for the first time in her life, Beatrice was afraid of this quiet sister for whom she had always secretly felt scorn. ''His name is—is Justin Strand,'' she stammered. ''He says he has paid off all his papa's creditors and can restore his family name by simply marrying any lady of noble birth. He boasts his gold can buy any woman he chooses, and—and that he has already put a—a down payment on—*you*.''

It should not have come as such a shock, God knows! Nor was there any reason why she should suddenly see Strand smiling down at Amanda Hersh in that quiet ante-room. Lisette stood for an instant, rigidly still. Then she whirled and, ignoring Beatrice's frightened cry, ran to wrench open the door, rush down both flights of stairs and along the hall. To how many people had Strand dared bandy her name? Had he, in fact, actually spoken to Papa, without so much as a word to her? She gave a strangled sob as she burst through the study door, but then she froze, her impassioned demands dying unspoken. Her father was crumpled over his desk, his shoulders heaving, while his wife bent above him, her own cheeks streaked with tears.

Horrified, Lisette gasped, ''Oh—my dears! What is it? Whatever is it?''

''You have no business coming in . . . like that, Lisette,'' said her mother, turning swiftly away to dry her eyes. "Leave us, if you please."

Despite those brave words her voice was cracked and trembling. Lisette ran to put her arm about the bowed shoulders. "No, Mama. I am not a child. Whatever the trouble, I belong here, beside you and my father."

Keeping his face averted, Mr. Van Lindsay stood and strode to the fireplace to stare down at the logs, his handkerchief busy.

Philippa leaned against her daughter, reaching out to grip that comforting hand. "You're a good child. Very well, you should know. It is finances, of course. We have for some time been quite desperate. You cannot know how often I have—have gone to your grandmama, which makes Papa feel so degraded. He could not bear it, and so he took a desperate chance and—and invested in one of the new canals."

"It could very easily," Mr. Van Lindsay croaked from the fireplace, "have made us all rich!"

"Yes, indeed it could, my dear," agreed his wife. "But unhappily it was a disaster. The rain this year—and it has stayed so damp. There were too many delays, you see. They ran out of funds, and no one else would invest, so those already having money in the concern had to—to add more, or lose everything."

"But—but if you *had* no more. . .?"

"I borrowed," said Mr. Van Lindsay, hoarsely. "And now the canal company has gone bankrupt. God knows how I ever shall be able to—to repay!"

"My God!" whispered Lisette, her eyes a dark blur in her white face. "Whatever shall we do?"

"Sell. Everything. House, furniture, carriages, horses—everything!"

There was a brief, heavy silence, as they each envisioned this grim prospect. Her mouth dry and parched, Lisette asked, "And—if we do? Shall we have sufficient to start afresh? To buy a small house, perhaps, and live together still?"

"We might," said Mr. Van Lindsay heavily, "have enough to repay the man who holds my notes—who has kept me going through all this, with never a word of complaint, nor ever pressed me for payment."

Lisette gripped the back of a chair with both hands. "Justin Strand . . ."

Humphrey swung around. "You knew?" he gasped. "Never say he told you?"

"No. He did not tell me," she said, thinking bitterly: Instead, he bragged of it to his friends! But she dared not further humiliate her father—not with him looking suddenly so old and drawn. Clinging very tightly to the chair, she wet her dry lips and croaked, "Perhaps I can help. Mr. Garvey is, I think, quite interested. Were he to offer—and I accepted—"

"Much good that would do!" her mother said tartly. "Oh, we thought at first it would be a splendid match, but now we hear the gentleman is not near so plump in the pockets as we had supposed. As Timothy would say," she added hastily. "There is a way, however, in which you could bring us about, Lisette. I, as you are aware, have excellent expectations of my Uncle Ian. The poor old gentleman cannot have many years left to him. If we could just keep our heads above water until then—but for these wretched debts. . . . At all events, another gentleman has expressed a deep interest in you, and has already spoken to your papa in the matter. He is—not quite of our class, I own, but—"

Lisette threw one hand to her trembling mouth. "No, Mama!" she sobbed. "Not Justin Strand! Oh—*please!* To wed into that shamed family! To have to name Rachel Str—Rachel Leith my *sister!* I *could* not. Oh—I *could* not!"

"Good God! What a Cheltenham tragedy!" snorted her father with considerable irritation. "The boy's not *that* repulsive! He may not come near to young Leith in looks—or gallantry. Certainly not in lineage, sad to say. But, by gad, he's a cut above—er—some."

"I would think," Mrs. Van Lindsay put in coldly, "that any loving daughter would be glad of the power to rescue her family from ruin! Not act like some weak-kneed blancmanger when offered the chance."

"Ah, I do not, ma'am," Lisette whispered, reaching out one hand in poignant appeal. "You know how I love you and Papa. How grateful I am for the m-many kindnesses you have shown me."

"Much you show it!" sniffed Philippa. "Years of uncomplaining self-sacrifice for the sake of our children! And—for what?

Rejection! Abandonment! Oh—what bitter fruit!'' And she dissolved into her handkerchief.

Anguished, Lisette sobbed, ''Mama—I beg of you—do not. Papa, there *must* be someone else? Suppose Mr. Vaughan should offer. Or—or Galen Hilby? They are both wealthy, and—''

''A dozen men *might* offer,'' said Mr. Van Lindsay, with barely repressed impatience, ''but who could hold a candle to Strand? He's come home as rich as Golden Ball, I collect. Besides, we cannot wait, Lisette. It must be soon. Strand will keep a quiet tongue, I am assured.'' He added despondently, ''If Garvey knew, then Prinny and all the Court would know I'd had to allow a nabob from an inferior house to tow a Van Lindsay out of the River Tick! I—I should never be able to hold my head up again!''

Lisette looked prayerfully from one to the other. ''Was it so dreadful to have borrowed from him?''

Mrs. Van Lindsay muttered a miserable, ''His mother was well born, but his sister Leith is of very low repute. And his papa was caught . . . cheating at cards!''

''Yes! Yes!'' said Lisette, gripping her hands in her eagerness. ''Assuredly you would not wish me to marry into so wretched a house!''

''Oh, he's a good enough catch,'' asserted Mr. Van Lindsay, hurriedly mending his fences. ''Half the ladies in the *ton* are dropping the handkerchief for him!''

''And it is quite a different matter to accept so eligible a bachelor as a bridegroom than to have it known he made us loans,'' Philippa decreed regally. ''His lineage is not so bad, I expect—just that wretched father. And his sister, but you'd likely seldom see her.''

''I hear the Leiths reside in Berkshire pretty much all year round,'' said Humphrey, treading closer. ''Strand's not a muckworm, m'dear, I'll give him that. Likely he'd agree to a magnificent settlement!''

Her brief hope shattered, Lisette stared blankly before her. Whatever had happened to all her hopes—her dreams of becoming the bride of a splendid fighting man like Tristram Leith? Camille Damon's quiet words seemed to echo in her ears: ''There is a time for pride . . .'' For the sake of her loved ones, she must swallow her own. But she would not think of it now. Surely something must happen to save her. Surely some valiant gentleman would appear to rescue her from this horrid fate. Meanwhile . . .

"Very well," she said dully. "If Justin Strand offers, I—I will accept."

Chapter 4

Justin Strand did not call in Portland Place next day, nor did he appear during the following week. Lisette's nervous fears eased a little; to all outward appearances she was bright and happy, delighting the beaux who had sorely missed her during her "indisposition." The most assiduous of these was James Garvey. He called at least once each day and was quick to notice that his reception, at least from the senior Van Lindsays, was cooler than had been accorded him previously, and that his fair Lisette occasionally seemed a trifle preoccupied. Mr. Garvey was a shrewd gentleman; he had waited a considerable time before contemplating so binding a step as matrimony. In Miss Van Lindsay, however, he thought to have found the ideal mate, and heiress, for everyone knew that her penny-pinching grandmama was rich as Croesus. He had thought to have a clear field, but the changed attitudes in Portland Place caused him some unease, and he proceeded to pursue his chosen bride with single-minded determination. Judith formed the habit of waiting for the florist's cart to arrive on the street each day, whereupon she herself would bear the current offering to her sister. It was usually impressive, and on the following Wednesday morning consisted of an enormous bouquet of white roses.

"Just like a wedding," she sighed, delivering the flowers to Sanders and the card to Lisette. "I doubt you'll need a shawl, dearest. It's warm out."

Tying the pink satin ribbons of her fetching little bonnet, Lisette admired the roses, smiled at the message Mr. Garvey had inscribed on the card, and said, "How lovely. And how nice to see the sun. Have you your books? Is Norman to accompany us?"

"No." Judith giggled. "Mr. Worth is taking him to see the Elgin Marbles. He was grumpy as a bear when he heard Miss Lovell has a bad cold and will not come for my lessons today."

"If you was to ask me," Sanders volunteered, "Miss Lovell should have never been allowed to go daily. A young lady needs a governess until she has made her come-out."

They all knew that Miss Lovell now lived at home and only came from ten until four each day because the Van Lindsays could no longer afford a resident governess. With a pang, Lisette thought that when she was wed Judith would be able to have a proper governess again. Aloud, she said, "I would think Mr. Worth might have offered to take you with them, dear."

"Go to a history lesson with my brother and his tutor?" squeaked Judith, incensed. "I should rather turn up my toes!"

"And I suppose your brother taught you that vulgar expression! Come along, then. Do not forget your box."

Judith glanced at the box she had dropped on the bed. "Oh, it's not mine. Another offering from one of your admirers, I suppose. It was on the hall table."

Lisette opened the small box. Inside was a simple bunch of violets. Again the card bore no message, only the name, Justin Derwent Strand. A coldness touched her, and she stared blankly at the fragrant blooms.

Peering over her shoulder, Judith gave a scornful snort. "Strand! Who wants *his* old flowers? And if he is as rich as people say, one would think he could do better than that!"

"If you was to ask me," said Sanders, who had taken Mr. Garvey in dislike, "they are in better taste than *some* of the floral offerings that is brought here. And what's more, it's in *very* poor taste for a lady to look down her nose at a gift."

"Exactly so." Lisette passed her the flowers. "Would you please put them in water for me, Sandy? Come, Judith."

It was indeed a bright morning, and their walk to the circulating library was enlivened by Judith's account of the novel she returned. This gruesome tale delineated the horrors besetting a young girl who was taken from her convent by her indigent father and forced to marry one Sir Montague Knaresworth, a villain of such depravity as would freeze the blood. "You could not *believe* what poor Fiona endures at his hands!" said Judith dramatically. "In the end a brave gentleman befriends her and they run away together."

"Good gracious!" exclaimed Lisette. "Does Mama know you read such things? It sounds most improper."

"Oh, but it is enthralling. If you would but read it, Lisette. Sir Montague must have been a veritable monster. I cried and cried. It was lovely. Poor Fiona! A lady is so helpless when she marries, is she not? I kept thinking of how fortunate Beatrice is to have wed someone as amiable as William."

Lisette's smile faded. For a depressing moment she saw herself in Fiona's role—forced into marriage with a man she despised. . . .

The porter was swinging open the library doors, and they entered to find the large rooms redolent with the fragrances of coffee and perfumes, and humming with conversation. Deciding to exchange their books first and perhaps have some coffee afterwards, they proceeded to the counter and handed in their returns, then went to the bookcases at the side. The library was enjoying a thriving business. Quite apart from the convivial groups gathered about the tables enjoying their coffee or tea, many patrons browsed among the bookcases, and Lisette soon found herself separated from Judith. Moments later, she was hailed by a familiar voice and found the dashing Earl of Harland at her elbow. Harland, who was always willing to chat with a pretty girl, spent some moments discussing the recent marriage of his son, Viscount Lucian St. Clair, and the charm of the Damon ball. They were considering the merits of a new book of verse that had been highly recommended to Lisette, when she became aware of a hovering presence and glanced around to meet a pair of shy hazel eyes and a rather flushed young face. "Lord Bolster." She smiled, holding out her hand. "How do you do? I see you have not brought your dog this time."

"Br-Br, Br-Br- He's outside," he gulped, shooting a glance at Harland's impassive features. "V-v-very n-nice to me-meet you again, M-Miss Van Lindsay." Even more flushed, he persisted doggedly. "H-he-hear he m-made himself a c-c-blasted nuisance of himself in y'house. Humble apol-apol-ogies."

She assured him Brutus had been no trouble at all. "I imagine he would be a perfectly splendid watchdog, sir."

His lordship appeared gratified, but about to essay another speech, was dismayed by a sudden wild outburst of barking and a few assorted shrieks from outside. Paling, he stammered an apology and left them.

Lisette turned amused eyes to the Earl. "I hope he may not be hauled off by the Watch."

"I hope not, poor fellow. He has trouble enough. But, I suppose you know about him."

"I knew he was wounded at Badajoz. And that he seems a very nice young man."

"Oh, Jeremy's a splendid fellow. One of my son's closest friends, I'm happy to say. He was speaking quite well again until recently. But when he and Amanda ended their engagement . . ." He sighed. "When Jeremy is upset, his stammering intensifies."

"What a pity. Indeed, I think it the saddest thing, for they would make such a delightful couple."

"Not sad, ma'am. Ridiculous. The only thing keeping them apart is my niece's totally unwarranted sense of unworthiness. One fails to convince her that people hold her blameless. The people who matter, at all events."

An even louder burst of barking sent Harland's worried glance to the door. "Your pardon, Miss Van Lindsay. I'd best go. Bolster may need a spokesman." He bowed over her hand, and departed.

It was time for her to leave also, but there was no sign of Judith. Suspecting her sister had been lured outside by the commotion, Lisette collected her books, went to the counter, and thence to the outer doors. Sure enough, Judith and Bolster were standing on the flagway, engaged in earnest conversation, Judith caressing the dog's unhandsome head while he panted at her with a decidedly crocodilian smile. Several elderly ladies inched past uneasily. Of Lord Harland there was no sign, but as she came up with them, Lisette was mildly surprised to hear Bolster extolling the virtues of his pet with scarcely a stammer.

"Oh, there you are, dear," said Judith. "I've been waiting

this age. You know Lord Bolster, do you not? And is not Brutus delicious? I am permitted to hold the leash while we walk home.''

Recalling Judith's previous reaction to the ''delicious'' canine, Lisette blinked, but said with a smile, ''How kind in you, sir. I fancy we will go quite unmolested, for no one would dare steal our books with you and Brutus guarding us.''

Bolster laughed, Judith claimed the leash, and they all set off. Lisette's hope to get to know this shy young gentleman a little better was foiled, however. They had no sooner crossed Bond Street than Brutus gave every evidence of being demented. He yowled, barked wildly, reared onto his back legs, and, with a great bound, tore free from Judith's grasp and galloped untidily in the direction of a slender gentleman walking towards them. With sinking heart, Lisette recognized Justin Strand's quick stride.

''Good heavens!'' gasped Judith. ''Brutus will knock him down!''

Lisette watched interestedly, but she was not to be diverted by such a scene. As the dog's mad charge neared him, Strand said a sharp, ''Brutus! Sit!'' and the dog flung himself down and sat wriggling and uttering little squeaks and snuffling barks of joy.

''Why w-won't he do that for m-me?'' Bolster asked plaintively as they came up with man and beast.

Caressing the ecstatic Brutus's ears, Strand caught a glimpse of Judith's suddenly mirthful countenance, and answered, ''Why, he will in time, Jeremy. You must be firm with him, is all. Good morning, Miss Van Lindsay.''

For the sake of her parents, Lisette returned the salutation with some vestige of warmth. ''I must make you known to my younger sister,'' she said, fixing that convulsed damsel with a minatory glare. ''Judith, this is Mr. Justin Strand.''

Strand bowed and, well aware that the youthful Judith was picturing poor Bolster's efforts to snap out a brisk command to Brutus, enquired as to whether she was a dog lover. Subdued by his steady stare, Judith replied in the affirmative and in very short order they were all walking together in the direction of Portland Place. Just how it came about, Lisette was unable to tell, but almost before she knew it, Mr. Strand was beside her, while Bolster went on ahead with Judith and Brutus.

''A beautiful morning, ma'am,'' Strand observed politely.

"Yes. It is nice to see the sun again."

"And to feel it. Quite a change."

She threw an oblique and suspicious glance at him, but his face was perfectly grave. "It may be warm, later on," she offered scintillatingly.

"That would be pleasant, don't you agree?"

She thought, Good God! What a conversationalist! but, much too well-bred to betray her boredom, responded, "I do," and was unable to resist adding, "So good for the flowers."

"Well, that's out of the way!" He gave a whimsical grin. "What next? Shall we turn to Brutus? That would be a safe subject."

Lisette smothered a laugh. "No, Brutus must wait. I have first to thank you for those charming violets."

"Dainty flowers for a dainty lady." He slanted an amused glance at her. "Had I supposed you the type to be impressed by pretension, I'd have sent three dozen red roses."

Lisette's heart began to beat a little faster. He was commencing his courtship, beyond doubting. Without much subtlety. Oh, if *only* he had been someone she could care for a little; someone unrelated to the Strands, who had helped her father because he was deep in love, not merely because he desired to purchase a socially acceptable bride. "Only three dozen?" she teased.

He chuckled. " 'Ware, ma'am. I never refuse a challenge. You may find it necessary to use a scythe to escape your front hall tomorrow morning!"

She threw up an imploring hand. "Pray—do not! I—"

"Is that villain upsetting you, Miss Van Lindsay?" James Garvey, driving a dashing black phaeton with wheels picked out in yellow, pulled up alongside and said laughingly, "How fortunate that I found you before he bullied you into forgetting our drive."

Lisette hesitated. Surely she had not overlooked an engagement? Garvey was handing the reins to his tiger and jumping lightly down. She glanced at Strand. His face was devoid of expression, but the smile had left his eyes.

"Surely you err, Garvey," he said, a pronounced sardonic ring to his voice. "Miss Van Lindsay could not have forgot so impressive a gentleman as yourself."

Garvey flushed a little, but at once riposted, "There, you see, ma'am? Even Strand knows a real gentleman when he sees one.''

Lisette stifled a gasp. Strand stiffened, and Bolster, who had watched this dangerous interchange uneasily, walked to his side. "C-come on, old f-f-f-" he said urgently.

"Fellow," Garvey finished for him, and stepped forward.

A large, growling, and muscular bulldog was suddenly between the group and the advancing Corinthian. Strand snapped, "Brutus!" and the dog checked, but did not relax his threatening mien.

Garvey also halted. "Gad, Miss Van Lindsay." He looked straight into Strand's cold eyes. "I believe you were right when you said 'twas a most unattractive creature!"

Beneath his tan, Strand was very pale, but those blue eyes fairly blazed, and the jut of his jaw was alarming. Lisette felt Judith's trembling hand slip into her own. In another moment there would be a challenge—and she the cause! She dared not offend Strand, and had no wish to hurt Garvey, and therefore said quickly, "Do you know, sir, you are mistaken. My engagement was to drive in the park with you this *afternoon*—not this morning."

"True," lied Garvey, wrenching his eyes from Strand to smile down at her. "But—*c'est tragique*—I find I am unable to be in Town this afternoon. Can you deny me?" His contemptuous gaze returned to Strand. "Under the circumstances?"

"Oh, very well." Lisette glanced to the scared Judith. "But, my sister—"

"Why, Bolster's a good fellow," said Garvey. "He will see Miss Judith safely home."

The slight was as cutting as it was obvious. Bolster frowned, but Strand ignored it and declared, "We will be most happy to escort your sister home, ma'am. The price you must pay is to allow me the time Garvey has relinquished this afternoon."

Garvey scowled, but before he could speak, Lisette turned and held out her books. "Thank you so much, Mr. Strand. In that case, will you be so kind as to take these home for me?"

Strand accepted the books. He was still pale and his eyes savage with anger, but he said in a controlled voice, "Gladly. I shall call at three."

It was earlier than was customary, but the weather was still too cool to make a later drive desirable. Lisette nodded, gave her hand to Garvey, and was assisted into the vehicle. Garvey took up the reins. His tiger released his hold on the bridles of the team, sprang back, then made a dash for the back of the phaeton as it rolled past. He clambered onto his perch and sat like a graven image, arms folded and back ramrod straight.

"The impertinence of that beastly fellow!" fumed Garvey. "I may find it necessary to teach him a lesson in manners!"

Very conscious of the pair of small ears behind them, Lisette was silent. If such a man as Mr. Garvey could really have been her champion, how gratefully she would allow him to shoulder her burdens. But in this situation, no one could help. Stifling a sigh, she said softly, "I could wish you had not repeated my remark about Brutus. I fear Mr. Strand may have placed a wrong interpretation upon it."

"I certainly hope he did! Oh, I know it was very bad in me, but truly, I could not resist. And if it should drive him off, it will have been worthwhile. I admit most of London's bachelors are my rivals, but *that* particular individual I will not tolerate! Some of the things I hear— And that such as he would have the gall to pursue so pure and highly born a—"

"Sir!" Lisette interpolated. "Your servant!"

"Who?" He glanced over his shoulder at the boy. "Lion?"

Lisette laughed softly. "Your tiger's name is Lion? But, how quaint!"

"I must have named him with a premonition that someday it would cause you to laugh in just that delightful way," he murmured. Lisette blushed. She said nothing, but Garvey sensed her embarrassment and said, "Never worry, dear lady, he would never betray me. Would you, Lion?"

" 'Sright, sir," said Lion woodenly.

"You'd not dare, you young rogue!" Garvey grinned. "At all events, ma'am, I must not complain of Strand's despicable conduct, since it has enabled me to have you here, beside me. Only see how the sun came out today—purely to shine on your beauty." He peered down at her. "I am *most* grateful you came."

"You must suppose me to be fast, I fear. But—you both seemed so angry, and I could not bear to be the cause of real ill feelings."

They turned into the park and, slowing his team, Garvey said grimly, "You are not, ma'am. What I feel for Justin Strand goes beyond— But enough of him! Likely you would prefer to walk for a little?" He drove along beside the Serpentine, then pulled the team to a halt and tossed the reins to the small Lion. "Walk 'em!" he said tersely, and springing out, reached up to aid Lisette from the vehicle.

He led her along a winding path until they came to a secluded seat, away from the water and the more travelled areas. It was improper, she knew, to be alone with him like this, but her heart was so heavy she scarcely heeded that knowledge. For a few minutes they sat in silence. Glancing up then, she saw Garvey patiently watching her. "Oh, your pardon!" she apologized. "I fear my thoughts wandered."

"And sadly." He took up one small, gloved hand. "Miss Van Lindsay, will you do me the honour to confide in me? What has brought such sorrow to those lovely eyes?"

"Sir—I am indeed grateful, but—"

"If you are truly grateful, then—oh, pray forgive if I rush matters. But from the very first moment I saw you—"

Appalled, she tried to free her hand. "No, do not. Please. You must not."

"How can I help myself? When first I called at your house I had no suspicion I was about to be dealt a leveller. I had thought only to—" He stopped, as though having been betrayed into saying more than he'd intended, then rushed on in a voice husky with emotion. "You are thinking I should speak to your father, and indeed I mean to do so. Ah, my dearest, most adored of ladies, can you not know how hopelessly I am fallen in love with you?"

The pleading intensity, the glowing warmth in his eyes vouched for his sincerity. Remotely, Lisette wondered why she felt trapped and afraid, instead of being delighted. It must, she thought, be because of the circumstances and her dread of wounding him. She drew her hand away. "No, oh, never say so! Truly, I had no thought to bring you sadness!"

He stiffened. "I am to be refused, then? I see." And in a tight, restrained fashion, "I should not ask, I know. But—is there someone else?"

She wrung her hands, wishing she had never come with him.

"Yes. No! That is—oh, I cannot say, but—but I am not free to—"

"Not free?" he echoed harshly. "No, by God! And not happy, either! You are not officially betrothed, but someone hounds you. Is that it?"

Her eyes stinging with sudden tears, Lisette shook her head.

Garvey again captured her hand and held it tightly despite her efforts to pull away. "You are being intimidated, I'll lay odds! Who dares to frighten you? If it is that wretched Strand—I've seen him go into your house several times. I knew he was about some devilment, but—"

"You have *seen* him?" she echoed unsteadily. "But how can this be? Have you been watching my home?"

He smiled ruefully. "Day and night, dear lady. I fairly haunt the neighbourhood. Just to be close to you brings me joy—even though you do not guess I am there."

Overwhelmed by such devotion, she blinked. "Oh—how dreadful! I had not realized your affections were so deeply engaged."

"They are. And thus I implore that you do not speak with such finality. Am I to be denied all hope? What is the hold he has over you? Do you love him? Lisette, *please* tell me if that is so, and I'll—I'll not trouble you further."

She said miserably, "I have not named Justin Strand, sir. Or—any other gentleman. My—my future is arranged. I can . . . say no more."

His voice low and throbbing with anger, he declared, "Strand was right! It is that same filthy idol—the god of gold! I never thought when he bragged—" He checked, bit his lip, and grated, "Forget I said that."

Horrified by his verification of Beatrice's warning, Lisette cried, "Strand bragged—in your hearing, sir? About—me?"

"I should not," he muttered. "But—oh, devil take him! If I hear him boast one more time that money can buy anything, I—" Again, he mastered himself, and did not complete the threat.

With tears of shame and rage glistening on her lashes, Lisette whispered, "Then, it *was* truth!"

"He *does* hound you, doesn't he? By heaven, I'll call him to account, the encroaching mushroom! And rid you of him."

Lisette was so distressed as to feel actually sick, but she fought off the sensation. It was not beyond the realm of possibility that Garvey would do just as he said. He had been out before, she knew, and was considered very dangerous. Quite apart from her natural horror of duelling, it would be to no avail. If he was wounded or slain she would have an even heavier weight on her heart, and if he killed Strand, not only would she consider herself to blame, but the man's affairs would certainly pass to his sister. The Van Lindsays would get short shrift from that jade, and thus be in even worse case. She therefore begged that Garvey not even think of so dreadful a thing. "It must only make matters worse. And besides, there are other considerations that I cannot reveal to you, that would make such a tragedy pointless."

Garvey's green eyes were very empty all at once. "Other considerations? Such as, ma'am?"

Lisette gave a weary gesture. "As I said, I cannot discuss them. Please take me home now, or my—"

He leaned closer, demanding, "*What* other considerations? Your father has been listening to idle gossip, perhaps? My friends do not please him—is that the sum of it?"

Lisette made as if to stand but, infuriated, he so far forgot himself as to catch her wrist and pull her back. "Perhaps I should speak with—"

A brightly coloured ball bounced around the bend, closely followed by a little boy in grass-stained nankeens. Lisette seized her opportunity and stood as two nursemaids wheeled their small charges along the path. She walked rapidly away, keeping her head slightly averted, praying they might not recognize her.

Her hope was vain.

"Oho!" breathed one of the nursemaids, her plump features wreathed in a grin. "If Miss hoity-toity Van Lindsay's *his* latest flirt, the cat's in with the chicks, and no mistaking!"

" 'Ere," said her friend, eagerly. "Oo was it, Ada? I know 'er, a'course. But oo was the genle'man?"

Ada imparted with relish, "That there 'gentleman,' me dear Flo, was none other than James Garvey! Him as is a bosom bow of our Florry Sell!"

"Our *oo?*" asked Flo, her brow furrowing.

"Ow, come on, Flo! You know who Florrey Sell is. Our Prince, duck."

"Prince? Oh, you mean George? *Wot* did you call 'im?"

"Florrey Sell! Lawks sake! Ain't you never heard that? It's what they called him when he was young and fair."

Flo uttered a disparaging snort. "Fairly fat, if you ask me!"

"The point is that Garvey's thicker 'n thieves with him. And you know what they say about the Regent!"

"No," breathed Flo, her eyes very wide. "Oo does?"

"Ow! Flo!"

Lisette entered the house through the areaway and asked Cook to send a light luncheon to the breakfast room. She further astonished that lady by washing her hands at the kitchen sink, for she had no wish to be seen by any member of the family until her nerves were quieter. She took off her bonnet and shawl in the breakfast room and ate her luncheon in solitude, her thoughts on the shocking truths James Garvey had divulged. She tried not to dwell on Strand's infamy. He was no gentleman, which she should have realized at all events, and to expect him to behave like one must only court disappointment and deepen her dislike of the man she was apparently doomed to wed. Garvey had apologized for his anger, but once they were in the phaeton, neither had spoken until they reached Portland Place. Lisette had stolen an occasional glance at him and discovered a pale face and frowning brow, the green eyes brooding. He had escorted her to the door, shaken her hand and said his goodbyes very properly, but the grimness had persisted, and she was left with a dread of what he meant to do.

She had no intention of mentioning his declaration, but it was evident that Judith had spoken of the earlier encounter, for when Lisette started up the stairs, her father called her down again and into his study, where he asked if she wished that he warn Garvey off. Something in his daughter's wan expression alerting him, he demanded, "What? Has he had the impertinence to address you?"

She pointed out, "You must remember, Papa, that at first you were all that was amiable. We can scarce expect the poor man to comprehend why our attitude has changed. He has been very kind, and—"

"*Kind,* d'ye call it? To subject two ladies to that disgraceful fiasco this morning? I call it damnably rag-mannered. Little Judith was still frightened when she come home, though Strand had done what he might to calm her. Had he not kept himself in hand, Lord only knows where things might have led! I'll be dashed if I don't begin to think well of that young fella!"

Relieved that his attention had strayed from the offending Garvey, Lisette pleased her papa by informing him that Mr. Strand intended to call, to take her driving.

"Then you will want to change your dress," he said, accompanying her to the stairs. "And I fancy Judith is waiting to speak with you. She is in the parlour. With Beatrice."

Lisette's pause was barely perceptible. Walking on, she thought that this day showed little promise of improving. Beatrice could be charming when she chose, however, and was evidently in good spirits, because upon entering the parlour, Lisette found her sisters laughing merrily together.

"Here you are at last!" exclaimed Beatrice, standing to give her a peck on the cheek. "Such an age you have been! But Judith has kept me entertained with her account of this wicked novel she has been reading. What Mama would say I dare not guess, but I could not keep from laughing when she told me of Sir Montague. She says his description fairly matches Justin Strand—tall and bony, with evilly glistening eyes. Is she not a naughty little puss so to mock him?"

"And ungrateful!" Lisette flashed an angry glare at Judith. "You forget, do you not, that Mr. Strand was so kind as to escort you home this morning?"

"Well, I did not need his offices," declared Judith, her nose in the air. "Lord Bolster and Brutus were sufficient of an escort. And besides, not only is Mr. Strand socially beneath us, but he's not near so handsome as Mr. Garvey."

Beatrice laughed, but Lisette exclaimed, "For shame! Whatever else he may be"—and little did they know how low!—"he is a—a friend of my father. And Grandmama thinks the world of him!"

"Scarcely a glowing recommendation." Beatrice sat on the sofa again, and tittered, "Lud, girl, why do you rage at us? One might almost think you were becoming fond of the creature."

"Then one would be most foolish! It is simply that I cannot

abide unkindness. Which reminds me, I had thought you were going back to Somerset with William?''

"Oh, he went back." Beatrice shrugged. "But I decided to stay in town for a while. I am invited to visit Dorothy Haines-Curtis. She is upset because she was obliged to send Harry Redmond about his business. The Redmonds are bankrupted, you know, so she is well rid of him. And why my plans should be any of your bread and butter, I cannot guess.''

Lisette, who was fond of Sir William, fixed her with a cold stare. "Can you not?''

Beatrice's eyes fell. She stood, exclaiming, "I declare, I cannot be in this house above an hour without coming to cuffs with someone! Nobody cares how *I* feel—nor what *my* life is like in that lonely old house . . . miles from any excitement!'' With tears coming into her dark eyes, she said on a sob, "Nobody even *tries* to understand!'' And with a flounce of silks, she sped from the room.

Lisette turned to Judith. "I think it will be as well, dear, if we forget what Beatrice just said. She likely does not mean it.''

"Oh, yes, she does. She is bored. She doesn't like that house in Somerset. And I doubt she likes William very much, either.'' Abandoning the air of sophisticated languor she had copied from Beatrice, Judith now bounced up, saying with ghoulish appreciation, "Was that not a famous confrontation this morning? I was sure Mr. Strand was going to take off his glove and cast it in Mr. Garvey's teeth! How thrilling that would have been! I probably would have fainted away.''

Lisette said dryly, "So might Mr. Strand. I hear James Garvey is a dead shot!''

Chapter 5

Promptly at three o'clock Mr. Justin Strand was announced and at once strode swiftly into the drawing room. Lisette had been idly turning the pages of *Ladies Magazine* and looked up, startled, schooling her features into a smile that died a'borning. In anticipation of a carriage ride, she had donned a high-necked gown of cream silk, the bodice overlaid with ecru lace, and had selected a fine straw bonnet with a high poke trimmed in the same shade of lace. Mr. Strand, however, was dressed very formally in an impressive dark brown velvet jacket, fawn knee breeches, and a magnificent cravat in which a great topaz gleamed. Not a little dismayed, she rose as he marched across the room to halt before her.

"Good afternoon," she faltered, holding out her hand. "I must thank you, Mr. Strand, for your—your understanding this morning. And for escorting my sister home. Perhaps I should call my mother. I'd not realized you meant to come up, and—"

His clasp was firm, brief, and icy cold. "And it is improper to be alone with me," he said in his brusque way. "I know. That is why I asked the footman not to announce me until I was up here. There is something I must discuss with Mr. Van Lindsay. I am told he is at home, but first, I must know. Miss Lisette—have you taken me in aversion?"

With the moment of truth upon her, she stared at him in blank shock. He was a little pale, and the thick light hair with its tendency to turn upwards at the ends was rumpled as though he had run a nervous hand through it. Those intense eyes seemed to burn through her defences so that she lowered her own and lied, "Why, no. But—but, I know you so slightly, sir. It is very—er, soon to—to—"

"You know my background; my family," he interpolated gruffly. "Tell me without frills if you please, ma'am. Would an offer from me be—repulsive to you?"

From under her lashes she saw that his jaw had set, and that a little nerve pulsed in his cheek. His hands, too, were clenching and unclenching, and she noted absently what long, thin, sensitive fingers he had. Could it be possible that he did care for her a little? What stuff! If he cared for anything, it was that he not be made to look ridiculous by suffering a rejection after his braggadocio! Recovering her poise, but her heart recoiling from this duplicity, she lifted her eyes to his. "For a lady to receive an offer of marriage can only be a great compliment, sir."

For an instant, something that might almost have been regret came into his expression, and was as quickly gone. "I see." He nodded, and stepped back. "Will you be so good as to excuse me, then?"

Lisette murmured, "Of course," and watched him stalk from the room. She sat down again, tears blinding her. What a perfectly horrid proposal of marriage. The antithesis of everything she had ever dreamt of. How stiff and cold he was. How totally lacking even a touch of romance. The odious creature had not so much as kissed her hand. After they were wed, she would likely freeze to death! And then, she thought miserably, everyone would be sorry.

The object of her thoughts paced along the hall, slowed, and stopped at the top of the stairs. With one hand resting on the banister, he stared blankly at the lower hallway. She didn't want him, that was very clear. But she would not refuse him. His brows drew together. Perhaps, if he waited . . . But he dared not wait. Garvey would not wait, and Garvey could upset the whole applecart! He squared his shoulders, ran an impatient hand through his hair, and hurried lightly down the stairs.

He had visited this house sufficiently often to find his way to the study but when he reached the door, he again paused. He could hear Van Lindsay talking very loudly inside, and Mrs. Van

Lindsay's voice raised in complaint. His knock received no answer and, looking about for a servant to announce him properly, he saw no sign of life. He opened the door, then stopped, blinking in astonishment.

The butler, footman, and two maids sat at one side of the room, watching their employer, who strode up and down, several sheets of paper close-covered with writing in one hand, and the other arm waving as he roared out a speech. Mrs. Van Lindsay, elegant in a gown of dark blue sarsenet braided with white at flounce and throat, ran along beside him, exhorting, pleading, demanding, all to no avail.

A slow grin curved Strand's mouth, and he watched, delightedly.

". . . the fields are being gobbled up!" thundered Van Lindsay.

"You will trample a hole clear through, do you not sit down, sir!" moaned Mrs. Van Lindsay, trotting just as destructively at his side.

"They do not farm! They buy up the land only for their own aggrandizement, and seldom set foot on it!"

"Your feet will touch the boards soon enough, do you not stop this horrid pacing!"

"*Thousands* have lost their place! Our valiant fighting men have been disbanded with neither thanks nor reward! The taxes are eating us up! And these reckless fools build their palaces, and—"

"Sit down! Will you not sit down, Mr. Van Lindsay? I beg! There are bare strands now! Another few strides, you will be through to the backing!"

The bedevilled orator halted. "By gad, madam! Can you think of nothing but your confounded floor coverings? I am striving to—" Here, chancing to encounter the amused glance of his guest, Humphrey gave a gasp. "Mr. Strand!" he cried with uncertain joviality. "Er—that will be all, you people."

Hiding covert grins, the servants fled. Mrs. Van Lindsay looked briefly ready to swoon, but recovered to extend her hand in a queenly gesture and assure Mr. Strand he was most welcome, although she would wish someone had been available to receive him.

Inwardly delighted that the lapse in protocol had enabled him to witness such a scene, Strand replied, "I am encouraged to feel sufficiently at home that I came on, ma'am. I trust I have not offended.''

"No, no!'' She granted him a rather toothy smile. "Never that, Mr. Strand. You are—always welcome. You have come to call for my daughter, I believe?''

"No, ma'am. I have come for a word with your husband. If I do not intrude at a difficult moment?''

"Never!'' Van Lindsay beamed, all but throwing his speech aside. "My dear, you will be so kind as to require that Powers bring a bottle of the 'seventy-four Madeira. Now, my dear Strand, sit down and be comfortable. Tell me—what may I do for you?''

"Do not cry! Oh, *please* do not cry!'' wailed Judith, fluttering about her sister with damp rag in hand and tears of sympathy filling her own eyes. "My poor darling! How could they be so *heartless?* Sold! Like sweet Fiona! I vow it is *inhuman!*'' She stood straight and flung up the rag in her distress, proclaiming, "We should *protest!* We must strike a blow for—''

"What the deuce?'' chortled Norman, stepping into the room. "Practising dramatics, Judith? Do you play the hero, or the abigail?''

"Odious wretch!'' his sister snarled, throwing the rag at him. "Can you not see that poor Lisette is dying of grief?''

"What? Oh, Lord!'' he gasped, dismayed by the sight of tears. "My—er, apologies, Lisette. It is not—Grandmama?''

"No. Thank goodness,'' gulped Lisette, trying valiantly to stop weeping. "It—it is only—''

"She has received An Offer,'' said Judith, eyeing her quailing brother with revulsion. "Men!''

"Good God! How many?'' he gasped.

Lisette could not restrain a watery smile. "One—this afternoon.'' She ignored the surprised glance Judith shot at her. "Justin Strand.''

Norman was so diverted as to forget discretion. He took out the piece of nougat he had been hiding in his pocket, removed a leaf from it, and popped it into his mouth. "Hmmn,'' he said indistinctly. "He's not a commoner, whatever they say of his family. And—at least it's not Garvey.''

"Garvey would be a—a paladin compared to Strand,'' Judith

declared with indignation. "And you thought him wondrous great when he first began to fix his attentions with Lisette."

"I doubt you know what 'paladin' means, even!" He did not add that he'd written to his brother Timothy in the matter, nor did he mention Tim's reply, now residing in his desk, but said merely, "Changed my mind about the fellow. Was it my decision, I'd have Strand, Lisette."

"And was it my decision, she should have neither, but wait until a Prince of the Blood offers!" Judith announced grandiloquently. "She has the looks, the lineage, and the grace, goodness knows."

"Well, *hee haw!*" mocked Norman. "From the look of her, she don't mean to have neither. Is that the sum of it, Lisette?"

"No." Lisette stood. "I shall wed Mr. Strand." She smiled sadly at Judith's agonized wail and, saying she must go and tidy her hair, went up to her bedchamber. Sanders was waiting and, taking one look at her favourite, held out her arms. Lisette walked into them and wept.

"My lamb." Sanders stroked the glossy hair comfortingly. "Never you mind. Things has a way of working out for the best. You'll find your happiness yet. Just look at Emily Cowper, married and a Countess, but in love with Palmerston as all London knows. Love don't always come where it's supposed to, my dearie."

"I know," Lisette sniffed, drawing back and drying her eyes. "That's what Grandmama said. Only . . . I had so hoped . . ." Her voice scratched into silence. She went over to sit down at her dressing table, and gave an aghast cry at the sight of her red and puffy eyes. "Oh, Sandy! They will be calling me downstairs!"

"Never you fear. We'll have you pretty as a picture in a trice. You just close your eyes now." Sanders proceeded to bathe Lisette's eyes with icy cold water, and then skilfully applied cosmetics. "Was Mr. Strand all loving words and flowery speeches, my lamb?" she asked.

"No! He—he was horribly cold and—and businesslike. He stamped up to me as though he were on a parade ground, and when I uttered a perfectly natural and maidenly demurral, he practically barked out that I knew his family, and demanded to know if an offer from him would be repulsive to me." Blinking away fresh tears, she said, "He—he might have been bidding at a cattle auction!"

"Poor lad," Sanders smiled, and as her lady's eyes flew open to fix her with an indignant stare, she shrugged, "Well, you know, Miss Lisette, some men has the gift of the gab, and some hasn't."

"Lisette!" Judith burst into the room, quivering with excitement. "Papa has sent Pauline to ask if you can please step into the drawing room only I came instead and what did you mean when you said one this afternoon did Mr. Garvey offer this morning?"

"Lawks!" gasped Sanders. "Whatever did you say, Miss Judith?"

Jumping up and down in agitation, Judith demanded, "Lisette! *Did* he?"

Lisette stood, smoothing her frock and knowing she looked fairly well restored. "Yes. He offered. And I refused."

Judith uttered a shriek and threw herself backwards onto the bed, to lie with arms wide-tossed. "What a waste! What an awful waste!"

Sanders muttered, "I doubt Mr. Garvey had any lack of flowery words."

Lisette said, "No. As a matter of fact, he did not."

And, sadly, she went downstairs to accept the hand of Mr. Justin Derwent Strand.

The newly betrothed gentleman politely refused an invitation to remain for dinner at the home of his affianced bride. Walking beside her to the front door, he directed a keen gaze at her composed features and said in his abrupt fashion, "I mean to make you a good husband, ma'am. I hope to make you happy."

Lisette looked steadily at him, wondering what he would think if he knew she was aware of the disgraceful way in which he had bandied her name about. Her silence apparently discomposed him, for he lowered his gaze, muttered, "I shall call to take you riding in the morning," accepted his hat and cane from the butler, and walked outside.

Turning about, he said with a flickering grin, "At half-past six," and left her speechless with shock.

She had not the remotest intention of arising at such an hour, but she began to harbour the uneasy suspicion that if she were not ready at the appointed time, Strand would not be above rousing the house. Vexed, she instructed Sandy to waken her at quarter to six, and by half-past the hour, clad in her most attractive habit, was peeping from the drawing room window.

"I'm over here!" announced a familiar voice behind her.

She spun around to find Strand watching her in obvious amusement. He looked different somehow in his riding clothes; more at ease, perhaps, in the brown corduroy jacket, beige breeches, and spurred boots. "Come," he said, holding out an imperative hand.

Resenting the suggestion of command, she sauntered to his side, tried to ignore that thin hand, but somehow found it clasping her own. He took a small box from his pocket, opened it, and revealed a ring that took her breath away. There were two diamonds and a round emerald, of superb hue and cut, mounted in a charming design of filigreed gold. "They were my grandmother's gems," he imparted, slipping the ring onto her finger.

"How lovely! And the fit is perfect. What a good guess!"

"Not at all. Your abigail gave me one of your rings to take to the jeweller. I commissioned Rundell and Bridge to design the new setting for you."

Frowning a little, she said, "You did? When?"

"Oh, last week," he answered airily, and stifling a smile at the immediate indignation in her face, said, "Come along. I cannot keep the horses standing."

"Nor can I make a practice of this. You must know, Mr. Strand, that—"

"Do you fancy you could manage to use my name?" he asked, suddenly wistful. "Since I did not ask for a kiss."

Colour flooded her cheeks. "You—are quite at—at liberty to take one, sir—Justin."

"Justin will do nicely," he said, kindly. "I have no title, you know."

Yearning to scratch him, Lisette swept from the room. Downstairs, he seized her hand as she started for the front door, and led her instead to the back of the house.

"What on earth?" she asked, curious.

"I came around the back, so that you would not see me arrive. Just in case you were peeping through the curtains, I mean."

Bristling, she resumed the attack. "Which reminds me, I do not make a habit of rising at this hour, and—"

"Never mind. You'll get used to it. This way."

He marched across the lawn as though this were his house instead of the home in which his seething fiancée had grown up, and opened the back gate.

Lisette walked ragefully into the alley. A groom held two fine horses, one a big chestnut stallion, and the other a black mare, all fine Arabian daintiness. Her vexation forgotten, Lisette went at once to stroke the mare. "What a beauty! You never found her at the stables? Is she yours?"

"No. She's yours."

She gave a gasp, and stared at him.

He said quietly, "Your engagement present, my dear." And, heedless of the groom's presence, he bent and kissed her on the cheek. An odd flutter disturbed Lisette's heartbeat. Instinctively, her hand went up to touch his face. For an absurd instant she thought she saw longing in his eyes, then he said, "Now you're paid up!" and bent to receive her foot and throw her up into the saddle.

The mare's name was Yasmin; she had a pretty, mincing gait and a spirited, playful disposition. "No cow-handed idiot has ever hurt her mouth," said Strand, adding a "yet," that caused Lisette to freeze with indignation until she glimpsed the twinkle in his eyes.

He rode towards the park despite the fact that his mount showed a marked inclination to climb into every passing vehicle. "I'm afraid," Strand said wryly, "I shall have to take this silly fellow for a gallop, but I'll only be a minute."

The park was almost deserted at this hour, and he was off, leaving behind the memory of his quick smile, his teeth a white gleam against the bronzed skin. Lisette sent the mare after him at a less headlong pace. The animal must, she thought, have cost a pretty penny, for her lines were magnificent, she moved like silk, and it was a joy to ride her. Never having been up at this hour, Lisette was unfamiliar with the peace of dawn and marvelled at how quiet was the great city. The skies were dotted with clouds that were grey at first, becoming gradually roseate as the sun touched them. The air was cool and invigorating, fresh after the rains of the night, and every leaf and blade of grass sparkled to the first rays of the sun. A distant hail penetrated her absorption with the beauties about her, and she saw Strand, far down the path, waving impatiently. On an impulse, she drove home her heels, and Yasmin bounded forward. Lisette crouched in the saddle, and the mare all but flew.

"Jolly well done!" cried Strand laughingly, as they came up with him.

"Oh, but she is splendid!" Lisette exclaimed breathlessly, cheeks and eyes aglow.

"And so are you, but I'd best not encourage you to behave so hoydenishly do we ride any later."

Lisette glanced nervously around, to find herself the recipient of a disapproving glare from a horsy-looking middle-aged lady, and of a decidedly approving smile from the lady's escort. "Good heavens!" she murmured, reddening. "I forgot myself! What a thing to do! I fear you are a bad influence on me."

"Nonsense. You should do it more often—in the country, at least. It becomes you. Come, we've plenty of time, and— Hello there!" He waved, calling cheerily as he rode to meet a solitary rider, Lisette following willy-nilly, and irked again by his abrupt manners.

Lord Bolster, astride a fine grey horse, looked nervously at Lisette, but shook hands and bowed politely. He had decided, he said, to go to Italy "on a repairing lease with Mitchell Redmond," as soon as he got Harry Redmond "settled." He seemed vague as to what this would involve, but in view of his mental condition and the great difficulty he experienced in enunciating, Lisette did not enquire. She had fully intended to invite Amanda Hersh to tea, and made a silent vow to do so. When they were alone again, she communicated this resolve to her fiancé.

"That would be kind in you," he nodded. "We could ask her to stay with us for a week or two, if you wish."

"Yes. But I had meant—in Town."

"Doubt there will be time. You'd best wait until we get to Sussex."

"S-Sussex. . .?" she faltered.

"Yes. My home is in Sussex. Good Lord! I must take you down there, of course. What a clunch I am! We shall have to go and see your grandmama this afternoon, but—"

"We—what?"

"I had thought you would want that. Do you not care for her?"

"*Care* for her?" She bridled. "Of course I care for her, sir!"

"Justin. No 'sir,' " he reminded her solemnly.

"It is merely that there is no cause for haste. My papa will put the announcement in *The Gazette,* and then—"

"It is already in, so you've no cause to worry your pretty head over that."

"Already *in.* . . .? M-my goodness, but you were sure of yourself, s—Mr. Strand."

"Not at all. Merely busy yesterday afternoon." He asked interestedly, "Are you going to do that every time you find me vexing?"

"Do what?"

"Call me Sir Justin, or Mr. Strand. You shall have to say my name in the ceremony, you know."

An uneasy suspicion deepening, Lisette entered what she feared might be a useless caveat. "Yes, but that will not be for some time."

He nodded. "True. Four long weeks. We had best get back now, if we are to get down to Richmond in time for luncheon. Do not just sit there, my dear. Pretty as you are, the flies are sure to pop into your mouth!"

He set a brisk pace, but before they were safely back to Portland Place, it was raining again. When the stunned Lisette was sufficiently recovered, she attempted to demand that they should at least delay the wedding until there was a chance of the weather improving. "Don't think it's going to improve, ma'am," said Strand, adding with a flash of his sly grin, "Do we delay until June, we'll likely have to be wed in a rowboat! Besides which, I doubt if I could persuade the Lord Mayor to keep up all the decorations until then."

Baffled, Lisette stared at him until he reached over to put one finger beneath her chin and lift it, thus closing her sagging jaw. "Very pretty, that astonished expression," he said with revolting condescension. "But it might not be an especially good habit to encourage, y'know."

Recovering her voice at length, she gasped, "What—*what* decorations? What have you done?"

He waved an arm expansively. "Have you not noticed? All

London wears her party dress. Flags, bunting, the parks full of lights, bands and parades and jollifications practiced these many days now."

She said indignantly, "But that is not for *us*, and well you know it, sir!"

"It ain't?" He blinked, disconcerted. "Never cast me down so!"

"Oh, for heaven's sake! You are as aware as am I that the celebrations are for the marriage of the Princess of Wales and Prince Leopold!"

"What? Then I've been properly gulled! Dashed if I shall ever heed the word of the Lord Mayor of London again!" The twinkle in his blue eyes very pronounced, he said solemnly, "I suppose that means *I* shall be expected to stand the huff for our own celebrations!"

The horses had slowed during this interchange, and, sternly suppressing a gurgle of laughter, Lisette spurred her mount to a trot once more, her covertly grinning betrothed following suit.

Despite his teasing, Strand's adherence to the immediacy of their union was firm, and Lisette soon discovered she had only begun to glimpse his unflagging zeal in achieving that—or any—goal. He did not so much ride roughshod over opposition as he outdistanced it, going merrily along at his energetic pace, apparently convinced that the plans he set in motion were sure to please everyone, so that by the time others caught up with them, it was too late to protest. A bewildered Lisette found herself whisked from Richmond, where her grandmother was not at home, to Windsor, where Strand's grandmother dwelt. This octogenarian *was* at home and, having favoured her grandson with a plaintive sigh and one faded cheek raised for his kiss, extended two drooping fingers for Lisette to shake, and offered Strand her congratulations on snaring "such a lovely girl. In spite of . . . everything." It was the first time Lisette had found her betrothed subdued, but he soon rebounded and next day the chaise was racing towards Esher and his Great-Aunt Therese. Therese was a large widow with an overpowering and delightfully erratic personality. She dwelt in a very large house to which she welcomed them warmly, and spent most of the day introducing them to visitors, more of whom arrived hourly. No one left, and the house became crowded, with each saloon seeming to contain a group of decidedly differing opinions to those aired in the next. Lisette was both bewildered and enchanted, the hours flew past, and she was genuinely sorry when they left.

They reached London at dusk. Lisette was thoroughly tired, but Strand arrived for dinner, as full of spirits as ever, and entered into a lively discussion with Mrs. Van Lindsay regarding the date of the wedding. Shocked when he expressed a desire for a morning rather than the customary evening ceremony, that redoubtable dame adopted her most chilling attitude. She was agreed with, smiled upon, told she was "a most delightful lady," and while still befuddled somehow agreed to the morning wedding.

Judith was no less summarily dealt with. Strand, interfering in matters to which gentlemen never paid the least heed, was horrified when he chanced to arrive a few days later while she was promenading in the elaborate gown she was to wear as a bridesmaid. "Why, it makes her look big as a house!" he exclaimed indelicately, and whirling to the murderously scowling Judith, demanded, "Do you like that abomination?" As always rather intimidated by his brusqueness, she stammered that she did. "But you cannot imagine it flatters you?" Sure she was being roasted, she sulked, "Flatters *me*? What could flatter *me*! At all events, it is too late now." Strand refuted this and demanded she go and bring "that periodical you ladies are always looking at, *My Lady*, or whatever it's called. Hurry now!" When she had fled, he turned to the astonished Lisette and expostulated, "Good God! Whoever chose that mass of frills and flounces?"

"My sister, Lady Dwyer, helped Judith make the choice. With which, I might add, she was perfectly happy until you condemned it."

"Hmmn. Thought so. Never mind, we'll come about!"

Judith returned with *Ladies Magazine,* and the pair of them spent an hour poring over this and that style until Strand decided on a very plain gown Judith thought deplorable. He convinced her it would be more becoming than the other and carried her off to a rather middle-class emporium called Grafton's, returning with a welter of pale peach-coloured satin and tulle, and the triumphant announcement that, Judith being a splendid seamstress, they would go along very nicely with this one. It was the first intimation her family had that Judith was a more than passable needlewoman, but to everyone's surprise, she set to work at once, thoroughly enjoyed herself, and turned out a truly charming gown that admirably became her.

The next item on the agenda was the possible location of the betrothal ball. It had been decided to hold this at the home of a friend until Strand came wandering in one morning with the guest list of his own friends and family. This was voluminous, but he cheerfully refused to shorten it and, since he was paying for the ball, which promised to be expensive even if it could not be expected to be a great occasion, it was clear that a much larger home would be required. Even so, they were all stunned when at his next appearance he casually announced that the Earl of Harland had graciously offered his London house for the purpose, and that Strand's majordomo, one Mr. Fisher, would "handle everything."

When the news of the betrothal appeared in *The Gazette*, London was deliciously shocked. As a result, a stream of visitors descended upon Portland Place in a flurry of excitement that was not soon to fade. One of Lisette's first callers was a man she dreaded to receive. Mr. Garvey was smiling and suave. He expressed his felicitations with grim insincerity, his eyes glaring his frustration. Bowing over her hand before he departed, he murmured, "I have not given up, ma'am. If there is any possible way to rescue you from this fiasco, it will be done!" Frightened, Lisette relayed the episode to her father. Van Lindsay pooh-poohed her alarm, telling her in some amusement that Garvey was merely a heartbroken suitor and must be excused this flight into melodrama. To his wife, he was less facetious. "Garvey is a vengeful man, m'dear," he said worriedly. "I told Lisette to forget the matter, but I'll not dissemble, he's a power to be reckoned with!"

Among the crush of those arriving the following day were two very different callers. The first of these was Amanda Hersh, whose green eyes still held the shadow of sorrow that had disturbed Lisette when first they met. Lord Bolster, she confided, had made a final attempt to persuade her to wed him and had been thoroughly routed when she had vowed to join the next group of emigrants sailing for the Colonies, if he did not cease to entreat her. "He is such a dear," she sighed, "and being extremely opposed to *that* notion, has agreed to deface himself."

Preserving her countenance with difficulty, Lisette said she had heard his lordship meant to go to Europe. "My betrothed," she went on, "has suggested you might agree to visit us in Sussex when we are settled there. I do beg you will consider it. I shall, I fear, find country life somewhat tedious, having been accustomed to Town."

This was not an idle remark. Strand had, at the first opportunity, taken his bride-to-be to visit her new home. Well aware that a certain pair of blue eyes watched her reactions with no little anxiety, Lisette had tried to be polite, but Strand Hall, with its pillared front and neoclassical architecture, she found cold and unattractive, and the housekeeper, a sharp-eyed woman named Mrs. Hayward, was respectful but unfriendly, so that, with sinking heart, Lisette had known there was a battle to be won there.

Shortly after Amanda departed, Lisette was receiving the Honourable Sarah Leith. Sally, who had once been a very dear friend, came into the room rather hesitantly. She was a kind girl, but blessed with few of the good looks so spectacularly evident in her brother Tristram. Her eyes were dark but not large; her clear skin was inclined to be sallow, and although her brown hair was luxuriant, it could not make her into a beauty. Her smile, however, was warm and sincere, and her gentle disposition soon won her friends to thinking her very pretty indeed. When she saw the smile Lisette summoned, she ran forward to clasp her in a hug and say rapturously, "Oh, Lisette! I am so happy! To think you will be my sister-in-law! Is it not wonderful? I never dreamed of such luck, for I always dreaded lest I be the victim of relations who would either bully or despise me—neither of which you will do! How thrilled I am for Strand—he is the very dearest boy. Indeed, you could not do better! And he, of course, is so deep in love he can scarce recall his own name most of the time!"

She laughed, and Lisette responded suitably, wondering how Strand, so very unloverlike, could possibly have given her such an impression. Drawing Sally to the sofa, she said, "How nice it is to see you again. It has been such a long time since we met."

"Yes—before my brother was married. And then, I heard you were ill. I wrote, but perhaps you did not get my letter. The postal service is so very bad these days."

Lisette blushed. She had received the letter and meant to respond, but never quite found the words. "You were so kind. I intended to write, but everything has happened so fast. How does your brother go on? I hear Mrs. Leith is—is very beautiful."

"Oh, she is! And so sweetly natured. They are beyond words happy! After Tristram lost Mia Buchanan, I began to think he would never wed. For a while I even thought—perhaps—" she smiled shyly—"you will think me foolish, but I hoped you had an affection for him, and that you would be my new sister. Then, when we feared him lost at Waterloo—heavens! What a ghastly time that was! You can imagine my joy when he came home at last, and so deep in love with his Rachel. But you know that story, I do not doubt, and the important thing is that he is happy now. Dear soul, he deserves it, and I could not wish a sweeter wife for him! Enough of my brother. Lisette, may I see your ring? Oh! It is beautiful! Do you know, I'd no idea you had even *met* Justin."

"I have known him a—a comparatively short time. It was all rather sudden."

Sally scanned her lovely face intently. "You are very brave to marry into our rather notorious family. I was a little surprised that your parents consented to the match."

"Oh, no, did you think us so very proud?" Sarah's colour heightened and, realizing she had thought just that, Lisette went on quickly, "Indeed, had my parents objected, I doubt they could have prevailed. Your brother-in-law is a most—ah—persuasive gentleman."

Sarah went into a peal of mirth. "Isn't he just? Tristram says that Justin quite wears him out." Her face clouded suddenly. "I only hope that long stay in India did not—" She checked and stood as Mrs. Van Lindsay swept into the room. "Good morning, ma'am. I am come to welcome my new sister-in-law into the family."

"Why, that is true, of course, dear Sally," gushed Mrs. Van Lindsay, extending her hand and managing to avoid her daughter's eyes. "A rather distant relationship, I fear, but one that will, I am sure, be a delight to Lisette. It is deplorable that I interrupt, but we simply must get to the modiste's shop for a fitting of the wedding gown. You do mean to come to our ball next week . . .?''

Miss Leith said warmly that nothing could keep her away and left them, and in short order Lisette was in the carriage with her mama and an eager Judith, en route to the exclusive little shop just off Bond Street. The wedding gown was lovely, but she was too preoccupied to show much enthusiasm. Standing patiently while the women fussed about her with tape measures and pins, her thoughts were on Tristram Leith. Sooner or later, she must meet him and his bride. The prospect made her heart cringe. She tried to force that terrible vision from her mind, and wondered vaguely what Sally had been going to say about Strand's sojourn in India.

The day of the ball dawned cloudy and threatening, typical of this depressing Spring, and Mrs. Van Lindsay went about with a glum expression, forecasting the Disaster of the Season. By noon, the rain had settled in with a steadiness that augured ill for attendance, and by dusk was an unrelenting downpour.

Mr. Van Lindsay, who adopted an air of tolerant condescension to his prospective son-in-law, was undismayed by the weather. He had jubilantly told Lisette that Strand's settlement had been magnificent. ''All our troubles are over, m'dear. You've done very well by your family, burn me if you ain't!'' The full extent of that settlement was unknown to her, but the purse strings were considerably relaxed, which was a joy to all. As a result, she had another new ball gown, a delicious concoction of pale blue satin, the low-cut bodice embroidered with seed pearls. With it, she wore long pearl drop earrings, and knew herself to look very well, a knowledge confirmed by the approval in the eyes of her betrothed when he arrived at seven o'clock for a light dinner. He looked quite charming in his ball dress, although she fancied to see a tiredness in his eyes: not surprising, she thought, considering the pace he'd set himself these past three weeks.

Lady Bayes-Copeland had arrived that morning, her sudden arrival in Portland Place having been a considerable shock to her daughter. ''I am here,'' she announced firmly, warming her frail hands by the drawing room fire, ''to see this young jackanapes my Lisette has accepted. Only ever laid eyes on him once before he commenced his courtship. Blessed if ever I saw such an unseemly rush to the altar! I collect you bullied her into accepting his fortune, eh, Philippa?'' It was not a propitious beginning and, when Strand arrived, the delay to which she subjected him while critically scanning him through her lorgnette before consenting to offer her hand, was even less encouraging. He seemed unabashed, however, meeting the old lady's keen gaze with twinkling eyes, though his manner was gravely respectful. She slanted several unkind barbs at him during dinner, and twice Mrs. Van Lindsay held her breath, her anguished gaze turning to her husband and quite clearly conveying the fear that Mr. Strand could scarce be blamed did he wash his hands of them all. The only time he gave the least sign that he comprehended the vitriol in my lady's remarks, however, was when she made a contemptuous reference to Tristram Leith's ''wretched'' existence. A hush fell over the tense diners. Strand had been sampling his wine. His hand paused briefly as he lowered his glass, then he set it down with precision. The eyes he turned to my lady's fierce ones were cool, and his brows slightly lifted. ''I fear, ma'am,'' he said in an uncharacteristically slow drawl, ''that you have been misinformed. My brother-in-law is one of the most truly contented men I know. I would not ask a happier marriage.''

''Happy?'' barked Lady Bayes-Copeland. ''What fustian! Who could be happy stuck out there at Cloudhills all year round? The man was a colonel! He is accustomed to activity and a full social schedule. The life of a country squire will soon pall, I'll warrant!''

''Perhaps it will, my lady. But for a man like Tristram Leith, the busiest and most socially glittering life imaginable must be a desolation were not the lady he loves at his side.''

It was far and away the most romantic thing Lisette had ever heard Strand say, and she stared her surprise. Beatrice sneered cynically. Sir William was so inspired as to utter an enthused, ''Well said, by gad!'' The old lady's eyes began to gleam. ''Huh!'' she snorted. ''And what of Justin Strand, sir? Is it to be Town or country for him?''

Strand grinned. ''Lord, ma'am, you must not speak of Leith and Strand in the same breath, or the latter must suffer to the point of extinction! Indeed, when I am in Tristram's magnificent presence, I sometimes find it necessary to pinch myself to be sure I'm still there!''

It was said with affection rather than rancour, and they all laughed.

Lady Bayes-Copeland did not so lightly lower her guns, however. "A clever evasion," she nodded grimly. "And I'm still without an answer."

"D'you know, ma'am," he replied, "I suspect you knew the answer before you asked the question."

For a moment she almost returned his unexpectedly winning smile, but instead snapped, "You're nobody's fool, I see. Yet had you been a little wiser, you would have come to see me at Richmond, young man. Not whisked my granddaughter off without so much as a decent meeting. You may imagine that because I'm an old widow, you can dismiss me from the reckoning in this family. But you are out there, and so I tell you!"

Mrs. Van Lindsay placed a hand briefly over her eyes, and her husband looked aghast. Strand said nothing, but Lisette felt constrained to point out that they *had* driven down to see the old lady. "I was dragged all that way in the rain, dear Grandmama," she said aggrievedly, "the very morning after I had accepted Mr. Strand's offer."

Contrarily, this advice served to send my lady's wrath flaring. "Then why in God's name could you not have said so, Strand? Making mock of me, eh?"

"Not at all, ma'am. But you were having such a lovely time trying to put me out of countenance, I hesitated to spoil it for you."

It was lightly said, but through another taut silence, his eyes met hers steadily. What she read in those eyes, only she knew, but suddenly her scowl relaxed. She smiled, then went into a cackle of mirth and, relieved, everyone laughed with her. "Very well, put up your sword," she wheezed at last. "I own you to be a worthy opponent. Have a care, Lisette! This brown-faced hank of skin and bone will be a sight more difficult to tame than would a gentleman like Tristram Leith!"

Lisette gave a gasp. Strand's narrowed eyes shot to her face. Mr. Van Lindsay, laughing heartily, missed the implication and said, "Well, he stood up to *you*, ma'am!"

"Indeed he did," chuckled her ladyship. "Game as a pebble!" She lifted her glass. "I give you joy. Strand—you've won yourself a rare girl. It will be up to you to see her beauty don't ruin her! Lisette—I venture to believe you have found a gentleman who is also—a man!''

Lisette met Strand's eyes. They were unfathomable; she dared not guess what he had read into her grandmother's remark, and why she should care what he thought was also a mystery. But she smiled, and for some odd reason felt proud. He returned her smile, and only Sir William noticed how tightly his fingers were clamped about the stem of his glass.

Chapter 6

At half-past eight Justin Strand's new town carriage was at the front door to convey the Van Lindsay party to the betrothal ball. The downpour had eased to a steady light fall, but the streets were deeply puddled, the carriage progressed with caution, and conversation in the large vehicle became desultory until Lady Bayes-Copeland remarked on the bridesmaids' gowns. "Who selected Judith's?" she asked.

"Well you may ask, ma'am," replied Beatrice with a vexed little titter. "*My* choice was rejected, and a dowdy thing she has sewn for herself in its place. She will look a quiz, I fear."

"If she does, ma'am, she may lay it to my door," said Strand quickly. "No doubt the gown would have been enchanting on another girl, Lady William, but—"

"But would have made Judith look as wide as she's tall," the old lady interpolated, adding a vehement, "You are to be commended on your good taste, Strand. I'd not known the gal was so fine a needlewoman, had you, Philippa?"

Lisette did not hear her mother's response. Seated between her betrothed and her sister, she felt Beatrice tense. She'd feared just such a reaction to Strand's interference, and could only hope Beatrice did not take him in such dislike that she launched one of her campaigns against him, which could prove painful for every member of the family. Such fears were forgotten, however, as the coach turned the corner on to Bond Street. Harland's house was a blaze of light. A long canopy covered the approach across the flagway, up the steps, and to the front doors, and despite the rain, carpets were already laid. Awnings had also been set up on each side of the entrance, where an eager crowd was beginning to form, pleased that they could watch the arrivals without being drenched.

"How nice of Harland to provide a shelter for the crowds," murmured Lisette.

"I suspect he wasted his effort," Beatrice sniffed. "There'll be no large turn-out to watch only a few guests arrive on such a miserable night."

"Stuff!" said her grandmother, as a footman ran to throw open the door and let down the steps. "If everyone waited for a mild night in England, we would have very few parties!"

The onlookers gave them a cheer as they entered the great house, and in the entrance hall Mr. Fisher, a lean, greying gentleman, was as immaculate as any well-bred butler at a *ton* ball should be. Already, strains of music were drifting down the stairs, although none of the guests would arrive for another half-hour at least. Strand offered one arm to Lady Bayes-Copeland, the other to his betrothed, and led the way upstairs and along the corridor to the doors giving onto the ballroom. A lackey hurried ahead to open those doors, and Strand, suiting his pace to the old lady's uncertain steps, was gratified as she cried an appreciative, "Aha! What a pretty sight!"

The great room was a picture: large golden baskets holding long-stemmed red and white roses were placed about the walls; the chairs and sofas were white, gold, and pink, and here and there on the walls hung two golden hearts, intertwined. Lisette darted a startled look at her fiancé and discovered him staring, wide-eyed, at this last touch.

"But it is charming!" exclaimed Mrs. Van Lindsay, entering on her husband's arm.

"Good evening," murmured Geoffrey, Earl of Harland, coming up behind them and, as usual, looking very well in his evening clothes. "Well, Strand," he said, having bowed over the hands of the ladies and exchanged firm handclasps with the men, "and how many of your family shall be here tonight?"

Beatrice uttered an audible gasp, and Lisette paled. Strand's brows twitched into his rare frown. "None, unfortunately, sir. I had hoped to persuade my sister, Charity, to come. But—it was not possible." His lips tightened as Beatrice sighed her relief, and he added a rather pointed, "But they will dance at my wedding, I assure you!"

"And so shall I," Lady Bayes-Copeland nodded. "But for the moment, come and sit beside me, Harland, and tell me all the latest *on dits*. I fairly thirst for gossip!"

The rest of the party adjourned to the ground floor to inspect the refreshment room where immaculate long tables awaited the many delicacies they soon would hold.

The guests began to arrive a little earlier than had been expected, and in far greater numbers, and by half-past eleven o'clock it was very apparent that the ball was a huge success.

Strand leaned to Lisette's ear during a brief lull in the reception line and murmured whimsically, "I trust the people outside did not give up hope too early."

She smiled. "I do not think we shall have to blush for our party, sir. Though my feet feel as if they are doing so."

"In a little while," he promised, "I shall take them in to supper, so they may rest."

"I'll say one thing for you, Strand. You move very fast." Resplendent in peerless evening dress, James Garvey went on, "What a great pity you was not with our Duke on the Peninsula."

"Isn't it?" Strand agreed, his handshake so crushing that his guest flinched. "And what a *good* thing you wasn't!"

Garvey glared. Strand smiled on him sweetly, then turned to take the hand of the Duke of Vaille. Gritting his teeth, Garvey sauntered on beside the elegant French Chevalier who had accompanied him. Lisette could breathe again.

Strand was soon enabled to keep his promise and take his betrothed to the refreshment room. He found her a place beside Sally Leith and Sir Frederick Foster and went off to the laden tables. Foster had been on the town for better than ten years and was an engaging young man. He was regaling the two ladies with the details of a horse race that had taken place between Sir Harry Redmond and Viscount Lucian St. Clair, when James Garvey slid into the vacant chair beside Lisette.

"I say, dear old boy," Foster remonstrated mildly. " 'Fraid that chair's reserved for our prospective benedick."

"And I shall hastily relinquish it when he returns. Fair Miss Van Lindsay, your dance card, I beg."

Foster stared at him for an instant, then turned to identify General Smollet for Sally.

Lisette seized the opportunity to murmur, "Mr. Garvey, I hope you—I mean, if I—if I gave you a wrong impression—"

"No, but you tried," he declared in a low, intense voice. "Very valiantly, poor creature! How terrible that such as you should be sold to the highest bidder!"

"No! Oh, please do not say so! You are—"

"I am—*ever*—yours to command! If you stand in need of help, only send me word, and I shall be at your side!" Despite the melodramatic declaration, his eyes were very grim. He signed her card, rose, bowed, and sauntered away.

The dashing Earl of Ridgley had claimed Lisette for his partner when the hour neared midnight, and he was leading her into a country dance when a slight commotion erupted at one side of the room. Lisette glanced that way, curious to see the cause of such a flurry of whispering and raised eyebrows. She saw Strand, his face alight, pull a frail, mousy-looking girl into a warm embrace, then reach an eager hand to the girl's escort.

Following his gaze, Lisette halted. She was accustomed to seeing Tristram Leith clad in the magnificence of his uniform, but even in civilian evening clothes he seemed to relegate all other gentlemen to obscurity. He was half turned from her, but his commanding height and the proud carriage of his dark head were unmistakable. She thought, No! Oh, no! And then he was glancing her way, so that she saw fully the vital smiling face, and the scars that now raked down his right cheek. It was the first time she had seen him since Waterloo, and although she knew he had been wounded, she was not prepared. She felt suffocated and, one hand flying to her throat, fought a sick dizziness. Dimly, she saw Strand staring at her, and then an arm was about her. In a voice that seemed to ring through the room, Beatrice asked, "Whatever is wrong, love? You are white as a sheet!"

"*You* must think me a regular pea goose," Lisette murmured, gratefully accepting the glass of water Strand offered. "I fear the heat and—and all that while standing downstairs, must have been too much for me.''

''I am fairly astounded,'' Beatrice admitted. ''I had always thought you strong as a horse.''

''Even a horse is sometimes caught offstride,'' Strand declared with disastrous loyalty.

Lisette's eyes flew to him. A corner of Leith's mouth twitched and in a chivalrous attempt to smooth a ticklish moment he said, ''My sudden appearance is enough to throw anyone offstride. My apologies, Justin. I thought you would want one of your sisters here, but perhaps Charity and I should not have come.''

Her motives not nearly so benign, Beatrice purred, ''But of course you should have come, Colonel. I am sure very few people hold *you* in any way disgraced.''

A chill came into Leith's fine eyes, and Charity Strand blushed painfully.

''For heaven's sake, do not encourage him, my lady,'' said Strand. ''Anyone so stupid as to lounge about under an exploding shell deserves to have his face remodelled.''

The tension eased. Charity gave a relieved little giggle. Leith reached out one large hand and deliberately dragged Strand's thick hair straight forward over his face. Strand grinned and shook his head and, careless of the fact that he looked considerably dishevelled, said, ''Let us ignore this military clod. Ladies, may I present my sister? Charity, you must meet Lady William Dwyer, and her sister, Miss Lisette Van Lindsay, my affianced bride.''

Beatrice bowed, but her brows lifted when Charity Strand essayed a markedly clumsy curtsey. Lisette held out her hand and murmured a polite but cool, ''I am so very glad to meet you, Miss Strand.''

''You see''—Strand smiled—''your fears were for naught, little one. Miss Van Lindsay holds *you* blameless, too.'' Lisette was surprised by the blaze of anger in his blue eyes. Nonetheless, he went on lightly, ''She has not much choice, of course, for when a lady takes a gentleman to husband, she takes his whole family, perforce.'' He looked at her levelly. ''Ain't that right, Lizzie?''

Beatrice uttered an outraged gasp. Lisette's eyes took on a

glassy hue. Charity lowered her lashes, her lips trembling against a smile, and Leith coughed suspiciously, behind his hand.

The suave James Garvey strolled up at that moment, to claim his dance, and numbly, Lisette tottered off beside him. Garvey found her vexingly inattentive throughout the boulanger, even when, in one of the few moments he could address her, he hissed a suggestion that she should fly with him to the Border, that very night. "If only to save yourself," he urged. Lisette scarcely heard this disgraceful proposal. In her ears lingered one repellent word: "Lizzie"!

She was dancing a quadrille with Lord Owsley before she really began to recover from such a shock and to plan her revenge. The wretch must be punished, and since the next dance was the waltz he had applied for long before the ball began, he would find her very hard to locate. She might, in fact, not be found in time to dance at all! Smiling in response to a singularly asinine remark of the adoring young Owsley, her teeth were unusually apparent. Furthermore, she thought, vindictively, does the wretch *ever* dare so address me again, he will have a taste of the Van Lindsay temper he'll not soon forget!

In point of fact, she had seldom been plagued by so unfortunate an emotion as temperament, but she was still seething when his lordship reluctantly restored her to her grandmother. Lady Bayes-Copeland was talking with Charity Strand as though she'd known her all her life, and Lisette at once turned aside, for she could not look at Charity without being reminded of Rachel, and it was all she could do to be civil to the girl.

"Come along, do!" called the old lady. "Never back and fill, so! Here is your sister-to-be, eager to know you better!"

Willy-nilly, Lisette sat beside them. "You should be dancing, instead of sitting here," she said, nobly turning her most bewitching smile on the shy girl.

"Oh, no, Miss Van Lindsay. I fear I would only make a spectacle of myself."

"Good gracious! Do you disapprove of dancing, then?"

Charity blushed. "I—I do not remember how to dance."

Lisette stared at her. Every young lady knew how to dance, and Charity was well past her schooldays. Surely they must have assemblies *somewhere* near Strand Hall? Or at least impromptu hops at parties, or in the Church Hall?

"I am learning again now," said Charity with timid eagerness. "But I still seem to lose my balance if—" She checked, seeing consternation come into the beautiful face beside her. "Oh—you did not know? I had supposed my brother would have told you. I was an invalid for three years. My horse threw me when I was seventeen, and I have only lately begun to walk again."

Horrified, Lisette was reminded of the scorn with which she had watched that pathetic attempt at a curtsey. What a wretched girl she was! "Oh, my dear," she said, her hand going out to the frail one that came so gladly to meet it, "I am so very sorry. Three years! How awful for you!"

"And for my sister. Rachel had such a frightful time, but I expect Justin will have told you all about—" She paused, her eyes opening very wide as Galen Hilby bowed before her and begged the honour of taking her down to supper.

The old lady gave Charity a gentle push, and she came to her feet and went shyly off with him.

"That was indeed kind," said Lady Bayes-Copeland. "I make no doubt Hilby knows of their reputation. Were you really unaware of her history, child?"

"Totally. Poor little thing, how frail she is. Grandmama, did *you* know?"

She was not destined to receive a reply, for Strand was bearing down on them. She had quite forgotten her plot to evade him, and, chagrined, viewed him with bleak eyes.

"I collect you've come to take her away from me," grumbled the old lady.

"In point of fact," he said gravely, "I've come to beg your granddaughter to hold me excused."

He *would!* The sly beast! "A more alluring partner, sir?" she said, in a tone that sent the old lady's glance flashing to her.

"If the lady will so honour me," he said, bowing low.

"G-Grandmama?" gasped Lisette. "She certainly cannot—"

"Speak for yourself, gal!" My lady held up one hand. Strand took it and assisted her to her feet. "Here!" She thrust her cane at Lisette and threw a saucy grin up at her gallant, murmuring as she slipped her hand onto his arm, "It had best be a very slow waltz, lad."

"I shall likely have my work cut out to keep up with you," he answered, and summoned the nearest footman. He sent the man off to the leader of the orchestra, and a few seconds later a fanfare preceded the introduction to a waltz. My lady Bayes-Copeland groped for her train, and one mittened hand lifted to Strand's shoulder. "Come on then, you young devil," she breathed.

He said belatedly, "I should perhaps have warned you that I am not a very good dancer."

"All you have to do," she said reassuringly, "is to take it slowly. And hold me up."

So he did. The orchestra played at a measured tempo that at first baffled other dancers. The Duke of Vaille, seeing Strand and his partner, at once left the floor and others followed, moving back to join the gathering onlookers until only a thin young man and very old and regal lady, who had not been known to dance for years, waltzed before them all.

A lump came into Lisette's throat. How tiny was the dear little soul, but with what proud grace she moved. Strand held her as though she were fashioned of finest porcelain, but he was smiling and talking to her, and once she laughed merrily.

They circled the floor once and then slowed, and the maestro at once ordered a final majestic chord. Amid a storm of applause, Strand made his bow, then steadied his partner as she rose from a rather wobbly curtsey. Fanning herself and vowing breathlessly she'd not enjoyed herself so much in an age, and why people should get into such a taking she could not comprehend, Lady Bayes-Copeland was escorted in triumph to a sofa, where Mr. Van Lindsay awaited her, holding a glass of wine.

Once more the orchestra played the introduction to the waltz. Strand glanced to Lisette. She moved smilingly towards him. Her unwanted fiancé had brought happy stars to the old lady's eyes; almost she could feel a fondness for him.

"La!" Beatrice sniggered. "But how monstrous clever he is. He has won his Lizzie back again!"

Life at the imposing house on Portland Place took on the aspects of a miniature Bedlam. Wedding gifts began to arrive, and notes of thanks must be written; the flowers selected for the bouquets were suddenly unobtainable due to the cold weather, and others had, at the last minute, to be ordered; Lisette's jewelled slippers were found to be a size too large, and another last-minute substitution was necessitated; the flower girl fell ill with measles, and her frock did not fit the child who happily took her place. And on top of all the countless and inevitable frustrations that have ever bedevilled brides and their families, Timothy Van Lindsay had not come home. He arrived only two days before the wedding, a typical Captain of the famous Light Bobs; sturdily built, with broad shoulders, muscular legs, the dark colouring that characterized his house, and calm eyes that, like those of his friend Harry Redmond, were inclined to narrow as though still countering glare of the Spanish sun.

Norman spotted his hackney from the drawing room windows, and his shouts of excitement roused the house and sent the occupants running out onto the front steps to welcome their soldier home. Several neighbours also hastened to join the celebrants, and it was quite some time before the joyous tumult quieted to the point where Timothy was able to steal upstairs and lounge comfortably in the chair in Lisette's bedchamber, as he'd been wont to do whenever he was at home.

He pulled a cheroot from his case and held it up enquiringly. Receiving her permission, he lighted it, leaned back luxuriously, and invited, "Come along, child. Tell old Tim the whole story. Why Strand?"

Perversely, for she had longed for this moment, she countered, "Why not?"

"You ain't exactly deep in love. A little bird told me you was only recently being courted by James Garvey. Was Strand aware?"

She gave a minuscule shrug. "Much he cares! Do you know him, dear?"

"Very slightly. He was at Harrow a year behind me. He seemed a decent enough sort, in spite of—" He paused, contemplating the glowing end of his cheroot. "He's the last type I'd have thought you would choose. And if you do not love him—"

"Love him!" she interposed. "He is the most odious, managing, braggadocio individual I ever met!"

"Good God!" he expostulated with a grin. "You *really* don't love him! Must I go and convince him to withdraw his offer?"

She sighed, her shoulders slumping forlornly. "Heaven forbid."

"I see. No, I do not see. Best tell me."

So she did. It took some time and, before she was halfway

through, she had made herself feel victimized to the point that she was fighting tears.

Her brother listened without interruption, then muttered, "Egad! I'd no idea my father was in so deep. I wish I could help. I must say I think it jolly noble of you to sacrifice yourself. Only . . ." he hesitated.

"Only—what?" Lisette sniffed, blowing her nose.

"Only, you know, I cannot help thinking that—er—that Strand is being sacrificed, too."

Raging, she whirled on him. "Oh! He is getting what he paid for! Our unblemished name to restore his own shamed one. Which is all he wants. And how typical that you would care more for a—a stranger than your own sister, just because he is a *man!*" Timothy blinked his surprise at this vehement outburst, but Lisette rushed on, "Does it mean *nothing* to you that he cares not a button for me? And that Rachel Leith is his sister?"

"Which brings us to another point," said Timothy, dryly. His tone of voice was not unfamiliar to his men, but Lisette had never heard it before. Deflated, she watched him in sudden apprehension. "Where does Leith fit into all this?" he asked.

A dozen evasive answers sprang to mind, but there was a deep affection between them; too deep for her to attempt to pull the wool over his eyes. She turned away and, gazing out at the city, said quietly, "He will become my brother-in-law, of course. Is that not delicious, Tim?"

He was briefly silent, then stood to rest a large hand comfortingly on her shoulder. "I'll have a word with Papa and with Strand. We will get you out of this, somehow."

"No." She nestled her cheek against his hand. "It's no good, do you not see? And at all events, Leith is married now. Happily, I gather."

The Captain scowled and returned to his chair, wondering why people always loved the wrong people. Leith must have been blind not to return the affection of this beautiful girl. Lisette might be a little high in the instep, but she'd a heart of gold for all that and, properly handled, would make some lucky man a splendid wife. "I like Leith," he grunted. "But, by God, if I thought . . ."

"Do not. He never by the slightest inference suggested a betrothal. If I was so foolish as to—to attach more importance to our friendship than he intended, I have no one to blame but myself. It just seems a singularly bitter twist of fate that I must now acknowledge his wife as . . . as my sister-in-law." She saw sympathy come into his eyes and added, "Never mind. Grandmama said I may yet find my own true love—quite apart from my marriage. As Emily Cowper has done. Now why do you glower, sir? This is 1816, after all."

"True," nodded Van Lindsay. "But, do you know, little sister, were I in your shoes, I do not think I'd try that game on Justin Strand."

Chapter 7

A shout went up from the crowd when the carriage came in sight, and a louder shout arose when the bride stepped out. Lisette had chosen a gown as romantic as her wedding was not. Copied from the one in which her grandmother had said her vows, the high-necked bodice of white lace rose demurely over a low-cut silk under-dress. The waist was tiny, and below it the skirts billowed out over moderate hoops in a cloud of silk and lace, caught up here and there by clusters of seed pearls. Her veil was also her grandmother's, descending to a twelve-foot train that her attendants lovingly guarded from contact with the wet flagway. She looked like a fairy princess, and the crowd cheered her dark beauty with enthusiasm.

Forcing her stiff lips into a smile, Lisette clutched Timothy's hand. The veil between her and the world on this rainy morning that should have been the happiest day of her life seemed to heighten a sense of misty unreality. This was not the culmination of her dreams, surely? She was not really marrying a man rich, but infuriating, alternately kind and brutally brusque, of inferior birth, and certainly not in the least in love with her. She could, she supposed wearily, become accustomed to his driving energy; to that eager look as if he expected always that something of import was about to happen; to the thin face and restless, nervous hands. If only he would show a little tenderness. If only once he had told her how beautiful she was, or expressed some affection for her. James Garvey had spoken, often and fluently, of his undying devotion. "Until death, my vision of perfection," he'd said yearningly. But, aside from that one half-heard suggestion at the betrothal ball, he had proven to be as loath to take action as he was eager to speak. Certainly not galloping to her window some night and riding triumphantly away with her across his saddle bow. Foolish thoughts. And she would not marry James Garvey today; nor would she marry the darkly handsome Tristram Leith, as she had done in so many happy dreams. For this was not a dream. This was grey reality.

They were inside the lovely old church now, and Papa came up and pulled her cold little hand through his arm, told her not to be nervous although his own hand was none too steady, and led her forward. The organist was playing; the church was filled. Heads were turning, kindly faces smiling, as with trembling knees she walked down the aisle. She hoped that Beatrice and Judith and her cousins were behind her, hoped that Strand would not attempt to hurry the priest through the ceremony. It was too much to hope that she would wake up and find it had all been a bad dream. . . .

Such the reflections of a bride on her wedding day.

Vaguely, she saw Strand watching her approach. The bachelor party must have been wild indeed, for he looked positively haggard. The priest was speaking, kindly but interminably. Music again, and the angelic voices of the choirboys ringing sweetly through the noble old sanctuary. More talk, and then Strand was making the responses in an odd, uncertain voice, stumbling over the words, but getting through it at last. She heard her own voice as from a great distance, clear and calm. "I, Lisette Hermione, take thee, Justin Derwent . . ." Unfaltering. Incredible. But it went on and on while she stood in that strange, trancelike state, hearing everything as though she were very far away. He was putting the ring on her finger, his hand hot and trembling. She stared down at it, reacting mechanically, waiting, while Strand put back her veil. He stared at her, his eyes reflecting a sort of awed confusion, as though he, too, were a captive in this dream. He kissed her perfunctorily, and they moved on to sign the register. Having somehow contrived to write her name, Lisette heard a sudden muffled snort beside her. What was he doing now? Surely he did not mean to disgrace them all? She glanced up in dismay. Strand took the quill from her hand, grinned, and winked at her. Bewildered, she looked down again and thought an appalled, My heaven! How could I have done so stupid a thing? But—there it was. Instead of "Lisette Hermione" she had written "Lisette *Heroine*"! She could have sunk and felt her face burn.

Strand pulled her hand possessively through his arm. "What a slip!" he chuckled. "Poor *ton*, m'dear! Or did you mean it?"

Poor *ton*, indeed! Facing the assembled throng, she smiled sweetly, and whispered, "But, of course! I deserve a medal, do not you think?"

"A small one, perhaps," he quipped. "But—you will likely earn a large one . . . as we go along."

The wedding breakfast was held at the Clarendon and was a whirl of gaiety and embraces, champagne and magnificent food, music and laughter and nostalgic tears. Much of the time the bride and groom were side by side, but sometimes they were parted, and a laugh went up when someone addressed Lisette as Mrs. Strand and she made no response. An extremely handsome young man came over with Charity Strand, who introduced him as Alain Devenish, a good friend of Colonel Leith. He was fair, with curling hair and features so perfect it was all Lisette could do not to stare at him. Fortunately, he possessed a cheerful, impudent manner so that one soon forgot his looks and was enabled to enjoy him for himself, and in a very short while he and the bride were on the best of terms.

Coming up behind them, Strand said, "So you have met my heroine, have you, Devenish?" and Lisette knew she would not soon hear the end of that slip. She joined in the laughter when her insensitive bridegroom told the story, and she was still smiling when a touch on her elbow caused her to turn and look straight at Rachel Strand Leith. The lady was small and fine-boned, with hair of a very pale dusty brown, great blue eyes, a straight little nose, and a beautifully shaped mouth just now curving to a rather wistful smile. Not all the accounts of how lovely she was had prepared Lisette for a girl so angelically fair; not all the defamatory remarks and vitriolic gossip could prevail against so sweet an expression. Struggling to ignore Tristram's magnetic presence, Lisette knew that Strand, who had been comparatively restrained today, watched her, and that Grandmama, leaning on his arm, was glaring at her.

For her part, Rachel Leith thought her brother's bride ethereally lovely, with the delicate lace framing her shining hair, her dusky eyes still lit by the smile that had faded from her lips. "Oh, Justin," she breathed. "How did you ever manage to win her?"

Lisette glanced with a trace of cynicism to Strand. He was regarding her gravely, but with an element of pleading at the back of his eyes that startled her. This notorious lady was his sister and, insofar as was possible for so cold a nature, he might be fond of her. Quite apart from that consideration, to even slightly snub the beauty would be to give the gabble-mongers grist for their mills. Therefore, she inserted at her most gracious, "I might well ask Leith the same thing."

Rachel laughed, reached out her hand impulsively, then withdrew it, as though anticipating a rebuff. Why Fate must be so fiendishly contrary, Lisette could not guess, but she felt a warm liking for this girl she had determined to loathe, and at once reached out to embrace her.

The two young husbands locked glances. "What lucky dogs we are," said Leith. "Did you ever see two such lovely creatures, Justin?"

Strand murmured an agreement, but his tone was cool, and there was no answering smile for his handsome brother-in-law, seeing which, the shrewd old eyes of Lady Bayes-Copeland grew troubled.

For quite some time after Denise left her, Lisette sat at the dressing table, staring blindly at her mirrored reflection. Mrs. Hayward had hired the petite maid to wait on her new mistress, but had said she'd thought Mrs. Strand would prefer to interview personally for a dresser. Lisette was pleased with her abigail. Denise was tiny and vivacious and blessed with a cheerful nature. The housekeeper was congratulated upon her choice and accepted these kind words with only a nod, no spark of liking warming her cold eyes. That the plump, impeccably neat woman adored Justin was very obvious, and equally obvious the fact that his bride was viewed with, at most, a deferral of judgement. It would be unfortunate, thought Lisette, if her first task at Strand

Hall was to dismiss an old family retainer! And as to hiring a dresser—that seemed the height of absurdity. What on earth would she need with a dresser, out here miles from anywhere?

She had not known until they were in the carriage, waving goodbye to the merry crowd of well-wishers, where they would spend their honeymoon. When Strand told her in his offhand way that they were bound for his country home, she'd been aghast, and had said sarcastically, "I must have misheard you, sir. This *is* my honeymoon, is it not?"

"And mine," he had pointed out. "I truly do apologize, but there are matters I have neglected too long. In a week or so I shall take you wherever in the world you wish, but for now, it must be Strand Hall, I'm afraid."

It was all of a piece, thought Lisette, standing and discarding the soft cloud of tulle that was her peignoir. A fitting start to this miserable marriage! She heard approaching footsteps and in a sudden surge of panic glanced at her reflection in the mirror. Despite her aversion to her bridegroom, womanlike, she'd been unable to resist the temptation to make herself as alluring as possible. Her nightgown was a diaphanous drift of light orchid, through which the graceful curves of her body were mistily apparent. She was pale against that rich colour, her eyes looking scared and enormous, but she knew she was pretty. Would her husband think her pretty? She began to shake as the footsteps came closer, then relaxed with a little sigh of relief as they passed by and faded into silence.

She extinguished the lamp, crossed to the great bed, and stood staring at it. Clenching her small fists, she prayed for courage, clambered in, and folded the sheet back tidily over her waist. She blew out all but one candle in the branch on her bedside table, clasped her hands, and waited. And, inevitably, her fears grew with each long moment. Mama had told her very little of what was expected of a wife, save only that she must be conformable, not hang upon Strand's sleeve (how utterly ludicrous!), and be willing to look the other way when he indulged in his "little *affaires*." Naturally, he would expect her to provide him with an heir, but he seemed a reasonable sort of man, and would likely not want a very large brood. Lisette gripped her trembling hands tighter. Beatrice had been less restrained. From her had come a warning to be prepared for sadistic brutality—for the lustful violation of every concept of maidenly modesty that had ever been inculcated into her mind, and for pain and savage degradation. Dear God! she thought, tears stinging her eyes. And to be thus shamefully handled by such as Justin Strand, who already considers me no more than a heifer purchased on the auction block!

She could see again the glitter in his eyes when he had looked at her, both in the church and at the reception. And his hand, when he'd helped her cut the wedding cake, had been very warm. She had heard the expression, "blazing with passion." Was that what it meant? Was she to be subjected to an orgy of unrestrained lust? Her spirits plummeted, and she was soon so depressed that her highest hope was to be so fortunate as to succumb at the birth of her first child. On second thought it did not seem quite fair to leave the poor mite without a mother. Perhaps it would be better did she instead contract some mysterious wasting disease and gracefully fade away until . . . Her heart bounced into her throat as a scratch came at the door. Shivering and overwrought, she called a faint, "Come . . . in . . ."

She was unspeakably relieved when Denise tripped into the room, curtsied, and handed her a folded paper.

Lisette smiled and thanked her, and, when the abigail had quietly closed the door, stared at the paper in her hand. It would be just like that wretched brute to have forgotten her altogether! Or to have gone merrily off to play cards with some of his vulgar friends to return at heaven knows what hour of the night, drunk and even more depraved than usual!

She broke the seal, unfolded the page, and read the words written in a near-illegible scrawl.

My dear wife—["Hah!" she snorted impatiently

How you may ever forgive me, I dare not guess, but I am called away on a matter that it is beyond my power to ignore.

Were you to turn your back on your unfortunate husband and go home to Portland Place, I could scarce blame you, and can only entreat that you not do so.

Know that, however grieved you may be, my own regret is tenfold, and try to be patient until the return of

Your contrite if absent husband,
Strand

One reading caused Lisette's eyes not only to lose every last vestige of the terror that had so recently filled them, but to widen to a surprising degree. The second reading caused them to positively spark, while, quite forgetting the fearful trepidation with which she had awaited the coming of her lord and master, she now was possessed by a boiling fury by reason of his absence.

"Oh!" she gasped inadequately. "*Oh!*" And lowering the hands that so tightly clutched the letter, she stared around the room as though it were filled with curious onlookers.

"Can you *credit* this?" she demanded of the bedpost. "He is . . . called *away?*" The bedpost maintaining a wooden stupidity, she threw back the sheet, sprang tigerishly from the bed, and began to prowl up and down. "It is not enough," she raged, "that he *bought* me! Not enough that he has—has *dumped* me here in this confounded desolation! Oh, yes! I said *confounded*— and meant it! It is not enough I have been wrenched from the arms of the man I love!" (A statement of somewhat dubious authenticity.) "He has been—*called away!*" Pausing before the mirror and catching sight of her flushed cheeks and wild eyes, she brandished the letter at her reflection and through gnashing teeth cried, "Look at yourself, Miss—Mrs. Justin Derwent Strand! Purchased like a slab of beef! And on your wedding night—your *wedding night*—abandoned by the wretched clod! Abandoned, humiliated, and made to look utterly *ridiculous!*"

Seething, she ran to the wardrobe and hauled out her valise and a bandbox. "He cannot blame me, can't he?" she panted, wrenching at the straps on the valise. "I am to—" She again had recourse to the letter, which was annoying since she was kneeling on it and, in retrieving it, tore it in half. Jamming the sections together, she snorted, "I am to—to be patient. *Patient!* Dear God! *Relieved* would be more apropos! Overjoyed! Delighted! May he *never* return! And when he does—" contradictorily— "when he does—I shall be *gone!*"

She stood and began to stuff gowns and habits ruthlessly into the inoffensive valise, then turned to trot, panting, to her dressing table, and gather up hairbrushes, combs, hairpins, and pots of creams and lotions. Running back to the valise, she tossed them inside haphazardly, all the while calling down male-dictions upon her absent bridegroom, until that worthy's ears, wherever they were, must have fairly frizzled. "How *dare* he!" snarled Lisette, pouncing on a candlestick which had somehow found its way into the valise, and casting it from her with loathing. "How *dare* he treat me with such flagrant contempt?" Only then came the ultimate horror: "What will the *servants* think?"

That was sufficient to give her pause, and she knelt there motionless, glaring into the chaotic valise. What *would* the servants think? What would everyone think? The fires of wrath began to yield to rationality once more. And slowly, she came to see how hopelessly she was caught. She could hear again her father's exultant voice. "The settlement is magnificent! All our troubles are over, m'dear . . ." And Mama, ecstatic because she might at last buy some new furnishings, and draperies, and even—joy unbearable!—new carpets! In the face of such generosity, how could she leave Strand? The man had already had his father's disgrace and Rachel's ghastly reputation to overcome. For him to be abandoned by his bride on their wedding night must be the *coup de grâce*. No one would blame *her*, that was certain, for her name was without blemish, but they would be sure to imagine all kinds of horrible things about *him*. Not that she cared, of course. He deserved the worst fate imaginable. He had, in fact, deserted *her!* Only . . . wherever he had gone, she was assured it would be with discretion. Whereas, if she went home, all London would know.

Lisette bowed her head, and wept bitter tears of chagrin, frustration, and—loneliness.

The sunlight poured into the bedroom and crept under Lisette's lashes so that she blinked and yawned sleepily. In another moment the bedcurtains were pulled aside, and the housekeeper stood there, smiling with astounding warmth and holding a tray containing an enticing display of hot scones with clotted cream and strawberry jam, an egg cooked just as she liked it, some rashers of bacon, and a pot from which emanated the delicious aroma of hot coffee. Memory returned with a rush. Sitting up, Lisette's guilty eyes flashed from Mrs. Hayward to the abandoned valise. Everything had been whisked away, and her dressing table was as neat as though nothing had ever been displaced.

"Good morning, ma'am," beamed the housekeeper. "We

wasn't sure what you preferred for your breakfast, so it's to be hoped as you'll find something to suit. It's a lovely day. So nice to see the sun again.'' She settled the tray across Lisette's knees, and glancing into the rather bewildered young face, still marked by tear streaks, her heart was wrung, and she murmured, ''How very pretty you are, if I dare be so bold as to say so, Mrs. Strand. Poor Master Justin! I said to him, no matter how he was needed, there's sometimes a 'no' must be said. But I don't need to tell you that he's not the kind to let people down who call on him. There now, I'll let you enjoy your breakfast in peace.'' And she was gone, leaving Lisette to stare after her, amazed at the changed demeanour.

By rights, a lady caught in so unhappy a web of circumstances should have found herself without appetite and picked at her food only for the sake of appearances. At least, that was the way of it in the romances Lisette had read. It was rather lowering to find that she was ravenous. She ate far more breakfast than was her usual custom, attributing it to the pure country air. She rang for Denise at length and lay back, wondering if Strand meant to return today and whether this was to be the pattern of her life. Perhaps he had a mistress in keeping somewhere nearby and, despite Mrs. Hayward's polite excuses, had actually rushed back to his peculiar once he had captured the mate who could restore some gloss to his tarnished name. The prospect of being abandoned in the country, while he amused himself elsewhere, brought such a surge of rage and self-pity that she was relieved when the door opened and Denise hurried in.

Like the housekeeper, the little abigail was full of light-hearted chatter. She was so sorry she had not quite finished unpacking last night, so that madame had found it necessary to seek out some of her toilet articles, but all was made right now. Did madame intend to ride this morning? Would madame wear the blue habit or the green? Was madame aware that there was in the house a water closet and that Monsieur Justin had had the entire building painted and refurbished? Madame had beyond a doubt been too weary to last night notice, but Mr. Fisher, the splendid butler, was of an anxiety to show madame about so soon as she was bathed and dressed. And Mrs. Hayward asked that if madame could spare an hour or so this afternoon, she might interview three women for the position of madame's dresser applying.

Suspecting that a determined effort was being mounted to prevent her from becoming lonely, Lisette was touched. When she went downstairs an hour later, clad in her green habit and a pert little hat with a matching green feather, her suspicions were confirmed. From the omniscient Fisher, who bowed and welcomed her, to the stableboy who eyed her with awed admiration as he led Yasmin from the stables, everyone seemed genuinely delighted to greet her. In return, she went out of her way to appear cheerful, her chin high, a smile never far from her lips and, however vexed she may be by the belief that she was the only resident of Strand Hall who did not know the whereabouts of its master, betraying no hint of that fact.

One of the grooms, a vigorous middle-aged man with a shy smile, mounted up and rode at a respectful distance behind her. She was not sorry for his company, since the neighbourhood was strange to her, and after a short while invited him to ride with her and serve as guide. It developed that his name was Best and that he had been in the service of the Strands for twenty years and more. "If ye would care fer to look round now, marm," he said in his soft Sussex voice, "ye can have a foine view o' the great house."

It *was* a fine view, thought Lisette. Always provided one cared for the pretentious neoclassical architecture, which she did not. Certainly, with the sun bathing its white columns, the breeze riffling the branches of the trees, and the flower beds a mass of colour, Strand Hall was an imposing sight. It faced west, toward the rolling wooded hills where she now sat her horse. The park that surrounded it was spacious and well kept, and many would have considered it a most desirable estate. She tried to be objective, asking herself if her dislike of the place was born of her distaste for her husband. But she decided this was not so. Perhaps in her mind the ideal of country living must always be the farm the Van Lindsays had once owned, where she had spent many happy childhood summers. The residence had been more an overgrown cottage than a manor house, rather on the style of a rabbit warren, with odd little corridors and unexpected steps that were a burden to the maids, and where one always worried lest Grandmama might trip. But the grounds were deliciously uncultivated, there had been many obliging trees where one could climb or erect tree houses or swings, with no thought of offending, and the house itself, a nondescript brick structure, had always seemed warm and welcoming, its charm so informal and delightful a departure from London's elegance.

Watching her, a half-smile on his face, Best said, "A bit grand, bean't it, marm? Would'ee care fer to see the Home Farm? It be a pretty—" He broke off with a shout of warning as a tawny shape hurtled at them from a clump of beeches, shot between the two horses, and raced for the house. Yasmin, the gentlest of creatures, was yet a spirited animal, and for a few moments it was all Lisette could do to keep her from bolting. Best's gelding, being of a less tractable disposition, shied wildly, and thundered off with the groom coming perilously near to being unseated. Best soon regained control of his mount and, turning, was immeasurably relieved to find Lisette riding up to him.

"I'm very sorry, marm. A foine help I'd have been if you had been thrown!" He glanced angrily to the house. "That worthless mongrel!"

"I rather doubt he is a mongrel," said Lisette, patting the still skittish Yasmin. "It was Lord Bolster's bulldog, I believe."

"Ar. Brutus. A good name fer 'un. If ye don't mind, marm, I'd better ride down to the road and see if his lordship be looking fer the beast."

They turned about and rode eastward until they approached the Petworth road. Lisette asked, "Does Lord Bolster live in the neighbourhood?"

"No, marm. His lordship's country seat is Three Fields, in Surrey. Likely he do be coming to see the master, and Brutus ran on ahead."

"Ran?" She smiled. "Flew, more like!"

Best muttered something, the words inaudible, but the tone making it clear that Brutus was not highly regarded at Strand Hall. Reaching the road, they parted, Best saying he would ride on a little way, and Lisette returned to the Hall.

It had become quite warm by the time she entered the yard. She saw no sign of visitors, or of Brutus but, deciding to walk around to the front in case he might be waiting there, spotted the animal in the shade of one of the pillars, lying on his stomach, panting cheerfully, with both back legs stretched straight out behind him. Lisette went over and bent to stroke him. He listened without apparent repentance to the admonition that he was a bad dog and had probably worried his kind master. His only response was an even wider canine grin and an apparent attempt to "shake hands." This gesture, being essayed from a prone position, was disastrously unsuccessful, the powerful paw raking down the skirt of Lisette's habit, one nail slicing the seam into a long tear.

"Wretched brute!" she scolded, and reflected that it was as well she might be taking on a dresser this afternoon. She returned to the back of the house. There was no one in sight when she entered the open side door. It was cool inside, but she was hot and thirsty and, suspecting Brutus was in like condition, walked along the hall towards the kitchen to ask that a bowl of water be put out for him. The kitchen door was standing open, probably to catch the breeze from the outer door, and as she approached, Lisette could hear the housekeeper speaking. " . . . quite clear to see on her pretty face, and her eyes so sad it would break your heart! It's not right, Mr. Fisher! She should be told!"

"Before you take such a step, Mrs. H.," Fisher responded dryly, "I would recommend you go down to Silverings and tell Mr. Justin what you mean to do."

"Very funny, I'm sure," the housekeeper retaliated. "But he shouldn't have gone. And *she* shouldn't have gone with him! A fine set-to! I vow I feel so sorry for that lovely little wife of his, I could just hug the poor, brave soul!"

The wind blew the outer door shut with a bang. Somehow gathering her scattered wits, Lisette fled.

By the time she reached her bedchamber, shock had given way to a quite different emotion from that which had so shattered her the previous night. There had been room for doubt then. There had been the possibility that Strand had been irrevocably committed—that he would return with some logical explanation. Now, she knew an icy wrath; an indignation that went past mere anger to inexorable condemnation. Sooner or later, Mr. Justin Strand would come home. And when he did, he would learn to his sorrow the price of insulting a Van Lindsay!

* * *

"*My* husband is away, I am afraid," said Lisette, walking across the saloon and extending a hand to Lord Jeremy Bolster. "He will be so sorry to have missed you."

Bolster sprang up, coloured hotly, bowed over her hand, and stammered out his apologies for having called at such a time.

"Not at all, my lord." Lisette seated herself and waved him to a chair. "I expect you have come in search of Brutus? He arrived this morning. I believe he is being—er—entertained in the stables, but Best will bring him to you when you are ready to leave."

"Oh," said his lordship, glumly. "I had hoped—Justin is away, you s-s-say? Dash it all, I th-thought perhaps he m-might . . ."

Lisette lifted her brows enquiringly. "Can I be of any assistance, sir? I am assured my husband would wish I do whatever I might."

Bolster explained painfully that he was soon to leave for Italy. "F-fraid old Brutus mi-might pine if I was to l-l-leave him. And I'd—hoped Justin m-might—er . . ." He checked, looking at her with his diffident, sideways glance.

"Take him back? Oh, but that would be famous! I am very fond of dogs, and—well, it's rather lonely here. I would be only too delighted to have Brutus."

Brightening, he said earnestly, "You are v-very g-g-good, ma'am. M-Mandy told me you was very k-kind, and I can s-see . . ." He gestured in a pathetically hopeless fashion, and finished forlornly, "D-don't want to go. But—b-best I do. What?"

"Perhaps it is, my lord," Lisette said kindly. "Time heals—so they say." Her own eyes became sad, and she sighed.

Watching her, Bolster asked anxiously, "N-nothing wrong, is there, Mrs. Strand? I mean—old J-Justin's not in queer s-stirrups or-or such like?"

"How kind you are. No, he was called away on an urgent matter he could not postpone."

He gave a relieved nod. "And you are quite s-sure he won't mind?"

"Perfectly sure," Lisette said with a smile.

Justin Strand did not appear at his ancestral hall that week. Surprisingly, however, Lisette entertained an unending stream of callers. Among these was her grandmother, who was as irascible as she was unexpected. She greeted Lisette with an almost fierce defiance and stamped about, grunting "Stupid!" from time to time, while rapping her cane violently on the highly polished floors. The architecture she viewed with a jaundiced eye; the lofty entrance foyer she found depressing, and she judged the splendidly restored tapestry which hung there an abomination. The lounges were draughty, the fireplaces probably smoked, and her bedroom was so vast she could scarce see across it. After one penetrating glance at her granddaughter's calm smile, she did not enquire as to where Mr. Strand had gone, nor once comment on his absence. She seemed at times preoccupied and, having stared into the fire for half an hour on the evening of her arrival, responded to Lisette's rather uneasy remark that she hoped the family was well, by saying testily that Judith seemed to be a shade improved and she hoped would grow up with more in her head than hair. "Not," she added, "like Beatrice!"

"Has my sister returned to Somerset, ma'am?" asked Lisette.

"No, she ain't!" barked my lady, with another rap of her cane upon the carpet. "She enjoys her freedom with the Haines-Curtis gal, who I doubt is any better than she should be, and given entirely too much credit for being responsible, which she ain't! Dwyer should take a stick to his wife! And not wait too long about it, neither!"

The old lady remained for three days, and although she was unimpressed with Strand Hall, the staff pleased her, and for one occupant she developed a passionate fondness. Brutus, who fawned upon her slavishly, was, she proclaimed, a splendid guard, a magnificent specimen, and a credit to his breed. Nobody's fool, he seldom left her side, even slithering into the forbidden dining room to accept tit-bits from my lady's hand whilst he hid under the table, and in general taking shameful advantage of the situation. When Lady Bayes-Copeland left, he was devastated and moaned for a full five minutes before discerning a visiting cat that must be chased from the premises.

The bulldog had, by this time, formed the habit of sleeping beside Lisette's bed. He snored, which was annoying, and his snores were broken by snufflings that were at times followed by a long silent pause. When Lisette first experienced this phenomenon, she jumped up in bed, convinced he had died, only to be shattered by a cacophonous explosion of snorts, snuffles, and grunts before the snoring rhythm was restored. Each time she was awoken by such a performance, she gritted her teeth and vowed never again to endure such a night. After several weakenings, she was driven to insist that Brutus sleep outside her door, but this was worse, for not only did he whine and tear at the panel but soon demonstrated that he was a dog of many parts. Lying sleepless and fuming, Lisette heard a new sound and correctly deduced he had seized the handle between his jaws and was wrenching at it. He'll catch cold at that! she thought, contemptuously. Brutus, however, did not catch cold; whether by accident or skill, the door suddenly opened. He raced in, leapt onto the bed, and bounced about in triumph until Lisette abandoned her enraged commands and broke her candle over his muzzle. He licked her face to show her that he held no grudge, then abandoned the bed, to settle down smugly beside it. The snoring began within seconds, but gradually Lisette became accustomed to the uproar and was able to sleep through it all.

On the morning after her grandmother's departure Tristram Leith and his wife paid a call. Despite her efforts, the sight of Leith's tall, athletic figure and handsome countenance made Lisette's heart contract. She was invited by Rachel to return with them to Cloudhills, but the prospect of being so close to Tristram—of seeing their happiness—was not to be borne, and with grace but firmness she declined, saying that she was sure her husband would return momentarily. She did not miss the swift, meaningful glance that passed between the two. From the moment of their arrival she had noted that Tristram seemed a trifle grim, and now the worry in Rachel's blue eyes, so like her brother's, was pronounced. Lisette guessed that they were pitying her, and her sense of ill usage was intensified. She stood on the front steps for a long time after they left, her wistful gaze following the carriage until it was lost to her sight, envying them the devotion that had manifested itself in so many small ways, and longing to be the fortunate lady now being happily carried off to Cloudhills. A large head was thrust under her hand; a snuffling bark dispersed her useless dreams. She petted Brutus gratefully, then sent a lackey to request that Yasmin be saddled, and went inside to change into her habit.

She enjoyed a long ride, Best guiding her to the Home Farm, which was a very pretty and orderly establishment, presided over by a cheerful, ruddy-faced farmer and his shy wife, who bobbed a curtsey each time she addressed the bride. Lisette, who had immediately won her admiration, now captured her heart by asking that each of the children be presented to her. She dutifully admired them all, kissed the baby, and left, thinking with a pang of her own brothers and sisters.

The house seemed awesomely quiet when she walked into the foyer. Upstairs there was no sign of Denise in either the parlour or her bedchamber. Walking to the bell pull beside the bed, Lisette's upstretched hand checked. A great white rose lay on her pillow, dewdrops still gleaming on the petals. Staring at it, her heart jolted. She frowned and did not pick up the bloom, but crossed to the dressing table where she sat down and started to tidy her hair. He was back! And he was watching her, she knew. She affected ignorance until her trembling eased, then glanced around, her brows arched enquiringly.

Strand leaned in the open door to the balcony, arms folded, regarding her with grave speculation. That he had been indulging in some very riotous living was evidenced by the pallor beneath his tan and the shadows under his eyes. How often had she seen that same look on Timothy's face during the Long Vacation, when he'd spent the night in that peculiar pastime the young Bucks and Corinthians called Boxing the Watch; or when he'd come home at dawn after a night of play (usually disastrous) at Watier's or White's. Resuming her task, she battled the urge to stroll over to her husband and claw his wretched face. Instead, "Good morning, Strand," she said politely.

His head lowered a little. Glancing up at her from under his brows, he murmured, "You are very angry. And rightfully so. But—"

"No, why ever should I be? You are perfectly at liberty to come and go as you choose. With whom you choose. Truly, I have had a lovely time."

He watched as she dusted a hare's-foot across her dainty nose, and said in a reluctant, halting fashion, "You are entitled to an explanation, and—"

"Oh, pray do not fret over so insignificant a thing. I thought it most considerate in you to give me a time to settle down. In fact—" she opened her jewel box and peered inside, saying carelessly, ''I had thought you might not return for several weeks. Would you mind if—''

The door smashed open. Brutus flung himself across the room. Caught by surprise, Strand was sent hurtling back onto the balcony.

For a very brief instant Lisette's heart leapt into her mouth. Then she heard the muffled explosion of swearing and, amused, hastened to survey the victim and the prancing delirium of his pet.

''Blast your ears!'' Strand roared, fighting off the ecstatic dog. ''Down, sir! Down, I say! No—not *on* me, curse you!''

Succeeding at last in extricating himself, he clambered to his feet, glared at his bride's smile, and demanded, ''What in the devil is *he* doing here?''

''He was a gift,'' Lisette said sweetly, bending the truth a little. ''Lord Bolster came and was—a trifle shocked, I suspect. To find me here all alone, you know.'' Glancing obliquely at Strand, she saw his lips tighten, and added, ''He thought Brutus might protect me.'' She raised limpid eyes to her husband and purred, ''So thoughtful.''

''And quite unnecessary. You are safe here. I will return Brutus this afternoon.''

''It is kind in you to offer. But if you do not object, Strand, I shall keep him. I doubt it is as safe here as you may think. And besides, when you are away on your—er—affairs, he will be company for me.''

Frowning into that angelic face, Strand's fists clenched. ''I do object. He goes back. This afternoon. Do you feel the need of a dog, ma'am, I'll buy you one.''

''But, sir, one cannot *buy* love. Or loyalty.''

The barbs went home. Strand thought, She marshals a strong counter-attack, and he bowed, saying nothing.

Lisette shrugged and turned away. ''However, if you must— you must. Now, will you please pardon me whilst I change for luncheon?''

He walked over to the door, and was about to open it when she called gently, ''Shall you be home for dinner, sir? I only ask because the Vicar and the Misses Hepplethwaite are to dine here and play some whist afterwards, and I possibly should warn them you will join us.''

The prospect was not enthralling. "I doubt I shall be home," he said, opening the door. "It's a long ride to Three Fields."

And a pointless one! she thought jubilantly.

Chapter 8

Lisette underestimated her husband. Although he did not mean to share the early evening's entertainment, Justin Strand had not the slightest intention of spending another night away from his bride. His return to his ancestral estate was not a propitious one, however. Before he was halfway home, it was raining hard. Brutus was afraid of storms, and when a sudden flash of lightning was followed by a great boom of thunder, he sprang onto the seat beside Strand and did his destructive best to dig his way underneath him. Strand was cold, furiously angry, and very tired. He allowed the edge of his rage to break over the burrowing dog, but was interrupted when the powerful animal's claws gouged his thigh. Instinctively jerking away, Strand lost ground and found himself unable to lower his knee save over Brutus. Snarling curses, he moved to the other side of the carriage. It was hopeless. The dog hurtled at him. Without the aid of two strong men it was doubtful the brute could be ejected from the carriage, and Strand had no intention of either sitting on Brutus or allowing the animal to sit on him. He draped a corner of his cloak over the shivering monster and favoured him with a succinct evaluation of his ancestors.

"I am sure you are aware, you miserable excuse for a watchdog, that I was thoroughly gulled today," he observed grimly. "My lady wife did not see fit to explain that she had promised to care for your revolting self while Bolster is away. She was certainly aware I'd not have the gall to dump such a plague on his lordship's servants. I have driven in excess of forty miles, Sir Shivershakes, to no purpose. But there will be an accounting! I promise you!''

Brutus quailed, whining heartrendingly, then sat up, eyeing his master in so frantic a way that Strand feared a resumption of the earlier chaos. He at once moderated his tone and at last was permitted the luxury of sitting peacefully, listening to the rain between Brutus's resounding snores.

It was half-past twelve when the carriage splashed into the stableyard, and the house was dark. He would light it, Strand thought mercilessly. Had it not been for his implacable resolve to spend the night with his bride and also to demand an accounting of her savage duplicity, he would have racked up for the night at the first tavern he'd come to and allowed Brutus to quake under the hay in the stables. Without an instant spent repining the disturbed slumbers of the inhabitants, he instructed his coachman to blow up a hail on his yard of tin. As a result, by the time he was climbing down the steps lights were already appearing in the windows of the long house beside the stables where the grooms and outside servants dwelt.

Best came staggering into the barn, dragging a coat over his nightshirt. ''Welcome—'' he began, then stopped, one glance at Strand's face freezing the words on his lips.

''Get that hound of Satan out of the carriage!'' snarled Strand.

Fisher, hurrying from the side door of the Hall, holding up an umbrella, said a concerned, ''Good heavens, sir! You must be tired out!''

''Ain't no dog in here, sir,'' called Best, puzzled.

''We may hope he is well on his way back to Three Fields!'' Strand said acidly.

Twenty minutes later, his hair brushed, his new red velvet robe tied over his nightshirt, and vengeance in his heart, he marched across his bedchamber and flung wide the connecting door to his bride's suite. The parlour was empty and dark. Pacing across it, he threw open Lisette's door. There was no light save for the flames still flickering in the fireplace, but by that faint glow he saw Lisette leap up in bed. She wore a filmy nightgown of some indeterminate pale colour, her cap was lopsided, and her eyes huge with fright. Retribution, he thought ragefully, was upon her. "Good morning, ma'am," he gritted. "I came home after all, you see."

He took three long strides towards the bed and the white-faced girl who trembled there.

Brutus had not essayed the long journey back to Three Fields, for he was decidedly a creature of habit. He was, besides, just dozing off, and did not hear the man's approach until Strand was almost on him, whereupon he sprang up hurriedly.

The result was unfortunate.

"Nothing to worry about, dear lady," Dr. Bellows uttered reassuringly, as he closed the door upon his recalcitrant patient and accompanied the bride (whom he privately thought to be exquisite) along the hall.

He has arrived in direct violation of Strand's orders and, walking into the book room where his patient was stubbornly attempting to read the morning paper, had announced a jovial, "Well, here's old Bellows-to-mend again, Justin. What now have you been up to, dear boy?"

Strand had groaned and covered his eyes with his left hand, whereupon Dr. Bellows had pounced upon the right and grasped it, drawing a shout from his patient and an instinctive flinch from Lisette. "Hmmm," he said mildly. "Something broken in here, I think. D'you have any idea how many bones there are in the human hand, Justin? No, of course you don't, for I keep forgetting you've a head of solid wood."

Surprised, Lisette had darted a glance at him, to find his face suddenly angry. She had been more surprised to see her husband colour hotly, drop his eyes, and endure in silence a careful but undoubtedly unpleasant examination.

When he had gone crashing down in the darkened room, Lisette, for one panicked moment, had fancied herself an early widow. He had soon sprung to his feet, however, and snarling hideous threats had raced into the hall after the fleeing Brutus. Fearing for the dog's survival, Lisette had followed, only to find Strand leaning against the wall, clutching his arm and looking white and exhausted. "Well, and is your revenge adequate, ma'am?" he'd asked unevenly. His fall was, she knew, only a trifling matter compared to the indignity she had been made to suffer. Nonetheless, she was not an unkind girl, and to see his eyes narrowed with pain had so wrought upon her that she had required Fisher to send a groom galloping at once for the family doctor. Strand had protested vigorously, but Fisher, being both fond of his employer and delighted by the bride, had not heeded him. Not a little frightened by both the accident and her husband's wrath, Lisette decided to play the part of the dutiful wife, which role she had since nobly maintained.

Now, she asked, "Then, there is nothing broken after all?" and wondered why, if that were so, the doctor had made such a fuss, insisting that her husband take to his bed so that the arm could be properly splinted and placed in a sling.

"To the contrary, I suspect several small bones may be either fractured or broken," Bellows said. "Shame it's his right hand. There'll be no keeping him inactive for long, even so. Still, for the time being he must stay quiet, ma'am. I cannot get laudanum down him, but I'll leave you these powders. Three a day in a glass of water. They taste foul, so he'll make a great fuss. But it will keep him quiet, at least. A very light diet, if you please, and I will come back tomorrow to see how he goes on. No need to show me out, m'dear. I know me way."

She expressed her intention of obeying his instructions implicitly and returned to the bedchamber.

Strand had already been subjected to one of the powders and lay watching her with a drowsy but irked look on his thin face. His hair was rumpled, and in the white nightshirt with his bandaged arm strapped across his chest, he looked rather astonishingly youthful and defenceless.

Discovering that Brutus panted beside the bed, Lisette knew a pang of guilt and said, "I am indeed sorry that you have had so much distress, sir. Is there anything I can do to make you more comfortable?"

"You can take out that revolting animal and shoot it," he muttered malevolently.

"But of course. I do not know what Lord Bolster will think of so flagrant a violation of my given word. But I must henceforth be guided by my husband in all things. Including—conduct." His eyes sharpened predictably, and she said with sweet martyrdom, "I should not wish to inflict such a task on Best, for he is so kind a man. Perhaps I could do it. I have watched my brother shoot at Manton's, so I am not afraid of handling a pistol.''

"Are you not? I shall have to remember that," he drawled thoughtfully. Lisette being unable to restrain a dimple, he stared at it, then growled, "You may well laugh, madam wife. The fact remains you've not yet begun to know that curst brute's habits! I was never so glad as to be rid of him, and I count it downright treacherous of you to saddle me with him again. He is a pest, ma'am. He eats like a horse, is totally unreliable as a guard, snores like a volcano, and—''

"And seems most fond of you, sir," Lisette put in meekly.

"Which verifies his stupidity, else he would comprehend that I cannot abide him.''

"Yes, but he might more easily comprehend that fact were you to stop caressing him.''

Strand glanced to the side and hurriedly snatched back the hand that had been absently fondling Brutus. "I—er . . . had not realized . . .''

"Of course, you are half asleep. I will remove him and take care he does not disturb you again." She moved closer to bend over him and seeing the look of shocked disbelief, enquired, "May I smooth your pillows?''

Strand's eyes were becoming positively heavy, but he propped himself on one elbow as Lisette plumped his pillows. "I wish," he yawned, lying back, "you would allow me . . . to . . .''

"Go to sleep," she adjured, and led Brutus from the room.

Strand lay quietly for a moment after the door closed behind her. Then he withdrew his left hand from beneath the eiderdown. For a long moment he gazed at the object he grasped. A small square of fine lawn, edged with dainty lace. He raised it to his lips and breathed the sweet fragrance of it. Awkwardly, he sat up and with painful care placed his prize in the drawer of his bedside table. Then he settled back down and went to sleep.

Dr. Bellows appeared to exert a powerful influence upon his patient, and for the two days following, Strand meekly submitted to lying abed, swallowing the noxious drugs and drowsing the hours away. By the third day he was beginning to grumble, however, and by the fourth, he was up and about. Coming downstairs at ten o'clock, Lisette was shocked to see him stride in at the front doors wearing riding dress, and arguing with a clerical-appearing individual regarding the benefits of allowing the south field to lie fallow for a season.

"Oh, there you are, my dear," he said, flashing Lisette an impudent grin. "This is my steward, Connaught. Connie—my wife. Now, I'm not at all pleased by the look of things at Silverings. The boat dock is downright rotted and must be attended to at once if we're not to lose the whole this winter. Mrs. Strand, would you please ask Fisher to step in here? As for—"

"No," said Lisette clearly.

A sparkle came into Mr. Connaught's faded brown eyes. Strand's head turned to his wife. Startled, he exclaimed, "Eh?"

"May I ask what you are about, sir?" She folded her hands and regarded him with cool disapproval. "Dr. Bellows said you were not to—"

He laughed. "Oh, you mustn't pay too much heed to our Bellows-to-mend. He's a good enough old fellow, but a regular gloom merchant. I'm doing splendidly. I've kept my arm in this confounded sling for—"

"Three days," she nodded. "Dr. Bellows said three weeks—at least."

"Nonsense. A far too conservative estimate, m'dear. I'll be fully restored long before that. Give you my word."

His eyes held a mocking glint. Lisette blushed and retreated, but at the door she turned back. "Did you have a nice ride, Strand?"

"Very nice. I shall roust you out soon, ma'am, for there's something I must show you."

"It shall have to wait, sir. I must insist there be no more riding today." Strand looked astounded, and she turned to his amused steward. "I am sure you understand, Mr. Connaught, that the master's recovery must not be impaired."

The gleam brighter than ever in his eyes, Mr. Connaught bowed and said he certainly understood. In fact, he was only going to stay another minute or two.

"Thank you," said Lisette. "That would be considerate in you."

Staring at the door as it closed behind her, Strand muttered, "Well, I'll be damned . . ."

"Nothing like having a lady around the house, is there, sir?" asked Mr. Connaught. "Especially so lovely a lady as your own."

Strand was silent for a long moment. Then, "No," he said slowly. "Nothing."

In the hall, Lisette encountered Mr. Fisher, winding the grandfather clock that stood at the foot of the stairs in the wide entrance foyer. "Good morning, Fisher," she said, captivating him with her smile. "Could you tell me, please, has there never been a music room in the house?"

"Years ago there was, madam," he answered, closing the clock with care. "It annoyed Mr. Rupert to hear practising, so the instruments were all moved into the children's room."

"The children's room?" Moved by a sly impulse, she asked, "Oh, is that at Silverings?"

"No, madam. Mr. Rupert never cared for Silverings, though it had at one time a quite splendid music room."

So Silverings belonged to the Strands. "I see. But my husband is fond of the place, I believe."

"Very fond. Would you wish to see the children's room, madam?"

Lisette indicating an interest, Fisher led her outside, past the barn and through a shrubbery having in the centre a cleared space in which stood what looked like an enclosed summer house. Unlocking the door, he said, "Shall I wait, madam? Or would you care to stay for a time?"

"I would. Thank you."

Left alone, she wandered about curiously. The room was surprisingly spacious and well kept up. In addition to chairs and tables, there was a small pianoforte which she soon determined was in excellent tune, a harp, a mandolin, and a case holding a fine violin. She sat at the piano and played for a while, well pleased with its tone and action. She did not turn when the door was softly opened, guessing that Strand had come seeking her, but when he did not speak a sudden unease caused her to spin around on the stool. She gave a gasp of shock. James Garvey stood in the doorway, smiling fondly at her. He swept off his curly-brimmed beaver and bowed low. "At last!" he breathed, coming quickly into the room and closing the door behind him.

"Oh, my poor creature. How wan you look! Does he ill-treat you?"

"Wh-whatever are you doing here? Mr. Garvey, I—"

"James—I beg! Just to hear it on your lips!"

"Oh, James, then. You must be mad! Does my husband know you are here?"

He shrugged, stepping closer to regard her with eyes aglow with adoration. "How could he? I understand he is confined to his bed after a small accident. I rushed here at once, to console you."

"Good gracious!" she exclaimed, walking around him to the door. "You are not very well acquainted with my husband, sir, else you would know he is scarcely the type to remain in bed."

Her hand on the doorknob was restrained as his own closed over it. "Lisette, my goddess of beauty, stay a moment, I implore you. All these weeks I have been desolate."

She said with asperity, "If my husband finds us alone here, Mr. Garvey, we are liable to be a good deal more than desolate. Now, you must please leave before—"

"Not yet! Do you suppose I rode all this way to be frightened off by the likes of Justin Strand?" He carried her hand to his lips despite her efforts to free it and, gazing down at her, murmured, "I love you still. You are everything feminine—everything pure and lovely. My adored Lisette, when may I see you? Can you get away from him? Could you come to—"

The door opened suddenly. Lisette gave a little squeak of fright and wrenched her hand free. Garvey turned lazily, quizzing glass upraised and a mocking smile on his lips. "Oh, but how very embarrassing," said he.

Charity Strand stood on the threshold. "M-my—my apologies!" she gasped, and fled.

Garvey laughed. Lisette said furiously, "Oh, but that was too bad of you, James. Now Justin will come, and—"

"Have no fear, beloved. I can handle your irate husband, should he object, which I rather doubt."

"What do you mean by that?"

"Merely that while he may not be very bright, I'd not take him for the reckless type."

"Be that as it may—" Lisette frowned—"he is my husband. I insist that you leave at once."

He instead stepped closer, and took her by the shoulders. "Did you despair, my lovely one? Did you think I had abandoned you? Never! I shall adore you for as long as I live."

His green eyes were soft with love, his handsome face hovered above her, and here was more romance in a few moments than she'd had from Strand in the two weeks she had been wed to him. Yet, oddly, she was more irritated that enchanted. "You are very good, and truly, I am most grateful for your concern, but I am a married woman now. Whatever might have been is—is past redemption." He looked so downcast that she was moved to add kindly, "Sir, you have every quality to charm a lady, and there are so many in London who must, I am sure, admire you."

He sighed. "But only one who has my heart." Lisette turned away, and he said, "Married, my lovely dream—married . . . but perhaps *not* past redemption."

"James," she said, searching his face, "you would not do anything foolish?"

He laughed easily. "I never do anything foolish—save to say farewell to you, my goddess. But before I go, promise me this. If you ever need me, if he ever ill-treats you, you will at once send word. Promise, Lisette?"

She nodded. "I promise." And thought it quite nonsensical.

Returning to the house, Lisette found Strand and his sister in the library. Their conversation terminated rather abruptly when she entered, but it soon became apparent that Charity had not spoken of what she had witnessed in the children's room. She had stopped, she said, for a brief visit en route to spend a month or two with the Leiths at Cloudhills.

"Which is quite absurd," said Strand. "This is your home, and always will be."

"Yes, and I should be most glad of your company," Lisette put in. "I miss my own family so badly, and it would be delightful if you could stay."

Charity was adamant, however. She would not dream of interrupting a honeymoon. "If the truth be told," she said with a glance at Lisette, "you will get little enough of privacy here, and will likely have a steady stream of visitors. You should have gone away, Justin."

He attempted a gesture, forgetting his broken arm, and winced slightly. It was sufficient for both ladies to demand he rest for a while before luncheon and, grumbling that his life was as ordered as though he were a small boy, he went contentedly upstairs to do as he was bid.

When they were alone, Lisette turned to her sister-in-law. "You did not tell him."

Charity shook her head. "I hoped there was nothing of import to tell."

"Thank you. And there truly was not. Mr. Garvey had just arrived with—with a message from my family, and sought me out in the garden." It must, she knew, sound false, especially since Garvey had been kissing her hand when Charity had burst in on them.

"I had heard Mr. Garvey is—er, devoted to you," Charity said in a worried voice. "But truly, he has a—a rather unsavoury reputation where ladies are concerned. If my brother thought—"

Lisette summoned a small laugh. "That I have taken a lover after less than a month of marriage? Good gracious! You must suppose me fast indeed!"

"Oh, no, no! I only meant that it might be necessary for you to tell my brother, does Mr. Garvey continue to annoy you."

It was said so earnestly, and the girl's sweet face was so troubled that Lisette could not take offence and, patting her hand, agreed, "Indeed it might. But not, I think, while Strand has only his left hand."

Charity paled. "Heavens! You never think it would come to a duel? Surely Mr. Garvey would not be so rash? *He* is the one challenges convention in pursuing a married lady!"

"I have tried to warn him away. We can but hope he will behave properly in the future."

Charity nodded, but when she was in the carriage and being driven to Cloudhills her heart was heavy. She had very little faith in the proper behaviour of Mr. James Garvey.

Something was tickling Lisette's nose. She brushed it away sleepily, and snuggled deeper under the blankets. Again came that persistent tickling. She opened one eye. A dewy pink rose lay within an inch of her face. Blinking at it, she heard a familiar and amused voice scoff, "Slugabed!"

She raised her head and discerned Strand, booted and spurred, standing at the foot of the bed. For a moment of foolishness she fancied him almost attractive as he leaned against the bedpost watching her with his quirkish grin, his blue eyes bright against his tan, the fair hair tumbled as usual, and his whip tapping restlessly against his top boot. Such an illusion must, she decided, be the result of insufficient sleep, and closing her eyes she muttered, "Go away."

The rose tickled her nose once more, and when next she opened her eyes, Strand's face hovered rather frighteningly close. "You desire help, madam bride?" he murmured. "I shall be glad to assist you . . ."

His hand closed over the bedclothes. Snatching at them protectively, Lisette, aware that he had every right to do as he chose, was spurred to hasty, if indignant, agreement. "Shall I ring for your abigail?" he enquired, moving back. "Or can you manage to dress yourself alone?"

Lisette imparted regally that although *she* might be forced to arise at so ungodly an hour, she refused to inflict such misery upon her hapless abigail.

Strand chuckled and left her, but she was shocked when the door again swung open just as she was getting out of bed, and he stuck his head back in. "If I chance to have dropped asleep by the time you arrive downstairs, please wake me." His eyes wandered downwards; he added appraisingly, "You've a well-turned ankle, I'm glad to see."

She gave a gasp of mortification and whipped her foot back under the covers. Dreading lest he again return with his odious offer of assistance, she dressed in record time, her rapid movements accelerated by the chill in the fireless room. Adjusting her petite grey hat, its large red feather a vivid complement to her dark hair and eyes, she appraised herself critically and decided that she looked well enough—well enough for her husband, at all events. She took up whip and gloves, paused beside the full-length mirror, and lifted her habit a little. She had suspected she had no cause to blush for her legs, but nonetheless, it was nice to know she had a "well-turned ankle."

Outside, the skies looked threatening and the air was cold. Lisette shivered as they started out of the stableyard side by side. "What a miserable morning. It looks like rain." She glanced at

Strand's right arm, carried in the sling. "I doubt you should be riding yet."

"It won't rain this morning. And I feel very well, thank you," he said cheerfully. "We'll give the horses a gallop. That should warm your blood a little." He added, *sotto voce,* "I hope."

Lisette turned a scornful glance upon the repellent creature but surprised such a whimsical twinkle she could not hold her anger and, fighting an impulse to smile in return, remarked, "I trust we do not have far to go, Strand."

"Oh, only a short way past Petworth," he said airily.

"*Petworth?* Why, it—it must be three and twenty miles, at least!"

"Oh, at least. But it's early yet, and we can breakfast along the—"

His words were cut off as Brutus came charging from the trees and shot under the horses, excitedly barking. Lisette had caught a glimpse of him an instant before he reached them and had tightened her grip on the reins. Strand was caught by surprise as his big chestnut gelding bucked in a frenzy of fear. Struggling to manage her own mount, Lisette shot an anxious glance at her husband. For a man with only one arm at his disposal he was doing magnificently, his wiry body swaying to counter the chestnut's gyrations as he fought for control. Reining the animal to a halt, his gaze flashed to Lisette. "That blasted idiot of a dog!" he exclaimed, a trifle breathlessly. "You might have got a broken neck out of this!"

"You terrify me, sir," she said meekly. "Shall I return home while you dispose of him?"

He glared at her, grunted "Come on!" and spurred to a gallop.

The horses were eager to go and fairly flew over the turf. Strand rode like a centaur, guiding the big chestnut unerringly with his left hand. Lisette, who had been used to chafe at the restrictions polite Society placed on young damsels and yearn for a gallop, contrarily was now vexed by Strand's breezy assumption that she needed no pampering. When her pert little hat was almost snatched off by the wind, she decided enough was enough and drew Yasmin to a sedate trot. Strand was soon out of sight, but since she had no idea whither they were bound, she surmised he would return for her. She was right. He came thundering up, his eyes bright and a becoming flush on his lean cheeks. "My apologies." He grinned. "I forget you're London bred and unaccustomed to exercise."

She was irritated, but smiled and said sweetly, "Alas, I fear I am a great disappointment to you, Mr. Strand."

"Never mind," he reassured her infuriatingly. "We'll have you up to snuff in no time."

Why was it, she wondered, that however right *she* was, however wrong *he* was, *she* inevitably was made to feel inferior? It was a new experience, and one she did not at all appreciate. Up to snuff, indeed! She rode on in a lofty silence, and Strand stayed more or less beside her, his horse fidgeting and fretting, snorting at every puff of breeze, sidling at shadows, and in general behaving so outrageously that several times Strand was obliged to allow him to circle Yasmin. Lisette was being drawn to a snail's pace and had to grit her teeth to keep from urging Yasmin ahead. They came to a low hedge the horses could have walked over, but Strand made a great point of insisting that Lisette wait, while he galloped off, the chestnut kicking up his heels in delight at the change of pace. In a minute or two Strand returned and led Lisette a short distance westward where he dismounted to open a low gate. Having ushered her through it with grave ceremony, he prepared to close the gate, whereupon his mount pranced sideways, colliding slightly with Yasmin.

"Brandy, you devil, be still!" Strand exhorted, and with laughter brimming in his eyes, said, "Sorry about this idiot, madam wife. He behaves in much the same fashion when I take my grandmother out."

It was the last straw. With a muffled but incensed exclamation, Lisette drove home her heels. Yasmin bounded forward. Strand's startled shout rang out, but bending low, Lisette urged the mare to greater speed, paying no heed to the wind now, and exulting in this gallop of her own choosing. Over lush meadows, down a gently sloping hill, and along a winding lane she raced, trees and hedgerows flashing past, the wind whipping her hair and sending her habit billowing. Her cheeks were tingling; she felt invigorated and ignored Strand's roared demand that she stop. He was coming up fast but, exhilarated by the chase, she made no attempt to slow the mare. They were following the path of the river and as Yasmin shot around a curve, the lane narrowed suddenly. Too late, Lisette saw that the heavy rains had caused the river to overflow its banks at a low spot just ahead. Floodwaters surged across the lane, having dug a deep channel in which debris swirled sullenly. There was no way to avoid that treacherous gulf. Tall hedgerows presented an impenetrable barrier at the left, to the right was the raging swell of the river, and the jump was by far too wide for Yasmin to attempt. For the first time in her life Lisette froze with terror and sat watching disaster rush at her.

A thunder of hooves, a gloved hand closing over her reins and wrenching back with surprising power. Yasmin reared, neighing in panic. Recovering her wits, Lisette jerked her about.

There was no time for Strand to do the same, besides which he had lost his own reins when he grabbed hers. He was leaning perilously from the saddle, but managed to pull himself upright. With his hand fast gripped in Brandy's flying mane, his knees tight, his weight on the stirrups, he guided his horse into that impossible jump. They soared into the air. Lisette gasped as Brandy's tucked-up back hooves skimmed an ugly splintered tree trunk. They could not hope to clear that deathtrap! They *could* not! But the chestnut landed on the far side. The earth crumbled away under his back legs. Strand had been flung forward and with a fluid leap was out of the saddle and tugging at the reins. For a breathless moment man and animal scrabbled and fought, then Brandy was clear and stood trembling, eyes rolling, and lathered with foam.

Lisette closed her eyes and breathed a silent prayer of thanks. "Are you all right?" she called anxiously.

Having already satisfied himself that she'd not been thrown, Strand did not so much as deign her a glance, his full attention bent upon an inspection of his mount's muddied legs. He patted the chestnut's neck and spoke softly to him. "Wait there!" he called curtly, and led Brandy along the lane.

Watching him disappear from sight through a break in the hedgerow, Lisette thought rebelliously that he had taunted her into essaying that gallop. The fact that he had shouted at her to stop conveniently escaped her, and she glowered at Yasmin's ears, quite sure she was about to be chastised.

Strand hailed her. He had circled around and, instead of having the common decency to rush to his shaken lady and determine if she was about to swoon, waited some distance behind her, gesturing impatiently. Her brows gathering into an irked frown, she rode back to him.

"What in the devil did you think you was about, madam?" he demanded, not mincing his words. "Trying to prove what a bruising rider you are? Did you not hear me tell you to stop?"

Unhappily conscious that his anger was to an extent justified, she lifted her chin and said with proud hauteur, "*Tell* me, sir? No man *tells* me what I may do! I do as I please!"

"You *did* as you pleased, *Mrs. Strand*. From now on, you will be guided by me!" His eyes fairly sparked rage; his chin seemed to thrust out at her, and his lips were a tight, angry line.

"How *dare* you address me in such a tone?" Lisette flared.

"Oh, I dare! Never doubt it. And shall do more than scold if you ever again commit an act of such reckless folly! Had you forgot you are my wife?"

Her lip curling, she retaliated, "I wonder how ever I might have come to do so!" She knew at once that she had erred, for the rage in his eyes was replaced by a dancing gleam of mirth.

"I do not wonder at all," he said, adding wickedly, "but I shall contrive to remind you of it. Just as soon as possible."

Her cheeks fiery, Lisette thought it best to ignore the vulgar boor.

Chapter 9

With wretched perversity the weather bore out Strand's forecast.
The sun burst through the clouds to bathe the rain-drenched
south country in its brilliance, the air became pleasantly warm,
and every bird in creation seemed determined to offer up a paean
of thanks for this respite from the gloom. At any other time,
Lisette would have been elated by so glorious a morning; under
the circumstances, however, she was all but oblivious of the
beauties about her. Strand's one attempt at conversation was a
banal comment on the improved state of the weather, to which
infamous behaviour his bride responded with justifiably haughty
courtesy. Had he cared even a mite, the wretch would attempt to
be conciliating, instead of which he was so heartless as to utter
not another word. Her own nerves ragged, she said nothing
either, and a deep, unbroachable silence settled over them.

It was almost nine o'clock when Strand turned into the yard of
a quaint old inn drowsing comfortably beneath three great oak
trees, its whitewashed walls somewhat weatherstained, but the
mullioned windows gleaming and with smoke curling from several chimneys. The proprietor of the inn, which was rather
inappropriately named The Pines, came hurrying out to them.
"Back again so soon, Mr. Justin?" he beamed, adding a disastrous,
"And I see you brought the little lady with—" His eyes, having
travelled to Lisette, widened. "Oh," he finished, lamely.

"You must allow me to make you known to my wife," Strand

put in, betraying no trace of embarrassment at this *faux pas*. "This is Mr. Drye, ma'am," and, as a fat little woman bustled out to join them, "and his lady, who is also the finest cook in Sussex."

Lisette summoned her most gracious smile. Strand assisted her to dismount and then went off to the stables with Drye, while Lisette was shown with much curtseying to a small chamber under the eaves. Viewing herself in the mirror, she was not surprised to find that the disastrous ride had reduced her hair to a windblown tangle, the collar of her habit was all awry, and her eyes looked red. She at once set about to correct matters, wondering what Strand must have thought of her appearance, and if the Other Woman ever allowed him to see her in such a state.

The parlour-maid brought up a jug of hot water. Lisette poured some into the china bowl and glared at it. Applying soap to cloth rather savagely, she decided that her husband's peculiar was likely an insipid blonde who laughed at every feeble joke he offered, and meekly agreed with whatever he had to say. The creature, whoever she was, had evidently visited The Pines a time or two, for it had been very apparent she was the lady Mr. Drye had expected to greet today. How infuriating, thought Lisette, that Strand would be so crude as to bring his wife to the same inn he had frequented with his mistress! But why should she expect anything else? He had not the slightest consideration for her feelings, or—

Conscience jabbed at her as she saw again the image of a lean, strong hand reaching out to grasp her reins. Had it not been for Strand's chivalrous intervention, she might have taken a very ugly toss this morning. He had, in fact, narrowly missed suffering such a fall himself. Apart from that, his fortune had been a boon to her hard-pressed family, and she had willingly entered a *mariage de convenance*. It would be shabby indeed to now require of him more than he had offered, or to fail to give credit where due. With this in mind, she completed her toilet, decided she looked passable, and hastened downstairs.

The coffee room was empty and the aroma from the kitchen so enticing that she was tempted to request that her breakfast be served. Her anxiety about Brandy was of prime importance, however, and she decided to go down to the stables while she awaited her husband.

She heard male voices as she entered the spicy dimness of the low building. Several men were gathered in a stall at the far end, and when she came nearer to them she was surprised to discover Strand was still here. He had discarded his jacket and was kneeling, carefully applying salve to Brandy's back legs, both of which were badly cut and scraped.

Aghast, as she perceived the extent of the animal's injuries, Lisette cried, "Oh! I am so sorry! Is it very bad?"

Strand glanced up. He looked dusty and grim and said wretchedly, "My own fault. How stupid that I allowed the mud to fool me. I should not have ridden the poor fellow."

She felt crushed by remorse and, perhaps because she had endured a good deal of nervous strain this day, was quite unable to cope with it. Not trusting herself to speak, she quickly left the stables and walked around to the side of the inn. Here, she discovered a pleasant garden enhanced by the rippling song of a little brook that meandered through it. She sat down on a wooden bench and strove to compose herself. Heaven knows she'd not intended to cause so bad a thing. Poor Brandy. If he was badly hurt, she would be responsible. Whatever had caused her so completely to lose her sense of propriety as to gallop about all over Sussex like some hoydenish gypsy girl? Whatever Timothy would think of her behaviour of late, she dared not imagine. He had been used to tease her because she was "always so curst serene." He had once said as much to Grandmama, and the old lady had remarked with her sly chuckle, "Still waters run deep, lad. If our ice maiden ever thaws, she may surprise us all!" Grandmama and her whims. . . . Lisette sighed. It was not to be wondered at that her temperament was suffering, considering all the sorrows and humiliation she had endured. She sighed again as one of those same humiliations slipped back into her thoughts. What was she like, his blond beauty? She *was* a beauty, beyond doubting, but was she of gentle birth, or nothing but a predatory opera dancer, or some—

"My apologies, ma'am." Strand's grave voice disrupted her reflections. "If you would wish to come inside, our breakfast awaits."

He had washed, his fair hair had been carelessly brushed into a semblance of tidiness, and he had again donned his jacket and tucked his broken hand back into the sling from which it had been removed while he worked with Brandy. Standing, Lisette noted these things absently, for she was searching his eyes. She cried a horrified, "Oh—no! Never say he must be destroyed?"

He took the hand she had reached out to him and looked at her keenly. "I shall most certainly say no such thing! I intend to leave him here for a few days. The head ostler's a good man and will take excellent care of him. Brandy will make a full recovery, I have no doubt." He frowned, and muttered, "Had I not made such a blasted mull of things, he'd have suffered less."

"Do not blame yourself," Lisette said miserably. "I should never have galloped off, *ventre à terre*." She looked down at the thin hand still clasping hers.

Strand's grip tightened. "Well, you would not have, had I not provoked you into doing so." Surprised, she looked up into a smile that astounded her with its kindness. "I am the villain in this piece, you know," he said.

"Villain?" She was oddly confused. "No, indeed you were splendid. Had it not been for you, I would have likely broken my neck. How you managed that jump with only one hand and no reins, I shall never know. I am truly most grateful. I wish—I wish we might—" She stopped, her lashes sweeping down.

Gazing at her, Strand breathed, "Might—what?"

"Might—cry friends." She felt him start and, glancing up, found him staring at her with an incredulous expression.

"*Friends . . .?*" he echoed. "Friends—with my own wife?"

She blushed and looked down. "Oh, I know ours is but a *mariage de convenance*, and—and that we do not care for one another, but . . ."

Strand released her hand and turned away. After a moment, he said in an odd sort of voice, "A terrible basis for matrimony, was it not? Had your father not been temporarily embarrassed, I'd have had no chance of winning you."

He was mocking her, of course, but she quickly lifted her eyes. He stood with his back to her, looking out over the busy brook.

"My father was not 'temporarily embarrassed,' as you so kindly put it, Mr. Strand. We were—I think my brother would say—'properly in the basket.' "

"And you were the price of the family reprieve." He turned,

smiling, but his eyes were empty. "I'm a regular Shylock, am I not?"

The tension seemed to have eased. Relieved, she said gaily, "You may find you made a poor bargain, sir. You seem to possess an uncanny ability to rouse the worst in me."

Strand brightened, and with laughter dancing into his eyes again, said, "No, do I? How famous!"

They talked easily through the meal, so that Mr. Drye was convinced he served an ideally happy couple and was encouraged to contribute to the conversation when bringing food or coffee to the table in the recessed window bay that was, he informed Lisette, "Mr. Justin's favourite spot."

"I can see why my husband comes here." She glanced from the mellow homeliness of the interior to the colourful garden. "Truly, it is delightful and greatly to your credit, Mr. Drye. May I ask why it is called The Pines?"

"Why, that were my grandfather." He beamed. "There had always been oaks here, y'see, ma'am, but by the time he come into the property he'd travelled about the world a bit, being a seafarer, and he'd seen some pines in foreign parts what he was much taken with. The inn was called The Oaks in them days, but he sent for his pines and planted 'em at last, and then struggled with 'em all his life. They never took, poor old chap. Year after year, he'd put 'em in and watch 'em wilt. Never would change to Scotch pines, though many there were as told him *they'd* take all right. Bound and determined he were, even to the extent of changing the name of the inn. When he was dying, he used to lie in bed and look out at the last of his prize trees, one he had great hopes for. Well, it started to wilt, so me father, being a good-hearted soul, and very attached to the old man, took it out quick one night, brought in a Scotch pine in a tub, and they told Grandfather his foreign tree had took at last. He passed to his reward quite happy—looking at that there Scotch pine, and never knowing it didn't come from Norway, like he thought. There it is, ma'am." He bent forward, pointing into the garden where a fine tall tree dominated a spot beside the brook. "You can see how nice it growed."

Strand laughed. "I wonder he doesn't come back and shake his fist at the imposter."

"No, but I think it very well done," argued Lisette. "How kind your father must have been, Mr. Drye."

"Aye, well, we all got to do what we can, haven't we, Mrs. Strand? Folks we love come and go, and sometimes we don't never know how much we care about 'em till they're taken and it's too late for to do anything to let 'em know. So it's best to be as kind as we may, whilst we may—if'n we don't want to have to look back with regret for the rest of our days. A little bit o' compassion is about the best investment a man can make, don't you agree, sir?"

Watching his wife's rapt face and thinking a great deal, Strand said, "Yes."

"What a wonderful philosophy," Lisette elaborated. "And is that why you never changed the name?"

"Partly that, ma'am, and partly because folks had got used to it and thought it was a bit of a joke. Folks always like a little mistake. Take my name, for instance—that's a funny one, ain't it? Me, a tavernkeeper, with a name like Drye! Cor, luvvus!" He grinned and, with his eyes brighter than ever, murmured, "Me missus has been standing over there waving at me something dreadful these past five minutes 'cause I'm jawing, and you be newlywedded, so I'd best go 'fore she hauls me out by the ear!" He nodded and went cheerily off to where, sure enough, his good wife awaited him with total indignation.

Her cheeks a little pink, Lisette glanced at her husband only to find him busily engaged in winding his pocket watch. "A little bit of compassion . . ." she said thoughtfully.

He glanced up at her from under his lashes. "I can see I must be a great deal more patient." At once Lisette's proud head tossed upward, and he went on gravely, but with a telltale quirk tugging at his lips, "With Brutus, that is."

By the time they returned to the stables, Yasmin looked bright and rested. The tall grey mare beside her looked more than rested: she looked, in fact, all but asleep, and Strand's decisive stride was checked at the sight of her. "Good God!" he ejaculated and, whirling on the apprehensive ostler, demanded, "What the deuce are you about? Where's Thunderbolt?"

"Sprained his hock, sir." The ostler added a placating, "We do be a bit short now, Mr. Justin, bein's a Lun'on gent come through and hired Sally-O and Pickles, and Mrs. Middle's eyes be all swole. 'Fraid Dasher here is all we got 'vailable-like.''

Strand grunted, swung into the saddle and, after a few minutes of hard work, succeeded in bringing Dasher's head up so that they might leave the yard.

By the time they had travelled two miles, Lisette was fighting to restrain hilarity, and Strand was equally occupied with curbing floods of profanity. Darting an irked glance at his bride as they sauntered up an inviting slope of the Downs—a slope created to be galloped over—he saw laughter brimming in her eyes and gave vent to a martyred sigh. "You'll note, ma'am, that I am moderating my speed?"

"You are all consideration," she nodded, the dimples beside her mouth peeping.

He laughed. "I suppose I deserve this poor slug. She puts me in mind of one of the horses I had the misfortune to acquire on the night I was returning home through a rainstorm with a certain repulsive dog."

Lisette blinked innocently into his accusing glance, then cried, "Oh! I had quite forgot poor Brutus. I cannot even recall where we were when last I saw him."

"Not far from home, to which he doubtless returned with all speed."

"I wonder why? He usually wants to be wherever you are."

"Why, the breeze came up, you see, and our Brutus is not as hardy as he appears. That's the reason—or one of 'em—that I palmed him off on that gullible dimwit, Bolster." Strand at once perceived that he had offended his bride, for Lisette's amused smile was replaced by a shocked stare. "Good Gad!" he groaned. "*Now* what have I done?"

"It just so happens, Mr. Strand," she said coolly, "that I like Lord Bolster."

" 'Mr. Strand' again," he mused. "Well, at least it wasn't Sir Justin." And failing to win a smile back to her eyes, said with a hint of impatience, "For heaven's sake, Lizzie, don't be so top lofty! I've known Bolster since we was in short coats. He's as good a man as one could meet, but if you expect me to speak of him with reverence, I—"

"I expect—Mr. Strand," Lisette declared in frigid tones, "to be addressed by my name—not that revoltingly common abbreviation with which you choose to taunt me! And I further expect that a poor soul who is not quite, er—right mentally, will be treated with kindness, at the very least!''

Mystified, Strand echoed, ''Not quite—*what?* Oh, d'you mean because he stutters? Well, that buys him no special privilege.''

''You know perfectly well what I mean. Poor Lord Bolster's mental impairment is—'' She stopped, frowning her displeasure as her husband succumbed to a shout of laughter. ''Well! Really!'' she said with considerable indignation.

Strand was so hilarious that Dasher woke up and turned to survey her rider with drowsy curiosity. ''Oh,'' moaned Strand, wiping tears from his eyes. ''How wretched of you to—to tease me so! And I properly believed you!''

Lisette blinked. ''Tease you? But—*isn't* Lord Bolster—deranged?''

''Oh, my God!'' And he was off again, his mirth so infectious that a slow answering smile softened her irate expression. ''Is that,'' he sighed at length, ''why you were so generous as to take Brutus for him? Oh, my poor wife! You have been properly hoaxed. Whoever told you so ridiculous a tale? Jeremy's bluedevilled just now because of his romantic muddle, but I do assure you he has every one of his wits intact.''

''But—but I heard Badajoz had left him . . . er—''

At this, the laughter vanished from his eyes. ''Bolster was badly wounded and buried under a pile of the dead. He was found barely alive and in deep shock. But there is nothing wrong with him mentally. Only try to get the best of him in any transaction! I wish you may succeed, in which case you will be the first one to do so! Why anyone would tell you such a rasper I cannot think. Everyone likes old Jerry!''

''Well!'' she proclaimed wrathfully. ''I think it positively disgraceful! Who would say such a thing if it were not true unless . . .'' She paused. James Garvey had said it, she was sure. And he had not been funning, which must only mean that James had really believed it. He was certainly not the man to—

They came over a rolling hill, and she gave a little cry of admiration. ''Oh, look! Is it not beautiful?''

Below, a river wound sparkling towards the sea, its course forming a wide loop about the ruins of a once noble house set amid lush lawns that sloped down to the riverbank. The grounds were well kept up, for flowers were everywhere and there were many fine old trees dotted about the spacious park. Whoever had dwelt here must have maintained a boat, for there was a small dock, just now in sad disrepair.

Watching her expressive face, Strand murmured, "Pretty, isn't it? But it burnt, as you can see."

She scanned the rambling old structure appreciatively. "Not all of it—see, at the western end the roof is still intact. And the owners have kept up the place; they must love it. What a tragedy."

He shrugged indifferently. "Would you care to go down?"

How insensitive he was, she thought, and asked, "Does someone live there? Do you think they would mind?"

"I suspect they'd be delighted that anyone was interested."

He led the way down the gentle slope and along a winding drivepath which was also well kept up and marked by the wheels of a carriage. The closer they came to the old house, the more Lisette was charmed. It must at one time have been quite large; a rambling half-timbered Tudor. Strand dismounted, tied Dasher—rather unnecessarily—to the charred remnants of a window frame, and turned to aid Lisette from the saddle. He shouted a "Hello!" to the livable end of the house, but there was no sign of life. They wandered through the burnt-out shell, crossing various thresholds until they entered what must have been a spacious chamber.

"What a lovely prospect they must have had," said Lisette, looking to the river. "Do you think this was the drawing room?"

"Main dining room," he murmured.

"Hmmnnn, then over here would—" She paused, noticing the soft dancing light that flickered all about them.

"The sun on the water," he explained. "It's a peculiarity of this particular spot, and is how the estate got its name."

"Silverings!" She turned to him in surprise. "Odious man! This is *your* house!"

"*Our* house," he corrected smilingly. "I'm glad you like the old place."

"Like it! I think it pure delight! But what a terrible loss it must have been."

"Yes. To my sisters and me. My father never cared for the house and would not have it rebuilt even when he could afford it.

I've restored the grounds, at least.'' A nostalgic light came into his eyes. "We had some happy times here when I was a boy.''

"I can well imagine. It has such a friendly, welcoming air, even now. May I see the other part?''

"Of course.'' Pleased by her interest, he led her to a half-open Dutch door at the side of the undamaged structure, peered inside, and called, ''Mrs. Ogden? Is anyone here?'' There being no response, he reached over to unlatch the lower portion of the door and stood aside, explaining as Lisette entered, ''The gardener and his wife live in a cottage on the estate, and she comes every day to put the house in order. She may have gone to the village.''

The room they entered was a good size, the walls whitewashed and the floors of random-width planks, dark and glowing with the patina of the years. An old-fashioned grandfather clock ticked companionably in one corner, and a fine carpet was spread before the wide hearth. Latticed windows were deep-set in thick walls, the seats below piled with thick, brightly coloured cushions. And through those windows came the pleasant light from the river, to dance over the large marine oil painting that hung above the mantel, and brighten the blooms of a bowl of spring flowers which graced a side table. The furnishings had clean lines and were luxurious without being ornate, and there were many books in the several bookcases placed against the west wall.

Entranced, Lisette wandered about, exclaiming over this or that, while Strand watched her. "You really are pleased with Silverings,'' he observed at last.

She swung to him, eyes alight. "Oh, yes. It reminds me of the farm we once owned. It was a funny old place, but we passed such wonderful summers there. May I see the rest?''

He assented readily and took her through a small dining room and up what had apparently been the back stairs, to a pair of bedrooms, in one of which Lisette's eyes were at once drawn to a small bottle of scent on a dressing table.

"This area originally constituted the butler's quarters,'' Strand explained with a touch of pride. ''And the room we first came into downstairs was used to be the servants' hall.''

Forcing her eyes from that betraying little bottle, Lisette said, ''Oh. Well, you have restored it very nicely.''

He glanced at her, surprised by the changed tone and more surprised by the sudden flush that warmed her cheeks. "Thank you. If you really like it, I thought perhaps . . . well, we could—ah—"

"Come down here?" she said eagerly. "Oh, I should love it! How nice to wake up in the mornings and look out at the river. So much more agreeable than—" She bit her lip, embarrassed.

"What's this?" He grinned. "Are you quite disenchanted with the Hall?"

"Oh, no! It is—er—very impressive. But—I prefer this."

He gave an exclamation of delight. "How famous! I was afraid you'd prefer our more dignified residence. For myself, I never could abide the place. And Tristram tells me that when first he saw it, he's sure he must have turned pale!"

Amused, she agreed, "Leith is not the type to be impressed by . . ."

"Pretension?" he prompted. "Never hesitate for my sake." He glanced to the window. "However, in view of my intrepid Dasher, if we're to be home by dusk I think we should be starting now, ma'am."

By the time they reached The Pines, the wind was rising and the clouds looked so threatening that Strand decided to take luncheon at the old tavern. Over the meal they enjoyed a long discussion regarding the possibilities of restoring Silverings, a venture with which Lisette was thoroughly in accord. She was mildly surprised when her husband not only encouraged her to voice her opinions regarding the reconstruction, but seemed sincerely interested in what she had to offer. When they were ready to leave, Strand was able to exchange his steed for a somewhat less somnambulistic animal. The storm had drifted away, and they started out in fair weather. Again, Strand proved a pleasant companion. He had taken quite a liking to Lisette's family and she was pleased when he suggested that she invite Norman to spend a week or two with them during the summer. All in all, she felt amazingly light-hearted by the time they rode into the yard at the Hall, and was more in charity with her husband than she'd been since first she saw him.

Best and another groom hastened to take their mounts. Strand responded to Best's anxious enquiries about Brandy, but it seemed to Lisette that the groom was not reassured. Glancing back as they walked away, she surprised a furtive anxiety in the man's eyes and, turning to her husband, realized belatedly that he looked tired. It must have been a wearing day; that jump especially had been taxing, and she knew a twinge of guilt that she'd not previously considered that his arm might be paining him.

"Strand," she said, "are you—"

"Lisette!"

"Surprise! Surprise!"

"Look who has come to pay a bride call!"

The shout, the squeal, and the amused, high-pitched cry brought Lisette running to embrace Norman and her two sisters. Judith looked plumply pretty and overjoyed, Norman was genuinely glad to see her, and Beatrice was a picture of elegance in a robe of green sarsenet over a slip of palest green cambric. She kissed her sister sweetly but not so unaffectedly as had Judith, taking care not to ruffle her coiffure.

"How lovely you look!" Lisette exclaimed. "And, oh, how very glad I am to see you all."

"I had supposed you might be," murmured Beatrice with a sidelong glance at Strand. "Which is precisely why we came."

Flustered, Lisette suggested they all return to the house, and in they went, Judith and Norman both talking at once, Beatrice's arm twined in Lisette's, and Strand quietly bringing up the rear.

Happily, the Van Lindsay party had arrived sufficiently early that the chef had been granted time to prepare his usual excellent meal. The dining room rang with chatter, and Lisette, delighted by this visit from her loved ones, was animated and—so thought Strand—glowing with happiness. The conversation swept from the wedding, to Strand Hall, which Beatrice thought enchanting, to Brutus, whom Norman thought a jolly fine dog, to Charity Strand and what a very charming girl she was. Strand wholeheartedly agreed with this, contributing his longest sentence thus far when he said that both his sisters were "rare human beings."

The faintest breath of unease touched Lisette. Her brows arching, she asked, "Did you meet Charity in town, Beatrice?"

"No, love. Here. Today."

"She came back?" Strand said sharply. "But she only left here yesterday afternoon. She was not ill, I trust, Lady William?"

"No, no," Beatrice answered, putting down her wine glass. "But it seems they encountered such bad road conditions between here and Godalming that they were compelled to put up at an inn for the night, and then your sister recalled something she had promised to take to Mrs. Leith, so she turned back." Her eyes sliding to Lisette, she smirked, "I could not have been more pleased, for we had such a delightful cose."

Lisette smiled. Inwardly, however, she was dismayed. Charity was so innocent and naïve; she would be no match for Beatrice.

"Well, I'm sorry we missed her," said Strand. "But we are fortunate to have more company. May we hope you mean to spend some time with us, ma'am?"

"Alas, but I cannot," sighed Beatrice. "Indeed, I should not have come at all, save to bring the children to you."

Lisette stared at her blankly. Amused, Strand raised his eyebrows and waited.

Looking from one to the other, Beatrice said, "Well, you must have got Mama's letter by now, surely?"

Lisette had received no such letter, but an enquiry to Fisher elicited the information that one had arrived this morning and would be brought at once. Lisette requested it be delivered to her in the drawing room, and they left Strand to his port.

Excusing herself, Lisette read her letter as hurriedly as her mother's flourishing hand would allow. Dear Great-Uncle Ian had, it would seem, received notice to quit and had sent word that he desired his near and dear to be around him at the end. Since "dear Great-Uncle Ian" was of a dour and reclusive nature and dwelt on one of the Scottish islands, this entailed quite a journey, but since he also was said to be an extremely wealthy old gentleman, Mrs. Van Lindsay had undoubtedly undertaken it without hesitation. Norman and Judith would benefit by a change from the London scene, she wrote, and since summer was almost upon them it would not do any incalculable damage for them to leave their studies now and spend a few weeks with Beatrice—at least until their parents returned, when they might possibly all remove to Worthing for a time. The rest of the letter was of small consequence and Lisette folded it and said thoughtfully, "Poor Uncle Ian."

Beatrice sniffed. "About time, was you to ask me. I vow I thought the man would live forever! Oh, never look at me in that silly, fusty fashion! You know he had his three score and ten at least a decade since. He's rich as Croesus and Mama was always his favourite, so perhaps she will now stop expecting me to open *my* purse each time they are in the basket. I declare, poor William has been *more* than generous. And patient? My dear husband is the very *soul* of patience, but there comes a limit, and you'll own Norman and Judith have not been strictly reared and their behaviour is not what one might wish.''

It was at about this time that Judith and Norman were jointly overtaken by the effects of the long journey and in a rare display of weariness elected to go early to bed.

''I am not at all surprised,'' said Beatrice, receiving a dutiful good-night kiss from each. ''Had you not felt it necessary to explore the entire estate with that horrid animal the instant we arrived, you might be less fatigued.''

''We might,'' Judith retaliated, hugging Lisette. ''But only think how it gave you the chance to worm as much as you could out of poor Charity Strand.''

Beatrice uttered an enraged screech and sprang to her feet, and the younger Van Lindsays fled, Norman's whoop echoing after them as he closed the door.

''Do you see what I mean?'' Beatrice asked angrily, sitting down and smoothing her robe. ''They are not to be borne!''

''From what Mama writes, dear, you could not have borne them longer than three or four days.''

Lisette had spoken mildly, but Beatrice fired up at once. ''And I collect you meant me to carry the *whole* burden—as usual! I vow it is so unfair. With Timothy away, *everything* falls on my head, only because I am the eldest. Nobody stops to consider that *I* might have plans! Or cares if poor William is reduced to a nervous wreck.''

Since Beatrice had never been known to offer the least assistance in time of crisis and would, in fact, go to considerable lengths to be suddenly ''called away'' in the event of illness in the family, Lisette found it difficult to summon much sympathy for this tale of woe. She knew ''poor William'' a good deal better than her sister imagined and was well aware that he both loved children and longed to set up his nursery. He was the most amiable of men and would, she had no doubt, have been delighted to host his niece and nephew on an indefinite basis. The truth of the matter was, she suspected, that Beatrice did not want to remain in the country, but had no wish to be cooped up in a town-house with a sister and brother who were, admittedly, rather a handful.

Watching her obliquely, Beatrice said a persuasive, "After all, it's not as though yours were a love match, dearest. Besides, since Strand is—is incapacitated—" She stopped, her eyes brimming, and went off into a small gale of mirth. "My clever Lisette! I thought I must burst with laughter when Charity told me the way of it!"

Lisette's hand tightened on her fan. "Told you—what?"

"Of how you drove him off for the first week and then was so fortunate as to have him trip over the dog! La, what a wretch you are! The poor man must be seething with rage. And—frustration! Did you—did you give the poor doggie a bone, love?" And again, she dissolved into hilarity.

This was exactly what Lisette had feared. Charity, obviously adoring her brother, had certainly said nothing malicious, but Beatrice's shrewd mind had very quickly put two and two together. She said stiffly, "That is not true, Bea! I must ask that you do not repeat—"

"Not true? Of course it's true! Mama told me how bitterly you wept when you were compelled to wed the creature, and—"

"Do I perhaps intrude, ladies?"

Strand's cool voice seemed to slice through Beatrice's words. Lisette's eyes shot to the door. He stood on the threshold. His lips were faintly smiling, but it was a rather grim smile and Lisette felt her cheeks blaze.

Showing not the slightest trace of embarrassment, Beatrice said blithely, "Oh, pray do come in, Strand. We are bored to death without a gentleman."

He walked in his quick way to poke up the fire and enquire if either lady desired a screen for the draught, for the wind was blowing ever more strongly. They both declined, however, and since each was busied with more or less the same strain of thought, a brief silence fell. Strand broke it, observing blandly, "It is rather chill this evening. I doubt you needed your fan, my love."

"Very true," said Beatrice. "I quite thought it would rain this morning."

"Did you?" said Strand.

"Yes, but it did not after all."

Strand's eyes, gleaming with mischief, darted to Lisette. She felt a surge of relief. He must not have heard! "Perhaps it will rain tomorrow," she contributed demurely.

He broke into a laugh. "You always can top me, my sweet."

He sounded genuinely fond, and an odd sensation shivered between Lisette's shoulder blades.

Beatrice looked wonderingly from one to the other, and Strand said politely, "Your pardon, Lady William. My wife was roasting me because of my scintillating conversation."

"Oh," said Beatrice vaguely. "Well, we cannot all be accomplished. I feel sure you must have *some* talent, Strand."

He grinned and admitted he was the dullest of men, but Lisette said defensively, "Save when a lady's life is in peril, do you mean? Words would not have saved me this morning, Justin."

He looked down, a flush burning his cheeks.

Beatrice at once demanding to hear the story, Lisette told her, Strand inserting an occasional mumbled complaint that she made more of the incident than was warranted.

"'Good gracious!" Beatrice exclaimed when the tale was done. "That was positively heroical in you, Strand. I'll allow I am surprised, for when we heard you had broke your arm on your honeymoon, so many thought it a downright silly thing to have done."

Strand's eyes, lifting slowly to Beatrice, contained a thoughtful and unsmiling hauteur. It was an expression Lisette had seen before, and she held her breath. Beatrice saw that glimpse of steel and, being nobody's fool, said hurriedly, "How you could have accomplished such a deed with but one hand defies imagination. I can scarce wait to tell William!"

The balance of the evening passed quite pleasantly, and since Beatrice announced her intention of leaving the following day, Lisette could only pray that no more such difficult periods would have to be endured—for a time at least.

It was a prayer destined not to be granted.

Chapter 10

Battle was joined the day after Beatrice's departure. Accustomed to lounging in bed until nine o'clock, at which hour he was usually sure of being variously implored, ordered, and sometimes actually threatened by his sorely tried tutor, Norman paid no heed to the first two attempts to rouse him, and was aghast to be ruthlessly awakened by the simple expedient of having the bedding torn from him.

"Good God!" he cried, leaping up in shivering dismay. "Is the house afire?"

"It will be, do you not look alive!" Strand, fully clad in his riding clothes, added, "I don't care to be kept waiting, young fella."

Staring at him with slack jaw, Norman gasped, "K-kept waiting? But—but it ain't even hardly *light!*"

"Lord! What wretched grammar! Come now, you'll find this is the best possible time to ride. Puts an edge on your appetite. I've a fine stallion saddled for you—a bit wild, but I think you can manage him."

Whether the challenge was the inducement, or whether Norman had taken due note of the set to Strand's chin, Lisette had no way of knowing, but not very many minutes after her husband had tossed her into the saddle, she was amazed to see her brother coming reluctantly to join them, his cravat a disaster, his hair uncombed, and a surly look in his dark eyes. Once mounted and out of the yard, he had all he could do to control the spirited animal Strand had chosen for him. The cold, bracing air and vigorous exercise had their effect, and it soon became apparent that the boy was thoroughly enjoying himself. Lisette was not surprised by the pace Strand set. Norman was. Despite his laziness he was a spirited youth and, concealing his unease, at once set to work to outdo his brother-in-law. Strand led them at thundering speed across a wide hilltop, and reined up at the start of the downward slope. It was a cool morning, the wind hurrying a flock of clouds across the pearly sky. The birds were already twittering busily, and the sun began to come up, gilding the clouds with gold that blushed slowly to a deep pink. Behind the neatly fenced meadows spread the darker bands of woodland, and beyond, smoke rose into the air, soon to be whipped about by the wind. Strand leaned on the pommel, looking out at the verdant panorama, and Lisette murmured, "How very lovely it is."

"Lovelier if you ain't starved and half froze!" grumbled Norman, and spurred his mount down the hill.

Strand grinned and followed.

Lisette asked, "Isn't that the Home Farm?"

"It is. And I've no doubt but that your brother saw the smoke and envisioned breakfast."

"Oh dear! Will they mind?"

"I suspect they'll be delighted." He added an amused, "But Norman may find the tariff rather high for his pocket."

An hour later, comfortably replete, Norman's round face reflected stark horror as he gazed from Strand's bland smile to Mr. Johnson's retreating form. "Help him . . . rebuild the chicken house?" he gasped, incredulous. "Why the devil should I do so? You own this place, do you not, sir?"

"Oh, yes." Strand nodded cheerfully. "But Johnson manages it for me, and I'd not dream of imposing on his hospitality without offering something in return."

Lisette concentrated upon her last piece of muffin and avoided her brother's imploring gaze.

Norman said with growing indignation, "Then toss the fellow a few coins and he'll likely think you most generous."

"Good God! Are you serious? Johnson would be most offended.

One don't offer to *pay* for hospitality in these parts. Come along now, we'd best get to it!''

Staring up at him, Norman stammered, ''We? Are—are *you* going to work, Strand?''

''But of course. I also enjoyed a hearty breakfast—did you not notice? Enough food to last me a week! Up with you!''

Slanting a half-worried, half-amused glance at her brother, Lisette was rather taken aback to note his mulish expression. However spoiled he might be, he was usually a good sport and the first to admit defeat was he bested. As he clambered reluctantly to his feet, however, it was apparent that he had taken Strand in dislike, a circumstance that made her heart sink.

Any suspicion Judith and Norman may have entertained that they had come into the country to eat and sleep was soon put to flight. In the days that followed, the indefatigable Strand kept them so busy that they seemed scarcely to have a moment's peace. He soon teased Judith into getting up and accompanying them on their early rides, a pursuit she abhorred and yet for some reason seldom missed. After breakfast, there would be a walk they must experience, or a visit to the village or some local beauty spot, with Brutus an occasional escort. Mealtimes constituted a source of despair to both Norman and Judith, for Strand ate sparingly, and even Lisette, who had a small appetite, was at times appalled by the meagre fare offered at table. If luncheon was served at all, it usually consisted solely of fruits, while dinners seldom amounted to more than one course of fish or cold meat with vegetables, and these in very short supply. Not only exhausted but half starved, Norman eyed Strand with ever-increasing hostility, while Judith complained bitterly that she'd not had a decent meal since she came, and would soon be reduced to picking berries to stay alive.

Despite these miseries, the days seemed to fly past. They rose early and went early and tired to bed. Their evenings were spent in playing cards or spillikins or Fish, reading aloud to one another as the fancy seized them, or the men playing dominoes while the girls sewed. Guests were few and far between, which, so Norman grumbled to Judith, was scarce to be wondered at, ''for they could get better food in the workhouse!''

Lisette was happier than she had been for weeks, partly because of the presence of her brother and sister, and partly because of an entirely unexpected development that brought a new joy into her life. They were playing croquet one warm afternoon when she inadvertently stepped on the hem of her dress. Hurrying into the house to change, she glanced out of her bedroom window and was aghast to see James Garvey riding nonchalantly up the drive-path. Frightened, she ran downstairs, hoping to reach the door first, but Mrs. Hayward already stood there. Dreading that Justin might come back into the house, Lisette crept to where she might hear, without being seen. Mrs. Hayward's voice was very low, but it was clear she was affronted. "I will do no such thing, sir!" she said angrily. "If you've a message for Mrs. Strand, I'll be glad to give it her, but as I told you, she is not at home." Garvey murmured something and laughed in his easy, good-humoured way, and Lisette saw the housekeeper's back stiffen. In a voice of ice, Mrs. Hayward said, "I would have hoped that a gentleman might have known better than to make such an offer, Mr. Garvey. Good day to you, sir!" And the door slammed.

Briefly, Lisette was tempted to intercede for him. That he had journeyed all this way to see her was indicative of a lasting affection, for which she was grateful. But the certain knowledge that Strand would be enraged, the awareness of the deep dislike already existing between the two men, and a fear of provoking what might very well lead to tragedy dissuaded her. It was not until they came inside to change for dinner that she found the note upon her pillow, with her name inscribed in a beautiful copperplate hand on the folded sheet. So James *had* left a message! Opening it, she read:

> *I recall when first I saw you,*
> *that the rain was pouring down.*
> *It was night and I was driving*
> *all alone through London Town.*
> *A chaise splashed up beside me*
> *and I saw your laughing face*
> *With the lamplight softly shining*
> *on your loveliness and grace.*
> *At once I knew*
> *my every hope was you.*

*   *   *

I remember the enchantment
*   when at last I learned your name.*
All my world was bright and glowing
*   never afterwards the same.*
Every dream was built around you
*   everything I owned I'd give*
To with happiness surround you
*   for as long as I may live.*
Because, I knew
*   all joy in life was you.*

I am warned you love another
*   and that I can never see*
In your eyes a glow of caring
*   or of tenderness for me.*
But perhaps I yet can serve you,
*   win a kindly word—a smile*
And my poor heart keep from breaking
*   if I dare to hope the while, that*
Someday you
*   may start to love me, too.*

Long before she reached the end of that poem, Lisette's eyes were blurred with tears. She pressed the so carefully written words to her bosom, her heart full. Here was devotion, indeed. How sweet of poor James to pen such beautiful words; how dear to be offered such humble love and devotion. She read it many times before she retired that night, and many times in the days that followed. Longing to write to express her gratitude, she could not do so. She was married, past redemption indeed, to a man with not a shred of romance in his soul, and although her own happiness was immeasurably increased because of Garvey's tenderness, to let him know that could only add to his grief. And so she did not respond, but carried the cherished poem carefully folded and wrapped in a perfumed handkerchief, in her bosom.

The antagonism between Strand and Norman reached its peak in a way she would never have expected. It occurred on a morning when she went yawning down the stairs for their morning ride and found her husband, as usual, booted and spurred, in the stables, laughing up at Judith, who was already mounted and looking down at him in an astonishment that changed to a squeak of delight.

"You never did! Oh, you wicked, wicked man!" she cried, leaning suddenly to ruffle up his light, crisp hair.

Why that gesture of affection should bring a little pang of irritation to Lisette, she could not have said, but looking at them she was shocked by two things that she would have noted before had she not been walking in a dream these past days, by reason of a certain letter in her bodice. Firstly, Judith was growing very pretty; and, secondly, the sling was gone from Strand's arm! That last was such a shock that she stood still and mute for a moment. Judith saw her and cried merrily, "Come and chastise your evil spouse, dearest! *What* a villain!"

Laughing still, Strand turned towards her. The smile died from his eyes. Lisette wore the new habit she had ordered in London and that had only yesterday arrived. It was of primrose cloth, with large mother-of-pearl buttons and foaming lace at cuffs and throat; her hat was new also, a chic little straw cap with short yellow feathers curling all along the narrow crown, and longer ones swooping at the back. He bowed. "My compliments, madam wife. A very pretty habit."

"Thank you, sir. My congratulations also—your arm is healed, I see." But having learned something of his impatience with infirmity, she added anxiously, "You *did* speak with Dr. Bellows before the splints were removed?"

"I did indeed. I have no wish to prolong my handicap, m'dear."

His eyes twinkled at her. Lisette blushed and trembled, and Judith called, "Never mind your husband, dearest. Look at *me!*"

She flung her arms wide. She had become quite slender. Marvelling, Lisette said, "You look charmingly. But, why did I not notice, I wonder?"

Norman came up, growled a greeting and swung into the saddle, watching Judith as she tugged at the waist of her habit, replying merrily, "Your evil spouse, Mrs. Strand! I *wondered* why he set such a wretched table!"

Lisette stared in astonishment at her husband's amused face, and he patted his own trim middle and said gravely that he had to be careful not to get fat. "You—did it deliberately?" gasped Lisette.

"What a filthy trick!" glowered Norman.

Judith chuckled. "No, but I think it delicious, and so kind. See, Norman, how slender I am become!"

He saw and, withholding his instinctive congratulations, said grudgingly, "Aye, well, I am not. My clothes fit so snug as ever, though I've starved since first we set foot here."

"Of course they do. Only look at yourself, Norman! You are positively svelte!"

Bewildered, he looked down. "I am? But—that cannot be. My coat is—"

"Strand asked Lisette's dresser to alter our clothes, so we would not notice when first we began to shed pounds," Judith laughed. "Are you not pleased?"

A grin trembled on Norman's lips, but he recovered and said gruffly, "I think it a foul trick! Much confidence you place in our willpower, Strand, that you must serve us so!" And he rode out of the yard.

"Pay him no heed," urged Lisette. "It was very well done, though I could wish you had let me in on the secret. No wonder we have set no covers for guests."

He laughed. "For that, I do apologize and will admit I had many trays carried to me in secret. But the boy looks well, do not you think? And our Judith will win hearts when we return to Town."

"Town?" Judith put in, eagerly. "Are we going back, Strand?"

"I've some business that takes me to London next week, and I'd thought you ladies might wish to shop at one of the bazaars— Bennet's this time, since I'm told it is the more elegant."

Judith's excitement was somewhat marred when they came up with Norman, and he grunted moodily that at least he did not have to go. Knowing better than to attempt to reason with him when he was in such a temper, Lisette was nonetheless irked, for Strand seemed to be going out of his way to be kind, and she could not but be grateful.

"We all shall go," Strand ruled. "You would enjoy a visit to London, I fancy, madam wife?"

"Oh, I would! Especially since it has not been a hot Spring."

This understatement provoked them all to laughter. They were riding along the Downs when Strand said, "Cheer up, Master

Gruff and Glum. I believe you may enjoy the gentleman I want you to meet.''

"Some crusty old tutor, I suppose," sneered Norman.

"He's crusty all right, but not a tutor. As a matter of fact, he's an old sea dog."

Norman's eyes shot to Strand eagerly. "A sailor?"

"Yes. I've noticed your preoccupation with ships. I think John Hawkhurst might—"

Norman all but fell from his horse and, reining up, gasped, "*Hawkhurst?* You never mean—you *cannot* mean Lord Wetherby?"

"I can, and do. Admiral Lord Jonathan Wetherby. He is— Do you know these fellows?"

Four rough-appearing young men were striding towards them. Norman took them in at a glance and said, "Let's go home. Quickly!"

Strand reached over to pull back on his reins and they all halted. "I do not retreat on my own lands, Norman. Lisette, you will please take Judith back to the house." And as she hesitated, he snapped, "At once!" in a tone that brooked no argument.

Frightened, the sisters turned their mounts and trotted back the way they had come.

"If it comes to a turn-up," Strand said coolly, "stay close and keep back to back. It's the safest way when outnumbered, and these look hefty fellows."

Norman looked at him remorsefully. Strand had not asked what was the trouble, but it was very clear that he was willing to share it.

"Hey!" cried one of the approaching bullies. "You wi' the red dicer! We want a word wi' you."

Surprised by the London accent, Strand said, "Since I am not wearing a hat, I presume you address my brother."

This announcement brought consternation to the new arrivals. They conferred briefly, then the apparent spokesman, a burly young man with a mop of curly brown hair and belligerent dark eyes, said, "Ee didn't say as 'e was yer bruvver. I s'pose we ain't goin' ter be give the right ter pertect ourselves."

Strand refrained from pointing out that they were trespassing. "I was not aware," he answered mildly, "that I was attacking you. If you've some complaint you should speak to my steward.

But if you can state your grievance courteously I can give you a minute or two. What's your name?"

"Jem Shell," said the spokesman, and jerking his thumb toward Norman, added, "'Ee owes us. A borde."

"Your pardon." Strand turned to the miserable Norman. "Did you gamble with these men?"

Shouts of laughter went up. Reddening, Norman stammered, "N-no, sir."

"'Ee bought me sister!" said Shell. "Then 'e wouldn't pay up!"

Astounded, Strand said feebly, "Bought . . . your *sister?* For a shilling?"

"Just a kiss, sir," Norman mumbled. "Only once we were in the barn, she ran—and they wouldn't believe when I said I did not get my kiss."

"I would say the girl showed good sense."

"And I'd say 'e's a liar!" snarled Shell.

"If you weren't four to one, I'd thrash you for that!" blazed Norman.

With an exaggerated shudder, Shell retaliated, "Lor'! I'm all of a quiver. You best run back 'ome wi' yer dainty bruvver wot hides a'hind bein' Quality so 'e don't 'ave ter face up ter the likes of us."

Strand regarded him thoughtfully.

"Ar," put in another youth with protruding teeth and a bitter expression. "Run orf an' 'ide—like y'been doin' all week. Scared t'set foot off'n yer big brother's land, ain'cha!" He spat perilously close to Strand's arm. "Quality!" he jeered, and donated a profane assessment of the aristocracy.

A little light began to dance in Strand's eyes. He dismounted and walked over to tie Brandy's reins to a branch. "You will recall," he reminded them, "that I said I would hear you out were you courteous. You are not courteous. Norman, d'you think we can beat some manners into the heads of these clods?"

To their credit, not one of them attempted to rush him until Norman had fairly leapt from the saddle. Then, the four toughs sprang into the attack.

It seemed, for a while, an uneven battle, heavily balanced in favour of the trespassers. Strand, however, had an odd way of fighting, for he sprang in and out, blocking and feinting with his left, unleashing his right only occasionally, but to astonishing purpose. Shell was the first to feel the power of that deadly right, and he soared backwards to lie groaning on the turf. Norman's stringent diet, taxing walks, and early rides stood him in such good stead that he was inwardly amazed. So were his opponents, and as another man reeled from the fray, Strand laughed cheerily. "Even odds, Norm. Good work!" Even as he spoke, his boot slipped on the wet turf, and he staggered, momentarily off balance. Unversed in the rules of The Game, the burly young man in the tattered brocaded waistcoat rammed home a solid left that smashed Strand to his knees. With a cry of rage Norman jumped forward, decked the waistcoat, turned back to his own challenger, and was in turn levelled by a flush hit to the jaw. As Norman went down, Strand got up, and the last survivor was neatly folded in half by the edge of Strand's left hand whipping across his midsection. His right cheekbone lurid, Strand bent over Norman. "You all right, old chap?"

Panting, Norman tried to sit up and fell back again. "Jove . . ." he gasped happily. "What a—jolly good—scrap."

"Wasn't it?" Strand manipulated his jaw carefully, decided it was intact, and went over to the sprawled Shell. "Your trouble, friend," he vouchsafed, "is drink. Too much of it. You'd do quite well, otherwise." He extended a hand. Shell took it and pulled himself to a sitting position.

"Guv'nor," he groaned. "Where'd you learn to 'it like that? A skinny gent like you?"

"Harrow," Strand grinned. "You would be surprised how miserable life can be for a boy who's not all brawn. If you're to survive, you learn fast."

"That last 'un," moaned Strand's final opponent, massaging his painful middle, "didn't come from no 'arrow! More like a chap I see in Singapore once."

"I say!" cried Norman. "Was you in the Navy, Bill?"

Bill allowed as he had been, but had been demobilized. "*Is* that where you learned that trick, sir?" he asked, eyeing Strand in awe.

"No. India. Are you all ex-servicemen?"

Shell got to his feet. "I was a rifleman, sir. Jim and Bob was artillery." Still rubbing his chin, he muttered bitterly, "Kicked us out, they did. No pension. No work. Can't even afford ter get 'itched up—wot girl'd 'ave us?''

Strand said, "I cannot answer for the girls, but it happens that I need some men. What kind of work can you do?''

At once they were crowding around him, their previous hostility forgotten, their eyes eager at this new hope. In very short order Strand had taken on four new men, who were instructed to report to Mr. Connaught at nine o'clock next morning. "One thing," he cautioned, mounting up and wheeling his horse, "I'll not tolerate a drunkard. Do your drinking in the time you do not work, if you must. But let me catch you gin-raddled on my property, and you'll never work for me again. Norman, have you anything to say to these men?''

Norman said earnestly, "I honestly did not get that buss, Shell.''

The big man grinned. "Know y'didn't, Mr. Van Lindsay. We was just tryin'. A man gets a bit desprit when 'e's allus 'ungry.''

Riding off beside his brother-in-law, Norman said fervently, "I know just what he means!''

Dinner that night was the merriest meal they'd yet enjoyed together. The battle had melted away all barriers between Strand and Norman and, rather typically, the admiration the boy had been fighting for some time now sprang to full flower and he became so enthused in his description of Strand's prowess in the noble art of fisticuffs that his exasperated brother-in-law was at last compelled to warn him to desist else he'd take him out to the barn next morning and demonstrate some of the "art" he'd held back from employing today. The girls, who had watched the fight from a stand of trees, were also full of admiration for the warriors, and, Lisette approving, Strand had permitted his frustrated chef to prepare an excellent meal, requiring only that Norman and Judith deal with it sparingly.

Afterwards, they played jackstraws in the lounge, Strand's thin fingers proving amazingly nimble at the game, although Judith won, her steadier hand prevailing in the last taut moments. It had been a close match, taking longer than they'd anticipated. By the time it was done, the teatray was brought in and within half an hour Strand was lighting Lisette's candle for her while one of the maids assisted Fisher to extinguish the lamps and lock up for the night.

Humming as she went into her bedchamber, Lisette was abruptly silenced. A great red rose lay on her pillow. Her heart seemed to leap into her throat as she stared blindly at the glowing bloom. Behind her, Denise giggled and spread her prettiest negligee on the bed.

By the time the maid left her, Lisette was gratified by the knowledge that she looked charmingly in the pink nightgown, her dark hair waving softly beside the dainty lace cap. Denise had extinguished all the candles and the flickering light from the fire played softly about the great room. Lisette leaned back against her pillows, hands clasped as they had been once before when she awaited her unwanted husband. She was not quite so nervous tonight. Strand had been more than kind—more than patient. Although, she thought defensively, he had only himself to blame both for having left her on their wedding night, and for rushing into her boudoir in such a rage he'd tripped and broken his hand. She smiled faintly and glanced to the side. Brutus was noticeable by his absence.

Time passed, and her apprehension began to mount. Strand would be gentle with her, of that she was quite sure, but to hope for a little romance, a few ardent words of love, was to ask too much of so matter-of-fact a gentleman. Only, how precious it would be to be approached with adoration . . . with words holding even a trace of the sweetness poor James Garvey had penned.

The door opened softly. Strand came in and closed it behind him. The long dressing gown he wore was dark red and made him look very pale. He walked to the end of the bed and stood there for a moment, staring at his beautiful bride, his expression veiled by the shadows. Her breath fluttering in her throat, her palms damp, Lisette could not know how his heart thundered or how his fine hands trembled with nervousness. She waited hopefully for a word of affection.

Strand untied the sash of his dressing gown. "You must," he said in a casual tone, "think me a sorry bridegroom only now to be able to—to come to you."

Lisette swallowed, and managed, "N-no. And—thank you for the rose."

He went over to blow out the solitary candle he had brought with him. Climbing into the bed, he paused, leaning on one elbow and gazing down into his bride's huge, terrified eyes.

As he bent to kiss her, a desolate and distant howling arose from the direction of the stables.

Justin Strand smiled grimly. "Not this time, Brutus," he murmured. "Not this time!"

Chapter 11

In anticipation of the visit to London, Judith and Miss Wallace,
Lisette's rather formidable dresser, put their heads together over
periodicals and pattern cards, spending hours closeted together
while Judith was instructed as to which fabric might be purchased for which style. Her experience at the wedding with the
plain gown Strand had selected and the compliments it had won
her had taught her much. Now, with Judith's figure much
improved, Miss Wallace said they could afford to be a little less
spartan, and Judith plunged happily into a glorious world of
India muslins, cambrics and gauzes, ribbons and frills and laces,
French knots and rosettes, and all the delicious accessories for
which Strand appeared perfectly willing—as a disgusted Norman
phrased it—"to stand the huff."

Norman, meanwhile, having discovered that Strand was fairly
knowledgeable in matters of ships and shipping, buttonholed his
brother-in-law to the extent that sometimes an entire day would
pass during which Lisette saw neither. One rainy afternoon,
having been thus abandoned, she was writing a letter in the book
room, with Brutus snoring deafeningly before the fire, when the
abrupt cessation of all sound attracted her attention. She glanced
around. Brutus was sitting bolt upright, staring out of the low
window that gave onto the front drivepath. Even as she watched,
he crouched and began to creep backwards in obvious terror.
Frightened, Lisette came to her feet. A firm hand touched her

shoulder, and she gave a gasp of relief to find Strand beside her. "Thank heaven!" she whispered. "He sees something! Justin—I'm afraid."

He slipped one arm about her and, with his free hand, slid open a drawer and took up a small brass-mounted pistol. Norman, coming in behind him, said an alarmed, "What is it, sir?"

"I'm not sure," Strand answered quietly. "Brutus has spotted something. Look at him."

"By Jupiter! He's scared to death. What d'you mean to do?"

"There's been someone hanging about of late, I think. Take care of your sister. I'm going to have a look." He deposited his trembling wife in her brother's arms and took a stride towards the window.

"No!" Lisette rushed to throw her arms about him. "Please! Do not!"

Touched, he looked down at the top of her glossy head, pressed against the lapel of his jacket. Then he said, "Better to find out now, love," and gently detaching her, flung open the window.

A bluster of wind and rain swept the draperies inwards and sent Lisette's letter fluttering to the rug. She ran forward, but Norman restrained her. Astonished, she glanced up. There was a new purpose to his eyes, a new set to his jaw, and by heaven but he was strong, his hands holding her in a grip there was no escaping. Her eyes flashed to Justin's straight, lithe figure as he jumped down from the porch and sprinted across the lawn. My God! she thought, he is a perfect target!

The thought had no sooner flashed across her mind than Strand checked, crouched in an attitude of intense concentration, then flung up his arm and fired. She uttered a small shriek of fright and, tearing at her brother's restraining hand, implored, "Go to him! For pity's sake! Go to him!"

Norman hesitated. "He'll have my ears," he muttered but left her and clambered through the window. He was about to run into the rain when Strand, who had walked towards a clump of aspens, began to hurry back to the house, the smoking pistol in one hand and a small branch in the other. He brushed aside Norman's anxious enquiries and swung easily through the window.

"Now I shall have to clean the stupid thing," he remarked, tossing the pistol onto the reference table.

Lisette quavered, "Are you all right? Who was it?"

"I'm perfectly all right." He shot her a grateful, if wet, smile. "Thank you for being concerned."

She stiffened. "*Concerned?* What on earth would you expect?"

"Brutus," called Strand. "You may come out now."

The only response was a faint whimper from a periodical that the wind had also deposited on the carpet. Brutus, having succeeded in burying his head under this, apparently believed himself securely hidden and made no attempt to come forth. Strand bent down and raised the periodical while Norman and Lisette exchanged baffled glances. Strand held the branch in front of the dog's craven eyes. "Look," said he. "It is quite dead."

Brutus glanced at the "defunct" branch, gave a yelp, and tried to hide under Strand's shoe. Strand sighed, shrugged, and replaced the periodical.

Grinning from ear to ear, Norman closed the window and chortled, "What the deuce . . .?"

Strand waved the branch. "He won't believe it's dead," he said solemnly, ignoring his wife's indignation.

Norman took up the branch. "By thunder, but it is!" He held up one leaf, a bullet hole squarely through the centre. "Look here, Lisette! Jolly fine shooting, Strand. Do you seriously tell us that great leviathan is afraid of leaves?"

"Oh, no. He employs a certain amount of selectivity. Only aspens—when they flutter. And the wind came up, you see. He really is terrified of 'em. That's why I had to send him to Bolster, in town. Fewer aspens."

Norman went off into peals of laughter, and Lisette, trying not to smile, said sternly, "I collect you care not that you frightened me—us—to death?"

He looked at her, his eyes dancing. "I tried to tell you about our craven canine after I broke my hand, but I could see you would not believe me. And, as a matter of fact—" he hesitated, then added awkwardly, "I care very much."

For a moment Lisette could not seem to tear her eyes from his steady blue gaze. Then, a horn summoned imperiously, the sound breaking a hush that seemed to have held them all mute. "You see?" she said. "He *did* hear something! How you malign that poor animal! If the truth be told, sir—"

"Justin," he murmured whimsically. "Plain Justin."

She chuckled, then a familiar voice was upraised in bitter complaint. "It is Grandmama!" she cried joyously, and ran to the front door, Strand following.

Secure in the knowledge that several humans were before him, Brutus boldly left his refuge and rushed into the hall, barking furiously. Norman picked up the periodical and stared down at it unseeingly, his eyes troubled. He had dismissed Judith's notions as being the babblings of a romantical schoolgirl, but dashed if he wasn't beginning to think she had the right of the situation. He sighed and put the periodical on the table. "Pity," he murmured.

Comfortably settled before the drawing room fire, Lady Bayes-Copeland damned the weather, the deplorable state of England's roads, and the fact that it had been necessary for her guard to fire a shot over the heads of several unsavoury looking customers who had attempted to stop her coach.

Strand had already noticed that the old lady, despite her usual ferocity, looked rather pale. She had suffered quite a shock, he realized, and therefore said lightly, "A mistake, I fancy, ma'am."

"Mistake?" she bristled. "What d'ye mean, Strand? They saw my coach, and—"

"And probably thought it was the Royal Mail," he said with a twinkle.

Norman and Judith laughed, but Lisette regarded her husband apprehensively. Her grandmama did not give him the setdown he justly deserved, however. "You may jest," she said angrily, "but with all this riffraff littering the country and turning their hands to violence and thievery rather than honest work, we are none of us safe!"

For once, the laughter that invariably lurked at the back of Strand's eyes disappeared. He said with respect but firmness, "Your pardon, my lady, but that same riffraff fought and died by the thousands for England. That same riffraff has been cut off by an ungrateful government with neither pension nor hope, and how many of the poor devils have died of their wounds in want and misery, I shudder to think. They are the greatest potential resource England has. If the government would offer them work, or—"

"Work!" the old lady snorted ferociously. "Who's to pay for

this work? Who can pay wages for thousands of shiftless vagrants in these bad times?''

''Had Bonaparte invaded as he threatened, ma'am,'' he argued quietly, ''none of us would have a roof over our heads, and perhaps not a head to cover! They preserved our way of life, yet how many will now lift a hand to help them? And we've no guarantee of safety in this little island. There are still fanatical despots willing to plunge us into another bloodbath, as my sister and brother-in-law can attest!''

Lisette turned a startled face to him, and Norman asked, ''What's this, sir? Another Gunpowder Plot?''

''You are not so far wrong,'' Strand nodded. ''Tristram says little of it. I suspect he's been ordered to remain silent, but I do know that he and Devenish escaped France by the skin of their teeth. Dev, in fact, will likely limp for the rest of his life by reason of one of Claude Sanguinet's crossbow bolts.''

''Good heavens!'' gasped Lisette. ''Was not Claude Sanguinet the gentleman to whom Rachel was betrothed?''

''He was. And a more vicious fanatic has not been born. Leith risked his life to bring Rachel safely away. It has all been kept very quiet, but we've not heard the last of Sanguinet, I'll be bound.''

''Very likely,'' said my lady irascibly. ''But I did not come all this way to be scared by your tales of some puffed-up Frenchman. I understand you've a pianoforte, Strand?''

''Yes, ma'am. But—''

''Do not 'but' me, young fella! I have been compelled to leave hearth and home and journey all this way to your ridiculous Grecian atrocity, so as to see my grandchildren. I demand some recompense!''

He hesitated, stood, and crossing to her side, bent to drop a kiss on her withered cheek.

With a cackle of laughter she shook her cane at him. ''Naughty rogue! That was not what I meant.''

''Why then, I shall take it back,'' he grinned, bending again.

She seized him by both ears, pulled him close, and bussed him heartily. ''Lisette,'' she said, still smiling up at Strand, ''I like your husband. Now, no more excuses, sir. After dinner—I will have music. Do you hear, Lisette?''

Strand glanced at his wife curiously. ''You play, my dear?''

"And very prettily," confirmed Lady Bayes-Copeland. "Though not as well as she sings."

Lisette said that she would be glad to sing if someone would play for her. "You know what a dunce I am when I try to play and sing at the same time, Grandmama. Perhaps Judith could—?"

Colouring up, that damsel replied that she'd not practised in weeks and there was no use asking her to play poorly in front of everyone.

"I found lots of music in the little garden house," said Lisette, "but it was rather old, and I doubt you could read it."

"I'll tell the men to bring it all to the house," said Strand. "If there is something you favour, I might be able to help."

"Famous!" The old lady rapped her cane emphatically on the floor, causing the dozing Brutus to leap into the air with shock.

Lisette murmured a surprised, "You play the pianoforte, Strand?"

He grinned. "One of my numerous accomplishments. I think."

"Such modesty," teased Judith. "I expect you play magnificently, Strand."

"Wait until after dinner," interposed the old lady, "and you'll see. Lisette, you may bear me company whilst I change my dress, and tell me how it comes about that Judith and Norman are so remarkably improved in looks."

Standing respectfully as Strand ushered his wife and Lady Bayes-Copeland into the hall, Norman winked at his sister and muttered, "Wait until dinner, dear Grandmama, and you'll see!"

Despite her alleged curiosity regarding her grandchildren, once upstairs her ladyship vouchsafed only a grunt upon hearing the explanation for their svelte figures, and at once launched into a tirade regarding their presence at Strand Hall. "I was never more shocked," she snorted, raising her chin so that her abigail might pin a snowy white lace fichu to the bodice of her violet silk gown. "I declare Beatrice must be all about in her head to dump two young people on a bridal couple! And what mischief is she up to that they must be hustled off so? I *warned* Dwyer to beat her! More fool he! She'll bring disgrace on us all yet, and you'll have no more cause to look down your nose at that fine husband you've caught!"

Blushing furiously, Lisette waited until her grandmother dismissed the abigail, then expostulated, "Really, Grandmama! I wish you would not say such things in front of your woman! And I most certainly do not 'look down my nose' at Strand. He has—has been more than good."

"More than good my mother's knickers!" rasped the old lady, delighting in her granddaughter's horrified gasp. "I have never yet succeeded in keeping a secret from the servants, and had you lived in *my* day, Lizzie—"

"Oh! Has he taught *you* that odious nickname? The man—"

"Is kept at arms' length, I do not doubt! Just as rumour says!" Lady Bayes-Copeland leaned forward and, having caught her bedevilled granddaughter as offstride as she'd intended, demanded keenly, "Is it truth? *Is* your marriage a farce?"

"Dear heaven . . .! How— Who—"

"Need you ask? How could you have been so addlebrained as to confide in Beatrice? The girl's got a tongue like a washerwoman, and for some reason loathes Strand. I put the fear of God into her, I can tell you! I hope I may not have been too late. If the clubs get hold of it, you'll have made that fine boy into the jest of London!"

Sudden tears stung Lisette's eyes, and she sank her head into her hands. "My God! How *could* she?"

"It is truth, then! You must be feather-witted! Do you not know that—"

"It is not true!" Lisette flared, lifting a stricken face. "Not now, at all events. But if it was, it would be *his* fault, not mine! You are quick to condemn me, ma'am, but precious little you know of it! And if you fancy Strand abused—what of *me?* Do you know what it is like to be married to a man who—who has never uttered a word of tenderness or—or passion? Who sees me as nothing save a social symbol to salvage his confounded—stupid name?"

Inwardly pleased by her granddaughter's spirited departure from her customary poise, the old lady snapped, "No, I do not. Your husband may not be clever with words, Lisette. He is, I venture to suspect, better with actions. And vastly more worthy than you warrant, madam! Now give me your arm. I trust you have an adequate chef, for I can scarce wait for my dinner."

Fortunately, her trust was not misplaced. The chef had outdone himself and after two excellent removes and several hearty laughs as a result of being given more details of her grandchildren's starvation, Lady Bayes-Copeland was in a mellow mood. By contrast, Lisette was unusually silent. She was filled with apprehension lest her sister's love of gossip should have tragic consequences. The very suggestion of criticism was sufficient to arouse Beatrice's animosity, and the fact that Strand had dared to interfere with her choice of a bridal frock for Judith and then been praised for *his* choice was quite enough to win her enmity. She tended to brood over real or fancied slights and might very well take revenge by scandalmongering, or—

"Wake up! Wake up!" cried my lady irritably.

With a gasp, Lisette saw that all eyes were on her. Murmuring her apologies, she stood and led the ladies to the drawing room. Here, the dowager saw fit to rhapsodize over Brutus and chatter with Judith about the forthcoming jaunt to Town, but she was becoming impatient when the door opened and Norman stuck his head in to announce that Strand was ready now, and that the pianoforte had been carried to the "blue salon."

"Fustian!" grumbled my lady. "The word is 'saloon,' boy, not that Frenchified fal-lal! Fetch my shawl, Judith, it's likely freezing whether it be misnamed or no! Great draughty place!"

A fire had been lighted some time since, however, and the saloon was quite comfortable. Strand had spread the music out on a sideboard, and Lisette leafed through it while he settled Lady Bayes-Copeland into a chair beside the fire. Lisette selected several songs, none of which appeared to dismay her husband. His rendition of the introduction to the first of these, however, caused her ladyship to throw up her hands and utter shrieks of mirthful consternation. "For heaven's sake, boy!" she chided. "It is a love song—not a military march! Must you always go at such a pace?" Strand took the criticism in good part and moderated his tempo. Lisette had a charming, if not powerful voice, and aside from launching into the fourth melody in the wrong key, Strand played quite well. Unfortunately, they were soon joined by another performer. Brutus, apparently feeling obliged to contribute to the evening, sat up and joined in, howling sonorously and reducing Judith and Norman to muffled hysteria. Strand struggled to preserve his countenance, and Lisette tried to finish her song, but the dog's full-throated accompaniment, plus the smothered giggles, conspired to defeat them. Strand collapsed over the keys with a shout of laughter. Equally overcome, Lisette leaned against the piano, and my lady, cackling hilariously, consoled Brutus with the outrageous falsehood that he "sang beautifully."

London was grey and chilly and, as usual, bustling. Best threaded the carriage with nice precision through the heavy traffic to Portland Place, where Judith and Norman were to stay, and Lisette went inside with them to greet the staff and hug her loved Sanders. "Might just as well have come down to you, miss," the abigail sniffed, much affected, "had I known the missus would be away for so long."

"We none of us knew, Sandy. Has there been any late word?"

"Mr. Powers got a letter this morning saying that Sir Ian has been took better. The master says if this keeps up another week, he'll come home. It seems like the weather's been a touch bleak, and he's got some chilblains, poor man."

Thoroughly conversant with her father's dislike of extreme cold, Lisette had no doubt but that they would soon be able to restore Judith and Norman to the bosom of the family, and she hurried back to the carriage to relay this information to Strand. He did not seem especially delighted to hear it, saying that he'd a project in mind that he was sure would keep Norman busily occupied for as long as he was able to stay in Sussex.

They proceeded to the house Strand rented in Sackville Street. Lisette had never visited this establishment. She thought it comfortable but austere, the furnishings a uniform mahogany and the colours of the upholstery and draperies rather sombre. Reading her expression aright, Strand said cheerfully that they would search for a more suitable house when his lease expired at the beginning of September. "Might as well purchase a town-house," he said. "We'll likely spend the Season here if— Well, I'll be dashed!"

He had opened the door of a small bookroom, where sprawled a gentleman, fast asleep in a wing chair.

Amused, Lisette said, "Why, it's Lord Bolster!"

Strand beckoned the footman who hovered nearby. "Has his lordship been here long?"

The footman cast Bolster a shocked glance but was unable to shed any light on the situation. The butler, being summoned, gave a little leap of dismay when he saw that softly snoring figure and exclaimed, "Good gracious! I'd no idea he was still here, sir. His lordship called last evening and said he would leave you a note, but I thought he had left."

"Good God! Do you not check the rooms before you retire?"

Reddening, the butler affected the air of a maligned deity and imparted that every room in the house was checked whenever the master was in residence, but since, to his knowledge, no one had used the book room yesterday, he had not felt it necessary to go in there. Furthermore, the note Lord Bolster had left was even now on Mr. Justin's desk in the study, wherefore—

His lordship snorted and stirred. Strand waved a dismissal to the butler and walked over to place a hand on his friend's shoulder. "Wake up, old man," he said, gently shaking him. "What a dreadful host you must think me, that you were abandoned here all night."

Bolster blinked up at him. His yellow hair was rumpled and untidy, he was badly in need of a shave, his garments were dishevelled, and there was about him a strong aroma of cognac. His bewildered gaze drifted from Strand's smiling features, to Lisette, watching him anxiously. Becoming red as fire, Bolster lunged to his feet, bowed, tried to speak and, failing, stood in quaking misery.

"Come along upstairs, Jeremy," said Strand kindly. "You can shave and refresh yourself in my room. Matter of fact, I think we may kidnap you back to Sussex with us. What d'you say, ma'am?"

"Why, that would be delightful," Lisette answered warmly, and then hurried out, well aware that his lordship's disrupted nerves would be better able to recover if spared her alarming female presence.

In the hall, a prim, tidy little woman was waiting. She identified herself as the housekeeper and presented two maids, a lackey, and the footman to their new mistress. Next, Lisette was shown to her suite, a spacious bedchamber, small parlour, and dressing room on the second floor, where Denise was already busily unpacking.

Bolster, meanwhile, allowing himself to be commandeered by his energetic host, was allowed small chance for comment even had he been capable at that point of making one. His rumpled clothing was whisked away, hot water was carried up for a bath, breakfast—despite his shuddering aversion—was ordered, and an hour later, feeling comfortably relaxed, the crick in his neck much eased, and his power of speech restored, he lounged on his host's bed, clad in a borrowed dressing gown and sipping gratefully at a cup of hot chocolate.

"D-dashed decent of you, Strand," he acknowledged. "Don't know wh-what you m-m-m- will be thinking. Your wife must fancy me to-totally looby."

"My wife," said Strand easily, "has taken a deep liking to you, Jerry. In fact, were I not assured she is madly in love with *me,* I'd be tempted to call you out."

He had spoken lightly, but to his surprise the expected laugh was not forthcoming; his lordship's eyes slid away and the ready colour surged into the pleasant face.

With an uneasy premonition of trouble, Strand asked, "Jeremy? Is something amiss?"

Bolster's hand twitched. "M-matter of fact," he gulped, nervously, "I th-thought—that is—well, the r-r-reason I c-came—" But here he became so inarticulate that Strand deftly changed the subject, then pleaded to be excused so that he might glance at his correspondence, and departed, leaving behind a guest both grateful for the reprieve and guilty that his warning had gone unuttered.

A small pile of letters lay on the desk in Strand's study. He identified two as being from friends in India, and several others of a business nature that he would peruse later. There was a short letter from Lord Leith and a longer one from Rachel, some statements that could be handled by Connaught, a cluster of invitations that he would go over with Lisette, a notice that the bracelet he had ordered was now completed, and at last, somehow having found its way to the bottom of the pile, the note from Bolster. The fact that this had been sealed and his lordship's crest imprinted in not one but four places along the fold, caused Strand to suspect Jeremy of having been well over the oar when he wrote it. The handwriting was, as usual, a disaster. The message, brief and to the point, drove the amusement from Strand's eyes. He read:

My Dear Strand—
   You have always been a good friend and your Lovely Wife is very kind. Especially to Amanda. I must repay you

*in a way I Abomminate. There is some ugly Roumours
about. Nothing to Dredfull but please do not rush of half
cocked untill you have Talked to,*

> *Yr. affecsionite and ever gratefull,*
> *Bolster*

His frowning gaze lingering on those four seals, Strand re-
folded the note automatically. Bolster, he thought, his mouth
settling into a grim line, had been wise in his caution, after all.
What kind of rumours? More of poor Rachel and that bastard
Sanguinet, perhaps. He wandered into the corridor, paused,
staring blindly at the black and white marble squares of the
entrance hall, and thus became aware of his wife's voice, very
low, in the small saloon. His frown deepened. If the gabblemongers
were at work, he had best caution Lisette. The last thing he
wished was to involve her in more scandal, yet . . .

His musings were abruptly severed as he entered the saloon.
James Garvey, resplendent in a primrose jacket that clung lovingly to his fine shoulders, fawn pantaloons that accentuated his
shapely legs, and a waistcoat of striped primrose and cream
brocaded satin, was clasping Lisette's hand while she smiled up
into his face. "You did get my note, then?" Garvey was
murmuring. "When you did not answer, I—"

"Forgive me, James. It was so very beautiful. But you should
not have come here!"

"Yes, yes. I know we must be very careful, but—"

The revelation that a clandestine love affair had been conducted under his nose was like a dash of icewater in Strand's
face. Emerging from that staggering shock, he said, "My love, I
would not disturb you while you—ah—entertain, but—"

Garvey spun around, his expression malevolent. Lisette, deathly
pale, managed to say calmly, "We are no sooner in Town,
Strand, than we have callers. Is it not delightful? Two gentlemen
already, and—"

"Oh, I don't know," murmured Strand, slipping Bolster's
note into his pocket.

Lisette gave a gasp. Garvey, yearning for an excuse to face
this man across twenty yards of turf, purred, "Your pardon,
sir?"

Ignoring him, Strand went on smoothly, "I cannot think of

Jeremy as a mere 'caller,' ma'am. He will, I trust, be with us for some time. It was kind in you to call, Garvey. May I be of some assistance to you?''

"I had not intended—'' Garvey began, with a sneer.

"To stay longer? But how very polite in you. Thank you, and do call again. I shall be very pleased to—er, meet you. At any time.''

Blue eyes, suddenly deadly, challenged narrowed green ones.

Her breath fluttering, Lisette extended her hand. "Good day, Mr. Garvey.''

"Allow me to show you out,'' offered Strand, his teeth gleaming in a wide smile. He tugged on the bell rope, and a lackey floated into the room so instantly that he could only have been waiting by the open door.

"Mr. Garvey's hat and gloves, if you please.''

Strand had no sooner spoken the words than a footman appeared, the required articles and a cane in his pristine grasp. Strand made no attempt to restrain his approving grin, though his servants remained woodenly impassive.

For an instant, Garvey stood there, seething. Then, he bowed low to Lisette, marched past Strand without a word, tore his belongings from the footman, and strode from the house. He had every intention of flinging open the front door and leaving it wide, but that little gesture was denied him as the butler hastened to perform the service, bowing him forth and closing the door gently behind him.

Strand turned to Lisette. She had changed her travelling clothes for a gown of beige muslin with brown ribbon fashioned into small fans around the low neckline and the sleeves, and little brown bows here and there around the flounce. He wondered if it was possible to find a dress that did not become her. Her eyes looked enormous and were fixed upon him. Anxiously, not fondly, as they had been for Garvey.

"I wonder,'' he mused, "if I erred in coming back to Town. It is so distressingly filled with—unpleasantness.''

"Justin, please do not imagine that—that Garvey and I—that we—'' She bit her lip and said a pleading, "Oh, you know what I mean.''

"Unfortunately,'' he conceded, dryly. "A deal sooner than I'd expected, I admit.''

Her cheeks reddened. "Regardless of what you may think, he is a very dangerous man. You would be—"

One mobile brow arched. He drawled mockingly, "A warning, ma'am?"

"No!" Her hands clenched. "How could you dare to think such a—"

The door opened. The butler announced, "Lady Hermione Grey, Miss Smythe-Carrington, and Mrs. Duncan, madam."

Nerves taut and heart pounding, Lisette fought for calm. "Show them to the drawing room, if you please." When the man had left, she turned to Strand. "That was a perfectly *dreadful* thing to say! You have no right—"

"Nor have we the time to discuss it while your eager callers wait." He stepped closer, his eyes bleak. "I fear the gabble merchants gather before we've had a chance to marshal our defences. If something is said concerning my sister or Leith, you had best pretend ignorance." He opened the door again. "As soon as they leave, madam wife, I shall require a little of your time."

Lisette walked down the hall to the drawing room, her thoughts churning. How enraged Justin had been to find her with Garvey. And how *dared* he imply that she hoped for a duel when her one thought in coming downstairs to see the man had been to thank him for his poem and to somehow make him go away before Strand saw him! What a miserable coincidence that her husband had walked in just as James uttered those unfortunate words. Naturally, Justin had read the wrong interpretation into the remark. She could still see his savage smile and hear the lazy drawl he employed only when he was very angry indeed. The antagonism between the two men had been an almost tangible entity, searing across that room, and the look on Garvey's face had been very clear to read. He wanted an excuse to call Justin out. And if they went out, he would kill her husband. With an ache of fear she knew that she did not want such a duel to take place, that she did not want Strand hurt—much less slain. It was not that she loved him, for he wasn't a very lovable man. Except . . . now and then, when his eyes crinkled at the corners, or when they twinkled at her, in his wretched teasing way, and, very occasionally, when she had thought to glimpse a wistfulness in his face that came and went so swiftly she could never be sure it had been there at all. As on the evening he had ''shot'' the tree for Brutus and she had scolded him, and he'd looked at her and said in his whimsical fashion, ''As a matter of fact—I care very much.''

She shook herself mentally. It was all fustian, of course, for he did not care. Not a mite. Or he would tell her so. Not once had he even uttered the words ''I love you.'' Tears stung her eyes. Not once. Not so much as a tender ''darling.'' He had been gently considerate in his love-making and had gone so far as to murmur that she was very beautiful, but his kisses were brief, almost careless, and of passion or real adoration there had been little trace. If anything, he tended to tease her even in those intimate moments, so that she was moved to laughter and her fears much lessened. She tensed. Was that why he never spoke of love? Did he know how frightened she'd been? Had he thought—

''Are you all right, madam?''

She jumped. A maid was watching her curiously, and small wonder, for she must have stood here an age with her forehead pressed to the door panel. Whatever was wrong with her mind? ''Quite all right, thank you,'' she said, managing to smile. ''A slight touch of the headache, is all.'' And she went inside.

Ten minutes later, aghast, she knew the disaster she had feared was upon her. Brenda Smythe-Carrington was the type of gentle, pretty, kind-hearted girl everybody liked, even Lady Hermione Grey, whose tongue was only a shade less acid than vitriol. Jemima Duncan was an inveterate gossip who could be vicious even while smiling fondly upon her victim. With a giggle here and a scold there, the latter two ladies welcomed Lisette to the ranks of the wives. Marriage was delightful, was it not? Even (and a spate of conspiratorial giggles) was it rather unwanted. Of course, if one really chose to repel a man—even one's husband—it could be done. Especially (with glittering smiles) by a really clever lady.

''Do you know, dear Lisette,'' confided Lady Hermione breathlessly, ''you may scarce believe it, but I once knew the sweetest girl, quite one of our beauties at the time, who was all but *sold* into wedlock with a—rather unfortunate gentleman. Not exactly beyond the pale, but—'' She pursed her lips and, before the stunned Lisette could comment, turned to Mrs. Duncan. ''You remember the case, Jemima,'' she said, with a sly wink of the eye that was beyond the range of her hostess's vision. "I simply cannot recall the poor child's name."

"No more can I, Hermione," purred Mrs. Duncan. "But it was indeed a tragic case. One could but hope the sweet girl knew that all London wept for her." She laid a gentle hand on Lisette's arm and said cloyingly, "Poor dear, a helpless victim of financial necessity."

"One can but hope," said Lisette, a flush beginning to glow in her pale cheeks, "that she was blessed by such true and loyal friends as you dear ladies."

"Oh, indeed she was," interpolated Miss Smythe-Carrington, looking genuinely distressed. "Surely she *must* have been, poor thing. What could be more dreadful than to be wed to a man one did not care for? I should think death infinitely preferable!"

"Oh, infinitely," agreed Lady Hermione. "And apparently the lady in question felt the same way, for it was said that for an inordinate length of time she would not allow her husband in her chamber." She giggled. "Is that not delicious?"

Mrs. Duncan trilled, "It is! And was the prime *on dit* for weeks! I doubt anything else has been—I mean *was*—spoken of for an age!" She glanced mirthfully at her crony, and they both burst into refined gales of mirth so that at length it became necessary to dab at tearful eyes with lacy handkerchiefs.

"How jolly it is," observed Lisette with a slightly tigerish smile, "to see you so enjoying yourselves. But I fear you must be talked dry. May I offer you a dish of milk?" Two startled pairs of eyes flashed to her. "Oh, dear!" she touched her cheek in dismay. "Whatever can I be thinking of . . .? I meant *tea,* of course."

After that, the conversation was a trifle less hilarious, although it ran along politely. The ladies sipped their tea and talked of commonplaces, with Lisette inserting an occasional blushful reference to her "adored" husband, so that when they left, my lady and Mrs. Duncan were rather tight-lipped, and Miss Smythe-Carrington said with a melting smile how wonderful it must be to be "so really happy" as her dear Lisette.

No sooner had the door closed behind them than Lisette all but flew to the book room, and thence upstairs in search of Strand. In the upper hall she nearly collided with his valet, one Oliver Green, a rotund, merry-eyed little man who looked more like a publican than a valet. He was carrying a pile of neckcloths and juggled desperately to retain them. "Oh, I am sorry, Green!" cried Lisette. "I must find my husband. Is he in his room?"

"No, madam." The valet gave a small gasp of relief as he steadied his collection. "The master has stepped out for a short while. I believe he said he meant to look in at his club." He stood there uncertainly for a moment, watching Mrs. Strand walk away, and wondering why her pretty little face had become so very white.

Chapter 12

Strand's confrontation with Garvey had left him in no mood to be cordial to anyone, wherefore, quite forgetting the presence of Jeremy Bolster in his house, he donned hat, coat, and gloves, and stamped outside. It was a drizzly morning, which did not in the least deter him from walking a considerable distance. Had he been more aware of what transpired around him, he might have noted many amused looks, and as many whispered asides, but he responded to hails with nothing more than an abstracted wave of his cane and strode on, his mind obsessed with the memory of the fond light in his wife's eyes as she had gazed up at the revoltingly dandified conniver who went by the name of James Garvey.

From the very beginning of their marriage, things had gone badly. He could scarcely have managed a less propitious beginning than to have been obliged to leave his bride on their wedding night. He could no more blame her for that than for the fact that on his return he'd stamped into her bedchamber and tumbled over the leviathan. When he had at last been able to mend his fences, he'd kept a rigid hold on his emotions, handling her very gently, afraid of scaring her off by revealing the depth of his love for her, and hurt because his attempt to impart his feelings had been coldly ignored. He'd never before been much in the petticoat line. There'd not been the opportunity. His father's gambling and spendthrift ways and ultimate folly of cheating at cards had decided his own fate. His years in India had been successful beyond his wildest dreams, but success had not come easily. It had taken backbreaking effort, an unceasing battle that had taken its toll of his health even as it had resulted in security for his sisters, and the payment of all his now dead father's bad debts. Having achieved what he'd set out to do, he had begun to look about for a bride. He'd hoped to find a lady of good family for whom he might also feel some affection. He'd not expected to encounter the embodiment of his every dream, who was also of lineage *sans reproche*.

His footsteps slowed, and he stared moodily at a sparrow hopping on an iron fence beside him. His courtship had, he acknowledged ruefully, been clumsy beyond permission. He sighed and, turning into Bond Street, knew that all his introspection had brought him nothing save the realization of defeat. His jaw set. However faint his hope of winning the love of his wife, he would see to one thing, by God! She never would become the foil of so unprincipled a libertine as Garvey!

Walking on with a resumption of his usual brisk stride, he entered a quiet little lane where was a discreet club known as The Madrigal. Here, as at White's or Watier's, could be found gambling, fine wines, and excellent dining. Lacking the exclusiveness of the larger clubs, The Madrigal gained from the membership of some of London's more successful artists, composers, and poets. Gradually, therefore, it had acquired a reputation as an interesting spot, where stimulating conversation crossed all political lines. The club began to thrive and had of late become the vogue, drawing in some very socially high ranking gentlemen, so that Strand had once laughingly told Bolster that had he not joined when he did, they'd now refuse to accept him.

The porter swung the door open with his usual polite, "Good morning, sir!" but Strand thought to see a troubled look also and, rather belatedly reminded of Bolster's note, at once forgot it again in his consternation that he'd abandoned his guest. In the act of removing his coat, he started to put it back on, but the horror in the porter's eyes dissuaded him. If something really ugly was circulating regarding Rachel and Leith, his abrupt departure must lend weight to it. He grinned at the porter, vouchsafed a blithe remark to the effect that he had forgot to collect Lord

Bolster, and allowed himself to be divested of his outer garments. The porter looked relieved and promised to tell his lordship Mr. Strand was here, did he arrive. Strand nodded and went into the ground floor lounge, where he wandered over to warm his hands at the fire. The room was not crowded at this hour, and the few gentlemen occupying it were more interested in their newspapers than in a new arrival. It seemed to Strand that General Smythe-Carrington stared at him with unusual intensity before retreating behind *The Times*. Lord Gregory Hughes, walking through from the stairs leading to the upper regions where were the card rooms, checked, started to say something to Strand, then coughed, shook his hand, and went out. A waiter approached, and Strand accepted the wine he offered, while wondering what was abroad to result in such obvious consternation.

A blow on the shoulder that almost knocked him into the fire disturbed his reflections and sent the wine in his glass splashing in all directions. A familiar voice cried, "Strand! You miserable varmint!" and he spun around to be seized in a hug that he gladly returned.

"Marcus!" He set down his depleted glass to grip Marcus Clay's uniformed shoulders. "And a Major, by gad! I've not seen you since—"

"Since the Spring of 'twelve when I was home on a repairing lease." The soldier's eyes, bright with affection, scanned the lean face of his friend. "What the deuce happened to you? You're brown as a berry!"

"I'm positively pale compared to when first I came home." And in answer to the questioning lift of this schoolmate's dark brows, he elaborated, "India. But enough of me, tell me of yourself. Did you see any of the action? You must have, I take it, to win all your rank. Lord, what luck! I demand—"

Here, an irked hissing warned that they disturbed the peace of others, and they adjourned to a pair of high-backed chairs beside the window. The dark head and the fair leaned closer together as they enjoyed a low-voiced conversation that bridged the years since last they had met. Clay was a personable young man, now happily married and the father of four hopeful children. He spoke lightly of his military career and said little of the exploits at Waterloo that had made him into a national hero, but Strand was enthralled. Too enthralled to notice the room filling and the level of conversation rising until he heard his own name, spoken in a contemptuous drawl that caused him to stiffen in his chair.

". . . gave Strand the devil of a run for his money." Holding forth at the centre of an amused group, James Garvey laughed, and went on, "She is incalculably far above the man, of course, and from what she tells me, everything you've heard is truth, and she is his wife in name only."

Strand, who had sprung up, reeled as though he had received a physical blow, and stood momentarily stunned with shock, while Clay, coming to his side, slipped a hand onto his shoulder and glared wrathfully at Garvey's back.

Quite unaware of their presence, Lord John Chester, his youthful face alight, demanded, "How the deuce did the lady manage it, I wonder? And how are you privileged to know, James? Have you seen the bride of late?"

"Very often." Garvey dug him in the ribs. "And often late. You must know that I worship at her shrine, and she returns my affection as fully. She never had any use for Strand, except that his—"

Battered by hurt and fury, Strand tore free from Clay's attempt to restrain him. Growling a curse, he caught Garvey by the arm and swung him around. "You," he stated unequivocally, "are a foul-mouthed, unmitigated liar, sir!" And he dashed the contents of his glass into that handsome countenance.

A chair went over with a crash amid an explosion of excitement. Then, a breathless hush fell. Every man present was on his feet, and new arrivals, at once becoming aware of the tense atmosphere, crowded the open doorway.

Garvey accepted the handkerchief Chester offered, wiped his face, and drawled, "Will you second me, John?"

"But, surely that will not be of the necessity immediate, my James?" The smooth voice with its pronounced French accent came from the door. Garvey tensed, paling, and his head jerked towards the speaker, a slight, very elegant gentleman, who watched the proceedings with a faint smile upon his mild features. "Claude . . ." breathed Garvey, his voice barely audible.

Strand had not seen Rachel's former fiancé for some years, but it seemed to him that the notorious Claude Sanguinet had not changed one iota. He must be forty, at least, but his dark hair was untouched by grey, his face unlined, his figure as trim as ever. "You mistake!" snapped Strand, still pale and trembling with rage. "This fellow bandied my wife's name about, and—"

"And you the felony compound, eh, Monsieur Strand?" Claude Sanguinet shook his head reproachfully. "Your indignation she is nonetheless warranted, for I also have hear my friend's so regrettable remarks. It would be well, James, did you make the apology, no?"

His eyes flashing, Garvey smiled. "Impossible, I fear, Claude. I have taken a glass of wine in the face, and—"

"Quite impossible," Strand confirmed grimly.

In some circles, Sanguinet was thought to be the most dangerous man in Europe, but there was no hint of this in his manner as he murmured gently, "*Mais non*, gentlemen. This cannot be. The bride would be *assurément*, devastated. As would I, dear my James."

Strand frowned from one to the other. Garvey was very white, his hands clenched at his sides, his narrowed gaze locked with Sanguinet's mild one. Through a quivering silence that battle of wills was fought. Then, incredibly, Garvey's eyes fell. He wrenched around as if impelled by an unseen hand and, his gaze fixed on the sapphire in Strand's neckcloth, said in a hoarse, strained voice, "It is . . . quite true that I . . . spoke without . . . without consideration of the feelings of the lady. I—I offer you my . . ." He seemed to choke, then gulped, "my—most profound apologies, sir."

Somebody exclaimed, "Well, I'll be damned!"

Strand's voice sliced through a flurry of comment. "You may tell your master over there that I shall take no apologies, Garvey. Not unless you also admit—before every man here—that you lied. My dear wife would never in this world have uttered such vulgar remarks."

"But you must own he *has* apologized, Monsieur Strand," the Frenchman pointed out softly.

"He apologized for bruiting about malicious gossip concerning my personal life," said Strand doggedly. "He has not admitted that he lied. My challenge stands."

There was a ripple of agreement. Mr. Garvey, it appeared, was not so popular as had been supposed, nor Mr. Strand as despised. Marcus Clay, however, groaned inwardly. Whatever the hold Sanguinet had over Garvey, it was too much to expect any man to take that ultimate insult.

Garvey's eyes slid to the Frenchman. "Only so far, Claude," he warned, in a voice low and cracking with rage and humiliation.

"For the sake of a lady who shall be nameless, but for whom I still hold a deep affection," Sanguinet persisted, "I am my every effort bending to avoid what must be a most *tragique* meeting, Monsieur Strand. My friend was perhaps—" he shrugged— "ill advised. He have repeat that which he is told. That which he believe come from the—ah, unimpeachable source, shall we say? And he—"

"Shall we rather say *he lied?*" said Strand very clearly.

"By . . . God . . . !" Garvey ground out between closed teeth. "If I—"

"You are, monsieur, a gentleman most *impitoyable*, I fear," sighed the Frenchman. He stretched forth an impeccably manicured white hand. "James—my James—I must insist that you your mistake acknowledge. Admit you—"

"Admit you lied!" Strand grated.

"For the sake of the Fair, I implore it," murmured Sanguinet.

"The devil!" snarled Strand. "For the sake of truth!"

Garvey was shaking visibly. His face was like putty, and beads of perspiration stood out on his forehead and trickled slowly down his cheeks. For an endless moment he stood there, while only the ticking of the mantel clock broke the deathly hush, and upwards of a hundred gentlemen stood scarcely breathing, waiting. Then:

"I . . . I . . . lied!" Garvey's voice, somewhere between a snarl and a sob, rose higher. "Damn you, Strand! You have it! I—lied!" He turned, thrust his way through the shocked crowd, and was gone.

Walking slowly down the steps of The Madrigal, very conscious of the eyes that watched from every window, Strand knew victory to be a cheap and hollow thing, and all his dreams like so many autumn leaves, dead and withered, scattering to the four winds. So many men had been eager to buy him a glass of brandy, to offer him their congratulations after Garvey's dramatic defeat. Even old Smythe-Carrington, making his majestic way across the room, had said a stentorian, "Well done, m'dear fellow. Must protect honour—'t'all costs. What?'' and amid a chorus of endorsement, rumbled off again. Bolster, who had been one of those so tensely watching from the doorway, glanced at the set smile on the pale features beside him, and uttered, "All m-my fault. Very bad."

"No such thing." Strand waved to Owsley and Hughes as they climbed into a brougham and drove away. "And you've my apologies for going off without you this morning."

Bolster gave a dismissing gesture. "Should have w-warned you. B-beastly mess!"

"It is." Strand glowered. "I wish to God he'd agreed to meet met."

"Much b-b- safer," Bolster concurred. "He's ruined, of c-course. You've made a dangerous enemy, poor fellow. Gad! But he was r-raving!"

"Cannot blame him," Clay pointed out glumly, coming up looking very gallant in his regimentals, with the pelisse slung across his shoulders. "Sanguinet properly forced him to his knees, and you all but stepped on his face, Justin."

"When I would so much sooner have blown his head off," muttered Strand savagely.

Clay met Bolster's eyes, and glancing up in time to see that meaningful exchange, Strand added, "You're thinking the situation would more likely have been reversed." He shrugged and, striving for a cheerful smile, informed them that he had learned a few things whilst in India.

"Have you perhaps learned how to mix a better bowl of punch than that hideous concoction we used to brew up at school?" asked Clay, also trying to be cheerful despite a heavy sense of foreboding.

"I have!" Strand slipped a hand through his arm. "And you and Jeremy shall come home with me, while I—" He stopped. Lisette would be at home. He could not face the treachery of his beautiful wife; not now. The wounds were too raw.

Bolster saw the suddenly stern look. "B-better not," he advised, taking Strand's other arm. "Cook there. Dreadful dragons, co-cooks. Now, at my place, we'll be undisturbed."

Strand threw him a grateful smile. "Ryder Street it is, then. And I'll brew you a punch you will never forget."

Clay cheered and hailed a passing hackney, and they all three piled inside.

Having changed into a peach velvet gown with tiny pearl buttons down the bodice, Lisette allowed Denise to arrange her hair in a soft and feminine style that she knew Strand admired. By two o'clock he had still not put in an appearance, and she dared not venture out-of-doors until she knew just what to expect, so she lunched alone in the breakfast parlour, listening to the rain patter against the windows and wondering where he was, and what was happening. Her appetite was poor. She ate sparingly, then wandered into the book room where the fire was well established. The novel she selected could not hold her attention. One horrible scene after another rose before her mind's eye so that she scarcely saw the printed page. Suppose Strand was jeered at wherever he went. That swift temper of his would flare, to Lord knows what effect! Suppose he guessed that Beatrice was responsible and drove straight to Somerset to challenge poor William? He would slaughter that gentle creature, beyond doubting! The very thought of such a disastrous train of events made her blood run cold.

Shortly after three o'clock she heard the door knocker and tensed, straining her ears. She could not detect Strand's brisk voice, nor the quick, light step. Still, her heart jumped with nervousness when the door opened. It was only Morse, bringing the salver to her, and she took up the card it held, irritated and determining that she would not be at home to any tabby who had braved this wet afternoon to sniff out whatever juicy morsel she might let slip. The card was inscribed "Miss Amanda Hersh," and, brightening, Lisette desired that her caller be shown in, and that tea be served.

She stood when Amanda entered and said a welcoming, "Good afternoon. How charmingly you look in that green gown, and how very kind in you to come and see me. Pray sit here beside the fire, it is so chill for this time of year."

She was mildly surprised when Amanda, her little face deeply distressed, seized her hand between both her own and said in a tragic rush of words, "I came as soon as I heard. Oh you cannot know how sorry I am you must be fairly retort and so soon after you are wed my poor poor soul!"

Lisette blinked and, drawing Amanda to sit on the sofa beside her, said, "I am humiliated, of course, but—"

Amanda breathed an astonished, "Humiliated? Good heavens!"

She looked quite shocked. Flushing, Lisette said, "I should have said 'ashamed,' I suspect. Is it not ghastly that such tales are—" She trailed into silence, for Amanda was regarding her with stark horror. Frightened, she demanded, "Mandy, what is it?"

"Oh, my!" cried Amanda, wringing her hands. "I was sure Strand would have told you by this time of the incantation at The Madrigal I did not think to be the one to have to tell you."

In a detached way, Lisette thought, She must mean confrontation, and felt for a moment as though she were wrapped inside a glacier.

"I am truly sorry," Amanda faltered, "but after what Mr. Garvey said Strand had no choice, and—"

"Garvey?" Lisette croaked. "Wh-where? When?"

"This morning. I am staying with my godmother Lady Carden you know and Lucian my cousin came and said it was a great pity Strand had not a whip in his hand."

Gaining some control over her numbed lips, Lisette asked threadily, "What happened?"

"Oh! Do not ask!" Amanda pressed her hands to hot cheeks. "Indeed I dare not repeat—"

Despite a flaring surge of anxiety and impatience, Lisette managed to be calm. "I know how difficult it must be for you, but I beg you, Mandy. If you are truly my friend, tell me."

"I am indeed your friend, Lisette." Amanda clasped her hand, her gentle eyes moist with sympathy. "I will never forget how kind you were to me and Strand also was so good and I know Lucian thinks him a jolly good fellow for he said so which he don't always about every man." Not appearing in the least short of breath after this scrambled utterance, she folded her hands in her lap and, fixing her green eyes on them, began, "Lucian says that Mr. Garvey was remarking how much he cares for you and that you care for him also." She heard Lisette gasp but, not daring to pause, swept on in her rushed fashion. "He laughed and said that you had given Strand a—a run for his money because you cared for *him*, Garvey I mean." Expecting a shriek or even a swoon, she slanted a fearful glance at Lisette and saw her sitting rigidly, staring at the fire, her face without colour, her eyes wide but not tearful.

After a moment, Lisette asked in a far-away voice, "And—my husband heard all this?"

"Yes and Lucian says he was absolutely splendid and threw a full glass of wine in Garvey's face!"

"Dear . . . God!" whispered Lisette, closing her eyes.

"Oh my heavens!" Amanda wailed, throwing an arm about her. "Do not swoon, please!"

Clinging to her, dreading the answer she must receive, Lisette whispered, "When do they meet? Did Strand have the choice of weapons? Yes—he must, of course. But he has no chance, Mandy. No chance at all! Oh, merciful—"

"Stop! Stop!" Quite unnerved, Amanda said, "There is not going to be a duel for another man was there and stopped it and I cannot recall his name but he was French and Lucian said he seemed to exert great influence over Mr. Garvey and Lucian dislikes him very much and says he is a menace which does not seem quite fair since he stopped the duel, does it?"

"No." Pressing a hand to her brow, Lisette tried to think. "Could it have been a Monsieur Sanguinet, perchance?"

"It was! How clever of you to guess and who would think *anyone* could make Mr. Garvey draw back from a duel when everyone knows he is such a dead—" She bit back the rest of that observation in the nick of time, and went on hurriedly, "But he did and Lucian said Garvey was so outraged he thought him like to have a seizure and went roaring off cursing like a bull! Garvey I mean not my dear Lucian."

Morse entered at this point, followed by a neat maid carrying a tray with the *impedimenta* for the tea ritual. Smiling mechanically, Lisette manipulated teapot, cream, and sugar, her thoughts in chaos and one dread fear uppermost: Strand must be mad with rage and humiliation. He certainly would attempt to trace the rumour to its source. Whatever would he say when he learned the source was her own sister?

At precisely the same time that Amanda was closeted with Lisette, two other meetings were taking place in rainy London Town. The first of these was held in the cosy parlour of Bolster's lodgings in Ryder Street; a fragrant parlour, due to Strand's precision with such things as a steaming bowl, lemon peel, and cloves. By reason of that same bowl, now set on a trivet in the hearth, it had for a time been a merry parlour, but now Clay was dozing in his chair, and conversation had become desultory. Bolster was still pondering the one problem, and Strand, his brow deeply furrowed, his brain clouded with the fumes of the potent brew, stared at his glass, seeing again Lisette's small hand resting so fondly in Garvey's clasp, her glorious eyes smiling up at the man; hearing Garvey sneer, ". . . she tells me she is his wife in name only . . . she returns my affection as fully."

Bolster muttered, "Women! They're the very devil, dear old boy. You're perfectly contented until they come into your life and show you how much more wonderful it could be—and then, dashed if they don't turn around and take it all away!"

"Jeremy," said Strand, "you're drunk. Y'never stammer when y'drunk. Why's that, d'you s'pose?"

The mystery held Bolster's attention for some moments. "Don't know," he admitted at last. "Y'right though. P'raps I'd best stay drunk all the time, eh?"

"Good idea. I'll join you. Drink up, ol' fella." Strand lurched over to the bowl to refill their glasses. He spilled considerable of his first ladleful, a feat that made them both laugh so much there was no point in again attempting it until they were able to stop chortling. He managed the task eventually, by which time they both were seated on the rug before the hearth. Strand saluted Bolster gravely with the ladle, put it aside, and remarked that the more he thought on it, the better the idea seemed.

"What idea?" asked Bolster, blinking at him owlishly.

"Why, t'join you. When y'go to—to Europe with ol' Mitch Redmond."

Bolster lay down on the rug and howled with mirth. Propping himself on one elbow, he peered at Strand, who was watching him approvingly, and said a succinct, "Went."

"Y'did?" Strand frowned, digesting this. "Y'mean—y'already back? 'Magine that! Clay, ol' fella, d'you know Bolster's back? He don't answer, Jerry. Why won't he answer? Don't want to talk to th' laughingstock, eh, Marcus?" And awareness knifing through the fog, he drew a hand across his brow and sat hunched over and silent.

Bolster placed a consoling hand on that bowed shoulder.

"Should have done as I told you," he pointed out with a slight hiccup. "Never fails. Worked f'me." He sighed. "For a while. . . . Why don't we go to Africa? Might get eaten by lion, course. Or elephant. Do elephants eat people, d'you know, Strand?"

"I did try it," muttered Strand, rather lost in the maze of his friend's monologue. "Took me an age, but—waste. She—she never even owned she saw it."

"Oh," said Bolster, his hazel eyes filling with tears. "Thass so sad, ol' sportsman. I—can't bear it!"

Clay opened one eye, failed to locate his friends, stood, and promptly fell over them. When the hilarity over this feat had died down, he sat on the carpet with them and told them sternly, if indistinctly, that they were both thoroughly foxed. Their vociferous indignation did not convince him. "Must be," he said judicially. "Stands t'reason. You wouldn't be sitting on the floor was you sober. 'Sides, y'can't go anywhere, Strand. Not now."

"C'n go anywhere I want!" Strand flared. "Oh, you think m'wife would 'ject? Well—" he bent closer and leered confidingly—"when I come home after my li'l trip to Sil'vrings, she said—y'know what she said? She said I'd perfect right t'come an' go as—chose. So I choose to—go 'way." Having delivered himself of which, he curled up on the floor and went to sleep.

Clay said solemnly, "He don't know how t'handle women. Never did, Jerry. Silly fella should've told Lisette th' truth. She's spoiled on 'count of being so pretty, an' awful high in th' instep, but she's a good heart, y'know."

Bolster thought about this for a while, then offered, "No. Couldn't've. I couldn't. Could you? Under circumstances?"

" 'Course I could!" Clay paused, then amended slowly, "Well, p'raps not, but you ask me, ol' Justin got just's much pride as lovely Lisette. An'—" He swung around, waving an emphatic finger, only to find he'd lost Bolster again. Relocating him, comfortably settled with his head and shoulders propped against Strand's back, Clay bent and went on. "'Nother thing—that r'dic'lous business with Garvey—"

"Gad!" Bolster opened drowsy eyes. "Wasn't it famous to see his high an' mightiness back down like that? Wonder I didn't—laugh out loud."

"Mus'n laugh at James Garvey!" Clay warned. "Matter of fact, Jerry, been thinking. You'd best keep an eye on ol' Justin. Garvey's not th' type to let this go, an' Justin ain't thinking clearly jus' now."

Bolster yawned. "Glad to. You goin' t'keep eye . . . s'well, Marcus?"

"Wish I could, but—" Clay shrugged wryly—"got to go to Horse Guards. P'raps next time, Jerry. P'raps next time . . ."

The third meeting involved only two gentlemen. It was quieter than either of the others, but by far the more deadly.

Claude Sanguinet was one of those present. Apparently engrossed in the cuticles of his right hand, he was seated in a comfortable Sheraton chair in the sumptuous suite he maintained year round in London's luxurious Clarendon Hotel.

James Garvey was the other occupant of the room. Standing with one shoulder propped against the mantel, his brooding gaze on the leaping flames of the fire, he waited through a long silence, then, flinging around, demanded harshly, "Well? You had me brought here. Say what you want, and be done!"

"Why, my dear James," Sanguinet answered in the French he invariably resorted to in private, "you were not obliged to obey my—er—summons, did you not so desire."

"The devil I wasn't! That peasant, Shotten, would likely have rammed a knife under my ribs had I refused."

Claude smiled. "He is a loyal soul."

"A soul is something he knows as little of as do you know loyalty! You humbled me today, Claude! Forced me to my knees in front of half London. And after all I've done for you! Tell me of loyalty!"

"But, my dear friend"—Sanguinet waved a languid hand—"you brought it on yourself. Has it become good *ton* in London for a gentleman to so publicly repeat the confidences of a lady—and with her unfortunate husband present?"

"Justin Strand ain't begun to know what 'unfortunate' means!" snarled Garvey, his handsome features twisting to a singularly ugly expression. "This is no lightskirt we speak of, Sanguinet! I want the girl. And I mean to have her!"

"Over his—ah—dead body?" Sanguinet prompted, amused.

"I had rather he was alive to see it, but—damn his soul!—

yes! From the moment I saw Lisette Van Lindsay I knew she was born to be my wife. He stole her from me, not by his charm, and not by reason of her love, for she despises the clod! But because—damme how it galls!—because his was the larger fortune!"

Sanguinet chuckled. "You might, I believe, have dispensed with the adjective."

His fists clenching, Garvey scowled at the elegance of the Frenchman. "It *was* large, until you ruined me, just as you ruined Rupert Strand! I wonder does his son know of it."

"Do you know, James," purred Sanguinet, "almost, you bore me. If you chose to gamble and lose in one or two of the clubs I chance to own, that is scarcely to be laid at my door. Did I not help when you were desperate? Did I not provide you with home, servants, all the luxuries of the fine gentleman?—which, I may add, you are not, my James." He laughed, his light brown eyes shining as they met Garvey's murderous glare. "We suit, dear my friend. You have the useful connections. You can open those certain doors in London to which I require admittance. And I—I have the bottomless purse. We suit. It is the satisfactory arrangement."

"It did not suit me this afternoon! But for your interference I could have called out that brown-faced cit and removed him from my path."

"Cit? Surely, you are too harsh, my dear. But I collect you crave an exercise for your so renowned marksmanship. A ball straight to the heart, no?"

"No. When the time comes I shall place my shot through the liver, I think. With luck, it will take Strand a week to die."

His eyes suddenly icy, Sanguinet came to his feet. "Brutality disgusts me. Even when my loved brother Parnell was alive, some of his traits—" He broke off abruptly.

Seething, Garvey did not dare to speak his rage and instead goaded slyly, "Do you tell me then that *you* bear no malice toward Tristram Leith, after he ran off with your intended bride? That *you* plan no vengeance?"

"My plans are not to be shared with you." Sanguinet's dark head lowered, and when he raised it the look in the brown eyes that glittered from under his brows brought a dryness to Garvey's mouth. "I will tell you that this insult, it shall be dealt with. In time. But it is a matter not to be compared to your puny bunglings. I am no ordinary man, Garvey. This fact it would behoove you to remember. Always.''

Garvey knew a nervous impulse to laugh, but one did not laugh at Claude Sanguinet, especially not while that strange red gleam lit his eyes. He was mad, egocentric, and totally ruthless, but as deadly as Garvey was, he knew himself puny indeed, by comparison, wherefore his eyes fell and he was silent.

His mood changing in one of those inexplicable shifts that more than anything else had convinced Garvey the man rightly belonged in Bedlam, Sanguinet said amiably, "As to Strand, *mon ami*, do whatsoever you will.''

"But—you said . . .''

"*Mon Dieu!* Am I so abstruse? If you wish the fool destroyed— destroy him. But I am known to have been wronged by the family, and you are known to be my friend. I can afford no further breath of scandal. I must remain the injured party. So it is that there must be no possible way of connecting you—and thereby me—to the foolish little affair. Were you wise, my James, you would simply hire an assassin. Lord knows there are sufficient available.''

Garvey scowled. "No. It must be by my own hand.''

"As you wish. But I shall make myself very clear. Because of this Leith I am delayed. It will take me now many months, perhaps, before my plans against this so foolish government of yours, they come to fruition. I do not permit, James, that these plans be jeopardized, nor even slightly flawed, by reason of the lust . . . the clumsiness . . . of one man.'' His voice a purring caress, Sanguinet raised one hand gracefully, and asked, "Is understood?''

For a moment Garvey stared at him in silence. Then his tight lips relaxed into a grin. "Is understood.''

Chapter 13

Whatever criticisms may have been levelled at Lisette Strand, that of disinterest in the problems of her friends had never been among them. Despite her own anxieties, she had become extremely fond of Amanda, and walking with her towards the front door, she murmured, "I simply do not see why you must feel so unworthy. Surely, everyone knows that Winfield is only your half-brother. From what St. Clair told me, you were never close, and nobody holds his crimes over your head. To break poor Bolster's heart for such a reason seems—"

Amanda halted and turned to face her. "He is a *peer*," she said miserably. "His family goes back—oh, farther than the Conqueror and people might sympathize now Lisette but what if Winfield should—hang and they say he will what then?"

Her own rigid standards rearing their heads, Lisette ignored them and said stoutly, "If Jeremy cares not, that should be enough. Indeed, Amanda, the poor soul looks so disheartened. I wish you will reconsider."

"I cannot," Amanda sighed. "Only I cannot really hope that while he is across the sea he will find someone else and—and forget me. Oh do you think he will?"

"No, of course not, you silly goose. But is he leaving again, so soon? He has said nothing of it."

Amanda gave a gasp. "Has—said? He—is *back?* Jeremy is in England?"

"Good graciously! Did you not know?" Lisette cast a rather vexed glance at the front door. The afternoon was drawing to a close, the rainy skies having already darkened to the point that candles and lamps had been lighted. From outside came the sounds of revelry; one gathered that some gentlemen were considerably inebriated, probably as a result of a prolonged and convivial luncheon. She was about to instruct the lackey not to open the door until the drunkards had passed by when, to her annoyance, the man sprang to life and flung the door wide.

Singing uproariously, but not felicitously, since each warbled a different ballad, Strand and Bolster reeled into the hall.

Lisette's relief was mingled with irritation. Amanda dropped her reticule and, with a little yelp of fright, stood motionless.

Swaying uncertainly, Strand peered at his wife. He drew himself up, bowed low, almost fell, but recovered. "Hail, madam wife," he enunciated thickly. "I am . . . quite 'toxicated. When sober I—shall bid you farewell." He reached out gropingly, and the butler sprang to support him. Strand gestured to the stairs.

"Wait!" cried Lisette. "What do you mean? Where are you going?"

"Africa. Jerry 'n me. T'be eaten. C'mon, old f'la." And he reeled off, singing heartily into the amused butler's ear.

Lisette glared after him. All her worrying! All her fears and anxieties! A perfectly horrid afternoon, and he had come home in this revolting condition!

At the foot of the stairs, Strand flung up a peremptory hand, and Morse assisted him to turn around. "'Minds me," he said. "I shall have some caps t'pull with you, ma'am." He started off, paused once more and flung over his shoulder, "Whole . . . damn hat shop, 'n fact!" This reduced him to imbecility, apparently, and he negotiated the stairs giggling hilariously.

Throughout this brief interlude, Amanda had trembled before Bolster, and his lordship, much less inebriated than his host, had stood in mute shock before her. At last, his voice returning, he croaked, "Mandy . . . Mandy . . ."

"Jeremy," she replied yearningly, then rushed on. "I did not know you was here else I'd not have come I hope you are well I must go."

He leapt to snatch up her reticule and, clutching it to his breast, gulped, "No, I'm not. I'm drunk. But when I'm drunk I can speak, so I'm going to beg—to implore you to wed me, my dearest girl. You know how I adore you. Please, Mandy. Without you—" he shrugged eloquently—"there ain't nothing, 't'all."

Amanda pressed one hand to her lips, but shook her head.

He glanced around. Lisette was nowhere in sight; they were quite alone. Dropping rather weavingly to one knee, he stretched forth a hand beseechingly. "Mandy, you *must*. I cannot live like this. And you, my sweet love, you are not happy."

"Happy! Oh Jeremy I cannot I will not ruin your life, if I must I will run away and hide do not ask goodbye." And staying for neither hat, umbrella, nor cloak, she ran out into the rain and to her barouche which was just pulling up on the flagway.

Bolster knelt there in the hall, Amanda's dainty reticule still clutched to his bosom. Then he sprang up and reeled after her.

Lord Bolster, having summoned up a passing hackney in order to pursue his beloved, did not return that evening. Strand failed to put in an appearance at the dinner table, but Lisette was joined by Norman and Judith. They obviously had not yet heard of the incident at The Madrigal and, postponing a discussion of that unhappy development, Lisette told them her husband was engaged with friends but that she hoped he would return before it was time for them to leave. Norman was eager to discuss their visit to Lord Wetherby, which was to take place on the following morning, and Judith was anxious to secure Strand's approval of a swatch of fabric she had obtained while shopping that day. Lisette's opinion was sought, and her endorsement noted but without much enthusiasm, it being very apparent that Strand had become Judith's oracle in matters pertaining to fashion, failing the presence of Miss Wallace, who, having contracted a heavy cold, had been left in Sussex. The evening slipped away, Norman and Judith said their farewells and were driven back to Portland Place, and still there was no sign of Strand. Lisette resigned herself to waiting until the following day to hear what had transpired at The Madrigal. It was, she decided, as well, since it was unlikely that he would recover to the point of being able to converse coherently with anyone.

She accepted her candle from Morse, bade him good night, and went slowly upstairs, pondering the events of this unpleasant day. It was beyond belief that a man as well bred as James

Garvey should have been so vulgar as to bandy her name about in a gentleman's club, especially in so crude a fashion. How she would ever again be able to walk out in public, she could not think. The shock had obviously been sufficient to drive Strand into a bout of heavy drinking—a typical male reaction! One might suppose he would instead have had the kindness to come home and warn her of the rumours that had been spread about them. With her hand on the doorknob, she knew a pang of guilt. Poor Strand. Here she was feeling hardly done by, when he must have suffered the greater blow of hearing it in so public a way. No wonder he had challenged Garvey. Yet how strange that Garvey had apologized in such craven fashion, and why on earth should Claude Sanguinet have intervened? From all she'd heard one would think he would joyfully have encouraged a duel that must certainly have seen Justin slain. She shivered at the thought and hurried into her parlour. There was no sign of Denise, who usually sat before the fire in the evening, reading or sewing, and Lisette walked across to open her bedchamber door, calling, "Denise? Are you—"

Strand rose from the armchair beside the fire. "She is gone to bed, madam," he said coldly. "You shall have to do without her tonight, I fear."

He had changed into a smoking jacket of dark blue velvet and had discarded his cravat, his shirt lying open at the throat and very white against his bronzed skin. He appeared quite recovered from his earlier disgusting condition; he must, of course, have enjoyed at least five hours of sound sleep since he had returned home, but anger radiated from him, the brilliant eyes seemed to hurl fury, the lips were thin and tight, the jaw a fierce jut. Suddenly apprehensive, Lisette wished he had slept until morning.

"That is of no importance, Strand," she said, coming quickly into the room and closing the door behind her. "What a dreadful day you have had. I have heard a little of it, and am so thankful you are not to go out with Garvey, for I—"

"How touching," he rasped, his eyes glinting ever more unpleasantly. "Were you so concerned for my welfare, ma'am, you'd have done well to keep your tongue between your teeth."

Lisette's jaw sagged momentarily. "*Wh-what?* Do you dare to imply—"

"No, madam. I *imply* nothing. I *state* that your vulgar and irresponsible gabbling has caused one man to be ridiculed throughout London, and the honour of another to be hopelessly fouled! I trust you are well pleased."

For an instant she was quite powerless to reply and simply stood there, all but gaping at him. Then, she said in strangled voice, "You dare . . . you *dare* to believe *I* would have spread such—such crudities?"

"If report errs," he sneered, "if you did not in fact vaunt abroad your cleverness in having kept me at arm's length through most of our so-called honeymoon, perhaps you will tell me who else might have done so. And why!"

"I need tell you *nothing!*" Lisette raged. "But *had* I spread such revolting gossip, can you suppose I would have been so noble as to have omitted all mention of your—your bird of paradise, or whatever it is you call such?"

Strand's eyes widened. "Bird of— The devil! So *that's* it! The incalculably superior Lisette Van Lindsay Strand guessed her unworthy husband had left her for another woman! Oho! How that insufferable pride of yours must have been hurt! And thus you thought to teach me a lesson, did you, ma'am?"

"After the disgusting boasts *you* made before we were wed," she retaliated furiously, "I doubt there is *anything* I could teach you! In vulgarity, at least!"

"I cannot be responsible for the gabblemongering of a set of women! I will admit you have surprised me, however. And what could be more vulgar than that revolting little flirtation you engaged in with Garvey this—"

"*Vile!*" Trembling with wrath, Lisette snarled, "Despicable *creature!*"

"A poor defence, ma'am! I said you had surprised me. It was because I fancied you had eyes for a worthier man, but I should have known when I saw you hanging breathless on Garvey's lips this morning, that—"

Crouching, livid, she hissed, "*That . . . what . . . ?*"

"That right under my nose you have been conducting a sordid *affaire!* And that—no matter how intimate—every incident that transpired between us, was at once whispered into *his* eager ear! For *shame* madam! If this is a sample of the famous Van Lindsay breeding—"

"*Peasant!*" she screeched, in a voice that would have stunned her grandmother. "Foul—loathsome—money-grubbing *nabob!*"

Strand was livid with rage. His eyes narrowed, their expression so threatening as to have daunted a lesser girl as he stepped towards her.

Lisette was far too infuriated to be daunted. She sprang at him, one hand flashing upward to be seized in a grip of iron, but the other eluding his grasp. He jerked his face away, but her sharp nails raked across his ear and down his throat.

Strand grabbed her flying wrist and rasped out a pithy sentence in Tamil which it was as well she did not understand. The sight of the crimson streaks she had inflicted sobered her, and the glare in his eyes was frightening.

Fear came too late. Strand had lived a nightmare this day. He had been publicly shamed, derided and, immeasurably worse, betrayed by the very lady he idolized. Lisette's attack was the last straw. Scourged by disillusion and with his head throbbing brutally by reason of the afternoon's excesses, he thoroughly lost his temper. For the first time, Lisette felt the full strength of him as she was swept up in arms that were more like steel bands. She uttered a shriek as he sat on the end of the bed, swung her face down across his knees, and reached across to seize the hairbrush from her dressing table.

"By God!" he snarled through set teeth. "It is past time someone taught you a lesson, you spoiled, prideful little snob!"

Kicking and struggling, beating her fists wildly against his leg, Lisette squealed, "Do not *dare!*"

For answer, he held her with crushing force and brought her hairbrush whizzing down. Lisette heard the *whack* more than she felt the pain. Her eyes grew as big as saucers; her mouth fell open. Never in her life had she encountered uncontrolled fury. Never in her life had she been really spanked. She experienced both now. Six times that hairbrush rose and fell, and at the finish she was sobbing with rage and humiliation and pain.

White as death, past caring, Strand stood up so that she collapsed in a heap at his feet. Glaring down at her, he said breathlessly, "Do you ever claw me again, madam tabby, you will get twice that treatment! And do you *ever* breathe one word of our personal relationship to anyone save your immediate family, you will really feel my wrath!"

"Beast . . ." she sobbed. "Savage! You s-speak of Garvey with—with contempt, but *he* would never treat me . . . s-so."

"Then it is as well you're wed to me and not to him. And wed you are!"

"*Bought* is—is what you mean. Bought and p-paid for!"

She crouched on hands and knees, tears streaking her cheeks, her great eyes filled with hurt and shock; and the enormity of what he had done penetrated his anger at last. He still held the hairbrush and now flung it from him with such violence that it sent a vase of flowers toppling.

Instinctively, Lisette shrank.

"Get up!" he growled, and when she only drew farther from him, he picked her up and tossed her onto the bed.

"Do not—touch me!" she gasped out, cringing back, her lips twitching pitifully. "Do not *dare* to—to strike me again!"

"I'll not touch you, never fear. I've not the stomach for it! But one thing I demand, ma'am. Your vicious little intrigues have spread over all London Town. As a result, we must face them down. Together. I'll own my pride inferior to yours, but I'll not be mocked on *this* suit. Now or ever! Good night, Mrs. Strand." He stalked from the room, but closed the door quietly.

Lisette turned and, burying her face in the pillows, wept until she fell asleep from pure exhaustion.

The rain stopped shortly after midnight, and an hour later the clouds had dispersed, allowing the full moon to paint all London with its glory, silvering alike shabby houses and luxurious mansions, shops and squares, slums and church spires and palaces; turning the wet streets to rivers of light, and dimming the feebler glow of flambeaux and street lamps. Slanting through a certain upper window of the now silent house in Sackville Street, it shone benevolently on the man who sat slumped forward across a table, his fair head cradled on one arm, whole the other hand, clenched into a fist, beat and beat at the inoffensive tabletop.

Strand was not called upon to waken his bride the next morning. Coming heavy-eyed down the steps, he found Lisette and the horses waiting. She was exquisite in a habit of dark red merino cloth and a high-crowned pink hat with a red ribbon around it that fluttered out behind her. "Good morning, Mr.

Strand," she said in a voice of ice. "I am here to receive my orders."

Flushing, he swung into the saddle, and when they were out of earshot of the grooms, he said, "I'd not intended to start this early, but it is as well."

"Perhaps you would be so kind as to inform me what I must expect."

His flush deepened before that contempt, but he said steadily, "We shall attend every possible event for which we receive invitations. We will be inseparable; we will ride in the mornings, drive in the afternoons, visit the galleries and museums and, in short, be seen everywhere. And everywhere we are seen, we will bill and coo like a pair of damned lovebirds."

"Sickening!" she judged with a curl of the lip.

"But necessary. You must appear to dote on me, madam. And I—" he looked away and finished harshly—"will worship you with my every breath."

Lisette gave a brittle laugh. " 'Twould require a consummate performance. Do you feel capable of maintaining such a fraud, sir?"

He did not immediately answer, looking straight ahead, his posture unusually rigid. Then he turned fully to her, a sternness in his eyes she had never before witnessed. "We either convince London of our devotion, Mrs. Strand, or become its laughingstocks. You may take your pick."

Her lashes drooped. She felt suddenly wretched and said defiantly, "Oh, very well. When do we begin this foolish charade?"

"Now. Scene One commences this very moment and will continue for as long as we are in the public eye."

True to his word, he maintained an air of devotion whenever they encountered other riders. He also held to a moderate pace, for which Lisette was thankful, since she was finding riding to be a somewhat uncomfortable diversion this morning.

When they returned to the house, they breakfasted together, Strand apparently engrossed in *The Gazette,* and Lisette going through her letters. While the servants were in the room, they engaged in light conversation, but the moment they were alone, silence settled over them like a blanket. Rising to pull back his bride's chair, Strand told her that he was leaving to take up

Norman. "We visit Lord Wetherby this morning. This afternoon, you and I are invited to a musicale at Hilby House, and this evening we go to a small dinner party at the Moultons. I trust these engagements will not inconvenience you."

"Your trust is misplaced!" Lisette snapped. "I plan to shop with Judith this afternoon, and am in no humour for dining— even with John and Salia."

"Adjust your humour," he ordered dryly. "I have already accepted. You may shop with Judith tomorrow. For an hour."

Lisette glared at him and went upstairs. Denise greeted her with awed timidity, and several times Lisette found herself being watched with such sympathy that she was sure the servants were aware of what had transpired the previous evening. She made a great effort to appear calm and, having changed her dress, went into the parlour to write letters. Alone, she sharpened a quill, but instead of writing her letter, drew small circles in involved designs all over a sheet of paper. Whatever, she wondered miserably, was to become of her? Although she had entered a *mariage de convenance,* an odd rapport had sprung up between her and Strand. She had begun to enjoy his cheery way of bustling them all about, his humourous grin coaxing them into whatever he wished. She had begun to feel comfortable with him, sure that whatever she attempted would win his encouragement, and that behind his teasing was kindness and an unfailing generosity. She had not dreamt he ever would visit so ferocious a temper upon her. Never in her wildest fantasies had she imagined that she—one of the most nobly born debutantes in all England—would be brutally beaten! And so unjustly, for she had not been the one to spread those wicked rumours. Common sense said, "You should have told him the truth." Pride said, "Why? If he was so base as to suspect me—let him suspect! At all events, the damage is done! Whatever understanding may have existed between us is gone forever, and besides, much I care what he thinks!"

If she told Mama and Papa what he had done, they would insist that she leave him. It was a comforting thought, but brief. She dare not leave him; to do so would be a sure acknowledgement that the rumours sweeping the Town were absolute truth. They would all be disgraced, and Strand—Strand would be livid! He would come after her, beyond doubting! She shivered, but at once decided that if ever he again attempted to brutalize her, she would shoot him. Had she a pistol handy. She had never fired a pistol, but Timothy would teach her. He had returned to his Regiment after the wedding, but he certainly would come home on leave, sooner or later. She could not tell him *why* she wanted to learn how to shoot, of course. It might be rather awkward to ask for instruction so that she could murder her husband, but she'd be able to come up with some plausible reason, when the time came. Meanwhile, she could always use a knife if the need arose. But Strand, she thought broodingly, was so terribly strong: he would probably wrench the weapon from her before she'd had the chance to plunge it into him. Her circle went sadly awry, the contemplation of so dastardly a deed causing her hand to shake. Perhaps, if she did it at night, and did not look, she could manage it. But that seemed unsporting. And to wake one's sleeping husband purely to inform him that he was about to be stabbed seemed to rather diminish the chances for success. She tried to wish that James had handled the business for her, but found it impossible to whip up much enthusiasm for a duel between the two men. She finally came to the conclusion that she would humour her husband—until the scandal had died down—and then get a Bill of Divorcement.

It did not occur to her that this would create an even larger scandal and, satisfied with her decision, she wrote her letter and went downstairs. She was reading in the book room when Norman rushed in, highly elated, and proclaimed Strand to be a prince of brothers-in-law. "Such a splendid time we had!" he exclaimed excitedly, straddling a chair and beaming upon his sister. "Lord Wetherby—he was used to be Admiral Hawkhurst, you know—is the very best of men. I thought him rather gruff at first, but Strand explained my interest in shipping and we got to chatting, and we both agree upon so many things, including the great possibilities of steam, Lisette! And the end of it was, Strand and I are to refurbish an old yacht now in dry-dock at Silverings, before the weather turns, we hope! Is that not famous?"

For Norman's benefit, Lisette slanted a warm smile at Strand, who had wandered into the room and was half sitting against the reference table, swinging one booted foot and watching the youth's enthusiasm with faint amusement. "Lovely," she agreed.

"But I was not aware the weather had ever settled into a summer style, and you certainly cannot work on a boat in the rain."

Undampened, Norman said, "Just like a woman to throw a rub in the way before we've even begun. The yacht's shored up in the barn at present, Lisette, and we can do some of the work inside, before we have to—"

He was interrupted as Judith rushed in, her eyes enormous and her bonnet still on her head. "Lisette!" she gasped, having entered the room at such speed she did not even see her brother-in-law. "I just heard! Oh, how monstrous it is! What Mama will say, I dare not think! And *Grandmama!* But how splendid of Strand to call out Mr. Garvey!"

Norman sprang up, and exclaimed, "*What?* Justin—you never *did?*"

"Oh, it's all right, Norman," Judith intervened, eyes sparkling. "Strand flung a tankard of ale in his face, but Garvey turned craven, and—"

Strand, who had come to his feet when the girl arrived, said bleakly, "And that will be about enough, if you please, miss!"

"What a bag of moonshine!" snorted Norman, his uneasy glance lingering on his brother-in-law. "As if a famous Buck like James Garvey would back down—even for Strand." Strand said nothing, and Norman wailed, "Never say it *is* truth?"

"No." Strand gave a faintly apologetic smile. "I believe my glass contained wine, not ale."

"Oh . . . my God!" Norman groaned, clutching his dark locks.

Strand's smile faded. The topic heightened Lisette's nervousness, and she interjected hurriedly, "Were I you, Norman, I would not offend Strand. He is quite capable of beating you."

Norman sat down, but he still looked troubled. Strand's eyes fell. His scowl vanished, and he changed the subject.

The musicale at Hilby House was an ordeal Lisette would long remember. She had chosen to wear a new blue silk round dress with six rows of tiny frills at the hem, and despite the inclement weather, carried only a gossamer scarf looped across her elbows. Denise was admiring her beautiful mistress when Strand came in carrying a small, flat leather box. Slipping it onto the dressing table, he bent to kiss his wife's temple and murmur lovingly, "I am glad you chose the blue today, my sweet."

The abigail sighed romantically, and left them. Lisette glanced to the closing door. "Bravo. A good touch, sir."

"So I thought." He shrugged. "Wear this, if you please."

"As you command, my lord and master."

He opened the box savagely and took out a bracelet of gold filigree. Finely cut sapphires were set amongst dainty golden leaves and flowerets of tiny pearls, the workmanship so exquisite that Lisette's breath was taken away. "Oh!" she gasped. "How *very* pretty it is."

"I brought it back from India," he imparted grudgingly, "but thought it too large, so Rundell and Bridge have sized it for me."

So he had not bought it purely for effect. Or perhaps he had intended it for his bird of paradise, and changed his mind so as to make a gesture in view of their present situation. Frowning, she watched him fasten it about her wrist and was struck by the thought that his thin fingers were so gentle now, whereas last night . . . She trembled involuntarily. Strand looked down at her in brooding silence, bowed, and went out.

They were quiet in the carriage, but from the moment they walked into the magnificence of Hilby House he was every inch the adoring lover, the bewitched slave. Struggling to appear as infatuated, Lisette more than once caught a glint of amused appreciation in his blue eyes, and when she sighed audibly as he provided her with a chair, he bent above her and murmured with a doting smile, "Not too much syrup, m'dear—lest they suspect."

Patting his cheek, she cooed, "I strive only to be as cloying as you, dearest love."

He nodded, took up her hand, and kissed it.

Each was aware of the many eyes that followed their every movement. Quite a number of those eyes surveyed Lisette with disapprobation. It was a new experience, and she apprehended with a distinct shock that Strand's belief that she had been engaging in an *affaire* with Garvey was not an isolated one. She had refused to believe that others would accept the tale and for the first time appreciated her husband's present strategy.

The Duke of Vaille came over to remark on Lisette's beauty and engage Strand in low-voiced conversation. His lovely fiancée, Charlotte Hilby, bending to Lisette's ear, said softly, "Don't be frightened, dear. Most of them do not really believe it. They will soon forget." Lisette was so moved by this kindness that a lump rose in her throat and she could not speak. She squeezed Miss Hilby's hand and blinked her thanks. The musicale began, and for a terrible few seconds she felt quite unable to face down all these critical, shallow people who'd not had the decency to know her above such despicable behaviour. She was shaking and, in her already overwrought condition, knew she would burst into sobs at any moment. Strand leaned to her and murmured with a tender smile, "Keep your chin high, best beloved. Concentrate on Leith—that should bring you safely through!" She was at first flabbergasted, then so infuriated that she did indeed come "safely through" the ordeal. But she did not concentrate on Leith. Instead, she dwelt with wicked delight on the scene in court when she should plead for divorce. And all the delicious things she would tell the judge.

Intermission came, and everyone adjourned to the large dining room where long tables held a tempting array of delicacies, and many small tables and chairs were set about. Strand seated Lisette at a corner table and went off to fill a plate for her. Returning, he made his way through the knot of dashing young gentlemen that had formed about her, and sat down. Her admirers scattered. Lisette breathed, "What a vicious thing to have said to me! And you've no reason for jealousy—there has never been a romance between Leith and me."

"Perhaps." He took up a macaroon and held it to her lips. "But you were, like Wellington's rope, about to break. So I tied a knot. You shall not disgrace me again, madam wife."

Raging, she opened her mouth to retaliate, but he popped the entire macaroon into her mouth, then watched with revolting admiration as she struggled to cope gracefully, her indignation effectively silenced.

The musicale ended, but for Lisette and Strand the masquerade had barely begun. Day after day their deception was enacted at dinner parties, routs, *ridottos*, and balls. They wined and dined and danced until the early morning, went home to snatch a few hours of sleep, then were up again and off to ride in the park. The days were a whirl of morning calls and callers, shopping or walks, luncheons, afternoon card parties, *soirées,* or concerts, and then home to put on their evening finery once more.

Strand seemed tireless, turning his mocking grin on Lisette if she dared commence a yawn, so that she would open her sleepy eyes very wide and fight to conceal her exhaustion. After ten days of this, she was so tired that when he ushered her into her bedchamber one night, she murmured a numbed, "Thank you, my dear one," and was mortified when he chuckled, "Oho, what a *faux pas!* We are quite alone, ma'am!"

"Whatever the words, sir," she said loftily, "my feelings remain the same. As do yours for me."

She stole a glance at him from under her lashes and saw a sadness come into his eyes. "What a pity it is," he said slowly, "that we cannot deal together better than this."

Lisette shrugged and strolled over to remove her earrings. When she looked up, he had gone, and she sat there, her shoulders slumping, tired and dispirited. She no longer carried Garvey's poem in her bosom, for she found of late that it was difficult to meet Strand's eyes when she did so. Now, she went to the drawer where her handkerchiefs were kept, and unearthed it from beneath the pile. Once again, the words brought a deep sigh, a yearning for the might-have-been. Replacing it slowly, she wondered if James still cared for her, if he sat somewhere in the great city at this very moment, breaking his heart for her. . . .

Her gaze drifted down the little column of handkerchiefs, all neatly ironed, their lace edges so daintily feminine. She did not at once discern the handkerchief Grandmama had fashioned for her—the last one she had crocheted before gout made it too difficult for her poor hands. Dear Grandmama had been used to make such exquisite lace. Because of her love for the old lady, that handkerchief was particularly dear to Lisette's heart. She began to search, but without success. Surely she had not lost it? Upset, she started for the bell pull, but it was almost three o'clock, she could not disturb Denise at this hour. She would ask her about it in the morning.

The next morning, however, all thought of the missing handkerchief was banished when Lisette awoke to a subdued murmur of activity. For a moment she lay drowsing, then it came to her that others were already stirring. She sat up with a start and snatched up the little porcelain clock from the table beside her bed. Half-past nine! With a gasp, she tugged on the bell pull and flung back the curtains of the bed. She was halfway to the window when the door opened and Strand strode in, booted and spurred. He marched past her, threw open the heavy curtains to admit a flood of sunlight, and turning to her said briskly, "So you're awake at last, ma'am!"

She drew herself up. She prided herself on not once having been late since her first initiation into his heathen custom of rising with the dawn. "I wonder you did not come and haul me out of my bed," she said regally.

His eyes flickered over the revealing nightgown she wore. "It would have been worth it, at that," he nodded. "But I judged you needed your sleep since we return to Sussex today."

Scurrying for a wrapper, Lisette pulled it closer about her. "You might have had the common courtesy to tell me!" she expostulated. "There were things I wished to purchase before we returned to the Hall!"

He frowned. "My apologies. I'd not decided until the day dawned fine. Can you send your maid for what you want? We can delay until eleven, but I would prefer to leave as soon as possible." The door again opened, and Denise started in, then paused uncertainly. Strand added a gentle, "Will that suit, my love?"

Lisette motioned to Denise to enter. "Of course," she purred. "I can scarce wait to get back to the country again. I'll be as quick as I can, dear."

He stared down at her, then suddenly bent, and pulling her to him, kissed her full on the mouth. For an odd moment, surprise had the effect of making Lisette feel giddy, so that she instinctively flung her arms about his neck, to keep from losing her balance. He released her, but his head remained down-bent, his lips very close as he gazed into her eyes with an ineffable tenderness. Then, the quirk touching his mouth for the first time since his confrontation with Garvey, he murmured, "How's that for acting, ma'am?"

Breathless, she answered, "Not . . . markedly amateurish, sir."

He nodded. "Probably out of practice."

* * *

A few subsequent discussions with Lord Wetherby had caused Strand to entertain second thoughts regarding the scope of their nautical undertaking. As a result, he'd sent an urgent letter round to Ryder Street, inviting the unsuspecting Bolster to accompany them back into Sussex. His lordship joined them shortly before they were to depart, and although Strand felt obliged to divulge the trap into which he had walked, Bolster was far from being dismayed and, in fact, welcomed the prospect of some hard work.

They set forth, the men riding, Lisette and Judith occupying the chaise, and the servants and the luggage following in a large travelling carriage. The little cavalcade enjoyed good weather for as far as Croydon, where they stopped to take luncheon at the Red Griffin. Before they left the famous old posting house, a few dark clouds had managed to spread over the entire sky and it began to rain. The gentlemen therefore decided to complete the journey inside the chaise. Always the best of companions, Bolster started a round tale in an effort to entertain the younger occupants of the vehicle. He had become comparatively at ease with them, so that he stuttered less, and having quite a flair for comedy had them all chuckling at his first chapter. Looking around at their amused faces, he said, "Chapter Two!" and pointed at Judith. Delighted, that damsel indulged her flair for the dramatic so that from a light love story it became full of gloom, dungeons, and sinister figures slinking about, wrapped in dark cloaks. Norman was selected as the next story-teller, and he launched with gusto into Chapter Three, whereupon the principal Evil Tyrant, Baron Klug, became very evil indeed, pursuing a fair and innocent clergyman's daughter, causing Sir Roderick, the gallant young hero, a great deal of misery, and bringing him at length into the very shadow of the guillotine.

"Lisette!" ordered Bolster.

"Oooh! Do hurry!" cried Judith eagerly. "I can scarce wait to hear what happens next!"

Lisette decreed that the innocent clergyman's daughter had not been standing idly by whilst all this was going on. She had, in fact, by means of an alluring disguise, gained admission to the dungeons where languished the hero's brave friends, and had so captivated the gaolers that she was allowed to take water to the miserable captives.

"An enterprising lass," murmured Strand. "Perhaps she's not quite as innocent as we thought!"

This brought a laugh from Norman and, from Judith, a scold not to interrupt.

Continuing with her chapter, Lisette said, "One by one, Isabelle lured the guards into the cell where they were swiftly and silently overcome by the prisoners. Seizing the weapons of their former captors, Roderick's friends also exchanged their poor rags for the fine uniforms the guards wore. Then, marching boldly into the square, they forced their way through the ululating mob to—"

"The—what mob?" Strand interrupted curiously.

"Ululating," said Lisette with a defiant stare.

"What does that mean?"

"You know perfectly well what it means! And if you spoil my—"

"Oh, never mind," Norman put in impatiently. "It means howling, Justin."

"Thank you," said Strand. "I likely forgot the expression whilst I was in India. Cannot recall it was widely used over there."

"From what I had heard," said Lisette, trying to restrain a smile, "you should have heard lots of ululating. You must have been in a very dull part."

"Then cheer him up with the rest of this exciting story!" wailed Judith.

"The—er—ululating mob . . ." prompted Strand.

"Oh, yes. Isabelle made her way to the guillotine just as poor Roderick's head was forced onto the block. Baron Klug's hand was upraised in the signal. The great blade glittered in the torchlight, and then Isabelle's knife sliced Roderick's bonds, and he sprang to his feet even as the blade of the guillotine came crashing down. 'Hold!' cried the Evil Tyrant, and—"

The cry of the Evil Tyrant woke Bolster, who had dozed off in the warm carriage. Feeling very remiss in his duties, he yelped, "Chapter Five—Strand!"

"Good heavens!" cried Strand. "Shoddy Rick flung—"

"*Rod*erick!" Lisette corrected sternly, over Bolster's hilarity.

"My apologies, m'dear. Roderick flung up his knife. The Evil Tyrant's sword flashed to meet it. And there on the gallows with the crowd hushed and silent about them, they fought; the blades hissing and ringing as they engaged, the two men striving in a desperate fight to the death, the crowd—a sea of upturned faces—lit by the torches' glare. And then gallant Roderick slipped on the uneven flooring of the scaffold. With a great sweep of his sword, the Evil Tyrant sent the dagger spinning from Roderick's hand. The hilt of Klug's sword flashed upwards and caught brave Roderick beneath the chin. Down he went, like a sack of meal upon the boards. A mighty roar went up from the breathless crowd, and—''

''Hey, wait up!'' cried Bolster, who had become interested. ''You've got th-things all wrong, old fella.''

''I have not,'' said Strand, affronted. ''It's my part of the story. I can do as I please, can't I, Norman?''

''Well, yes, but—''

''But what became of poor Isabelle?'' asked Judith anxiously.

Strand took up Lisette's hand and kissed it. ''Oh,'' he said, ''she married the Evil Tyrant. It is the way of real life, you know, Judith.'' He turned to his wife and, remarking the dimple that swiftly vanished, asked with his teasing grin, ''Ain't that right, beloved?''

With perfect justification, Lisette refused an answer.

Chapter 14

Strand Hall was gleamingly impressive in the late afternoon sunlight. Mrs. Hayward and Fisher came out onto the porch to greet the family and welcome his lordship, and Brutus went quite berserk, rushing from one owner to the other, barking madly, and leaping about, succeeding in muddying everyone until Strand cowed him with a firm *"Down!"* Despite the warm welcome they were accorded, Strand was quick to note the trace of worry in the eyes of both his butler and housekeeper. Rumour, he realized, had spread on the usual lightning links between servants' halls, and his people likely were aware of everything that had transpired in London.

Since the supplies for the boat venture were to be delivered at Silverings, the men left directly after breakfast the following day to supervise the unloading. Returning to the drawing room after watching them ride off, Lisette asked Judith what Miss Wallace had said of her various lengths of material.

"Oh, she thought it very well done," Judith said happily. "We were to start on the beige wool half-dress today, but I neglected to buy the braid, so we'll likely make up the pink velvet instead."

"I *am* sorry, dearest! That wretched Strand! He rushed us so, I knew we would forget something."

"No, but he has been so good." Judith slipped an arm about her as they started to the stairs. "I often think how he has changed all our lives. Can you credit the difference in my brother? I wonder Strand can bear it, he pesters him so.''

''He does?''

''Why, yes. Have you not noticed how Norman trails after him? He has taken your husband for his model, I suspect, and I doubt could have found a finer one.'' Slanting an oblique glance at her sister, Judith read surprise in that lovely face, and added hurriedly, ''Norman fairly badgered Strand to hurry our leaving yesterday, so we can scarce blame the poor man that I did not have time to purchase my braid.''

Lisette pondered those words in the morning when she began to sort through the correspondence she'd not had time to attend to the previous day. She had not known their hurried departure had been the result of her brother's manoeuvrings, and wished she had not scolded Strand so. Still, Judith might find less to admire in her brother-in-law did she know he beat his wife! And afterwards made not the slightest attempt to woo her forgiveness. The only time he'd really kissed her since the spanking episode had been in her bedchamber yesterday morning, and that only to impress Denise. The abigail had immediately left, of course, but her merry eyes had later conveyed quite clearly that she had seen that warm embrace. Lisette blushed a little as she remembered the touch of Strand's lips, the strong hands gripping her shoulders. How wonderful to be kissed like that by someone who really cared; how wonderful if so sweet a caress was followed by words of passionate adoration, instead of being quizzically asked if her husband's acting was adequate. . . . Did he treat his blond bird of paradise so? Or was there no need to act with that lady? She frowned and tore an invitation to fragments without first having read it. He would doubtless have again sought out his peculiar had he not been so busied with convincing all London Town that he adored his bride. Now that they were back in Sussex, however, he would probably lose no time in going to her. Lisette scowled at the torn scraps of paper between her fingers. Was that why he had offered to help Norman work on the boat? She'd thought it an excessively kind gesture, but perhaps it was merely a means to leave his wife while he consoled his amour. If truth be told, Strand actually meant to spend very little time at—

"Your pardon, madam," murmured the lackey, carrying in a calling card.

Lisette whirled on him. "What is it?" she snapped.

The lackey blinked, and made a rapid readjustment of his private opinion that Mrs. Strand was as calm and gentle as she was lovely.

A picnic was prepared the following morning, the girls having indicated an interest in viewing the efforts of the amateur shipbuilders. Two hampers were loaded into the chaise, together with the kitchen maid who was to preside over the feast. Her qualifications were evidently questionable, for no sooner were the hampers installed than Brutus leapt into the vehicle. The maid's resultant hysteria alarmed the animal, but did not undermine his guarding instincts. As a result, demands to "get out at once!" were met with a craven crouch and much whining, but a marked disinclination to obey. Bolster, feeling responsible for the dog's behaviour, volunteered to ride in the chaise and protect the maid, an excitable French emigrée who was niece to the cook and quite sure she would be devoured was "the beast *énorme*" not allowed into the hamper. Strand said with some heat that no servant or guest of his was going to be inconvenienced by a confounded bacon-brained mongrel, but his preparations to oust the dog brought forth nervous protests from the ladies, while the maid declared she was about to fall into a fit. Outnumbered, he abandoned the effort and they started off, only an hour later than had been originally intended.

The day was misty but with a promise of brightness that materialized to warm sunshine by the time they reached Silverings. Once again, Lisette's heart lightened when they dismounted before the ruins, and Judith, who had not previously visited the estate, was enraptured and roamed about eagerly, exploring and admiring. The supplies for the boat renovations had been stored in the barn, together with the *Silvering Sails,* just now looking like nothing so much as a derelict fit only for firewood. Lisette said as much, but her brother indignantly proclaimed that the "old lady" was perfectly seaworthy and that a few repairs and new paint and varnish would work wonders with her.

"But it is enormous!" said Judith dubiously.

"It!" Norman snorted. "*She*, Judith! *She!*"

"Whether an 'it' or a 'she,' the fact remains that you have, as usual, bitten off much more than you can chew, brother dearest!"

"Pooh! Nonsense! Strand and I will have it done in the wink of an eye!"

"Well, we—er—might require some helpers," Strand said cautiously.

"Oh, no!" cried Norman in tragic accents. "I had thought this was *our* undertaking, Justin. Just the two of us!"

"And m-m-me," Bolster put in aggrievedly.

"Yes. You, of course, Jerry. Strand, never say you mean to import common *workmen?* Only think, we have Silverings close at hand. Do we decide to work late, we can always stay overnight."

"From the size of your boat," remarked Lisette, watching Strand from under her lashes, "you might be obliged to move down here for a year—or more.'

He considered her with a level, dispassionate gaze and said quietly, "It's an idea, ma'am."

The gentlemen now became extremely occupied with an inspection of the vessel. She was a small yacht but, being shored up, did indeed look enormous in the barn. A flying spark from the fire that had gutted most of the house had ignited her sails, burnt the roof of the cabin, and well scorched the deck and the rails before the fire had been extinguished. The hull was sound, said Norman, but all the woodwork needed refinishing, new masts would have to be fitted, and the cabin rebuilt. The talk here became very technical; Lisette became lost in a discussion of shrouds and jibs and something called "the mizzen." Judith drifted quietly away and, eventually following her example, Lisette wandered into the sunshine.

There was no sign of Judith, but a merry conversation was being conducted in the livable part of the house, so it was likely the girl was inside, talking with the gardener's wife. Lisette started to join them, but a sudden image of a dressing table holding a small bottle of scent rose before her mind's eye, and she decided she did not care to go in just at the moment. Brutus was sitting beside the Dutch door, either guarding the house or the picnic hamper that had been carried there. Lisette sat on a bench for a while, enjoying the sunshine and stroking the dog. He howled when at length she stood and started to walk away, but although she called him and he wriggled eagerly, he could not bring himself to desert his post and sat moaning as she strolled away.

There was such peace here, thought Lisette. The cries of mudhens and ducks, the soft splashing sounds of the river, the sweet fragrance of flowers. How Rupert Strand could have disliked Silverings, was—

"Pssst!"

Startled, she glanced around. She was by now out of sight of house and barn and it was quite lonely. . . . And then the low hanging branches of a willow tree parted. A handsome, eagerly smiling face was revealed. A gloved hand beckoned imploringly. For an instant, Lisette was too shocked to move. Then, hurrying to him, she cried, "Garvey! My God! Are you mad? If Strand sees you—"

"Much I care." He took her hand and drew her into the leafy privacy created by the gracefully trailing branches. Pressing her fingers to his lips, he murmured, "Oh, my dear—my beautiful love! If you but knew how—"

Recovering her wits, she pulled her hands away. "I do indeed know, sir! I know the dreadful things you said to my husband! Flagrant untruths! And I know why! You thought to provoke him into a duel!"

"Of course." His adoring eyes searched her face. "You must have guessed what I was about. I know of no other way to free you from your wretched bondage, and can only offer my deepest apologies that I failed you."

"Failed me!" With a little cry of horror, she stepped back. "Mr. Garvey, I fear your intellect must have become disordered. When did I ever suggest so dreadful a thing? Why would you suppose I—"

For answer he all but sprang to take her in his arms, saying breathlessly, "Your eyes, your smiles—you have told me in a thousand ways that my affections are returned. Never feel ashamed, beloved. You were not to blame for that travesty of a marriage!"

"Stop! Oh, stop!" she cried, fighting to free herself. "If I gave you such an impression, I am heartily sorry for it. I was deeply moved by the poem you writ me, but I'd not meant to encourage your hopes."

He stared at her. "My poem? You—ah, liked it, then?"

"Liked it! I thought it the loveliest thing. And it came at a time when I was rather downhearted. Truly, I was exceeding grateful, but—"

"It came from my soul." He smiled. "Lisette, you do not love that ill-bred boor. He has neither looks nor address, and aside from his fortune is totally beneath you! If—"

Her hands clenched into small fists, her eyes flashing, Lisette flared, "How dare you speak so of my husband! Ours may not have been a love match, but Strand has been all that is good! Our only real quarrel was occasioned because you told him such wicked lies!"

"For which the brute beat you savagely, so I heard!" He sank to one knee before her, looking up, and said in a near-groan, "Lord! When I heard of it I thought I must run mad! Your beautiful self abused by that crudity who is not worthy to kiss your little shoe! And now, in your sweet loyalty, you defend the creature! How like you! Oh, Lisette! Lisette! To think I brought such misery upon the lady I worship!"

His voice broke with the intensity of his emotion, and bending lower, he seized the hem of her dress and pressed kisses upon it. Aghast, Lisette drew away, staring down at him. Judith was not the only Van Lindsay to harbour a romantic nature. Beneath Lisette's cool and graceful poise beat a heart yearning for the romance she now feared would never come her way save, as Grandmama had implied, through the "side door." She had been revolted by Garvey's behaviour, and she had no wish to take him for a lover, but his tender poem and this abject display of worship could not but move her. Thus, instead of firmly rebuking him, as she knew she should do, she said rather unsteadily, "What you have heard or—or been told, I cannot guess. But, I do assure you that Strand has never—"

He came to his feet in a lithe bound and gripped her arms. "I have heard only what all London has heard. Ah, never look so pale, dear loyal soul! Did you think to silence servant-hall gossip? Rumours swept Town like wildfire and before noon the next day everyone knew. Many discounted the tales. Not I! I knew all too well how that crude savage would serve you, God forgive him!"

"No!" she cried in desperation. "Whatever people say, Strand has never been really brutal to me. You should not have come here, James. I am married, and—"

"Yes, so you told me once before, my dearest. Married past redemption, you said, but—"

"I did not! That is—I did not mean it in *such* a way. I was—I had not— Oh, *why* will you persist in—"

He tightened his hold as she attempted to draw back. "You promised," he intervened tenderly, "to send for me if he ill-treated you. Why did you not? Did you think I had failed you in the matter of the duel, and would fail again?" He overrode her shocked denial, and went on in a louder voice, "I was compelled, my adored Fair. Claude Sanguinet once discovered a slight indiscretion committed by a member of my immediate family. He threatened to make the matter public if I oppose him in the Strand situation."

Intrigued, despite herself, Lisette asked, "But why? One would think he had every reason to loathe the Strands after Rachel jilted him and married Leith. Why would he choose to stop your duel?"

"Because I am known to be his friend. He does not want it thought that my challenge to Strand was issued at his instigation."

She frowned. "It all sounds most weird. But the important thing is that you must go at once, and forget about me. How you found me here, I cannot think, but—"

"I followed you. I have been staying in Horsham, praying for a chance to see you, and was watching the Hall when you left this morning."

Touched, she said, "James, I am so sorry. But you must find another lady!"

He drew her closer. "Foolish little love. How could I exist were I to give up hope that someday you and I will—"

"Lisette? Lisette . . . where are you?"

Lisette paled. "Bolster! Oh, heavens! James, you *must* go!"

"Only if you promise to meet me."

He bent to kiss her, but she swung her face away. "No! Can you not accept my refusal? I do not want to hurt you, but you *must* not continue to pursue me!"

"Li-sette . . . ?"

The voice was very close. With a frightened gasp, she tore free. "Go! For pity's sake, *go!*" she hissed desperately, and stepping

• *211*

into the sunshine again, came almost face to face with Lord Bolster. "Here I am," she cried smiling, but her heart racing with fright. "Is the boat finished then, my lord?"

She could not know how white and frightened she looked. Bolster frowned, and his eyes shifted to the leafy screen behind her.

"Yes. And S-Strand and Norman ready to sail off to sea, taking our f-foo f-foo- luncheon with them. I thought you had become lost and have been looking for you this age."

"I am sorry to have wandered off," she said contritely, "but it is so lovely here."

A branch snapped behind her. His expression unwontedly grim, Bolster stepped towards the tree. Horrified, Lisette took his arm and all but babbled, "You must explain this strange business of restoration to me, for I would—" She stopped, her great eyes becoming wider as she saw that Strand was coming briskly towards them.

Bolster's suspicions were by now so thoroughly aroused that he would not have been in the least surprised had James Garvey leapt from concealment brandishing a pistol. But because he was both fond of Lisette and sincerely sorry for Strand, he essayed the travesty of a laugh and stammered, "I f-found your b-br-br lovely w-w-wife, J-Justin."

Stand looked at him thoughtfully. "So I see."

Justin Strand had contrived to exist for close to thirty years without experiencing the adoration of the waters that inspired so many of his fellow Britons. He had read Thomas Traherne's immortal observation, "You never enjoy the world aright, till the sea itself floweth in your veins . . ." and had been unmoved by it. He had been obliged to spend a good deal of time on shipboard and, although not plagued by sea sickness, had considered the interminable journey to India (which had taken the better part of four months) a dead bore. It would, in fact, never have occurred to him to go to the trouble and expense of rebuilding *Silvering Sails* had he not become fond of Norman. He had soon realized that the youth he'd at first been inclined to write off as a lazy do-nothing had all the makings of a fine young man, whose greatest vice was boredom. Suspecting that the boy's initial hostility towards him had been inspired by a deep devotion to Lisette,

Strand judged this not only understandable, but commendable, while the pranks were more the products of youthful spirit and a sense of humour than an intent to harm. He should have been sent away to school. It was a great pity that Humphrey Van Lindsay had been unable to provide the needed funds to permit this. Strand, however, did have the funds, and with typical zest he set about arranging for Norman's future. It would require time for his schemes to materialize, and meanwhile the refurbishing of the yacht might not only keep the boy happily occupied for the balance of the summer but also provide them with a boat once again, if only for use on the river.

By the end of the week it became very apparent that Strand's earlier misgivings had been justified. The task would take a deal more time than he appreciated. In an effort to expedite matters, he drove himself and his small crew hard. Bolster and Norman were thoroughly enjoying themselves, but by the end of the day they were all so tired and dirty that they took to remaining at Silverings, just as Judith had foretold.

Strand Hall seemed quiet and subdued with no gentlemen about, and Lisette commenced to feel a grass widow, for once again her husband had vanished from her life. She was grateful for Judith's company and warmed by the knowledge that her brother was undoubtedly having the time of his life.

On Friday of that week, Bolster succeeded in severely wrenching his elbow while carrying a heavy board. Strand accompanied the casualty back to the Hall. He was mildly surprised not to be met by Brutus, whom Lisette had insisted on retaining "for protection." The dog usually staged a welcoming ritual that might have led the uninitiated to suppose he was suffering severe convulsions. Today, however, although there was not the slightest breeze, Brutus was noticeable by his absence. The entire house, in fact looked deserted and, assisting Bolster from the saddle, Strand was relieved to find Best and a stableboy running to greet them and take charge of the horses.

"I'm glad to see there's someone about," he said. "What's to do, Best?"

"The mistress and Miss Judith has gone to a fête at Park Parapine," said the groom, looking worried. "They was expected back afore this."

"Then they will undoubtedly arrive at any moment. Mrs. Strand is very punctilious in such matters. I've left Green at Silverings with Mr. Norman. Is Fisher here? Or Mrs. Hayward?"

"Mr. Fisher and Lang do have goed to Dorking for supplies, sir. And Mrs. Hayward be all on end."

"The devil! Well, then, you must come. Let the boy take the horses. Lord Bolster's knocked himself up a trifle and will need our help."

With the stableboy obediently leading the horses stableward, Best accompanied his master and Lord Bolster to the front door, at which point Strand said curiously, "Dorking? Why Dorking?"

"Fer supplies, sir. Mrs. Hayward said Horsham would not do."

"Why ever not? Have we company?"

They stepped into the deserted hall. Strand thought to hear voices upraised in dispute, and Best nodded toward the back of the house and muttered, "I'll help his lordship upstairs, sir. Belike you'll wish to greet your people."

Bolster grinned, but his eyes were strained; the ride he had insisted would be child's play had not only taxed him, but had served as warning that the foolish little accident had done more than wrench his elbow. The old wound in his shoulder was making itself felt in such a way he would be obliged to take himself to Town and let Lord Belmont prod and poke about again. "Go-go on, Justin," he urged. "Cannot neglect your—ah, people."

Exasperated, Strand fumed, "Of all times for the house to be empty as a confounded drum! Who the deuce do we entertain?"

"Your lady's family, sir," Best offered glumly.

"Oh, good God!" groaned Strand. "My apologies, Jeremy, but I must welcome them. Should you wish that I send for the midwife?"

"*Midwife?*" Bolster echoed in a near-scream. "What the d-devil—?"

"'Fraid it's the best we can do, my dear fellow. There's no doctor close by. Old Bellows always visits his mother in Wales at this time of year."

"Oh. Well, I'll have n-no midwife laying her hands on my p-poor elbow! Matter of fact—" Bolster paused on the stairs and resting one hand on the railing, said reluctantly, "M-may have to go back to T-town. Dreadful of m-me, but . . . there 'tis."

Strand's heart sank. He had hoped, selfishly, the Bolster would, in his good-natured fashion, bear Norman company for a week or two, so that he himself could come back here occasionally during the process of rebuilding the boat. Norman was working well, but he should not be left down at Silverings alone. It was utterly reprehensible, of course, that he'd even entertained such inhospitable notions, but dear old Jeremy had seemed to enjoy the work, and it might have taken his mind off his own troubles. Scanning his friend's face, he saw the strain in the hazel eyes and, his scheming forgotten, said sharply, "Damn it! You twisted that shoulder! I should have driven you straight to Town! What a gudgeon I am! I'd clean forgot! I should never—"

"Confound you, Justin!" Bolster interrupted angrily. "*Will* you b-be still? I shall d-do nicely if I rest a little." He lifted one hand to quiet Strand's impassioned attempt to intervene, and went on, "You forget I was in a b-blasted great brawl with St. Clair last year, without no trouble. Except I lost a tooth. I'd have d-done well enough had I not t-tripped over my own f-feet. Now get on about your business." He winked, took another step, then threw over his shoulder, "And do not *dare* let that m-midwife near me!"

Best aided his lordship up the stairs, listening with amusement to the young nobleman's indictment of friends who threatened their guests with such fiendish ploys as to visit midwives upon them.

Strand stood for a moment, listening to this profane monologue and watching his friend anxiously. What Bolster said was true; the war wound had not bothered him for a long time. He should have remembered, though, and would have given a good deal not to have been responsible for Bolster being plagued by a resumption of the trouble. A muffled shout recalled him to his present obligations and, accepting the inevitable, he ran a quick hand through his rumpled locks and hurried along the hall.

Turning the corner, he halted, astonished. The under-footman knelt with one eye pressed to the keyhole of the book-room door, while the lackey hovered mirthfully beside him.

"There he goes!" whispered the footman, waving his arms excitedly. "Oh, what a sight! I wish—"

"You had best wish I do not send you packing!" Strand's thunderous growl brought the footman springing up so hurriedly that his head slammed against the lackey's nose. Two horrified faces whipped toward their employer. The lackey gave a gasp and fled. Scarlet, the footman, opened the door, but was too unnerved to utter a single word of announcement. Fixing him with a smouldering glare, Strand walked in, only to again check, his eyes widening.

The Van Lindsays had arrived some time earlier, and Humphrey had decided not to waste his time. Holding several sheets of paper in one hand and gesturing dramatically with the other, he paced the room, blasting forth his rhetoric while his wife trotted around and about him, alternately cajoling, raging, and scolding, all to no purpose. Brutus pranced along beside her, thoroughly enjoying his new indoor sport. Even as Strand, his lips curving to a grin at this scene, entered the room, Philippa halted and cried in a voice of martyrdom, "Humphrey, desist! You'll not tramp holes in my daughter's house!" Snatching up a straight-backed chair, she set it behind her retreating husband's back, trotted over to claim another, and placed it beside the first, then stood grimly awaiting the result.

Brutus deduced there could be only one reason for her efforts. He sprang onto the nearest of the deterrents and sat panting.

In full cry, Mr. Van Lindsay swung around and advanced at fair speed. Strand's jaw dropped. Behind him, the footman peered in joyous anticipation. Brutus was a large dog. Crashing into something, Van Lindsay lowered his page, roaring an irate "What in thunder?" and came nose to nose with a grinning canine countenance and a large pink tongue that flapped around his face. With a startled yelp, the orator leapt away, collided with the second chair, and fell into it. Brutus jumped companionably into his lap. Philippa shrieked with laughter. Humphrey howled his indignation. Nothing loath, Brutus joined in the chorus.

It was too much for Strand. Clapping a hand over his mouth, he tottered backward. Weeping but faithful, the footman pulled the door to. Master and man leaned against the wall and succumbed together, their mirth the more delicious since it must be smothered.

* * *

"*Had* I dreamt you were here, Mama, I would never have allowed Judith to remain at Park Parapine!" Already dressed for dinner and seated on the sofa in her mother's room, Lisette said remorsefully, "I feel dreadful, and Judith will be disappointed beyond anything."

"With no cause, my love," Mrs. Van Lindsay smiled fondly, adjusting her pearls as she sat at the dressing table. "Papa and I will drive down and collect her, for we've a standing invitation to visit the Drummonds."

Watching Sanders arrange a fine lace cap over her mother's luxuriant hair, Lisette asked, "Do you mean to take Judith back to Town with you, then?"

"I most certainly do! Both she and Norman have been from their studies for too long. Besides, the Season will be commencing, and I am thinking it time for Judith to attend a few parties. Nothing more daring than country dances and such, but she will be fifteen next month, you know, and I have never held with taking a girl straight from the schoolroom and throwing her into Society. I do hope she has not been allowed to enlarge herself during my absence."

"You will scarce know her," smiled Lisette. "How very fetching you look. A new gown, Mama?"

Marriage, Mrs. Van Lindsay decided, suited her beautiful daughter. There was a subtle difference in the girl's manner. Not so much a lessening of poise as a relaxing of formality; a new assurance and warmth that made her seem infinitely more approachable. And yet, also, there was something at the back of those great eyes that might almost be sadness. Disturbed, Philippa nodded, "Thank you, Sandy. That will do nicely. Lud, but I missed you when we was in Scotland!" She waited until the door had closed upon her gratified minion, then turned to her daughter and added, "And should have taken her had I known Judith would not need her! What on earth was Beatrice about to have brought the children to stay with a bridal couple? I dare swear I was never so vexed as when we reached Town and Sandy told me of it! And what your grandmama will have to say to me I dread to contemplate. I have had a dozen letters if I've had one, warning that Beatrice was up to no good, and that wretched old hag Monica Hughes-Dering had the gall to say flat out she had heard Bea has taken a lover, and that fool Dwyer properly into the hips over it!''

"I assure you, Mama, we did not object to hosting my brother and sister," Lisette evaded. "Indeed they have been a great delight, and Strand has been so good with them.''

"Has he, indeed?" said Mrs. Van Lindsay, a grim set to her mouth. "And as good with you, child?''

Her face hot, Lisette faltered, "That—would depend, ma'am, upon—upon what you have heard.''

"What I have heard is a proper Cheltenham tragedy, and likely holding less truth than would fill a flea's thimble! I am assured you would never be so gauche as to spread such vulgar scandal!''

With a wan smile Lisette said, "Thank you for that, Mama. I am grateful that *you* believe me innocent.''

"More to the point, your husband does." Lisette's heightened colour alerting her, Philippa probed sharply. "He does, does he not? You *did* assure him you are guiltless?''

Never had Lisette lied to her parents. She found it horrendous to do so now and hung her head, stammering, "Well I—er, of course—''

She was rescued by a scratch at the door, presaging the entrance of Norman, his dark young face none too clean, his clothes rumpled, but a son such as Philippa had longed to see.

"Mama!" he cried joyously, coming to sweep her into a hug with a new assurance that further bewildered her. "Oh, but this is famous!" He dropped a buss onto her astonished face. "Wait till you see the boat Strand and I are renovating. How long do you stay with us? Did my poor Great-Uncle go to his reward?''

"No." she gasped faintly. "Norman, my heaven, but you have *changed!* Lisette said—but I never thought—good heavens!''

Pleased, he laughed, and bowed with theatrical grace. "Did you not tell my mother, Lisette? I collect you were too busy chattering of—er, other matters! Egad, what a family. You two up here, and my father downstairs, probably giving poor Strand beans over the duel!''

"Duel?" echoed Mrs. Van Lindsay, aghast. "What duel?''

"*You* may count yourself fortunate there was no duel!" Humphrey advised, holding up his glass so that Strand might refill it for him. "Garvey's a fine shot and, I'll be honest, I'd not care to be in his black books. Were I you, my boy, I'd watch my back. If Sanguinet won't allow him to call you out, he's not above resorting to other means to even the score."

Much restored after a few hours' rest, Bolster agreed. "Pre-pre- just as I said, sir."

"I thank you both for the concern." Strand smiled, returning to stand by the drawing room fire. "But surely you judge him too harshly. Garvey is a womanizing lecher and runs with a set I'd want none of, but save for his extraordinary behaviour when I challenged him, I know of nothing to cause me to question his honour."

Humphrey sipped his cognac appreciatively and, frowning into the flames muttered, "I'd thought more along the lines of his pride. The fellow was wild for Lisette before you won her, and regrettably, we encouraged his suit until—but you—ah, probably know all about that. From what I heard you emptied a wine bottle over his head."

"A glass, merely, sir."

"Even so, I'd never have believed Garvey would swallow that!"

"A very little of it, I should think."

"It ain't no laughing m-matter," warned Bolster sternly. "Don't like Garvey. Never did. Nasty temper."

"Then how fortunate I am to be surrounded by such devoted champions," Strand laughed. "You do mean to return, I trust, Jeremy? And Norman—"

"Must return to Town," decreed Humphrey, "for he—"

Coming into the room at that unpropitious moment, Norman said in a voice of stark tragedy, "Town? Me? Oh, sir! Never say so!"

Humphrey frowned. "I do not care to be interrupted. I vow I don't know what you young people today are coming to. Of course you will return to Town. I've a new tutor hired for you, since poor Worth tells me he had sooner be nibbled to death by newts than suffer another month with you!"

"But, sir," Norman pleaded desperately, "our boat is—"

"Be damned to your boat!" snapped his father huffily. "I shall discuss your future with you when these two gentlemen are not obliged to have to endure so depressing a subject. I'll own myself pleased by your improved appearance, at least. How old are you now? Older than Judith, I know. Fifteen, is it?''

The old sullen look creeping back into his eyes, Norman muttered, "Sixteen, sir.''

"Very well, you may take a glass of ratafia with us. With your approval, Strand.''

"By all means.'' Strand dropped a hand on Norman's drooping shoulder as he walked to the sideboard where stood the decanters. "Matter of fact, we've had a busy time here. Norman and I got into a fine brawl, and—''

"The young puppy!'' exclaimed Mr. Van Lindsay, spluttering over his brandy. "He dared raise his hand against you? Why, I'll—''

"No, no. *With* me, sir. We took on a few of the town bullies who thought to—er—have some sport with us, eh, Norman?'' He gave the boy a glass of ratafia and his most friendly smile.

Norman took the glass, but said in quiet denial, "No, sir. They came after me, Papa. In regard to—''

"In regard to having—er, 'bought' their sister,'' Strand grinned.

Mr. Van Lindsay's eyes all but started from his head. Bolster gave a shout of laughter.

"You—you young dog!'' chortled Humphrey.

"Tell us, for Lord's sake!'' urged Bolster.

So Strand told them of the incident, finishing, "And he fought like a Trojan, sir, do I say so myself!''

Vastly entertained, Mr. Van Lindsay slapped his knee. "God bless us all!'' he exclaimed. "I do believe you'll make a fair copy of your brother after all, Norman.''

"Oh, I doubt that, sir,'' said Strand blithely.

Bolster glanced to him in surprise. Norman, on the other hand, looked at Strand as though this man he had come to admire above all others had sunk a knife in his breast.

"What's that?'' asked Mr. Van Lindsay, somewhat startled.

"I don't think Norman will be a copy of his brother, sir,'' said Strand. "As a matter of fact, with your permission, I am negotiating to get him commissioned a naval ensign.''

Norman dropped his glass.

Lisette entered the room moments later, when the excitement had died down a little. She had chosen to wear a robe of pale pomona green over a cream under-dress, and her only jewellery consisted of dainty diamond drop earrings. She had thought she looked well, but her mama said she was positively delicious, and, to judge from the expressions of the gentlemen as they stood to greet her, that opinion was shared. Norman was so ecstatic as to be all but incoherent, but when Lisette had drawn forth the details of his brilliant future, she was almost as excited and, having hugged him with enthusiasm, went to Strand and thanked him prettily for his help and interest. He was pleased but said in his brusque way that it was a lot of fuss about nothing and that anyone would have done it. Humphrey voiced the opinion that his little girl had found herself a fine gentleman for a husband, to which Lisette said demurely that she was quite aware of Strand's many qualities.

Bolster stood beaming at her, and she went to urge that he sit down and not further tire himself. Not wishing to embarrass him, she lowered her voice and murmured, "I was so very sorry, Jeremy, to hear that you hurt yourself while helping my brother. Strand will be remorseful, I do not doubt."

"And for n-no cause," he smiled, grateful that she spoke too softly for her father to hear. A shrewd judge of character, Bolster had no doubt that the bombastic politician would seize upon the trifling accident and not only enlarge it into a full-fledged disaster, but also draw a great deal of the attention he dreaded to himself. "Feeling much imp-improved already, y'know. Wouldn't go back to Town, except—"

"Except Strand insists, and rightly so," she put in, sitting down, so that he perforce followed suit. "You will be very welcome to return, if Lord Belmont allows it. Indeed, I think my husband is counting on it—so long as you do not work too hard." She saw that he was about to protest, and added with a mischievous twinkle, "We cannot have Miss Hersh becoming overset with nerves, can we?" Bolster's face fell. Leaning closer, she said kindly, "My Lord, *do* go and see her while you are in Town. Perhaps you could take a letter from me."

He looked up eagerly. "No, would you? Oh, but that would be sp-splendid. If only she will receive me . . ."

Chatting easily with his father-in-law, Strand's eyes drifted often to the pair on the sofa. They made a handsome couple. How softly they spoke, almost secretively. . . . Bolster was looking at Lisette as though she were something holy. As if—he drew himself up short. What in the deuce was he about now? Jeremy was the most honourable of men and so in love with his Amanda he could scarce see any other woman. If he was less shy with Lisette than was his usual way, it was probably because she'd gone out of her way to be kind to him and because he knew she was fond of Amanda. For shame, Strand! he thought impatiently. For shame!

Lord Bolster left Strand Hall early the next morning, Best driving him back to the metropolis, from which his lordship cheerfully vowed to return the instant the mighty Lord Belmont pronounced him fit enough to do so. "M-might be back tonight!" he called, as the curricle started off along the drivepath.

A few hours later, the Van Lindsays departed, taking with them a son alternately rhapsodic because of his rosy future and cast down because the *Silvering Sails* was far from completion. Strand was appealed to with the greatest pathos, until he laughingly agreed to work his "poor nails" to the bone to finish the task.

Lisette took leave of her family in the drawing room, the evils of her situation suddenly making it more than she could bear to watch the carriages disappearing from sight. While awaiting the rest of the party, Strand and Mr. Van Lindsay wandered together onto the front porch, beside which could be heard a faint grinding marking Brutus's attention to a rediscovered bone. A brief silence fell between the men, both having much they would like to say, and struggling to put their thoughts into words. Van Lindsay succeeded first. Clearing his throat he said gruffly, "I'm most devilish grateful to you, Strand, for your interest in Norman. I vow I was never more shocked than when I saw the tears in the poor lad's eyes last night. I'd not dreamt he entertained hopes for such a career. Gad! How can I have been so blind?"

"I think we all are when it comes to our own, don't you, sir? Perhaps it is that we are so close to them every day, we no longer really see them. But I am perfectly sure your son knows you wish only the best for him."

"It is good of you to say so. I'm not totally unaware, however. I have for instance, noted something about you and my little girl."

Strand tensed, the smile in his eyes fading into a guarded expression.

"She's miserable," alleged Van Lindsay, bluntly. "And, dammit all! I know why!"

His hands clenching, Strand wondered bitterly if all England knew of the barriers between him and his wife.

"I'm sorrier than I can say, that such a thing should have occurred," Van Lindsay went on. "Especially right at the start of your married life. It was dashed decent of you to say nothing to my wife. She don't know yet. Lisette would say nothing, of course, for she's the soul of loyalty. What you must think of us, I dare not guess. We're responsible. No way out of that. Though Lord knows, we tried hard enough to guide the girl." He sighed, and thrust out his hand. Strand took it and gripped it hard. "She ain't all bad, y'know," Van Lindsay said pleadingly.

Considerably taken aback, Strand responded. "You may believe I am very well aware of that, sir!"

Shaking his head, the older man said heavily, "If he would only refrain from spoiling her to death—the poor booberkin," Strand started, his eyes glued to Van Lindsay's troubled face. "I've told and told Dwyer to spank her," Humphrey went on, "but telling pays no toll. I don't hold with violence, but"—he shrugged—"I pray you don't reproach your sweet little sister, m'boy. Doubt she had the faintest notion of what Beatrice would make of her unguarded words."

Strand stood rigid and silent, the implications striking him with numbing force.

Philippa and Norman came out onto the porch then. Brutus pranced up the steps and succeeded in getting under everyone's feet, but at last the baggage was stored in the boot, the goodbyes had all been said, promises of frequent visits exchanged, and the carriage rumbled off along the drive, Philippa's dainty handkerchief fluttering from the window.

Chapter 15

Strand stood staring after the departing carriage for quite some time. Brutus returned from having assisted the horses to negotiate the drivepath and went panting in search of his bone. He found it, made his ponderous way up the steps, and paused for a minute or two beside the quiet man, but Strand did not address him so he went on about his business, carrying the bone into the house for burial. Van Lindsay's words seemed to roar in Strand's ears: "Lisette would say nothing . . . she's the soul of loyalty . . ." His clenched fists tightened until the nails drove into the flesh. It had been *Beatrice,* all the time! Beatrice must have pried a few confidences from Charity and then flitted-about, spreading her mischief. He could have groaned aloud, so searing was his remorse. He had captured the loveliest girl in England for his reluctant bride; he had even begun to fancy she no longer quite despised him. And then, tricked by that bastard Garvey, he'd allowed hurt pride to rule him, to the extent that— His head bowed under the weight of guilt. He'd spanked that glorious girl for no reason! Dear God, how could he have been so stupid? So lacking in faith? Lisette had been so good as to conceal the truth about poor naïve little Charity, and in return he had beaten her. And cherishing his sense of ill usage, had since make no slightest effort to apologize—to try to heal the breach between them. The memory of several slights he had dealt her returned to lash him until they were magnified out of all proportion. How she must loathe him. How she must despise the man who had so selfishly claimed her, and then mistrusted and maltreated her like some feudal savage.

A less sensitive man might have run into the house, fallen to his knees before his love and, confessing his contrition, begun to win his way into her affections. Despite his bride's impression of him, however, Strand was an extremely sensitive individual, too sensitive to be easily able to express his deepest feelings. Therefore, he instead wandered down the steps and across the lawns, hands deep-thrust in pockets, and frowning gaze on the ground before him. There was, he knew, only one reason that she had not left him: she considered herself to have made a bargain and, no matter how repulsive it might be to her, she was too honourable to fail to live up to it. The thought made him writhe, but the prospect of giving her up, of stepping out of her life and permitting her to seek a Bill of Divorcement was even more harrowing. It would be an example of perfect love, and she would have a chance to find happiness with someone she could really care for. . . . He gritted his teeth and knew he could not do it! Not yet, at all events. Such unselfishness was surely more of angels than of mortal men, and Justin Strand was very mortal.

The sun sank lower in the sky, the golden light of afternoon began to warm into a roseate sunset, and still Strand wandered blindly, striving to reach a decision. He concluded at last that his best course would be to keep his promise to Norman and finish the renovating of the boat. In his heart of hearts he knew that his decision was a craven one. It would be simple enough to engage a shipwright to effect the repairs. The truth was that he shrank from facing the accusation in the lovely eyes of the girl he had so wronged. He argued defiantly that he had given Norman his word and that he alone was responsible for seeing that the work was properly completed. And perversely, hoped that while he was away and his presence not a constant reminder of his brutality, Lisette might begin to forget. She might even welcome him with a kindlier attitude. But if he stayed away too long, if he came back to find the great house bereft of her gracious presence, the halls lacking the sound of that quick light step and rippling little laugh, the air not holding the haunting perfume that was so uniquely Lisette . . . it did not bear thinking of! And it would not happen, by God! He'd tell Connaught to send the four new men down to help, and it should all be done in jig time. He would come home then, and woo his bride with every ounce of ardour he possessed. He would *make* himself utter the phrases that burned in his soul but froze on his tongue.

He squared his shoulders and, looking up, was startled to discover that he had been wandering for hours, and shadows were lengthening across the meadows beyond the Home Wood. Turning about, he strode briskly towards Strand Hall.

With Strand busied at Silverings, Lisette decided that this would be the perfect time to take inventory of all the household linens and chinaware, both of which items she felt needed replenishing. This domestic task was deferred before it was properly begun, however, when Amanda Hersh arrived with her abigail and so many bandboxes and portmanteaux that it was clear she intended to make a long stay. Lisette was delighted to have such pleasant company and touched when she learned that Strand had despatched his groom to London armed with a request that if at all possible, Miss Hersh accept an invitation to join Lisette in Sussex. Peering at her hostess narrowly, Amanda exclaimed, "Good heavens you did not know!"

"No. And could scarce be more pleased!" Thinking to detect a trace of apprehension in the sweet face, she added, "Unless—my husband did not cause you to feel *obliged* to come?"

"Good gracious, no! Strand was most polite as he always is with me though I can readily see he must be a great trial to you for he is not the most robust of men and to be working outside in every weather must worry you even if you are very brave and I wish I was but I was quite afraid to come and wonder that I did at all."

Instinctively drawing a breath at the end of this scrambled sentence, Lisette asked, "Why? Do you not like the Hall? If you prefer, we can go into Town. Or should you like to journey to Berkshire, perhaps? My sisters-in-law are there, and I have been intending to visit them for some time."

"Please do not suppose me ungrateful of your hospitality for indeed I am and I love the country save only that—" Amanda hesitated and said shyly, "You are trying not to laugh so I have said something silly but we have become such special friends I need not mind only Jeremy is also your friend."

Both touched and amused, Lisette said teasingly, "And you fear I may nurse a *tendre* for him?"

Amanda burst into a peal of laughter. "Of course not for how should you when you have such a wonderful marriage, it is that I fear he may come here he will not do you think?"

Lisette concentrated on straightening her wedding band and said that she was sure they would have plenty of warning did his lordship decide to do so. "Meantime," she went on, able to meet Amanda's trusting eyes again, "I promise you shall not be bored, for I have so many invitations, and more callers than you could believe. I am become slightly—er—notorious, you see. We shall have a lovely time, Mandy."

And they did. After the few sunny days, the weather became inclement again but this deterred few hostesses, only a proposed boat party having to be cancelled. Since it was redesigned into a masquerade requiring that all guests wear nautical costume, it became, instead of a failure, one of the hits of the summer. The hostess, Lady Salia Moulton, decorated her charming old house to suggest the interior of a packet and drew a large and enthusiastic crush of guests. Lisette and Amanda were escorted to this party by Jocelyn Vaughan, who had become a frequent visitor to Strand Hall and was always an attentive and charming companion. It was but one of many social events that filled their days, and since they each were blessed with a rich sense of humour and in their various ways suffered the pangs of romantic afflictions, their friendship deepened and they dealt so well together that time passed swiftly. One thing marred this period for Lisette: the fact of her husband's continued absence. When she had blithely told Amanda he would be gone for a week or more, she had uttered the remark more as a safeguard against that remote possibility than from a belief he would really stay away. She had to struggle to keep from animadverting on the likelihood that he was with his Fair Paphian and, being convinced that they would see him over the weekend, had to exercise considerable restraint not to betray her vexation when they did not.

On Sunday afternoon they attended a church bazaar and later dined with the Vicar and his family, spending a delightful evening at the Vicarage. Monday was their first comparatively quiet day, and after luncheon they sat together in the lounge, Lisette writing to Timothy and Amanda struggling with some beading on a reticule. That this task was not proceeding satisfactorily eventually penetrated Lisette's absorption, and she glanced up to see her friend squinting at the finely set stitches, her little face contorted into an expression of frowning concentration. At once offering the services of her dresser, Lisette was told that Miss Wallace had already been so good as to volunteer to repair the sadly torn lace flounce of the gown Amanda had worn to the nautical masquerade party. "Besides," Amanda remarked, "I really love to work my designs only I sewed this one so well I simply cannot see the stitches and I do want to replace the beads with those pretty French ones we bought at the bazaar yesterday."

Lisette's attempt to help was as ineffectual. Amanda was a fine needlewoman, and her stitches were practically invisible. "If only we had a magnifying lens," Lisette murmured, blinking. "Oh, I have it! Strand's quizzing glass!" She stood, waving away Amanda's protests that she not put herself to so much bother. "I've got to go upstairs at all events, for my mama particularly desired me to send Timothy the direction of a friend of hers in Paris, and I cannot recall it. I'll see if I can find the glass while I am up there."

She found the Parisian's direction neatly inscribed in her address book, but did not fare so well in her husband's bed-chamber. Strand was not the type to affect such things as fobs and seals, and possessed but one quizzing glass that was brought forth only occasionally. Lisette's hurried scan through his chest of drawers unearthed such unlikely objects as a collar obviously purchased for Brutus, a solitary spur and several whip thongs, a small brass-mounted pistol, and an old map of East Anglia—but no quizzing glass. The dressing room was equally unproductive, and Lisette was about to admit failure when her eyes fell upon the small table beside Strand's bed. There was one slim drawer, but since Green was either very indulgent of his master or of an equally haphazard nature, it was possible the missing glass might be there. Lisette opened the drawer carefully. She moved aside a folded letter inscribed in the writing she had come to know as Rachel's, but could see no sign of anything resembling the quizzing glass. Preparing to close the drawer, she paused. A dainty handkerchief, trimmed with lace, had been beneath Rachel's letter; a lady's handkerchief, surely? Her hand trembling, she took up the neatly folded square and uttered a shocked gasp. The lace was unmistakable—it was the handkerchief grandmama had fashioned for her. But why on earth was it here in Strand's drawer? Something dark showed through the fine cambric. Unfolding it, her heart began to thunder. A small blue feather had been carefully placed there; a feather from a bonnet that had found particular favour with her husband. He had once casually remarked, in fact, that she had been wearing that same bonnet when first he had seen her.

The implications were inescapable. A lump came into her throat; she could not seem to think coherently, and stood there, her eyes wide and unseeing, until a call shook her from her trance.

"Lisette! Lisette!"

Mandy's voice, and extremely agitated. Lisette started, folded the handkerchief with its small enclosed treasure, replaced it, and went into the hall.

Amanda waited there, her face white and frightened. "I must leave at once!" she imparted tremulously. "A messenger has come I heard him tell Mrs. Hayward that Lord Bolster sends his compliments and is delayed in Horsham but will come tomorrow if it is convenient, oh but I am so sorry and must leave at once!"

Nothing Lisette could say would move her. Thoroughly distraught, Amanda fled to her bedchamber, astonished her formidable abigail by snapping out sharp orders, and within the hour the carriage was rumbling down the drivepath carrying its shaken occupant back to London Town.

Lisette went back into the house, entertaining the distinct suspicion she dwelt in the midst of some strange dream. Adding to this impression was a sense of unfamiliarity in the hall, explained when she noted that the large tapestry had disappeared from the wall. Mrs. Hayward was summoned and all but burst into tears at the sight of the nude expanse of plaster. "Mr. Justin was so proud of it!" she mourned. "It was dreadfully shabby when he come home from India, ma'am, but he had it restored so lovely. Wherever can it have gone? I know it was here this morning, for I saw how the sun was hitting it and wondered if we should ought to draw the draperies over the east windows."

Lisette thought absently that the sun's appearance had been brief. The sky was clouded over now, and a brisk breeze had come up. "I am perfectly sure that Miss Hersh did not tuck it into her reticule,'' she said with a faint smile. ''Perhaps—oh, why did I not think? Mrs. Hayward—it is quite windy outside.''

The housekeeper blinked at her. ''Brutus!''

''Yes. That wretched animal has made off with it!''

Together, they initiated a search for the Intrepid Watchdog, and he was located in the red saloon, quaking beneath the small mountain of the tapestry. Shaking her head, Lisette watched footman and housekeeper bear off the prized wall hanging and, leaving Brutus moaning his anguish over the treachery of humankind, returned to her room. She picked up her address book, intending to return it to the drawer, but instead stood gazing blankly at it, thinking of her handkerchief, and the little feather so betrayingly hoarded within it. Surely, a gentleman would behave in so tender a fashion for but one reason—that he was deep in love with the owner of the purloined articles. But Strand did not love his wife. . . . Did he? Her face was burning suddenly. She felt shy and restless so that she began to wander about the room, carrying her address book, alternately elated and disbelieving. Was it possible that he had wed her because he *had* fallen in love with her? Had he believed his suit so hopeless that he'd seized upon what he believed his only possible chance of winning her and concealed his inner feelings, fearing they would be repugnant to her? And even if this was true, why should it cause her heart to leap about so crazily? She came to an abrupt halt. She was forgetting that Strand had deserted her on their wedding eve: scarcely the act of a man passionately in love with his bride. She scowled at the andirons, gleaming in a brief ray of sunlight. How foolish she was to have become so enraptured and hopeful over a man whose heart belonged to another lady. His blond enchantress. She must not allow herself to lose her perspective. She was lonely, that was all.

Through her solitary luncheon she strove to think of other matters and failed miserably. Attempting to read that afternoon, her thoughts strayed constantly from the printed page. She found herself smiling at the recollection of Justin's teasing, and the way his blue eyes tended to crinkle at the corners when he laughed. Her eyes grew sober as she remembered his livid fury when he thought she had betrayed him. And he really, she thought rather wistfully, had not spanked her very hard with the hairbrush. Not as hard as he might pardonably have done, under the circumstances. The memory of the afternoon when he had "shot" the tree drew a little gurgle of laughter from her.

"It must be a most amusing novel," observed an unwelcome visitor.

Her cheeks scarlet, Lisette sprang up. "Beatrice!"

"Yes, love," gushed her sister, hurrying to embrace Lisette while assuming her most charming smile. "I heard you was alone, and determined to come and cheer you—"

"I wonder," Lisette interpolated coolly, "you would dare come here."

A wary light crept into Beatrice's hard eyes. She had put off her cloak and gloves and, moving to the fire, began to warm her hands, saying innocently, "Ah, you are in a funning mood, I perceive. Poor dear, how lonely it must be for you, with Strand away so much of the time."

"I am not funning. I know that you were responsible for setting those wicked rumours about, and—"

"Oh!" gasped Beatrice. "How *can* you say such a thing of your own flesh and blood?" She tugged a handkerchief from her reticule and held it to her lips, sobbing a muffled, "You should be *ashamed,* Lisette. Oh, I vow I am quite shattered!"

"Nonsense! Very few people knew that Strand had gone to Silverings that first week of our marriage. And those who *did* know believed us deeply attached. You wormed the tale from Charity, and embellished it to—"

"Wicked! *Wicked* girl!" Beatrice wailed. "To accuse your own loving sister! Oh, it is too much. *Everyone* hates me and chooses to believe the very worst! I have done nothing! Nothing! If you had but an ounce of sisterly affection for me, you would know better."

Lisette was beginning to tremble because of this bitter confrontation, but she said bravely, "It is because I know you so well that I understand what happened."

"Never have you spoken to me so!" Beatrice wept her way to a chair and sank into it. "To think Strand should turn you against me in such a way! Oh, I know how it must have been, for he has never liked me, even as—" she sniffed, watching her sister covertly— "even as he never loved you."

Unexpected strength surged through Lisette. She said calmly, "My husband has never sought to turn me against you, Bea. But he was much hurt by all this unpleasantness, and his well-being must now come first with me. Even as you would place William first in your life.''

Beatrice's head jerked up. She demanded suspiciously, ''What is that supposed to mean? Do you imply—''

Still standing, her hands loosely clasped before her, Lisette said a quiet, ''I do not imply. I warn you openly that both Grandmama and our parents have heard you have taken a lover, and—''

Springing up, Beatrice gasped, ''My heaven! Mama and Papa are back?'' She shot a nervous glance to the door. ''They do not stay with you?''

''No. They have left.''

''Thank heaven! I could not stay were they here.''

At this, a tiny frown puckered Lisette's brow. ''I wish I might ask you to stay. Unfortunately, I—''

''What?'' With an expression of total horror, Beatrice faltered, ''You will not allow me to overnight with you? But—but you must! You cannot turn me out, Lisette! You cannot. I—I have nowhere to go!''

''Fustian! You have your own home, and a loving husband waiting.''

''Loving husband! Pah! William has heard all the nasty little gabblemongerings, even as have you. And was so heartless and cruel as to believe them. I did not stay to hear his foolish recriminations, I do assure you! Surely, there never was a lady more ill-used by her family and friends!''

''My heavens! Do you tell me you have left him? Bea, you cannot! The scandal!''

Sinking down again, Beatrice sobbed, ''Much you care. You married a man whose—whose sister is sunk . . . beneath reproach! That scandal did not . . . weigh with you!''

Reminded of how harshly Beatrice had berated her for hesitating to accept Strand, Lisette shook her head in exasperation. ''That has nothing to say to the matter. You must go home. No, Bea, it is of no use to entreat me. To allow you to stay here at this time must offend my husband and embarrass me. Besides, I am invited to visit my sister-in-law Leith at Cloudhills, and leave tomorrow.''

Beatrice sat very still, an arrested expression on her face. Then, to her sister's dismay, she ran to kneel before her, clutching at her skirts and weeping hysterically. "Please! Oh, please, Lisette! I *dare* not go home, to say truth. William is—is furious with me. And if Mama and Papa should come—oh, I could not bear it! I could not! And—and even were I to stay with friends, or—or my cousins, everyone would—would know. Please!" She raised a tear-stained and pathetic countenance. "You are my only hope. Oh, I know I am naughty sometimes . . . and—and vex you. But I did not mean to cause the talk about you and Strand. I swear I told only Jemima Duncan, and—"

"And might as well have announced it in *The Gazette*!" But Lisette was shaken, and took her sister's upreaching hands, begging that she not kneel in such a way. "Whatever would the servants think? Come now, do be sensible."

Beatrice was too unnerved to be sensible. She seemed so close to lapsing into complete hysterics that Lisette had no recourse but to coax her into a chair and insist that she sip a little brandy while she strove to calm her. Sir William, she pointed out, was very obviously devoted to her. Were Beatrice to agree to set up the nursery he so longed for, he would probably be more than happy to forgive her. Her response interspersed with gulping little sobs, Beatrice confessed to having been a fool. "If only—oh, if *only* I had not . . . been so utterly *bored*," she choked. "But, William is too cross now, Lisette. That's why I thought . . . if you would but let me stay—even a few days—he would have time to—to overcome his pride, and I could . . . beg his forgiveness." She took up her sister's hand and, nursing it to her cheek, begged, "Only say you will. Dearest, I promise never to trouble you again. *Please* say I may stay with you. Just for a day or so."

And the end of it was, of course, that Lisette sighed and agreed Beatrice might remain, even though she herself must leave early in the morning. She was promptly hugged, kissed, and wept over. Her offer of dinner was rejected, however; vowing herself too overwrought to be able to do anything but repair to her room. Beatrice was ushered upstairs, delivered into the care of her abigail, and soon comfortably settled into bed.

Exhausted by the emotional scene, Lisette ate a light and solitary meal and retired early. She looked in on her sister before she went to bed. The room was dark save for the firelight. Beatrice, lying limp and wan against her pillows, was still awake, however, and professed herself quite unable to express her gratitude.

"Perhaps we have all learned something from this bumble broth," sighed Lisette with a tired smile.

"You are too good . . . too sweet," Beatrice acknowledged tremulously. "And never fear, dearest, does you husband return tomorrow, I shall tell him I must needs leave at once, for you are perfectly right, and my presence here could only distress him."

"You will go back to Somerset and try to reconcile with poor William? You promise this?"

"Yes. Oh, I do! I shall be a good wife to him. You will see."

Lisette pressed her hand, and left her. Once in her own bed, sleep eluded her, an endless succession of worries pressing in upon her. It dawned on her suddenly that her wickedness in having lied to Beatrice about visiting Cloudhills could scarcely be improved upon. Rachel and Charity would be there, and— was she very tactful, she might be able to learn something of Strand's *affaire de coeur*. She did not give one thought to the fact that her admired Tristram Leith might also be in Berkshire; nor why her need to know more of her husband's *incognita* had become a near-obsession. Drowsily considering what to wear for her journey, she fell asleep.

Her slumbers might have been less sound had she again looked in on her sister. A tray on the bedside table held the remains of a healthy supper. The room was a blaze of candles, and Beatrice, cuddled against her pillows, was writing a note. She looked smug, and not in the least contrite.

Denise was unhappy, Mrs. Hayward was troubled, and the coachman mumbled that weather was a-blowing up and Mr. Justin didn't like his horses to be tooled in the rain. Lisette could do nothing about the admittedly heavy clouds, but she had not been schooled by her mama to no purpose. Her upraised brows and look of astonishment devastated Denise, silenced Mrs. Hayward, and defeated the coachman. Within the hour her portmanteau was in the boot, two bandboxes were in the carriage, the coachman was on the box, and a burly groom was riding guard. Beatrice was still fast asleep, and only a very uneasy Mrs. Hayward stood on the porch to wave goodbye.

"There," said Lisette, settling back against the squabs. "It is only nine o'clock and we are safely on the road. And there is not a drop of rain falling.''

"No, madame," Denise agreed glumly. And added under her breath, "Yet . . ."

She was right. By the time they reached Horsham a light drizzle had begun to fall. They passed Chiddingfold in a steady rain and, while eating luncheon in a private parlour of the Pease Porridge Inn at Farnham, Lisette was cowed by a blinding flash and an earth-shaking bark of thunder. She tried to appear nonchalant when the coachman scratched on the door to suggest respectfully that so soon as the storm had "blowed itself out a mite" they should return to Strand Hall. "You must resign yourself to the fact that I have no intention of doing so," she said coolly. "When the rain eases, we will continue to Berkshire." She ignored the small wail from Denise and became engrossed in a novel she had brought with her, hoping her trembling would not be too noticeable as thunder clamoured overhead.

It was half-past one o'clock before the storm lifted to the point that they dare resume their journey and, although preserving an air of assured calm, Lisette was inwardly shaken to hear an incoming traveller remark to the host that it had thundered like the Waterloo cannon when his coach had passed through Horsham. With a sudden pang of anxiety, Lisette turned to the gentleman's stout wife and said, "Your pardon, ma'am. Are you of the opinion the bad weather is widespread? Could it, do you suppose, have extended throughout Sussex?"

"I'm afraid it very well might have, ma'am," replied the lady. "What do you say. Mr. Gresham?"

Her spouse echoed her fears, pointing out that he'd encountered a friend in Horsham who had driven up from the coast and experienced heavy weather all the way. "Were I you, madam"— he nodded to Lisette—"I would terminate my journey so soon as is possible. Certainly before light fails. Looks as if we're in for a bad night!"

Lisette thanked him, and hurried out to the coach, Denise moaning behind her. Settling into her seat, Lisette tried not to worry, but Strand was so determined to finish that wretched boat. It would be just like him to pay no heed to the weather, and press on! But she was being silly; likely he was not outside at all, for the *Silvering Sails* might still be in the barn. With a lift of her chin, she thought it very possible that his occupation had little to do with either boats or weather!

The rain lightened and then ceased, but their progress was slowed by the condition of the roads that was not good at best and had now deteriorated to a degree that caused the coachman to curse fluently, if softly, as he attempted to guide his team through a sea of mud. The surface improved when they approached Aldershot, but Denise's timid plea that they overnight at that old city was gently but firmly refused. An odd unease was driving Lisette, and she had no intention of being balked in her desire to reach Cloudhills that day. She was not a foolish girl, however, and told the coachman that they would not proceed if it was unsafe to do so. "By all means, make enquiries as to what conditions lie ahead of us."

The enquiries resulted in an assurance that the roads were perfectly passable as far as Basingstoke, at least, where there were several fine posting houses in the event the storm should roll back again. They reached Basingstoke at half-past four, and again stopped. Even as they pulled into the yard of a busy inn, the Oxford to London stage arrived with a great trumpeting of the guard's yard of tin, a scrambling of ostlers, thunder and splashing of sixteen muddy hooves, snorting and blowing of wet horses, shouts of passengers, and bellowed commands of the driver. Lisette's coachman clambered down from his perch and, waiting his opportunity, slipped a florin into the stagecoach driver's ready palm and was graciously informed that the Newbury Road was passable so there wasn't no cause for to suppose as the road to Aldermaston wouldn't be likewise. This piece of optimism was unhappily ill-founded. By six o'clock they not only were engulfed in a veritable downpour, but the road had all but disappeared beneath the mud so that with every lurch of the carriage, Lisette expected them to overturn and land in a ditch. Denise began to sob with terror. Calming her as best she might, Lisette watched the skies darken, her heart leaping when a distant rumble of thunder announced the return of the storm. She had seldom been more relieved than when the coachman opened the trap to shout that they were now on Lord Leith's preserves, and the gatehouse just ahead.

Soon the carriage slowed and then stopped. An individual crouched under a piece of dripping sacking hove into view and waved urgently at Lisette. Denise let down the window, admitting a rush of colder air and flurry of raindrops. Pulling her hood closer, Lisette leaned to the window.

"Sorry I be to tell ye, ma'am," called the lodgekeeper hoarsely, "but the great house do be closed. The family is away just now, and workmen be painting the whole downstairs."

Denise whimpered. Her own heart dropping into her shoes, Lisette gasped, "Away? Is—is there no one at home at all?"

The lodgekeeper shook his head and replied lugubriously that the Colonel was gone off somewhere, to London, he thought, "And Mrs. Rachel and Miss Charity be gone too. Ain't no one up there saving only the housekeeper and a couple of parlourmaids, ma'am.

"Well, for heaven's sake, why did you not say so? Certainly the housekeeper will not turn us away on such a night!"

"Belike she won't," he agreed dubiously. "But it bean't fitting, it do stink so drefful of paint!"

"A deal more fitting that this horrid storm," said Lisette, and required that her coachman drive on.

Cloudhills hove into view like a great and welcoming refuge, then suddenly became a monstrous black shape against a vivid flash of lightning. The coachman's blast on the horn was answered by a lackey who came running out to hold the horses, and as thunder bellowed deafeningly, the front doors opened wider to reveal a brightly lit interior and a motherly woman fumbling with a large umbrella. The guard opened the carriage door and let down the steps. Lisette was greeted by the housekeeper, the umbrella, and a stifling reek of fresh paint. The back of the house, explained Mrs. Keene, when the unexpected guest had identified herself, was "not nearly so bad." Hurrying Lisette and Denise into the great hall, she said firmly that Mrs. Strand and her servants must not think of journeying on, smell or no smell. Another booming roll of thunder caused the buxom housekeeper to jump and remark with a grin that she could scarce be more pleased to have company arrive, for thunder and lightning plain terrified her.

The sprawling and luxurious Tudor house, set, as its name implied, on the rim of a hill, commanded a wide view of the surrounding countryside, and was renowned for its beauty and comfort. Today, however, it presented a bleak appearance, for the view was shut out by the grey curtain of the rain, and most downstairs rooms were either empty or had their furnishings encased in Holland covers. Offering profuse apologies for the state of the house, Mrs. Keene bustled her beauteous charge upstairs. Mrs. Leith and Miss Charity, said she, would be oh, so sorry to have missed their sister-in-law. Were there any more in Mrs. Strand's party? Another coach following, perhaps? Well, it was as well, for there was only one guest room made up on this floor, which would do nicely, however, and madam's maid could have a room in the servants' quarters. No call to worry over the coachman and guard for there was plenty of room for them. Mrs. Strand could likely do with a cup of tea before dinner, and she should have one quicker than the dog could wag his tail!

The chamber to which Lisette was conducted was spacious and comfortable. Velvet draperies were quickly drawn against the lowering dusk, and the glow of candles brought a warmth to the heart, if not to the room. The fire was already laid, and Mrs. Keene had it flickering merrily in no time. Within half an hour Lisette was seated at a small table before leaping flames, an ample meal set before her, and several books and periodicals brought in for her pleasure. Mrs. Keene stayed for a few moments while two soft-footed maids hovered about. The weather looked to be clearing, she thought, but if Mrs. Strand cared to remain until the family returned in a day or two, no effort would be spared to ensure her comfort. Meanwhile, madam's bed was ready with a warming pan tucked twixt the sheets, and she'd only to give a tug on the bell pull did she need anything.

By the time the hospitable lady left, Lisette was beginning to feel drowsy. Between the tiring journey, the pleasant meal, and the warmth from the fire, she no sooner started to leaf through one of the periodicals than her head was nodding. She rang for Denise and an hour later was in bed and fast asleep.

At about the same time that Lisette had been leaving Farnham that rainy afternoon, a light travelling chaise splashed up the drivepath and stopped before Strand Hall. The panelled door bore the crest of its noble owner and, upon the groom jumping down to swing it open, Lord Jeremy Bolster alighted, smiled his thanks, and ran lightly up the steps. Fisher admitted him and swiftly put him in possession of the fact that Mr. Strand was still down at Silverings, and Mrs. Strand had driven up to Berkshire to visit her sisters.

"Good God!" exclaimed Bolster. "In th-this weather? You noddicock, you should not have allowed her!"

"Madam was quite determined on it, milord. In fact—"

"Bolster! Why, how delightful to have callers in this lonely old place!"

If his lordship shrank inwardly at the gushing tones, he nonetheless bowed with unfailing courtesy over Beatrice's hand. "Lady W-William. Didn't expect to f-f-f- see you here."

"Why ever not? Lisette is my sister, you know. Do you mean to stay? I hope you do. It is a crushing bore here alone, and I must say I think it shabby that I no sooner arrive than Lisette goes jauntering off to Berkshire!"

Bolster, however, thought Lisette had employed shrewd tactics indeed and, having every intention of emulating them, smiled and was silent.

"She said she promised to her sisters-in-law at Cloudhills," Beatrice swept on, walking back with him to the drawing room. "I think she must have mistaken the date, and she will be provoked with me not to have remembered until I arose this morning that Mrs. Leith and her sister are in Town. I saw them on Bond Street only the day before yesterday, and Rachel said they mean to pass a few days with the Mayne-Warings."

"You'd think she'd have reme-membered that," said Bolster, frowning a little.

"Well, of course she does, you silly boy," teased Beatrice, rapping his arm with her fan. "The Mayne-Warings are Tristram's aunt and uncle and were at his wedding, even if very few of the *ton* were in attendance. I believe Rachel and Lady Mayne-Waring hit it off famously, in spite of—er—everything."

"I m-meant that if L-Lisette was promised to Mrs. Leith, she don't seem the type to f-f f-forget the date."

Beatrice's brow puckered. "No," she said slowly. "For she has the most excellent memory in all things, and—" She stopped. One shapely hand drifted to her cheek in an aghast fashion, then she said a little too hurriedly, "But there is a first time for everything, no? Oh, there you are, Fisher!"

The butler slanted a rather affronted glance at her as he carried in a silver tray on which were decanters and glasses. Beatrice gave a trill of nervous laughter, causing the frown in Bolster's honest eyes to deepen. Pouring ratafia for Lady William and Madeira for his lordship, Fisher murmured an enquiry as to whether my lord would be overnighting with them.

"Came down to help Mr. S-Strand," said Bolster, accepting his glass with a nod of thanks. "Still at it, is he?"

"He is, indeed, sir," sighed the butler and, with a troubled glance at the rain-splashed windows added, "I only hope he may not be working outside."

"Hmmnn. I'd best get d-down there. Ask Best to find me a suitable pair, w-would you?"

"Best is at Silverings with the master, sir. But I am sure your own man can select the horses he wishes." He bowed, took himself off, and paused in the doorway to enquire how soon his lordship wished to be on his way.

"At once," said Bolster, an unusually firm set to his jaw.

Beatrice began to chatter about his kindness in having come all this way to assist her brother with "that silly old boat," complaining that Norman should never have plagued "poor Justin" until he agreed to restore it. Bolster scarcely heard her. He was thinking that Lisette was a glorious Fair, no doubt of it, but it was rather painfully obvious she was not deep in love with her husband. Already there had been one unpleasant scandal. If she'd gone trotting off to see Rachel or Charity and they was away, she would be alone at Cloudhills. Unless Leith was there. He scowled down at the amber wine in his glass. Perfect gentleman, Tristram Leith. Totally besotted over his lovely wife. But there was an ugly little rumour drifting about to the effect that Leith had enjoyed more than a casual acquaintanceship with Miss Van Lindsay and that the girl had, in fact, expected to become his bride. Nothing to it, probably. Still, if word should get out she'd gone running up there as soon as her husband's back was turned, and with the two girls away . . . gad!

"Is something amiss, my lord?" asked Beatrice, innocently.

Bolster jumped. "Eh? Oh, no! Why?"

"You were frowning so."

"Oh. Well, it's—er—it's a d-deuced n-n-nuisance to have to g-g-g- drive all the way down to S-Silverings in this rain, ma'am! I'd better leave before I ch-change my mind."

In point of fact, his lordship had already changed his mind. Hurrying to the stables, he informed his groom that he would not be needed past the first stage, and could bring Mr. Strand's horses back as soon as they were rested.

"First *stage*, sir?" echoed the groom. "What—between here and Silverings?"

"No, you hedgebird. Godalming."

"Godalming, sir? But I thought as your lordship were going to help Mr. Strand with his boat."

"Just remembered," Bolster said nonchalantly. "Pressing engagement in Oxford."

Chapter 16

During the night the storm rumbled itself back toward the city, but although the wind and rain lessened and eventually stopped altogether, Lisette did not enjoy a restful sleep. Once, she half woke from a dream in which Justin invaded her bedchamber at dead of night, while singing a decidedly naughty Spanish lovesong. Typical of dreams, the song was delivered in a fine true baritone, whereas her husband's singing left much to be desired. Despite her broken slumbers, habit decreed that she wake at dawn and, having lain staring at the bedcurtains for half an hour, she arose, reached for the bell rope, then relinquished it. Denise had been thoroughly worn out last evening; it would be cruel to waken the poor little creature at this early hour. Still, she would go down and see if there was some hot water to be had.

She put on her peignoir and started along the hall. It was a wide hall, richly carpeted and charmingly appointed. She had been too wearied last night to notice much of the house and now looked about her with interest. Her interest became consternation, however, as one of the doors she approached was flung open. She came face to face with Tristram Leith, considerably in need of a shave, his thick dark hair tumbling untidily over his brow, and his dressing gown tied carelessly so that a hairy chest was exposed to her startled eyes.

"Good God!" gasped Leith.

"T-Tristram!" Lisette squeaked, shrinking against the wall in horror.

"Your—your pardon!" He ran a hand hurriedly through his hair. "I came in very late and did not waken the servants. I'd not realized you and Strand were visiting us."

"W-well, we are not!" she gulped. "Did Rachel and Charity come back with you?"

She knew from his sudden pallor that they had not and uttered a whimper of dismay. "Then—you . . . and I . . . have been here all alone? All *night?*"

Leith forced a grin. "None so dreadful, is it? I *am* your brother-in-law, after all. Come now, never look so scared. Perhaps I can creep away again before anyone knows I—oh, devil take it!"

A maid carrying a steaming copper jug was followed by a lad with a bucket of firewood. Both halted, staring in amazement at the two who stood as if frozen in the hall.

"Is—that for me, I hope?" called Leith with hoarse cheeriness.

"N-no, sir." With her stupefied gaze fixed upon her employer's broad chest, the maid said faintly, "It is hot water for—for Mrs. Strand."

Leith glanced down and stifled a groan as he snatched his dressing gown into a belated propriety.

Ready to sink, Lisette contrived to walk gracefully back into her bedchamber, and knew only too well that her face was scarlet.

It was late afternoon by the time Lord Jeremy Bolster left Aldershot, his mood considerably less amiable than usual. The job horses he had hired in Godalming had been the best of a very poor lot. They had proven to be slugs as he'd feared, and as he had told them frequently but without result for the balance of their hire. The state of the roads compelled him to change teams at Aldershot, but his situation had not improved, for the pair he now drove were poorly matched and no more inclined to lean into their collars than had been their predecessors. He would, he realized glumly, be compelled to rack up at Basingstoke, a development he viewed without delight since the bad weather would undoubtedly result in overcrowded conditions and harassed servants.

Arriving at Basingstoke in the middle of a crashing thunderstorm, he was cold and irritable and wished he'd dared bring his groom. He'd not done so, of course, for fear of what he might encounter at Cloudhills, though with luck there would be nothing to encounter. It was unlikely that a lady would persevere with a journey in the face of such wretched conditions.

The yard of the fine posting house he selected was crowded. Despite the crested doors of his chaise, his lack of attendants was noted, his consequence suffered, and he was fortunate to be allocated a small and noisy room located directly over the kitchens. The sheets were so questionable that he tore the bed apart and aired the bedding before the fire. In the dinning room he endured an execrable dinner, his misery lightened only by some tolerable Burgundy and the conversation of a wealthy local merchant who was so jovially ill-mannered that Bolster was fascinated. He slept poorly, falling soundly asleep at dawn and not awakening until eleven o'clock, the early call he had requested having been totally ignored. The thought of breakfasting in the crowded coffee room was unbearable, and he set out for Cloudhills under bright skies, but over roads clogged with mud. He stopped at the first promising hedge-tavern he came to and was restored to spirits by plain but good fare. He was soon on the road again and pulled into the stableyard at Cloudhills shortly after one o'clock. A groom ran to take charge of the team and tossed his lordship a sympathetic glance.

"Do not d-dare to ask if they're mine!" warned Bolster, jumping down and peering into the stables.

"Be ye lookin' for the Colonel, sir?" the groom enquired.

Admirably concealing his dismay, Bolster lied, "Yes. Have they all re-re-come back, then?"

"Just the Colonel, I do believe, sir. Comed in late last night, he did. Left 's'marnin' though. Don't blame him. Stinks up there. Drefful!"

Undaunted, Bolster pressed on but reaching the house, he was obliged to agree. The painters were busily and vociferously at work in the great hall. Following Mrs. Keene, he was guided through a welter of planks, ladders, buckets, brushes, and rolls of wallpaper to the kitchen and the small office beyond it where the butler handled his transactions. "Sorry I am to bring you back here, milord," she apologized, "but the paint smell is not quite so bad, you'll notice. Did you wish to leave a message for Colonel Leith?''

He shook his head and, feeling like a spy, said, ''Wanted to t-tell you that Mrs. Strand m-might come. She th-thinks her sisters are here. I'll try to head her off, if I can, but—''

''No need for that, sir,'' the housekeeper assured him with a rather tight smile. ''Mrs. Strand overnighted with us. Poor soul was that disappointed, but I gave her the ladies' direction in London, and she left early this morning.''

''I see. And—er, the Colonel?''

Mrs. Keene's eyes dropped. Reddening, she began to fuss with a neat pile of statements on the desk. ''He stays with—with Mr. Devenish, I believe, sir.''

After a brief pause, he said blandly, ''The roads are very b-bad. I f-fancy Mrs. Strand will go straight home—to Sussex, I m-m-mean.''

''Oh, I doubt that, milord. She was most anxious to see Mrs. Leith.'' Fixing him with a defiant stare, she added, ''That was why she come, you see. I doubt the roads will intimidate such as Mrs. Strand. Likely she will drive straight on and try to reach Berkeley Square before dark.''

Bolster thanked her, said his farewells, and made his way outside.

Climbing into his chaise, his eyes were very grim indeed.

Despite Mrs. Keene's faith in her, Lisette's hope of reaching London that evening was foiled by the state of the roads. Mud was everywhere, fallen trees blocked thoroughfares, and clogged traffic resulted in interminable delays and confusion. They arrived in Stoke Poges as the light was fading, and were able to bespeak some passable rooms at a small hostelry. A private parlour was not to be had, however, and Lisette ordered dinner sent to her room, where she shared the meal with Denise and then tumbled into bed, close to exhaustion.

Had she known it, she had fared better than the faithful young Corinthian who followed her so doggedly. Lord Bolster's job horses were not pleased by the littered highways and short of lashing at them with his whip, he could not convince them to travel above a snail's pace. Leaving Reading, one of the animals took violent exception to a wagonload of pigs that jolted raucously past. My lord's hack reared, startling his lazy companion into a buck. The chaise went off the road, the wheel demolished a signpost and fell off, and the chaise lurched and splashed into the mud. Bolster was thrown clear and, shaken and muddied, all but danced his fury. Fortunately he was a well-known young gentleman and the occupant of a passing phaeton, chancing to recognize him, came to his rescue. The wheel, however, was badly sprung, and it was necessary that Bolster, horses, and chaise be returned to Reading to join the many travellers awaiting repairs to their vehicles.

"*Not* work today?" Strand reached up to halt Green's ministrations and over the lathered shaving brush regarded his faithful valet incredulously. "Why the devil not? It's stopped raining, hasn't it?"

"Yes, sir." Misliking the glittering brightness of his employer's eyes, Green said carefully, "Only—well, you did become very wet yesterday, and I—"

Lowering his hand, Strand interrupted hurriedly, "How the deuce was I to know the skies would fall just as we were dragging the old tub down our slips? Anyway, she's launched, and watertight, at least. Mr. Norman will be proud. It would have been a fine bobbery if he'd stepped on the deck and she'd sunk like a stone!"

Green smiled politely in response to the mischievous grin that was slanted at him. He said nothing, but turning Strand's head, his fingers lingered on the strong jaw a shade longer than necessary. Frowning, he murmured, "I doubt one more day would prove disastrous, sir."

Strand, already chafing at the innumerable delays that had kept him from returning to his bride and determined to be done with this business before he left, said with a trace of asperity, "Likely you do. But the boy's to come down next weekend. I want it done!"

The valet's bushy eyebrows lifted, and his lips tightened. It was comment enough.

"Oh!" groaned Strand. "Had I but known in India that you were going to be such a confounded mother hen! You are angered because I did not give over yesterday when you bade me, is that it?"

"You were soaked, sir." Since it was now out in the open, the valet applied more lather to his master's upper lip with rather unnecessary vehemence, so that Strand sneezed. He then bent a grim stare on his victim and nodded, "Quite so, sir. You've took a chill is what."

"Damn you! You splashed soap up my nose is all!"

The indignation in the blue eyes brought a softening to Green's brown ones. "Sir, your skin is very warm, and—"

"Aye. I'm alive! Not the bloodless corpse you will make of me do you not cease brandishing that razor about! Have done, man! I feel splendid. Besides, I mean only to see *Silvering Sails* varnished and I'm off! I'll not wait to have the sails fitted. I'll send my amateur shipwrights to convey them here, but we'll allow the professionals to attend to that business. There, does that suit your Finickyness?"

Green bowed, and his demeanour became of polar propriety. Aware that he was in disgrace, Strand cursed him roundly, teased him, and finally, unleashing the brilliant grin the valet was never able to withstand, brought him neatly around his thumb. He agreed to a request that he at once return to the house should it start to rain again, and even submitted to having a wool scarf wrapped around his throat. Whistling cheerily, he then strode outside, stubbornly ignoring the fact that his head ached annoyingly.

Watching that jaunty stride, Green pursed his lips. "I doubt," he muttered, "that scarf will stay in place above five minutes."

He was right. However, since the sun now smiled down on drenched Sussex, awaking the dancing light of the river and bringing a welcome warmth to the damp air, Green ceased to be quite as concerned and went about his own affairs.

With his customary zeal, Strand threw himself into the final sanding and varnishing of the rails, so that he was soon very warm indeed and his jacket was shortly tossed down on the deck beside his scarf. The work went along well, and the final brush stroke was applied shortly after noon. The little crew gathered up their materials and repaired to the dock, turning back to survey the results of their labours. Strand mopped perspiration from his brow and joined the men in a cheer. The battered and burnt old hulk that had occupied the barn was now, to his eyes at least, a splendid sight, the cabin rebuilt and bright with white paint trimmed in yellow, the decks immaculate, the masts tall and proud and, thanks to a talented village artist, the name tastefully emblazoned on bow and stern.

Strand told Shell and the men to report back to Mr. Connaught, who would instruct them in the matter of transporting the sails, and they moved off, passing Best, who came up and, surveying the craft with a less loving eye, suggested that she appeared to lean to the right a bit. "Just a teensy bit, mind."

"There is," said Strand loftily, "a deal of work remaining to be done."

"Ar, fer ye got to get something to hang on they masts," observed the groom knowledgeably. "Ship cannot sail 'thout sails. Not nohow."

"But she can drift, blast it!" Strand exclaimed, and sprang quickly to secure the aft mooring line that had worked loose, probably by reason of the surging of the rain-swollen river invading even this quiet inlet. By the time he finished, he was considerably warmer and irked by reason of having forgetfully rested his hand on the newly varnished rail. Straightening, he was dismayed by a sudden chill that caused him to shiver violently. He groaned and cursed his frustration. Green had been right as usual. He'd spent altogether too much time in the rain, but—

"Pssst! You deef, or wot is it?"

Turning sharply at this, Strand discovered a small but very pugnacious-appearing personage who scanned him narrowly.

"I'll be gormed if you ain't shot the cat!" observed this youthful apparition with considerable righteousness. "And 'fore noon, too! 'Ere, you best take care, my cove! You'll be proper lurched if old swivel nose catches you wiv a ball o' fire!"

Not unfamiliar with cant, and aware he also presented a most inelegant appearance, Strand grinned and vouchsafed the information that, contrary to the belief held by his visitor, he was not in the least over the oar.

"Garn!" scoffed the boy derisively. "You're clean raddled, you is!" He ran a shrewd eye over Strand's dirty and occasionally varnished shirt and ragged old breeches and shoes and, concealing his incredulity, stepped closer, and lowering his voice asked, "Want to earn a borde? Good clean work. Nuthink smoky. All y'got t'do is take a writing to 'er nibs up in the palace yonder.''

Something in Strand's eyes became very still. "Do you mean Mrs. Strand?"

" 'Course! Didya fink I meant the Queen o' Sheba? 'Ere''—a grubby, folded paper was thrust out—''take it. And you wanta be cagey-like. It's—er—'' the small countenance twisted into a leering smile that was ageless. ''It's from 'A Friend' as they say. See?''

Strand's gaze travelled from the wizened face that had seen too much of evil to the paper he held. "Yes," he said quietly. "I see."

"Orl right.'' The boy dug into his pocket, unearthed a shilling, and handed it over reluctantly. ''I bin 'anging about all mornin'. Tried to get it ter the 'ouse, but ol' swivel nose—Mr. Green to you, my cove—was allus about. Don't ferget now. Cagey-like. Fer the lady, and no one else, eh?''

Strand nodded and, the smile quite gone from his eyes, agreed to be cagey.

When he reached the Dutch door, Green swung it open for him. "Good gracious, sir! You'll be wanting to bathe. I—"

"Tell Best to saddle Brandy," Strand interposed shortly, and strode past.

Staring, Green protested, "But—"

"At once!'' Strand flung over his shoulder. "I must return to the Hall. Follow me as soon as you've packed."

Green knew the tone and scurried for the stables. The cat, he thought, was in with the chicks. Though why, he could not guess.

Strand washed hurriedly. Green came to him then and silently assisted him to change clothes in record time. One look at that bleak expression had frozen the valet's final attempt to reason with his master, nor did he request to rush with the packing and accompany Strand back to the Hall. He knew he would be refused.

Once in the saddle, Strand rode out at the gallop. He avoided roads and by-ways and headed straight across country, violating several warnings anent trespassing as he sent Brandy to the northeast. He had been riding for some time when he felt the chestnut stagger. Appalled, he reined up. The horse was lathered and breathing hard. Enraged with himself, Strand dismounted and walked until the pleasant structure that was The Pines hove into view. He handed Brandy over to the ostler, flushing slightly because of the amazement in the man's eyes. The parlour of the usually cosy inn was positively frigid. Mr. Drye, hastening to welcome his favourite customer, was checked by the jut of the chin and the thin, hard line of the mouth. "Alone today, sir?" he said mildly. "If you'd care to sit here at the window, Mrs. Drye will have some—"

'I'l take the table by the fire," said Strand. "It's blasted well freezing in here, Drye."

The host blinked. He had lit the fire only because the walls were almost two feet thick and tended to be clammy of a morning. Already, two travellers had complained of the heat in the low-ceilinged room. Showing Strand to the table he had requested, Drye poked the logs into higher blaze and went into the kitchen, fanning himself.

Left alone, Strand contemplated the hearth. It would, he told himself, be despicable to read the letter he carried. It would be utterly disloyal to pay heed to the insinuations of that grubby little boy with his too-wise eyes and leering mouth. If Garvey still pursued Lisette it was only to be expected, was it not? And he had, after all, not yet begun his own campaign to win his bride. He had no right . . . no right at all. . . .

He drew a hand across his eyes, wishing his confounded head would stop aching so. How the letter came from his pocket to the table, he could not have told. But it was there. Creased and none too clean. Mocking him. Daring him to read it. Tempting him to dishonour.

He was relieved when Drye came back to set soup and bread before him. The hot soup warmed him a little, but the bread seemed to stick in his throat. And ever as he ate, the greyish edge of the letter peeped from beneath the breadboard as though it whispered, "Take me up. See the message I have for her. Take me up—if you are man enough!" But he would not. He was not that base. Not yet, by heaven!

"Oh, your pardon, sir!" The serving maid set down a tankard of ale at the same instant Strand reached for the salt. "Now look what I've gone and done!" she gasped, using her apron to wipe the splashed table. "Oh! All over your letter it do be! Let me

. . .'' She dabbed anxiously at the paper, Drye running over to add his own efforts and apologies.

"Oh, it is nothing! Nothing!" said Strand pettishly. "Have done, man!"

Drye caught the girl's surprised eye and jerked his head meaningfully and they retreated to the kitchen.

His fingers trembling, Strand took up the letter. It was not very wet, but the ink might smudge. He would dry it at the fire. The blasted seal was already loosened and, perhaps, did he spread it, it would dry faster.

He unfolded it and held it to the flames, resolutely keeping the writing turned away from him. But he could not keep his eyes from that horribly tempting page, and with the glow of the fire behind it, the words began to be clear. One word fairly jumped out at him . . . Leith. *Leith!* Muttering a curse, he snatched up the page, and read:

> *Dearest beloved*—[Strand swore]
>   *You married Strand reluctantly, and knowing you had my heart. Nor did I feel constrained from pursuing you, since I held his ''courtship,'' if one can call it that, to be dishonourable.*
>   *I cannot condone what you now mean to do (and do not ask how I learned of it, for I'll not betray a confidence). I entreat you to abandon your plans. I know you have long nourshed a* tendre *for Tristram Leith, but do not, I beg of you, go to him! To do so can only bring heartbreak upon the Leiths, more and perhaps fatal rage from your unpredictable husband, and grief to—*
>
> Yrs, forever,
Garvey

Lisette's original intention to go straight to her parents' home on Portland Place was abandoned when she realized this must necessitate further delays. Her need to talk with Charity had become of such importance that all else must be set aside, and to that end when they at last came into Mayfair late next morning, she directed her coachman to drive straight to Berkeley Square and the residence of Tristram Leith's uncle, the Earl of Mayne-Waring.

Being a well-bred individual, with long years of experience in his profession, the butler who opened the door of the impressive mansion evinced not the slightest surprise upon discovering a morning caller upon the porch, with behind her an extremely muddied travelling coach complete with coachman, groom, and what appeared to be an abigail peeping from the rain-beaded window. He bowed deferentially to Mrs. Strand and imparted his regret that neither Mrs. Leith nor Miss Strand was in Town, they and Lady Mayne-Waring having gone down to spend a week or two with Lord and Lady Moulton in Sussex.

Lisette could have wept her frustration. Greenwings, the Moulton's lovely old country home, was not above five and twenty miles southeast of Strand Hall! These three miserable days had been wasted in searching for a girl who had all the time been only three hours' drive from home! She thanked the butler, returned to her carriage, and instructed the coachman to proceed to Portland Place.

Lord Jeremy Bolster was despondent. For three days his frenzied pursuit of Lisette Strand had all but banished his own problems from his mind. This morning, however, he had reached Town and learned from his valet, an unfailingly reliable source, that only an hour since Mrs. Justin Strand had called briefly at the mansion of the Earl of Mayne-Waring, and then proceeded to the home of her parents. The danger was, it would appear, past. Bolster was nothing if not thorough, however, and so it was that he strolled up Stratton Street, his heart as heavy as his steps.

The porter admitted him to number 15, and he climbed the stairs to Devenish's rooms. The door was opened by an impressive valet who advised that his master was not presently at home, but expected to return before noon so as to change his clothes for an afternoon engagement. Since it was then half-past eleven, Bolster accepted an invitation to wait, rather than again venture into the rain in search of his quarry. He bestowed his long drab coat upon the valet, tossed hat, gloves, and cane onto an already littered sideboard, and settled himself in the comfortable chair beside the fire of the cosy parlour. He was scanning *The Racing Calendar* when he heard a carriage rattle at a spanking pace along the street and stop nearby. A moment later, someone pounded on the door, and voices in the hall were followed by a quick, light step that Bolster knew all too well. His heart sinking, he sprang up to confront the man he was least desirous of beholding.

"S-Strand!" he said nervously. "You here?"

Strand carried his hat and whip and was still wearing a many-caped drab coat. He looked haggard and grim, and returned a pithy, "Evidently. Have you seen Leith?"

"Leith?" Bolster echoed, his voice squeaking a little. "N-n-no. Not here, dear old b-boy." To which he added a reinforcing, "I come to s-s-see Devenish. D-Devenish lives here."

"So I understand." Strand passed his hat and gloves to the hovering valet, but retained his whip. He then flung himself into the one remaining armchair and glowered at the fire.

Bolster thought he looked ripe for murder. "Catch cold in here with your c-coat on, old fellow. Want to walk? I'll come with you."

"Thank you," Strand muttered. "But I shall wait for Devenish. He may be able to tell me where I can find a filthy snake that calls itself Tristram Leith."

Anguished, Bolster thought, He knows! But springing to his feet, he tried to look shocked, and expostulated, "Confound you, Justin! Here you go r-rushing off half-cocked again! What is it this time? Tristram's a spl-splendid fellow."

Strand leaned his head back against the wing chair and with a curl of the lip observed, "The kind of 'splendid fellow' who marries my sister and within a year seduces my wife!"

"No, no! That ain't so! I swear you are quite out there!"

"Devil I am!" Strand uttered a mirthless bark of laughter and stood to take off his greatcoat and toss it over the table. "I chance to have intercepted a letter warning my devoted bride against going to Leith. I reached home to discover she had already done so!" He paused, his face turned away, and added as though the words scourged him, "I traced her as far as Cloudhills."

"Yes, but she d-did- did not st-stop there."

For a moment Strand was very still. Turning his head, he looked at Bolster enigmatically. "She didn't?"

"No, no, old fellow. Saw her m'self. In Oxford."

"Did you now?" said Strand in a soft, almost caressing tone.

"How very remarkable. I was told the road to Oxford was flooded and that the military was turning back all travellers."

"Oh . . . well, I must have dr-dr- passed through b-before that."

"Indeed you must," Strand said dryly. "And come away by means of a rowboat, eh? Do you mean to explain away the letter also?"

"Er—likely it was more of Garvey's no-no-nonsense is all."

"And he tricked Lisette into driving to Berkshire also, no doubt? Good try, my friend, but . . ." He stood, rummaged under his coat, retrieved his whip, and sat down again.

Bolster eyed the heavy whip uneasily. "Wh-what d'you m-mean to do?"

"Call Leith out," Strand grated. "The sneaking, lying cur!"

"Good God! You mustn't talk like that, Justin! He's wed t-to your sister!"

"The more reason to slaughter the—" Strand paused, listening intently.

To Bolster's horror, wheels sounded outside, followed by a sudden burst of male talk and laughter.

Strand came to his feet in a fluid, pantherish movement. Jumping up also, Bolster gripped his arm. "Justin! For the love of God! Do not!"

"Stand clear, Jerry." Strand wrenched free. "I'd not have you hurt."

"You're m-mad! C-consider Rachel! Consider Lisette!"

"Consider the marriage vows! Consider honour and decency!"

"Aye, but if—"

Footsteps were in the hall. Devenish's voice said laughingly, ". . . but it *was* his wife, eh?"

Strand's lips pulled back and from between gritted teeth came a low, menacing growl.

Attempting to seize the whip, Bolster pleaded, "Give over, man! You will never b-be able t-to—"

Strand shoved him away. "I shall *kill* the swine who was with my wife last week-end!"

"But—I swear it w-wasn't Leith!"

Strand caught his breath. His eyes, turning to Bolster, put that earnest young man forcibly in remind of two sabres. "Then . . . who . . ." he breathed, "*was* she with?"

The door was flung open. Desperate and thinking only to prevent the impending tragedy, Bolster cried, "Me!"

Alain Devenish and Marcus Clay paused on the threshold, struck to silence by the dramatic pose of the two before them: Bolster's hand clutching Strand's wrist, Strand, pale and rigid, every inch of his lean frame reflecting restrained fury.

For Strand, time seemed to stand still. A series of cameos flickered through his mind with blinding speed: Lisette, saying so casually that Bolster had visited her during that first horrible week of their marriage—ostensibly to leave Brutus in her care. Bolster, usually so painfully afflicted with shyness at the presence of a female, yet conversing merrily with Lisette. The two of them, standing very close together before the weeping willow at Silverings, and on Bolster's face that almost ludicrous expression of guilt. Lisette's deep concern when Bolster had wrenched his arm while working on *Silvering Sails* . . . the way they'd sat together on the sofa later, whispering so softly, so secretively . . . Lord! How could he have been so blind!

"By *God*!" he snarled. "*You? Of all men? You?*"

His lordship blinked. It had never occurred to him that Strand might think *he* had cuckolded him, and briefly, he was stunned with surprise. If ever there was a moment when it was imperative that he enunciate clearly, this was it. But the more nervous Bolster became, the worse was his stammering, and thus, belatedly attempting to extricate himself from this deadly development, he uttered an unfortunate, "N-no! Not—I didn't—*we* didn't—L-L-Lisette and I d-d-did—but we didn't mean t-t-to—"

A red haze was before Strand's eyes. Quite forgetting he still held the whip, he struck out, the blow catching Bolster across the left side of his face so hard that he was sent reeling back.

"*Foulness!*" spat out Strand, advancing on his dazed victim. "Judas!"

Recovering their wits, Devenish and Clay jumped forward; Devenish, to support Bolster, Clay to leap before the enraged Strand.

Appalled, Clay demanded, "Justin! Are you run mad? Bolster is your closest friend!"

With an effort that left him shaking, Strand overmastered his fury. His face very white, he said with devastating and deliberate clarity, "Lord Bolster is no friend of mine! He is a damned cheat! A lecherous, conniving, disloyal, womanizing vermin I can scarce wait to shoot down so I may wipe my boots on his worthless carcass!"

"Good . . . God!" gasped Devenish. "What in the name of—"

"Name your seconds, Bolster!" thundered Strand.

With deepening horror, Clay noted that the door to the hall stood wide and that the porter, who had been conductiong two military gentlemen on tour of some available rooms, stood with his charges gazing across the small vestibule at the dramatic confrontation. Stifling a groan, he raced to close the outer door, his heart plummeting as he recognized one of the officers as Captain Butterfield, a likeable but garrulous young man. There was, he thought miserably, no quieting this now!

"J-Justin," Bolster managed faintly, one hand pressed to his cheek, "you m-must not—"

"If your friend, Mr. Devenish," sneered Strand, "lacks sufficient backbone to meet me, I would as soon bring my pistol here and shoot him down like the dog he is!"

To swallow this, added to the former insults, was unthinkable, and Devenish and Clay exchanged stricken looks. His lips tight, Devenish turned to Bolster. "Jeremy, do you wish that I act for you?"

Bolster lowered his hand, revealing a great darkening welt across his cheek. "No! Justin, I b-beg of you to l-l—"

"Observe the whining coward," sneered Strand. "What is your next move, poltroon? Shall you fall on your knees and beg pardon?" Bolster flushed, and Strand snarled, "Can you suppose I would *ever* pardon such treachery?"

"N-no!" Bolster said with a faint frown. "B-but I am n-not—I did not—"

"You convicted yourself with your own mouth," Strand raged. "Unless—" The glaring, murderous light in his eyes softened. He said an all but pleading, "There can be but one reason for your refusal to meet me! You are innocent and it *was* Leith, as I suspected! Jeremy, for the love of God! Only tell me that is so, and—"

"No!" gasped Bolster. "But there is no n-n-need for us to fight, and—"

"*No need?*" Strand thundered. "Damn you! Do you rate her favours so cheap?" He sprang forward, but Clay stepped between them, and said, a touch of frost in his voice, "Bolster. You have no choice, you know."

Bolster sighed. "I know," he muttered, and drawing himself up, added with the odd judicial dignity that occasionally marked him, "Gone too far now. Quite r-right. I th-thought Leith was c-coming in with you, else I'd not have said—oh, well. Too late n-now." He glanced at Devenish. "Thank you for the offer, D-Dev. I'll accept it."

Devenish nodded gravely.

Strand turned his glittering gaze on Clay.

"I'll act for you, Justin," the Major said with frowning reluctance. "When?"

"Now!"

Devenish gave a gasp and, with sudden and uncharacteristic propriety, remonstrated, "Cannot fight at this hour! Ain't done!"

"Don't be so damned prim!" growled Strand.

"If you were caught," Clay pointed out reasonably, "you'd have to make a run for it. Better be dawn, Justin, or—"

"*Now!*" Strand reiterated. Green had been right, as usual, and he had contracted a heavy cold. Already he felt hot and feverish, and his head so wooden that to think was an effort. Lord knows if he'd be able to fight at all tomorrow! He said stubbornly, "I've to leave Town first thing in the morning. No one will see us in this miserable weather. We can meet in Wanderer's Spinney off the Wimbledon Road. If"—his lip curled unpleasantly—"you can get your man there, Devenish."

With his wide gaze fixed on the hearth, Bolster did not hear this latest slur. He was instead experiencing a vague and foolish sense of pride that Strand *had* suspected him of engaging in an *affaire* with the lovely Lisette. This emotion was followed at once by regret that the beauty had proven so faithless. She *had* spent the night at Cloudhills, alone with Leith. That much he'd been able to determine. It was a pity he had been unable to come up with a believable explanation for her activities—or his own. But at least Strand no longer suspected that Leith had been his betrayer. Perhaps, did Strand wound him a little . . . for he certainly would not shoot to kill, would he? Bolster frowned thoughtfully. Perhaps he'd best write a note to Lisette and to

Leith, warning them. Just in case. He thought with regret of his love and of the life they might have had, save for her high sense of honour. And with a sudden stab of guilt, knew that his mother would mourn him deeply. And there was good old Harry Redmond and his tempestuous brother, Mitchell. And Lucian St. Clair, and Vaughan, and . . . He started when Devenish touched his shoulder and repeated a gentle, "Well, Jeremy?"

"Eh? Oh, whatever. I shall choose pistols if you d-d-do not mind." He looked to Strand apologetically. "Never was much good with swords, you know."

Not glancing his way, Strand nodded. "Two o'clock!"

"Good God, no!" Devenish was nursing the hope of reaching Leith and somehow calling a halt to this, and he expostulated, "That's ridiculous!"

Bolster gestured fatalistically. "Two o'clock is acceptable to me, Dev."

Strand took up his belongings and marched to the door. Bolster called to him. He scowled and swore under his breath, but turned back.

Bolster held out the fateful whip. "F-forgot this," he said quietly.

A wave of grief racked Strand. His exquisite and wanton wife . . . and *Jeremy* . . . ! He took the whip and strode out, leaving the door open.

Chapter 17

Passing Mrs. Strand's cloak to the footman, Powers relayed the news that her family had been delayed due to the weather and was not yet returned from Park Parapine. "Meanwhile, Miss Lis—ah, madam," he intoned, "we are so fortunate as to entertain my lady."

Lisette was ill-prepared to cope with Beatrice, and, her heart sinking, could not restrain a dismayed, "Oh, dear!"

"Wicked, wicked girl!" snarled an irate voice. "How I wish I might box your ears!"

Turning joyously, Lisette cried, "Grandmama!" And ran to kiss that vexed *grande dame* and say fondly, "Oh, but how famous to find you here! Do you stay with my parents? Please say you do not mean to rush away."

Mollified, Lady Bayes-Copeland allowed herself to be ushered tenderly to the drawing room, settled into a chair by the fireside, and begged to wait while her granddaughter hastened upstairs to change her gown and tidy her hair. Returning very soon to the old lady, Lisette drew a chair closer, expressing her concern that her grandmother should have journeyed to Town in such weather.

"Is a new form of madness," declared my lady, sourly. "No sooner does heaven visit a second Flood upon us than everyone takes to the roads! Beatrice, yourself, Jeremy Bolster, my new grandson and, most unwilling and innocent of victims, myself!"

Surprised, Lisette asked, "You have seen Strand? And Bolster? Here?"

"I have seen neither. Only arrived half an hour before you. I was at Brighton. My footman brought the post down to me, and there was a letter from Strand which disturbed me. On my way back to Town, I detoured, suffering my poor old bones to be jolted over more miles of cart ruts for his sake, only to reach the hall and find him gone!"

"I am so sorry, dearest. Justin is at Silverings, working on the yacht."

"Ain't. According to Fisher and your housekeeper, that skitterpate Jeremy Bolster rid in, was closeted with Beatrice, and went off uttering some fustian about being called to Oxford. *Oxford!* From what his mama told me of his undergraduate years there, the town would throw up barricades to keep his disastrous person from the environs!"

Trying not to dwell on what Beatrice might have said to alarm Bolster, Lisette probed, "And—my husband, ma'am?"

"Galloped in as though the devil capered on his shoulder, to hear Fisher tell it. Threw some necessaries into a valise, ordered up his chaise, and drove off again!" She rapped her cane on the floor, then shook it at her bewildered granddaughter. "Well you may stare, miss! The man's betwattled, just as I always held! You should never have married him, and you'd best not set up your nursery, for it will surely be inhabited by caper wits!"

Lisette was silent and, her heart touched by those great frightened eyes, the old lady said in gentler tone, "Now, for Lord's sake, child, never look so scared. I did not mean it. Is a fine boy, else I'd not have gone to such lengths to find him. For that is why I came here. Truth to tell, I feared you had—er—bolted, and that he'd followed you."

Lisette flushed. Evading her grandmother's shrewd gaze, she explained that she had become bored in Sussex and decided to visit Rachel and Charity for a few days. "But the roads were dreadful," she appended, and to forestall the comment she dreaded, went on hurriedly, "Indeed, I find it most unkind that Justin would ask you to come to us in such a storm."

"Well, he did not. Matter of fact, he wrote asking if he might visit *me.* But—well, here. Read it for yourself." Lady Bayes-Copeland drew a crumpled sheet of paper from her pocket and offered it with an impatient jerking of her frail hand.

Lisette unfolded the page and read:

"Dear Grandmother B.C.—"

"D'ye see the way he names me, the saucy rogue?" demanded the old lady, stabbing a finger at the letter. "B.C. indeed!" She cackled mirthfully. "I'll B.C. him! Well, never sit there like a lump! *Read* the thing, girl!"

Dear Grandmother B.C.—

You once told me that I know nothing of how to treat a lady. You were perfectly right, and I stand in need of help.

May I come and see you? If I do not hear to the contrary, I shall drive down on the morning of the twelfth inst., and call upon you. I am desperate, ma'am, else I would not beg that you please receive me. Pray forgive this invasion of your privacy.

> *Your devoted admirer,*
> *Strand*

Lisette lowered the page slowly. Retrieving it, my lady sniffed, "Now tell me what has gone amiss. Have you quarelled because he spanked you?"

Startled, Lisette gasped, "You knew about that?"

"My spies are everywhere! Did Strand believe the tales Beatrice set about he was well justified, but I doubt he beat you half as hard as you deserved!"

"Deserved! I had done nothing! *Nothing!*"

"Save tilt your haughty nose in the air because you fancied him beneath you, which he ain't! Child, oh, child!" The old lady leaned to place one hand on her granddaughter's wrist. "Never be so foolish as to throw away the love of a good man for the smooth words of a pretty scoundrel like Garvey!"

Sudden tears stinging her eyes, Lisette answered huskily, "I am not that big a fool, Grandmama. But Strand has an odd way showing his love. On our wedding night, he—"

"I know all about that and am sworn to say not a word." My lady leaned back in her chair, both hands clasped atop her cane, waiting with smug anticipation. She had not long to wait.

"You—you *know?*" stammered Lisette. "Oh, Grandmama! I implore you to tell me. Who is she? Have I met her? Is—is she very beautiful?"

The twinkle in the old lady's eyes brightened. "A suprising degree of concern from a girl who cares naught for her husband!"

Lisette drew back, turning her face aside, and, after a contemplative moment, my lady murmured, "She is young. And of a very kind and gentle disposition, and—"

"Not a spoiled little shrew—like me!" Lisette interpolated through suddenly clenched teeth.

Lady Bayes-Copeland scanned her thoughtfully. "No. Not at all like you, my dear." She noted the way the white hands gripped the sides of the chair, and how the sweetly curved lower lip trembled, and went on, "But he loves her very deeply. She has something better than mere looks, you see. A compassionate soul; a warm and tender heart." Lisette's proud head bowed low, and the old lady added slyly, "But that does not concern you, since you have interests elsewhere."

"Much chance I shall have of—of finding another interest," said Lisette, blinking rapidly. "If Strand served me so brutally over a silly rumour, heaven knows what he might do did I take a lover!" Flashing a glance at her grandmother, she surprised a grin on that wise countenance and cried indignantly, "Well you may laugh, ma'am! Had you ever known how it feels to be beaten, you . . ." The mirth on the old lady's face faded into nostalgia, and Lisette interrupted herself to breathe an awed, "Grandmama . . . ? My grandfather—he did not—you were not . . . ?

"Ah, but I was, child. Such a gentle soul was my Donald. And I, the rage of London—and Paris! I was promised to him in my cradle, but despised his quiet ways, and he so patient through all my tantrums. I thought I could do as I chose, but he showed me my error. . . ." My lady sighed, her eyes very soft by reason of that distant memory.

Leaning to her, Lisette breathed, "And did he strike you very hard?"

"No." Her grandmother chuckled. "Not really. It was the humiliation hurt the most, and the knowledge I had indeed been most naughty. But never had I admired him more, through I did not let him see that, of course, and wept so that he was horrified by what he had done and—oh, so sweetly repentant."

"And—and so you forgave him?"

"Of course." My lady cackled and gave Lisette a conspiratorial dig in the ribs. "But not before I had made him promise never to raise his hand to me again. He never did, and although we had our squabbles and differences from time to time, I gave him no cause to doubt me, and I always held him in respect—to the day he died, God rest his dear soul. . . .'' With another sigh for yesterdays, she put her snowy head back against her chair and closed her eyes for a moment. Strand's letter slipped from her hand, and taking it up to fold it absently, Lisette said, ''But I thought you had many lovers!''

''So I did!'' The fierce eyes snapped open again. ''*Cicisbeos* merely, but I'd the largest court of any woman in London, I'll have you know. In fact—'' The door burst open. Irked, she swung her head around and began, ''How dare—''

Amanda Hersh rushed in, dropped the old lady a hurried curtsey, and turned a distraught countenance to her friend. ''Thank heaven I found you Lisette! You must stop him you *must!*''

Standing to greet her, Lisette was struck by foreboding. ''What is it? Has something happened to Lord Bolster?''

''I pray not!'' cried Amanda, wringing her hands. ''I do not know the cause but Strand struck Jeremy in the face with his whip!''

Lisette gasped, ''He—*what?* Oh, your pardon, but you must be mistaken. They are the very best of friends.''

''They were! No longer. Strand must be all about in his head but he struck him I tell you!''

''The devil he did!'' Lady Bayes-Copeland rose with unusual alacrity and, proceeding straight to the heart of the matter, said ''They'll go out, then?''

''This—this afternoon!'' wailed Amanda.

Too stricken to utter a word, Lisette stared at her.

''Where?'' barked the old lady. ''When?''

''Alas I do not know ma'am I can discover naught of it I am sure Mr. Devenish knows but he would not tell me.'' Amanda moved to clasp Lisette's arm imploringly. ''I *cannot* understand it but they are to fight with pistols that much I did learn and it means—that— Oh, Lisette help me! For pity's sake *help* me!''

Lisette raised a trembling hand to her brow. ''Yes, but what—whatever are we to do? This afternoon! My God! Why ever must it be so soon?''

''Because men are incredible ninnies!'' raged my lady, rapping her cane on the floor in frustration. "And this is no time to stand on ceremony. Come!"

Two terrified pairs of eyes turned to her. "Where?" asked Lisette.

"To the servants' hall." My lady began to march to the door, her step surprisingly brisk. " 'Tis the one sure source of information. But if those two idiots kill one another before we can stop them, I shall never speak to either of 'em again! And so I warn you!"

The drizzle had stopped by the time the carriage halted, and pale rays of sunlight were beginning to slant through the warm, misty air. Strand drew the collar of his greatcoat higher about his throat and, shivering, started off with his usual rapid stride, only to check as a shattering howl blasted the damp silence. "That damnable hound will raise every constable for miles around does he keep that up!" he gritted.

Marcus Clay nodded and, praying that Leith would receive his message, offered to go back and let Brutus out of the carriage.

"Lord, no! He would hang on everyone's neck, blast him!"

Walking on, Clay asked, "Why did you bring him if he's such a nuisance?"

"I didn't *invite* him! The brute jumped in just as my groom was putting up the steps and raised such a fuss when we tried to drag him out that two old ladies who chanced to be passing threatened to have me arrested for cruelty to animals! It seemed less trouble to haul him along, but that is why I'm late." He scowled to see Bolster's chaise drawn up beside some trees. "Damn it! I knew he'd be punctual!"

Clay muttered that he'd best consult with Devenish and wandered over to the small group awaiting them. The surgeon, a cold-eyed man with a military bearing, vouchsafed the information that he'd not been in attendance at a duel since "poor young Hedges" was killed in May. Clay and Devenish exchanged grim glances and went off to measure the distance.

"Any word?" Devenish asked, low-voiced.

"None. Even if my man finds Leith, I doubt anything can be done. What a *damnable* coil this is! Poor Bolster's face looks dreadful. How's he taking this?"

"A sight calmer than I would do. But there's an air of resignation about him. I've an idea he means to delope."

"Good God! He must be mad! But if he *does* fire in the air, I give you my word Strand won't! He's like a man possessed. Have you learned what set it off?"

"Something about Lisette, which I cannot fathom, because Bolster's crazy for his Amanda. This spot's level, eh? Strand's— Jupiter! What was that?"

The long-drawn-out howl echoed eerily through the swirling vapours. Glancing in some amusement at Devenish, Clay saw the fine young face was pale and scared—a most uncharacteristic reaction from this fire-eater. "It's only Brutus," he said reassuringly. "He stowed away in Justin's chaise. Something bothering you, Dev?"

Devenish snorted. "Oh, no! Only that two of my good friends are about to slaughter one another!" He then offered an apologetic, "Sorry, Marcus. Nerves a bit tight. I'd have sworn we were followed here. You didn't see a black brougham lurking about, by any chance?"

Before Clay could respond, Strand marched up to ask with some ire what was causing the delays. "I've an—an appointment," he said curtly.

"If you will move out of the way, we'll finish here," Clay answered.

Strand stamped off. Devenish and Clay marked the distance, then went to inspect the pistols. There was some further delay when Devenish affected to mislike the balance of his principal's weapon, but Strand, managing somehow to avoid looking at Bolster's calm but cruelly bruised countenance, snarled that he would take the offending pistol, and moments later the protagonists faced one another across twenty yards of mist-wreathed turf.

Strand stood very straight, the gleaming pistol held at his side. It all seemed quite unreal, but that, he knew, was because the chill he had taken on the boat was tightening its hold on him. His head felt wooden and stupid, he knew he was feverish, and his hand was none too steady. Still, it was done. The seconds had conferred and argued and procrastinated for as long as they possibly could. The final instructions had been given by Clay, his pleasant features very grave. The only thing remaining now was the count—and these last moments of grief and farewell. He recalled Lisette's face as he first had seen it, angelically lovely, framed by the dark window of her coach. How little he had dreamed then that his foolish heart, so instantly and irrevocably given, would lead him to this bitter moment. She'd never cared, of course. He was no Don Juan, not like that blasted Leith! Yet what a blessing he did not face Leith today. Poor Rachel would have been—

"One . . ." Devenish's voice echoed across the quiet meadow.

Scarcely hearing, Strand frowned. Why was he thinking of Leith? He did not face that tall, dark Adonis. The yellow hair that gleamed in the diffused light of this mist-shrouded afternoon belong to Jeremy Bolster. . . . It was Bolster who had betrayed him, who evidently, having lost his own love, had decided to trifle with another lady. The wife of his good friend! Bolster! Had it been Garvey, now, that would have been logical enough. It would have fit. He'd thought it *would* be Garvey, and never dreamed—

"Two . . . !"

That ominous call came slightly muted through the trees, and the man who moved so stealthily forward stopped, then sighted carefully along the barrel on his fine Manton. To anyone observing the actions of Mr. James Garvey, it must have seemed that he directed the pistol at Lord Bolster's broad back, but actually, he aimed past Bolster, his target the heart of Justin Strand. Even with his hated rival at last in his sights, however, Mr. Garvey, that pink of the *ton*, was not a happy man. He had fashioned a very neat little scheme whereby Strand, having read the letter cunningly misdelivered to him, would be maddened with jealousy. By rights, he should have returned home to find Lisette gone, pursued her to Cloudhills and discovered her with Leith, who had also been deftly tricked into returning to his estate. Very neat, Garvey had thought, and the inevitable duel would have resulted in both men (one way or another) being killed. So tidy and convenient. Leith's death would have pleased the Frenchman; Strand's death would have wiped out the insult against himself and paved the way for his courtship of, and eventual marriage to, the beautiful and by that time extremely wealthy widow. A delicious touch would be that there was nothing to link him with the matter. He could scarcely be held responsible for the deaths of two men who faced one another in an affair of honour. It was most regrettable that things had not progressed according to plan. Bolster's curst intervention had been as disastrous as it was quixotic. Firstly, it had removed Leith, and thus one could not count on the reaction of the Frenchman. Secondly, Bolster was not nearly so reliable a shot as the intrepid Colonel, and anyone willing to incur the wrath of a jealous and justifiably incensed husband might also be so addlebrained as to delope—especially a marplot who had cried friends with Strand since childhood!

Nourishing feelings of betrayal, Garvey had embarked on his present course with considerable reluctance. It was risky. He had at first intended to follow Claude Sanquinet's advice and hire a professional assassin to ensure Strand's demise, but the threat of blackmail at some later date had deterred him. Besides, his own marksmanship was second to none, and this shot must not be missed. He was quite sure that even if Bolster did fire, it would be with the intent to inflict some superficial wound. There was the possibility that his lordship would aim wide, which would be obliging. One could not take chances, however. Two wounds on Strand's lifeless body could prove embarrassing, and to ensure his swift departure from the scene, Mr. Garvey had brought his hired brougham up as close as he dared. His tiger was holding the nostrils of the horses at this very moment, to ensure they did not whinny and betray his presence. There was, at least, no cause to doubt the discretion of his tiger. That young villain had committed many indiscretions, any one of which would be sufficient to ensure his transportation, to say the least!

"*Three* . . . !"

The fatal word resounded through the stillness. Two hands gripping the deadly, long-barreled pistols were flung up simultaneously. Garvey, his pistol already in position, timed his shot exactly. But again, the unexpected occurred. Having succeeded in coercing a groom to open the carriage door so as to quiet him, Brutus leapt forth with the full power of his muscular body, toppled the groom, and raced off in search of his master. His path was chosen for directness rather than good manners, and took him straight between Garvey's team, who at once reared, screaming their terror. Jolted by the sudden outburst at that crucial instant, Garvey's hand jerked.

Three shots rang out, the third sounding merely an echo of the first two.

Bolster fired into the air. He heard a scream from somewhere close by. In the same instant, he was dealt a sledgehammer blow which sent him sprawling.

Strand, the smoking pistol falling from his hand, stared numbly at Bolster's motionless form. He had aimed for the arm, but must have erred. What a ghastly error! But God knows he'd not meant to kill Bolster! He'd *not!* Shattered, he stumbled away; Brutus, who had been petrified by the shots, creeping out from beneath a bush to slink after him.

Clay, Devenish, and the surgeon were running to the downed man. Tristram Leith suddenly burst through the trees, flashed a grim glance at Strand, then raced to Bolster. Lisette and Amanda followed, and Strand checked and stood rigidly as they halted before him. Amanda's horrified gaze darted to the quiet little group hovering above someone who lay very still on the ground. With a strangled moan, she crumpled in a faint. At once dropping to her knees, Lisette took up one of Amanda's limp hands and began to chafe it. Looking up at her husband, she demanded, "What in heaven's name were you thinking of? Must you al—"

Strand stepped back, an expression of such agony on his pale face that she was struck to silence. "Do you not *know* what has brought me to this pass?" he cried in distraught fashion. "My closest friend lies there—dead belike! And by *my* hand! Go, wanton! Go and look upon your handiwork!" And with a wild, despairing gesture, he turned and strode rapidly away.

Bolster, however, was very soon struggling to sit up. "Where's S-Strand?" he muttered, but encountering the firm hands of the surgeon, he winced and sank back again.

Alain Devenish straightened, drew a deep breath of relief and, meeting Clay's equally relieved gaze, said a thankful, "Jove! I thought for a minute . . .!"

"So did I," Clay nodded. "And I perfectly loathe funerals!"

"W-well, you may have to go to one, at all events," asserted his lordship, faint but persisting. "Of all the filthy tricks! I am so n-noble as to delope, and Strand d-damned well shoots me in the back!"

Bending over him again, Devenish smiled. "A neat trick, I

grant you, Jerry, old fellow. But hardly possible, you know. It may have seemed that way, but—"

"D-devil take you, Alain! You ain't the one lying here! I tell you, I was hit from behind! Ask the sawbones."

Clay glanced enquiringly at the doctor, who condescended to remark that he preferred to be addressed as Dr. Cholomondeley, and that the ball had scored Bolster's side and may have broken a rib, but did not appear to have penetrated the lung.

"*Could* the shot have come from behind him?" asked Clay, humouring his incensed friend. "I heard Strand's horses going wild about something or other."

"Brutus," said Devenish succinctly. "He all but turned inside out when he heard the shots."

"His lordship did appear to fall forward," vouchsafed Cholmondeley, working deftly. "Shock, however, effects odd reactions at times, and I scarcely think that—" He glanced up. "Hello, Colonel. Are you a party to this?"

Devenish started and turning, said, "Jove, Tris! I wish you'd come a sight earlier!" His gaze shifting, he added a shocked, "Gad! Is that Miss Hersh? Poor girl. Looks like you've another patient, Cholmondeley."

"*What?*" Bolster hove himself upwards.

"Lie back, you idiot!" said Leith. "No, Cholmondeley, I am *not* a party to this insanity! Mandy is better now, Jerry. There, she's already starting to get up. Play your cards properly and we may yet turn this tragedy to good account."

Struggling, Bolster gasped out, "D-d da-da- now *blast* you, Tris! Mandy swooned! Let m-me—"

Noting Amanda's wavering approach from the corner of his eye, Leith swore under his breath. "*Will* you lie still?"

Bolster, however, had one thought in mind, and that to catch a glimpse of his beloved. He glimpsed instead a flying fist which, connecting with his jaw, obliterated all thought for a time.

"The devil, sir!" exploded the physician, outraged.

"By God, Leith!" Clay protested.

"Quiet!" hissed Devenish, as Amanda tottered to them, Lisette standing back so as to be out of the way.

The Colonel said gravely, "Do not lose hope, Mandy. Poor old Jeremy just *might* pull through."

Amanda viewed the limp and bloody form of her love and,

dropping to her knees beside him, wept, "Oh, Jeremy . . . my dearest one do not die I implore you else I must die too."

Opening dazed eyes, Bolster saw the adored face above him. "Mandy . . ." he uttered faintly. "You c-came! D-don't leave me—please, Mandy."

"Oh, I won't. I won't!"

With this, he was happily content until a hard and most unkind pinch in his left arm drew a yelp of shock and pain. Looking up, he met Leith's eyes and an imperative grimace. For a moment baffled, he suddenly comprehended. He sighed gustily and closed his eyes.

Amanda clutched at one unresponsive hand and gasped, "Doctor! Is he—"

Dr. Cholmondeley had been securing the temporary dressing about Bolster's hurt, while benefitting from a tersely whispered explanation from Devenish, and save for a grim shake of the head, made no response.

Bolster was in not a little pain, but he was so overjoyed by the close proximity of his love, that he performed quite creditably, saying as one at the gates of death that he could have gone with less regret had he only known his Amanda might have borne his name. And callously disposing of the several relatives who would most willingly move closer to the title in that unhappy event, added, "It d-dies with me . . . you know . . ."

Amanda gave a stifled wail, and Leith bent to her and whispered, "Offer him some encouragement if you can, Mandy. Old Jerry's too good of a fellow to go without hope."

"Oh!" sobbed Amanda, nursing Bolster's hand to her cheek. "I love you, my dearest one. Only get better and I will prove how much!"

Bolster was so encouraged that he gave every indication of being about to spring up and smother her with kisses, wherefore it was necessary for Devenish to pinch him again, which he did so heartily that Bolster was hard put to it to refrain from cursing him. Fortunately, he bit back that impromptu utterance. Misinterpreting the set of his jaw, Amanda supposed him to be restraining his groans, and deposited several damp and sympathetic kisses in his palm. "As soon," she gulped, "as you are better I will marry you and—"

"You *will?*" beamed the ecstatic Bolster. "Did you hear that, you fellows? I am *betrothed!* If th-that don't beat the—"

With rare tact, Dr. Cholmondeley chose that instant to tighten his bandage, otherwise his lordship might have ruined the entire thing.

"*Thank* heaven you are come home!" Hurrying into the entrance hall, only slightly leaning upon her cane, Lady Bayes-Copeland stretched her thin hand to her granddaughter, and demanded, "Tell me quickly. Is someone killed?"

"No, ma'am." Lisette was cold and felt drained and bereft of all hope. "Lord Bolster was shot, but he is alive. Amanda is with him now, and—"

"And where is my grandson?"

"Why, I suppose Norman is—"

"Is here!" Shaking her cane impatiently, and hindering Powers by assisting in the removal of Lisette's cloak, her ladyship barked. "You know very well to whom I refer. Don't be missish! Ain't the time!"

Lisette submitted to being hurried to the stairs. "If you mean Strand, ma'am, I neither know nor care! As usual, he blamed me for this, as though—"

"Stuff! The poor lad had good reason, I suspect. Beatrice is here!"

Lisette's lips tightened. The perfect end of a perfect day! "How nice," she said dryly.

"It ain't. At all. Good gad, how these stairs tire my poor old limbs. Your arm, Madam Hauteur! Now, when we meet your sister, you will be so kind as to follow my lead!"

Gently aiding this frail old tyrant into the drawing room, Lisette checked momentarily. Beatrice sat huddled on the sofa and was in the act of accepting the glass of wine Norman offered. Much shocked, Lisette thought her sister looked to have aged ten years. Her usually elegant coiffure was tumbled and untidy, with wisps hanging at all angles. Her dress was creased, her half-boots muddied, and she looked positively shrunken. But worst of all was the expression on her ashen features, an expression that went beyond grief to a dulled resignation that was appalling.

Forgetting everything except that this was her sister, Lisette started forward with a little instinctive cry of sympathy. She was restrained by a claw of a hand.

Norman turned to them and gave a gesture of helplessness, then put down the wine and came to give Lisette a kiss, and whisper, "Another bumble broth! Gad! What a family! Is poor Bolster killed?"

Lisette shook her head, but before she could speak, the old lady said harshly, "Well, madam?"

Beatrice raised haggard eyes, then cowered back against the sofa.

"Your machinations, Lady William," my lady said in that same acid tone, "near cost Jeremy Bolster his life, which would likely have resulted in that ninny Amanda Hersh grieving herself into an early grave." Tears brimming in her dark eyes, Beatrice began a plaintive response that was ruthlessly overriden. "To those two lives," observed the old lady grimly, "we may well add Justin Strand, of whom I—at least—am extremely fond. On top of that, you have very likely broken the heart of your husband, who is so foolish as to love you!"

The effect of this indictment was shattering. Norman, who had retreated to the side of the room, quailed in horror as Beatrice burst into a storm of sobs, and began to sway back and forth in a frenzy of grief.

Unmoved, the old lady snorted, "A pretty display! And one that will avail you nothing. You had best make your peace with your sister, madam!" The only effect this had was to increase the volume of the lamentations, whereupon my lady barked, "Norman! Run and get a pitcher of cold water!"

Only too glad to escape, he shot for the door.

"No-no . . ." Beatrice raised a wet face and reddened eyes. "I know what—what I must do . . ."

At the door, Norman looked back, pleadingly. Lady Bayes-Copeland nodded, and he fled, closing the door quietly behind him. The old lady settled herself on the edge of a loveseat, but Lisette, chilled by apprehension, remained standing.

"I—I will confess," Beatrice announced between sniffs. "Though—though I am not the first lady ever . . . to take a lover, I suppose."

"To take a lover if one has an inattentive, repulsive, or unfaithful husband is one thing," said my lady tartly. "In your case there was neither excuse nor justification. And to plot with that lover to the jeopardy of another member of your own family is despicable!'' Her cane rapped on the floor to emphasize that terrible denunciation and she repeated it in her harsh, cracked old voice, ''*Despicable*, I say!''

Her head down-bent, Beatrice said tremulously, ''Yes. Only—only I thought James loved me. He said—''

''James?'' echoed Lisette, astounded. ''*Garvey?*''

Beatrice nodded. ''He said he had a score to settle, and—and so I told him what Charity said about—about Strand leaving you on your wedding night. And about him staying away a week or more. It was James circulated the rumours that you had deliberately repulsed your bridegroom. When Strand confronted him in The Madrigal, James said that you had told him you were a wife in name only and that you were in love with James.''

One hand flying to her throat, Lisette exclaimed, ''Oh, my God! No wonder Strand challenged him! How I wish he had told me the whole and I'd not have—'' A bony finger jabbed into her ribs. She cast her grandmother an irked glance, but said no more.

''James was like a madman after their quarrel in The Madrigal,'' Beatrice continued, staring blindly at the rug. ''I tried to comfort him, but all he could say was that his honour must be satisfied. He begged me to—to convey to him anything I learned about you. He said . . .'' She closed her eyes briefly, her hand beginning to tear at her handkerchief. ''He said that if he could just wipe out that stain on his honour, he would—would take me away. That William could obtain a divorce and James would wed me. Lord help me! How little I guessed . . .''

She began to weep wretchedly, but Lisette was appalled and made no move to go to her.

''When you arrived at Strand Hall and discovered Lisette meant to visit her sisters-in-law,'' rasped my lady grimly, ''you *knew* that Rachel and Charity were not at Cloudhills. You did not apprise her of that circumstance, but instead sent word to your scheming lover. Correct?''

Lisette gasped out a disbelieving, ''Oh, no! You never did?''

Hanging her head, Beatrice whispered, ''Yes. It—it was wicked in me, I know. But . . . I loved him so, and I thought— Oh well, never mind about that. I sent a note to James by my groom that very night. When he received it, he writ a letter to *you*, Lisette, begging that you not run away to Tristram Leith. And he had the letter taken to Strand at Silverings—as if in error.''

"How vile!" uttered my lady in accents of loathing.

Very white, Lisette muttered, "Strand already suspected that I cared for Leith. If he—if he read *that* . . ."

"He did, of course," my lady interpolated dryly. "He'd have to be a ninny or a saint not to! And so he set off at the gallop to intercept you."

Lisette threw both hands to her cheeks, but after a moment's puzzling said, "But if Strand learnt I spent the night at Cloudhills, alone with Leith, why did he call out *Bolster?*"

Lady Bayes-Copeland directed a chill stare at Beatrice. "Ask our traitor."

Wincing, Beatrice explained, "He did not discover that. But Bolster did."

"And was so gallant as to attempt to spare you—all of us— the stark tragedy of having your husband shoot down your brother-in-law!" said my lady.

"But—but . . ." stammered Lisette, "surely he knew that Justin would call him out?"

"That simpleton?" The old lady gave a scornful bark of derision. "He is brave as he can stare, I grant you, but not one for deep thinking. Nor imagine I think the less of him, for he is a fine boy. Do not forget, my dear, that he and your husband have been friends all their lives. I suspect our quixotic peer traded on that friendship. He probably had no notion Strand would really believe him to have been your secret lover, and hoped merely to confuse Strand into delays, thus providing time in which to reason him from his rage. Instead, Strand called him out and then shot him. Utter folly!"

Beatrice's head sank even lower. Almost inaudibly, she whispered, "N-no."

"What the deuce d'you mean, *no?*" demanded her grandmother fiercely. "Do you add an admiration of duelling to your incalculable idiocies, madam?"

Beatrice wet dry lips. "Strand d-did not shoot Bolster, Grandmama. James was there. He followed Devenish and then hid behind a tree, intending to shoot Strand in case Jeremy should delope." She heard a startled exclamation and, flashing a frightened glance upwards, saw that her grandmother had come to her feet and that the two women stood there, like some familial tribunal, watching her in horror. Cringing, she faltered, "Only

B-Brutus upset James's team, and James missed his shot and—and wounded Bolster by accident.''

There was a brief, stunned silence, even the unquenchable Lady Bayes-Copeland rendered speechless by this shocking disclosure. Then, ''Now . . . now here's shameful treachery, indeed!'' she breathed. ''Which I shall ensure is well circulated among the *ton!* Must I name you a party to this dastardly plot, wretched girl?''

''No! Oh, no!'' Clasping her hands together prayerfully as she blinked up at them, Beatrice sobbed, ''I beg—I *pray* you believe me! I thought James would manoeuvre Strand into a duel and—and wound him—just a little ¬. . perhaps. But I never *dreamt* he meant murder! I was waiting at his lodgings when he came home.'' She saw her grandmother's lip curl contemptuously, and rushed on. ''He was like a man possessed, and took a—a sort of cruel delight in telling me what he had tried to do. I was—absolutely appalled. I taxed him with having deceived me, and he laughed. I was so frightened! I begged that we run away, and be married in Italy when William gave me the divorce.''

''Little fool!'' snorted her grandmother. ''Garvey never loved *you!* It is Lisette he wants.''

''Yes,'' Beatrice wept, covering her face once more. ''So he admitted, at last. And taunted me so—so savagely. It had all been lies from the very beginning. Strand had never boasted of having 'bought' Lisette, as James told me. He said he had at first intended to kill Strand, but then realized that if he waited until after they were wed, Lisette would be a—a very wealthy widow—''

''*Foul!*'' screeched my lady, her cane striking the floor in a staccato outburst of indignation. ''And you could *listen* to such—such wicked infamy, and not come to me—or your papa—with it all? Oh, for *shame!*''

''I dare not come to you,'' choked Beatrice. ''James said if I told one word of what had happened, he would say I planned it all with him! And he boasted that he would s-soon wed the lady he—he really loved, and be a rich man besides. Oh . . .! When I think what I have done! And—and my poor, good, grieving William! Oh, how I wish I was dead! I wish I was *dead!*''

''Very Drury Lane-ish,'' sneered her grandmother, giving the bell pull a tug. She glanced at Lisette, who stood in white-faced silence, staring down at her sister. "What is in your mind, love? That we must warn Strand?"

"Yes," Lisette answered numbly. "And that I once was so unpardonably foolish as to wish I could wed James Garvey—instead of Justin!"

Chapter 18

All night the rain beat down steadily, drenching the waterlogged countryside and turning the usually gentle drift of the river to a boiling race, the roar of which penetrated even the thick walls of Silverings. With the dawn, the *Silvering Sails* rocked uneasily in her small inlet, protected to some extent from the mainstream, but occasionally caught by a surge of waters so that she strained at the ropes securing her. One might have supposed that the man who had toiled for so many hours refurbishing the vessel would evince some concern at this sight, for the river became more littered with mud and debris, the safety of the inlet more threatened, with every hour that passed. In point of fact, however, Justin Strand, seated in the windowseat, his back against the walls, his legs across the length of the cushions, saw neither storm, river, nor boat. Wherever he looked, even if he closed his eyes, three faces haunted him: the white, still features of Jeremy Bolster, poor little Amanda's stricken expression, and the scornful countenance of the girl he had worshipped and wed, and who had so carelessly betrayed him. All the way back to Sussex he had been able to think of nothing else. Throughout the hours of darkness he had paced the floor, racked with guilt and fear for Bolster, and scourged by the knowledge that Lisette, denied the love of the man to whom she had given her heart, knowing how deep was the devotion offered by her husband, had still rejected him, choosing to take his best friend for her lover.

He ran a distracted hand through his rumpled hair, reminded that he had come within a hair's-breadth of calling out Leith—a mistake that would surely have broken Rachel's heart. There were levels to tragedy, he acknowledged; for instance, his personal grief was intensified because it had been Bolster who betrayed him. Bolster, whom he'd always held to be the very soul of honour, and totally above such base treachery. Yet, even so, he had not intended to—

A hand touched his shoulder gently. A troubled voice asked, "Sir! Be ye all right? It do be almighty hot in here, so hot as a furnace, yet ye be a-shivering and a-shaking like any aspen tree!"

Strand looked with a smile into Best's honest eyes. "I'm afraid I may have contracted a cold."

"Ar," said Best, uneasily. "Well, I do wish as how Mr. Green would come."

Until they reached here last evening, Strand had quite forgotten that he'd left instructions for his valet to return to the Hall. He had sent the other groom off at once, with instructions that Green was to come down to Silverings, but after the heavy rains of the night, it was quite possible that the roads were flooded. "I'm sure he will get here as soon as he can," he said. "Are the horses dry?"

The stable roof, Best admitted, was beginning to drip in a few places, and he was in fact going down there now, to see if he could make some temporary repairs. "It do be a great pity," he added with a reproachful glance at his employer, "as that fancy French cook bean't here, seein's young Johnny bean't able to have come back in time to do the job."

The image of the lofty René condescending to look at the stable roof, much less soil his talented hands upon it, brought a gleam to Strand's tired eyes. "Then let us hope," he said bracingly, "that young Johnny returns with Mr. Green. Meanwhile, do you need help, let me know."

Best grunted. The last person he would ask for help, he thought, was a man who looked fair wrung out. But he said nothing, and went clumping off to the stables.

Left alone, Strand gave himself a mental shake. All this brooding was achieving nothing. To have left the scene of the duel without first determining the condition of his victim had been reprehensible. But very likely Bolster was not dead at all and would make a full recovery. The thing to do now was to come to some decision regarding his marriage. It was very obvious that Lisette did not want— His gaze having returned to the rain-streaked window, he was much shocked to see the *Silvering Sails* drifting erratically, secured by only the bow line. If she once got into the mainstream of the littered river, she'd have little chance, and Norman would be heartbroken was she sunk! He sprang up hurriedly, only to reel to the wall and lean there, fighting a sick dizziness. The apprehension seized him that this was not a cold that plagued him, but a recurrence of that abominable fever. He rejected the notion at once. It could not be! Not this soon! He'd had little sleep last night and that, coupled with the chill he'd taken on the boat, had not helped matters. His head soon cleared, and he went over to the sideboard and poured himself a glass of cognac. The potent liquor burned through him, and be began to feel more the thing. Lord, he thought, as he hastened upstairs to get his greatcoat, how Green would rail at him if he should fall ill! He'd never hear the end of it!

The door to his bedchamber was slightly open. Brutus was comfortably disposed in the armchair and his master's new four-caped coat had been fashioned into a burial ground from beneath which peeped the remains of a bone. Exasperated, Strand retrieved his coat while advising the animal in pithy terms of his probable ancestry. Brutus was sufficiently interested as to yawn, raise his head and watch the proceedings. Deciding a walk was in the offing, he sprang down and collected his property before accompanying Strand to the stairs with much enthusiastic, if muffled, yelping.

Outside, the wind was approaching gale proportions. Strand full expected his canine companion to bolt back into the house when he saw the trees whipping about. Apparently, there was not an aspen in sight, however, and neither the sight of drifts being blown across the lawns nor the trees bending before the gale caused the animal to become alarmed.

"I collect," remarked Strand cynically, "that you are very discriminating as to what may cause your intellect—what there is of it—to become disordered! Come along, then. But be warned that I've no least intention of jumping in after you, should you fall in!"

Undaunted, Brutus trundled ahead, tracking down and attending to several enticing distractions along their route until, a likely depository for the bone presenting itself, he proceeded to excavate the middle of a flower bed.

Lost in thought and unaware of these depredations, Strand made his rapid way to the dock. The *Silvering Sails* rocked and pitched at the end of her solitary rope, masts swaying and boards creaking. The aft mooring rope trailed over the side, and must be secured if she was to have any chance of riding out the storm. Strand waited his chance, then sprang nimbly aboard. The erratic motion of the vessel slowed him, but clinging to the rail he staggered aft and began to haul in the rope. The rain was a steady, soaking drizzle, and the wind so strong that at times it buffeted his breath away. It was not an icy wind, but his teeth began to chatter, and the headache which had plagued him for the past two days was becoming more intense. The boat pitched violently, and unable to hold his balance, he swayed to his knees, swearing lustily.

Only the fall saved him. A boathook whizzed past, missing his head so narrowly that it ruffled his hair before it smashed against the rail. Beyond it, James Garvey's face loomed, contorted and dark with hatred. With a bound, Strand regained his feet, barely avoiding a second fierce lunge of the boathook. That Garvey meant murder was very apparent. A pistol would have been swifter and surer, but also, he realized, would both attract attention and rule out the possibility of accidental death.

"Maniac!" he shouted, edging back and from the corner of his eye searching for something to use as a weapon. "Do you want to hang?"

"I want you dead! I want your wife, to whom you have no right! Never fear—I'll not hang!" And on the last word, Garvey sprang forward, the boathook flailing in a mighty sweep. Strand had to leap for his life. He eluded that murderous attack, but landed on a coiled length of rope, and fell heavily. With a triumphant shout, Garvey drove the boathook downward. Strand rolled desperately, and the iron hook ripped through the back of his jacket and slammed into the deck. Snatching up the rope, Strand flung it at Garvey's face. Garvey jerked back, slipped on the wet deck, and staggered, fighting to retain his balance as the boat yawed drunkenly. He recovered almost immediately, but

Strand had seized the opportunity to jump up and grab a belaying pin. It was only half the length of the boathook, but he swung around, gripping it in both hands, just in time to block the shattering blow Garvey had launched at him.

Again and again, driven by hatred and avarice, Garvey attacked. Again and again, Strand deflected his blows, but he also battled fever and the disadvantage of an inferior weapon, and he was driven back relentlessly until he was at the stern. The roar of the river filled his ears, and as the *Silvering Sails* swung straight out from the dock, the littered swell of the mainstream was terrifyingly close. If he fell there could be no survival; the strongest swimmer could not prevail against that furious boil of mud and debris. His arms were aching from the shocks of Garvey's maddened onslaught, and his vision began to blur. As he blocked another attack, Garvey's form drifted in twain. Two murderous assailants faced him; two boathooks hurtled at his head. Dazed and uncertain, he peered through a thickening mist from which a harsh laugh sounded triumphantly. The splintered boathook flashed down and Strand was able to deflect it only partially. He felt a mighty shock, a blinding wave of pain, and the deck flew up to meet him.

Vaguely, he knew that he was lying prone, his cheek against the blessed coolness of wet boards. Crimson stained those boards. He blinked at it and was shocked by the knowledge that it was his own blood. His head pained so savagely that he felt sick but, stronger than pain, the instinct for survival demanded that he get up, for to lie here was death. He strove feebly to lift himself, but his head whirled and his bones were sand, and he could only get an elbow under him. Gleaming, tasseled Hessians were very near, and yet not advancing. Puzzled, Strand heard a strange new sound.

"Nice doggie . . ." said Mr. Garvey, placatingly.

Blinking, Strand perceived Brutus a few paces distant. A transformed Brutus, who was the very epitome of canine savagery. Below his upcurling lip protruded long, gleaming fangs; the hair across his broad shoulders stood straight on end, and from deep within that powerful chest rose a rumbling growl calculated to give pause to any man.

His boathook at the ready, Garvey coaxed, "Here, boy . . ." He held out one hand, tightening his grip on the boathook with the other, but when Brutus's jaws snapped only inches from his fingertips, Mr. Garvey forgot the boathook and jumped backwards.

The wind flung his coat wide, and the ends fluttered. Brutus quailed, howled, raced for the fallen coils of rope, dug his head under them, and crouched. shivering.

Garvey gave a shout of laughter. "A fine champion, Strand!" he gloated, and with both hands, swung the boathook high.

Brutus might not have earned the right to be dubbed "a fine champion," but his intervention had given Strand the chance to catch his breath. Mustering all his wiry strength, he leapt to his feet. The belaying pin was within easy reach, but he disdained it; only his bare fists would do for this task. He was very fast; his right rammed in hard under Garvey's ribs. The boathook fell from suddenly nerveless hands. Garvey's face purpled as he doubled up. Strand straightened him out with a left uppercut that lifted Mr. James Garvey to the toes of his fine Hessians, and caused him to sink downward with all the grace of a sack of potatoes.

Swaying drunkenly, looking down at his vanquished foe, Strand heard a shout. His head weighed a ton, but he raised it slowly. Best and Oliver Green were running along the deck towards him.

"Take this . . . carrion," he said faintly, "and—lock it up. Tried to . . . to . . ." And sighing, he crumpled to the deck.

Despite the fact that they had left Croydon at first light that morning, the condition of the roads was such that is was late afternoon before Lisette's carriage approached Silverings, and her coachman advised the groom that not only was it a miracle they had arrived, but they would be marooned here, that was certain, for there wasn't no way to go back up them roads till the water drained away. Silverings' ruins looked forlorn and sad under the lowering skies, but from the mullioned windows of the old house came the warm glow of candlelight. The Dutch door swung open, and Oliver Green came out and started towards them. Lisette drew a deep breath of relief and, beside her, Norman shouted, "Hurrah! You guessed rightly, Lisette! Strand *is* here!"

Their joy, however, was short-lived. Running to meet the carriage, heedless of the rain, the valet had no welcoming smile, his broad features instead reflecting a deep anxiety.

Norman had the door open and the steps let down almost

before the carriage stopped and, springing out, reached up to hand down Lisette.

"Thank God you've come, ma'am!" said Green. "We've had trouble here."

A hand of ice clutched Lisette's heart. She faltered, "My husband?"

"I'm afraid the master is—is very bad, ma'am."

She whitened and began to run to the house, the man keeping pace with her and Norman demanding with a rather surprising air of authority to know if James Garvey had been at Silverings.

"He has, sir," said Green, swinging the door wider for Lisette to pass. "And tried to kill Mr. Strand."

Lisette put back her hood. "I heard Dr. Bellows has returned from Wales. Has someone gone to fetch him?"

"Best will bring the midwife from the village, can he get through. He would have no chance of reaching Dr. Bellows, not in this storm."

"The devil!" Norman exploded, helping Lisette take off her cloak. "Where is the beastly rogue? Did he get away? We came hoping to warn my brother—is he shot?"

"The master was struck on the head. He managed to overpower Mr. Garvey, Lord knows how! Best has taken Mr. Garvey to the village constable."

Lisette was already running upstairs. The door to the front bedroom was partially open, and she could hear someone talking inside. She pushed the door wider and went in, then stopped, her heart twisting. Strand lay in the big bed. A bandage was taped to his forehead, and he was muttering to himself. He was very pale, but his eyes were open, and she felt an almost overpowering surge of relief to find him conscious. Approaching the bed, she said softly, "Justin?"

He turned to look up at her, his eyes unnaturally bright. "You *know* I did not mean to kill you!" he muttered fretfully. "Didn't mean it, Jerry . . ." And in a sudden burst of rage, "Traitor! Filthy damned traitor!"

With a gasp of fright, Lisette drew back. Behind her, Green said gently, "Perhaps you should wait downstairs, ma'am. Mr Justin doesn't know what he's saying. When he is like this—" He shrugged helplessly.

For answer, she began to strip off her gloves, but made no

move to leave. Strand's ravings had faded to that unintelligible mumbling. He looked so ill; so terribly ill. The fear in her heart deepened. She handed the valet her gloves and asked, "Green, what did Mr. Garvey hit him with?"

"I could not say, ma'am. But I rather doubt it is the head wound we have to fear, for that does not look to be more than a bump and a nasty cut."

Norman, who had halted just inside the door, now came up to the bed, saying in a low voice, "My grandmama told me Strand contracted some kind of fever whilst he was in India. Is that the trouble?"

Lisette threw her brother a shocked look. The valet nodded and, speaking softly also, answered, "It is called malaria, sir."

For a moment, Lisette could not breathe. The room seemed to close in upon her, and she reached out gropingly. At once, Norman's arm was around her. "No vapours from you, m'dear, surely?" he asked, and as her terrified eyes lifted to meet his, he added with a lightness he was far from feeling, "Strand's all steel—do you not know that yet?" He glanced to the valet. "How frequent are the attacks?"

"Not so frequent since we come home, sir. I'd hoped we might have seen the last of it, but—" He broke off, biting his lip, then blurted out, "Well, he pushes himself so. He should never have worked on the boat in the rain the other day. And then—to drive all the way to Berkshire, and knowing he was feeling unwell—but there was no stopping him!"

Lisette turned her face against her brother's shoulder, and Green went on hurriedly, "You know something of the malady, sir?"

"We'd a cousin who contracted malaria in South America, but—" Norman closed his lips over the rest of that sentence. A faint whimper emanated from Lisette, and the valet looked aghast.

The sick man moaned and began to toss restlessly. Recovering her wits, Lisette moved to rest one cool hand on his brow. Dismayed, she looked up at Green, who stood watching, her cloak and gloves clutched to his bosom. "He is on fire!" she whispered. "Is this an unusually bad attack?"

"He'll pick up once Best comes with the midwife," he evaded. But, seeing how frantically those great dark eyes searched his face, he could not deceive her and admitted sadly, "I have never

seen the master become so very ill quite this fast before, ma'am."
He looked down at Strand, his own eyes clouding. "I'd give everything I have, if—if only—"

"Good God!" said Norman indignantly. "He ain't dead yet! Don't *you* turn into a watering pot, Green!"

Green's answering smile was bright, if rather lopsided.

Trembling and stricken, Lisette rallied her forces. With a calm that astounded both men, she said, "Norman, please bring me a bowl of water and a cloth, and ask Denise for my lavender cologne. And she will have to prepare some barley water or lemonade for Justin. I'm afraid I must ask you to see what you can do about dinner, Green."

He regarded her uneasily. "Gladly, ma'am. But perhaps I should stay with the master. When he becomes violent it's all I can do to hold him. And you've had a long journey. You should rest."

"No." Her chin went up. "My place is beside my husband. If he becomes violent we shall just have to tie him down. Hurry, please."

They both left. Drawing up the chair from the writing table, Lisette sat close beside the bed and leaned over to gently stroke back the tumbled fair hair. Strand's head tossed, and he stared at her without recognition. To see his forceful vitality reduced to this total helplessness was shattering. She blinked tears away and prayed, "Please God, let the midwife come quickly."

The afternoon slipped away, however, and Best did not come. When darkness fell, the steady beat of the rain increased until it was a driving downpour, while the wind became ever more forceful, the gusts rattling the windows and sending smoke puffing down the chimneys. By nine o'clock Lisette was forced to accept the fact that the roads must be totally impassable, and that whatever was to be done for the sick man would only be achieved by those already gathered in what was left of the old house.

The battle that followed was one she would never be able to forget. Strand's fever seemed to mount hourly, his outbursts of delirium accompanied by wild thrashing and attempts to get out of bed that sometimes required both Norman and Green to hold him, the threat that he would severely overtax his strength terrifying Lisette. Soon after two o'clock, he fell into a motionless silence that petrified them all, but by the expedient of holding a small mirror to his lips, Green discovered he was still breathing.

"Must be exhausted, poor devil," said Norman, himself owly-eyed from the combined effects of the long journey and this ghastly night. "Come, Lisette, to your bed. I'll wake Denise and she can watch Justin for a while."

The respite was brief. Barely an hour later, the abigail shook Lisette awake, sobbing that the master was raving and she must come at once. She found Strand sitting up, Green's arms wrapped about him, while the sick man again fought his duel with Bolster, shouting anguished curses because of his friend's duplicity. Running to him, Lisette soothed, "It is all right now, dearest. I'm here with you. Lie back, Justin. Please, dear, lie back."

For a moment there was no change. Then he sank down, and she sat beside him once more, bathing his face gently. She glanced up to find Green waiting, his drawn features filled with an expression of despair. "Green," she whispered, "I am so afraid. Is there nothing—no medicine we can give him?"

He wrung his hands. "Mrs. Rousell—the midwife, ma'am— has some. Dr. Bellows left it with her last time Mr. Justin was taken ill. It is made from the bark of a tree." He knit his brow. "Something 'ona.' Brincona, or Vincona . . . oh! Cinchona, that's it! They call it quinine. Dr. Bellows told Miss Charity it would mean the difference between life and death for Mr. Justin was he to suffer another attack. If *only* Mrs. Rousell would come!"

Neither of them had heard the door open softly. Norman stood with his hand on the latch, listening to them. His eyes were on Strand, still now, save for the endless plucking of his long nervous fingers at the eiderdown. It was devilish, the boy thought miserably, that in so short a space of time one could become so attached to a man that should he die the hole left in one's life would be unthinkable. And what it would do to Lisette . . .! As quietly as he had come, he closed the door.

In the sickroom, hour succeeded weary hour. Sometimes Strand was quiet for a long interval, sometimes he tossed and moaned, crying out half-finished sentences in English or Tamil, or striving to sit up, fighting Green's efforts to restrain him. But always, running through his delirium like a continuing thread was one name, and whether it was whispered or shouted, the tone was always the same—a yearning disillusionment that wrung the hearts of those who heard him: "Lisette . . . Lisette . . .''

By dawn he was perceptibly weaker, his eyes still holding the feverish glitter, but his movements less violent, and his voice almost inaudible. Green, who had slept for several hours in the chair beside the fireplace, awoke to find Lisette holding a glass of barley water to her husband's cracked lips, while Denise propped his shoulders. Coming swiftly to aid them, the valet murmured, "Mrs. Strand, you *must* get some rest. We'll have you ill yourself if you keep on like this. We should take turns. Perhaps, if Mr. Norman could sit with him now . . . ?''

"He is gone," vouchsafed Denise. "He leave the note for madame. He have to the village go to try and find the medicine for monsieur.''

Her heart warmed, Lisette thought that the rain seemed a little lighter, and the wind was definitely less furious than yesterday's gale. If anyone could get through, it was Norman. Once the boy set his mind to something, he was just as doggedly determined as was her husband. She looked down at Strand, and his face seemed to ripple before her eyes. Capitulating, she stumbled to her bed, murmuring a demand to Denise that she be awakened if there was the slightest change in her husband's condition, but falling asleep before she could complete her sentence.

When she returned to the sickroom shortly after noon, she found an unexpected change. Strand was now as cold as he had been hot yesterday. He lay there shivering convulsively, his teeth chattering. She thought at first that he was rational, but when she approached, he sat up, shouting, "Do not . . . walk on the carpet! Are you addled? Got to . . . get new . . . carpet!'' She eased him down on his pillows and took up his hand and he turned blurred blue eyes to gaze at her. "Must let her go," he muttered between shudders. "Have to—let her go . . . only decent thing . . .''

And their battle began all over again. She did what she might to keep him warm, prayed for Norman's return, and talked gently to the sick man whenever it seemed that he might hear her.

At three o'clock Green came upstairs. He had shaved and changed his rumpled clothes, and he looked refreshed. He brought with him a tray, which he placed on the table by the windows, and proceeded to pour a cup of coffee, the aroma drawing Lisette despite her intital avowal that she did not want anything. She was, she found, ravenous, and eating toast and marmalade while she kept one eye on Strand, she asked in the low tone they all employed in the sickroom, "Will the medicine the doctor left still be potent, do you suppose? How long ago was it that my husband suffered an attack?"

Green hesitated a moment, then, pouring more coffee into her cup, said, "Why, it was when you first were wed, ma'am. Mr. Justin knew he was ill before the ceremony. I begged him to delay, but he would not."

Incredulous, Lisette gasped, "He—he was *ill*? But I thought— Oh! Why on *earth* did he not tell me?"

"He'll have my ears for telling you now, ma'am," Green sighed. "The thing is—well, I've been with him these four years, and—and I—"

"You love him," she nodded gravely. "I am well aware."

He reddened. "Why, he took me up, ma'am, when no one else would. God knows what would have become of me, else. I'd been cast off without a character by a very powerful gentleman high up in the East India Company, because I'd chanced to see him in—well, doing something he'd no business doing. Mr. Justin risked the ruination of everything he'd half killed himself to build up when he hired me. But he did it and earned the respect of a lot of gentlemen who had cause to dislike my former master. Still, it was a dreadful chance he took; you'd know how very dreadful if you knew how he longed to come home. The climate didn't suit him, and every day he was breaking his heart for England. I'll never forget it, ma'am. And that's why I—I suppose I take an interest in—in anything having to do with him."

Lisette smiled. "I understand, and indeed am grateful for your loyalty. But what I *cannot* understand is, why he did not postpone the ceremony. I remember noticing how hot his hand was when he put the ring on my finger, but—" She remembered also the interpretation she had placed on his heated touch, and on the glitter in his eyes, and she felt sick and ashamed and was silent.

"If you will forgive me for speaking plain," Green said hesitantly, "Mr. Justin dared not postpone the wedding. Oh, he never spoke of it to me, but I knew, because Lord Bolster kept at him to change the date, and one day he rounded on him, and said it was more than he dare do. Mr. Garvey was courting you also, and the master was deadly afraid of losing you. Afterwards, well, you see how it is when the fever really has him in its grip. He couldn't bear you to see him like this—and on your wedding night." He looked at her pleadingly. "You can scarcely blame him, ma'am."

A soaring joy was lifting Lisette's heavy heart. She said, "So he came down here, and this—Mrs. Rousell nursed him?"

"No, ma'am. Mostly, it was Miss Charity."

"*Miss Charity?*" Lisette gave a rather hysterical little trill of laughter, and Green stared his astonishment. "Charity!" she exclaimed again. So the blond paramour she had so resented all this while did not even exist! Strand had left her, not because he loved another woman, but because he did not wish her to see him racked by this dreadful fever. "Oh!" she said in a half-sob, her eyes bright with unshed tears. "Oh! If *only* I had—"

"Oliver . . . ? Are you here? Is—is *anyone* here . . . ?"

Fighting the impulse to run to the bed in response to that feeble call, Lisette rose and went swiftly to bend over the invalid. "Hello, my dear tyrant," she said gently. "Are you—"

She had quite forgotten the circumstances under which they had parted, and was shocked to see his eyes widen in horror. "No!" Strand gasped. "No! Go away from me! I do not want you here! No!"

Sinking to her knees beside the bed, she implored, "Stop! Justin, I beg you—it was all a ruse, my darling. Garvey planned it, hoping you would call out Tristram. Dearest, please listen to me! I went to see Charity and Rachel, it is not what you—"

But it was useless. As rapid had been his return to normalcy was his relapse into delirium. This time, however, his frenzied ravings swiftly grew feebler, his strength so obviously failing that Lisette was distracted with fear and scarcely dared leave his side for a moment without dreading what she might find upon her return. She prayed as she had never prayed in her life that Norman would come, but the hours crept past, and the afternoon was waning when at length Strand's faint voice again asked lucidly, "Are you still here . . . Lisette?"

She had been sitting close beside the bed, a hand over her eyes, and at once, fearful of the possible response, said timidly, "Yes, Justin. I am here."

He peered at her uncertainly. "Did—did I dream . . . ? You said—Garvey . . . ?"

With a muffled sob, she knelt and, nursing his hand to her cheek, said a tremulous, "Yes. Oh, yes. Justin, I did not betray you. My dearest, I never shall."

He smiled in a faint shadow of his mischievous grin. "You are . . . very kind. And—and I'm glad you—Jeremy!" The sunken eyes opened wide. "Is Bolster dead?"

"No. Very much alive. And with Amanda's promise to wed him. You did not shoot him, love. It was Garvey. Beatrice told us."

He sighed, "Now, thank God!" and closed his eyes wearily, but after a moment peered at her again. With an ineffably tender smile, he whispered, "I think, my dear . . . that you will not be burdened . . . with your tyrannical husband, much . . . longer. I wish you would kiss me . . . just one last—"

"*No!*" With a wail of anguish she leapt up. "You *shall not!* Not now!" She climbed onto the bed and lay down beside him, sliding an arm beneath his shoulders, totally uncaring that Green, tears streaking his cheeks, stood by the fire as if rooted to the spot. "You are not *trying* to live!" she accused fiercely. "Wretched, wretched man! I will not *let* you leave me!" She turned his pale, surprised face towards her and began to kiss his brow, his lean cheeks, his eyelids, between kisses whispering she knew not what terms of endearment and pledges of devotion, interspersed with scolding and demands that he make an effort to cling to life, for her sake. How long she held him thus, how much she said, she could not afterwards have told, but when Norman crept in later, the precious medicine bottle clutched in his hand, he found them both asleep, Strand's head cradled on his wife's shoulder, her cheek against his tumbled hair, her arms fast about him.

Chapter 19

"Dashed if ever I saw such a scaly set-out!" Norman proclaimed, his indignant tone belied by the twinkle in his dark eyes. "What I went through! Soaked to the skin; fording raging floods; slogging through mud up to my knees; tossed onto my head when my blasted animal balked at a puddle he could have stepped over! I was forced to detour fifteen miles out of my way because two stupid bridges had been washed away! A lesser man would have given up, eh? But no, I persisted, got to the village, and sought out that cantankerous old midwife. I had to roust her out of a room where a lady was shrieking her head off because she—"

"My heavens!" said Lisette, her amusement giving way to consternation. "You never made Mrs. Rousell leave a confinement?"

Straddling a chair in the kitchen while he watched her prepare a breakfast tray for the invalid, he grinned. "I thought the same, but it turned out it was only her daughter, objecting to having her locks cut into a short style. Lord! And after all that misery, I arrived back here, bedraggled, bruised, battered, half frozen, and exhausted, bearing your beloved his vital draught, only to find you both cuddled up as snug as—"

"Norman!" Lisette exclaimed, blushing. "What a thing to say!"

"What a thing to see," he countered, adding gruffly, "and

never have I been more happy, I'll allow. But after my heroic efforts, to come and find them all for naught, and the medicine no longer needed! Gad!''

Her cheeks hot, Lisette nonetheless met his eyes squarely. "It *is* needed. He is not out of danger, although this long sleep has worked wonders, I do believe.''

"You *both* slept the clock around.''

"Never look so smug, brother. You did, too, so Green tells me!''

He chuckled. "From sheer frustration, no doubt.''

"There is no cause. Justin is much improved, but we—we almost lost him, Norman. We still could, though we've a better chance with the medicine you brought. I will *never* be able to tell you how grateful—''

"Oh, pooh! Nonsense!'' He stood and made for the door. "Do you mean to talk such fustian I'm off. Cannot bear it. May I look in on Strand?''

"For a minute or two only, if you please. I so dread lest the fever come back. Green says it could. And until the doctor has come, I'll not rest easy.''

"Get away with you. What you mean is that you want to keep him all to yourself! If ever I saw such a pair of lovebirds!''

"Horrid boy!'' she said, but she laughed and her eyes were sparkling as he had never seen them sparkle, for his remark was not so far removed from the truth. Lisette's burgeoning affection for Strand had come to full flower during her desperate battle for his life. She knew now that her heart was for all time given to the husband she had married with such reluctance, and that knowledge lent her a glow and a tenderness that immeasurably heightened her beauty.

She had looked in on Strand the moment she awoke and had been elated to find his fever broken and his eyes clear again. He had been too weak to do more than lie and gaze at her, and she had quickly left Green alone to care for him. How much did he remember, she wondered. Would he speak now of his love for her? She knew beyond doubting that he loved her just as she loved him, but it would be so wonderful to hear him say it. . . .

Green came busily into the kitchen. Their shared vigil of terror had brought them to a closeness that would last through many years to come, and almost unconsciously the valet had slipped into the way of longtime retainers, his demeanour towards Lisette never less than respectful, yet containing the faintly proprietary tone that one might use to a beloved child. "I'll take that, Mrs. Lisette," he said, deftly appropriating the tray. "Just the gruel, eh? I'd thought I would bring us some tea later. Not too strong, mind, but you and the master might like to take a cup together, being as he's feeling so spry today."

Norman left the bedchamber as they entered. He said nothing, but threw an amused wink at his sister. When she walked in, she saw why. Strand was propped up by several pillows. He had been shaved, and his thick hair brushed into the careless style she had come to think very becoming. He was drawn and pale, his eyes sunk in deep hollows, and he lacked the strength to stretch out his hand to her as he tried to do, but Lisette's blush was intensified by the awed look of worship in his eyes.

Stifling a smile, Green drew up her chair and placed the tray on the table beside it. "Here's your lady come to give you a spot of breakfast, sir," he said cheerily. "Do you see how much better our invalid looks, ma'am?"

"He does, indeed." Lisette concentrated upon arranging a napkin across Strand's chest. He did look stronger. Perhaps, when Green was gone, they would be able to talk a little.

The valet plumped up his master's pillows, hovered about for a minute or two, then took himself off. Lisette began to wield the spoon, guiding it carefully to her husband's lips, very aware of the fact that his adoring eyes never for a moment left her face.

He behaved dutifully for a while, but at last sighed and shook his head. She put down the bowl and lowered her lashes, waiting.

"Lisette," Strand murmured.

"Yes, Justin?"

"I—I—want—I wish—I mean—er—what became of Garvey?"

With only a trace of wistfulness, she thought, So much for romance . . . Then, seeing his hand lift very slightly but fall back onto the coverlet, she took it up in her own vital clasp, and smiled, "Gone, I'm afraid, love." The thin fingers tightened a little at the term of endearment, and his eyes were saying everything his lips apparently could not speak. She forced herself to be sensible and said, "Constable Short was no match for the likes of James Garvey, and when he went to the gaol yesterday morning, he found his prisoner flown. Even so, Garvey will have to leave England, I am assured. Grandmama has vowed to set about the word of his infamy, and I doubt he'll ever dare show his face to the *ton* again.''

''Good,'' said Strand.

Lisette restored his hand to the coverlet, but when she made to draw back, he clung to her fingers. With her heart beginning to beat faster, she looked down and again waited. He was still very ill, of course, but . . . ''Justin,'' she prompted in a shy little voice, ''is—is there, that is, do you remember—anything?''

He made no answer. Looking up at length, she sighed. He had fallen asleep once more. Shaking her head, she gently disengaged her hand and bent to kiss him lightly on the brow. ''Odious, odious man!'' she murmured.

Strand smiled contentedly.

So long as Strand was within a stone's throw of death's door, weak as a kitten, and still racked by the effects of the fever and the head injury, his behaviour was exemplary. He never complained, always obeyed those who cared for him, and when he occasionally spoke, it was to utter such faint words of appreciation for their tender solicitude as touched their hearts. Within a very few days, however, he was on the mend and, like most energetic individuals, proved a dreadful patient. He demanded from Norman a complete inventory of the damage resulting from the storm, and then fretted and fumed because he was not allowed to get up and at least supervise the necessary repairs. He insisted that Best ride to the Hall as soon as the roads were passable and send a groom to Bolster's lodgings in Town, or to Three Fields, to determine his lordship's present state of health. He became exceedingly irate over his diet, terming it pap, or slops, and eventually threatening to hurl at Green's head the next bowl of broth that was presented him. Green, nobody's fool, had noted that with one person his master was meek to the point of slavishness, and mercilessly using that weapon, the valet murmured that he would speak to Mrs. Lisette in the matter, though it was by her orders that the food was prepared.

''Oh, never mind,'' Strand grumbled, accepting the despised offering. ''And that's another thing—I want some help brought here. Send down a couple of housemaids from the Hall, and the cook. The roads must be safe by this time and there's no reason why René cannot man the stove instead of you and Denise doing all the work. My poor wife must be damn near exhausted, fetching and carrying for me!"

Aware of the fiery René's opinion of the tiny kitchen that had been installed at Silverings after the fire, Green glibly resorted to his infallible remedy and murmured that he would talk to Mrs. Lisette.

"You will do as I say!" snapped Strand irately. "My wife has enough to concern herself with and— Where is she, by the way?"

"She is with Dr. Bellows. He just arrived, sir."

Strand groaned. "That old fidget? He'll be reading her a fine Jeremiad, poor girl." His eyes softened. He sighed, "I wonder she puts up with me, Oliver."

"I—ah—venture to think madam does not find that task— er—*entirely* reprehensible," murmured Green, his eyes twinkling.

"Do you, by God!" flashed Strand. "You impertinent scoundrel! Wait till I'm up out of this blasted bed! I'll show you what's reprehensible!"

"*He must not* get up yet," decreed Dr. Bellows, accepting a refilling of his glass and knowing he should leave this beautiful lady and get to his patient. He ran a tidying hand over his thinning sandy hair and crossed his short legs as he observed that malaria did not thrive in England's cold climate. "Does Strand only give his system time to repair and recover from its effects, he may well go thirty or forty years without another attack. I've known such cases. But I know your husband also. A walking volcano, ma'am! Always must be up and doing. It would surprise me did his man not have to tie him to the bed to keep him from wearing himself out before he's had a chance to recuperate."

Sitting opposite the small physician in the sunlit parlour, with Norman perched on the arm of the sofa beside her, Lisette said worriedly, "We shall contrive to keep him quiet, doctor. But he was so terribly ill. I never saw such a violence of fever and delirium, and I have often helped Nurse when one of the family was sick. If it should recur, Dr. Bellows . . . it—it will not . . ." She bit her lip, watching the doctor with an anxiety he thought enchanting, and that brought to mind the remarks of certain of his learned acquaintances, to the effect that the Strand marriage was solely one of convenience. When next he encountered those individuals, he would advise them with considerable vehemence that if Justin Strand had entered into a *mariage de convenance* he wished *he* might have undertaken such a liaison! Meanwhile, he said kindly, "Will not carry him off? I pray not, dear lady. Your husband's problem—and it is a major one—is that he refuses to follow an ancient and wise Chinese maxim, 'Exercise moderation in all things.' You would be amazed at how nicely it works. Strand, however, has a boundless enthusiasm, a passionate interest in his people and estates, a driving need to be always changing something for the better. Admirable traits, but unless harnessed to a common-sense understanding of human frailty, well calculated to wear down health to the point—" He pursed his lips. "Strand, ma'am, has no patience with the simple needs of the body. He eats if the notion strikes him; he rises at dawn and works till all hours; he forces his physical form to keep pace with his plans and ambitions, and—" he shrugged and spread his stubby hands expressively—"it simply cannot be done."

"I see," said Lisette, her brows knit. "But if he *did* live at a—a somewhat less hectic pace? If he were—er—persuaded to be more moderate in his pursuits, could I then hope not to be an early widow?"

The doctor stood, took up her hand, and saluted it reverently. "My dear, with you at the helm, I predict Justin Strand will live to a ripe old age!"

Walking with her sister-in-law into the small saloon at Strand Hall, Rachel Leith's lovely face reflected stark astonishment. She sat in the Sheraton chair next to the green brocade sofa and said in aghast tones, "Justin has left you again? I cannot credit it! I thought he must be ripe for Bedlam when I learned he had believed such evil of poor Bolster, but—"

"You must not forget that Strand was desperately ill at that time," Lisette defended reproachfully.

Encouraged by this unexpected reaction, Rachel said, "Yes. And you saved his life, for which I shall never be able to thank you enough." She reached out to squeeze Lisette's hand affectionately. "Charity stays with Amanda now, and is having such a lovely time helping her choose her bride clothes. As for

Bolster, he is in transports. I do not believe the dear man has come down to earth for weeks. Have you seen his idiocy?"

Lisette smiled and nodded. "He came to see us soon after we returned here. Strand was delighted, but was at first so humbly apologetic for having doubted his dearest friend that poor Jeremy was fairly appalled."

"It was an appalling business." A frown touching her eyes, Rachel lapsed into thoughtful silence.

"Yet—could have been so much worse." Lisette hesitated, then said, "Rachel, who is Claude Sanguinet?" Her sister-in-law's startled face turned to her, and she added, "Oh, I know he is a Frenchman of great wealth, to whom you were once betrothed, but that is all I know. How is he so powerful?"

All mirth was gone now from Rachel's face. She said in an odd voice, "He is *horrifyingly* powerful. You know that Tristram helped me get away from that terrible . . . magnificent château near Dinan?"

"I know very little. But Justin once said you had been told not to speak of it. I saw Monsieur Sanguinet once. He did not look very terrible."

"No." Rachel's hands gripped tightly and her wide eyes were fixed on events that only she could see. "But he is," she half whispered. "He is a savage. A cruel madman. He befriended me at a time when we were in most desperate straits. I did not know . . . what he was really like. Few people do. But I am afraid. Someday—" She shivered and bowed her head. "I must not say more, but, as for me, if it had not been for Tristram . . ."

Dismayed, Lisette stammered, "Oh, my! I am terribly sorry. I had no idea it was so bad. I have upset you."

"No, no!" Rachel looked up and smiled brightly. "Only, I try not to think of those times. They were bad—and yet, that was when I met my dear husband, so you see there were happy moments, too. Enough of that. Now you must tell me of my brother. If I know Justin, he has been a most intractable patient and quite driven you out of your senses."

"Oh, dreadful," Lisette agreed, laughing. "As soon as he began to get better, he was impossible!"

"Poor girl. You must be very glad he is gone away."

Lisette looked down at her hands and managed a rather scratchy, "Yes."

Rachel Leith was a most warm-hearted girl. She had always thought this beauty pretty-mannered and charming, but a shade too self-possessed. When her brother had fallen so desperately in love with her, she had encouraged his hopes outwardly, and inwardly had despaired of his chances of ever having his affections returned. Intrigued now, she said, "I can tell that you have had a dreadful time. Justin is so hopeless about resting, or taking care of himself. Even so, I would not have supposed him capable of being so unfeeling as to abandon you again, after you were so good as to nurse him day and night, when we all know you did not—" She caught her breath, her eyes horrified because of what she had almost said.

Looking up through a veil of tears, Lisette sniffed. "Did not care for him? Well, you are right. I did not—when I married him." She dried her eyes, aware that Rachel had stiffened. "It was supposed to be a *mariage de convenance*," she imparted miserably. "Is it not the height of stupidity for the bride of such a match to—to have fallen madly in love with her own husband?"

"No!" Rachel moved impulsively to hug her and say in her winning, eager way, "I think it wonderful, for Justin has been in love with you since first he set eyes on you."

"So I—I thought. But ever since he was ill, he—he has not . . . not so much as . . . kissed me!" She raised tragic eyes and went on, "And now he has gone away again and I know Charity was not his Fair Paphian, but I cannot help but wonder if there *is* one after all."

Stifling a smile at this naïve muddle, Rachel commiserated, "He is the outside of enough, and no mistaking! I wonder you do not leave him."

"*Leave* him? How could I, when he is the dearest, kindest, most gallant, and unselfish man who ever lived?" Lisett's lower lip trembled, and she added a forlorn, "Only, I do not think I can endure it, does he mean to be endlessly coming and . . . g-going like this."

"The wretch! Did he say *nothing?* Did he leave no word at all?"

"Only this." Lisette drew a very wrinkled note from her pocket and handed it over.

" 'Dear Ma'am' " read Rachel aloud. She flashed an irked upward glance at her sister-in-law's woeful countenance. "Typical!

So very romantic! 'Dear Ma'am, I am called away on a matter that must be completed with all possible speed. By your leave I shall call upon you next Thursday afternoon at three o'clock. Please receive a man who is—yours forever, Strand.' '' She looked up and said with incredulity, ''*Call* on you? Today? In his *own* house? Good God! Did Leith write me such a note I would have him put under restraint at once! Though I am glad to see my brother's writing is improved. When he is ill his hand shakes so he can scarce form the words. And, do you know, dear, the ending *is* rather—''

She stopped as Fisher entered. He presented Lisette with a large, beribboned box, and at once trod his stately way from the room without uttering a word.

Intrigued, Rachel said, ''Good gracious, how theatrical! Is there a card, love?''

Untying the pink velvet ribbons, Lisette said, ''No. Perhaps it is inside, but— Oh! Rachel, *look!* Is it not *exquisite?*''

At first Rachel saw only a charmingly arranged posy of pink roses and maidenhair fern, but in the centre was a velvet cushion containing a large diamond set in an intricately wrought gold filigree pendant. Lisette jumped up, ran to take a small pair of scissors from a drawer, and began carefully to snip the stitches holding the chain in place. Rachel assisted then in fastening the chain about Lisette's white throat, and clapped her hands when she finished. ''Oh, you must see it! Here—in the mirror. It is adorable! I would not have thought Justin had the sense!''

Lisette admired her reflection, then ran eagerly back to the box. She found a note inside. Unfolding it with hands that trembled, she uttered a shocked little cry that brought Rachel hastening to read over her shoulder:

> *I saw a maid who set my soul to dreaming*
> *Sweet, tender dreams of love that haunt me yet.*
> *A girl with eyes like dusky velvet, seeming*
> *To make my heart a shrine just for*
>   *Lisette.*
>
> *Her hair a cloud of midnight, richly glowing.*
> *Her voice a silvery peal I can't forget.*

Her lips curved in a smile, as if she's knowing
Deep is the love I bear for my
       Lisette.

I'll gather all my courage and pursue her.
I'll kiss away her sorrows and regret.
I'll worship and adore and gently woo her,
And win myself an angel, named
       Lisette.

Astounded, Rachel breathed, "Why, it is beautiful . . ."

"How *dare* he!" raged Lisette, tearing at the clasp of the pendant. "Oh, that wicked, *wicked* man! After all the pain and grief and suffering he has brought on us!" She was panting, so deep was her disgust and chagrin. "Rachel, help me! Help me get this wretched thing off!"

"Do not! Please, do not! You will break it. And I am sure Justin did not mean to offend. I—I do not understand. You said you loved him, yet—"

"This horrid diamond did not come from my husband! Garvey sent it, just as he sent the other poem! To think he would *dare*—" She succeeded in opening the clasp, tore the offending pendant from her throat, and hurled it across the room.

"Garvey?" Rachel echoed in bewilderment. "No, but—but this is Justin's hand, dearest. Surely, you must know it."

Shock drained the high colour from Lisette's cheeks. She stared at Rachel blankly. *Justin?* Justin had not writ that poem. He *could* not have done so. Justin's writing was atrocious. Would she ever forget that first dreadful note he had sent, telling her he was leaving her on her wedding night . . . Like a physical blow, she thought, But he was *ill* that night! And Rachel said when he is ill his hand shakes *so that he can scarce form the words!*

Regarding her anxiously, Rachel held out the note Justin had written to say that he would call today. Numbly, Lisette looked from one to the other. The writing was identical! She gave a gasp, remembering the note Grandmama had received from Strand. Why ever had she failed to notice the difference in the writing? "My God!" she moaned. "It cannot be . . . it *cannot* . . .!" And to Rachel's bewilderment she suddenly fled, in a most ill-mannered abandonment of her guest, flinging open the door and running down the corridor with a flutter of draperies and a rustle of the two letters she held.

Following at a less precipitous rate, vastly entertained, Rachel informed a bowl of chrysanthemums that while this household had never been of an exemplary nature, it had of late deteriorated into total insanity. She climbed the stairs, marvelling at the progression of events, gleefully anticipating sharing them with Tristram and Charity. But she hastened her steps when she heard sobs coming from Lisette's bedchamber. Entering, she found her sister-in-law kneeling on the carpet, weeping over three letters spread before her. "Oh, my dear!" Rachel cried, running to kneel with her. "Whatever is it?"

"They are . . . the *same!*" sobbed Lisette, a glory shining through her tears. "Oh, Rachel . . . all this time, I though him so . . . so unromantic. All this time I thought that wicked Garvey had writ my first poem! How I—I longed for Justin to speak such beautiful words! How I *yearned* over them . . . never dreaming my . . . my own beloved husband— Oh, Rachel!" And clasped in her sister-in-law's arms she dissolved into floods of happy tears.

Well before the appointed time, Lisette was seated in the drawing room, her hands clasped in her lap, her face pale with anticipation. She wore a new gown of pale orange velvet, the low square-cut neck edged with tiny scallops, the skirt falling in a slim, straight line from beneath the bodice, and the puff sleeves also edged with the embroidered scalloping. An orange velvet ribbon was bound through her glossy dark hair, and her only jewellery was the diamond pendant that had been joyously reclaimed (luckily intact) and reverently replaced about her throat. She was quite alone, for Rachel, overcome with wonder that her loved but prosaic brother should have hidden such a flair for the art of flirtation, had vowed she'd not stay like a marplot in a house where a man obviously meant to court his own wife. She had summoned up her carriage and her maids and been swept away, fairly beside herself with eagerness to share all this deliciousness with her husband.

The clock on the mantel suddenly chimed the hour. Lisette jumped. Strand had said three o'clock. Oh, how she longed to see him! How did he intend to "pursue and woo" her? Had he stayed away so as to make plans for——

Fisher swung the door open. "Mr. Justin Strand," he announced, his face commendably enigmatic.

Lisette's heart was pounding as though it must break through her ribs. She could not know how brightly her eyes shone, how charming was the blush on her smooth cheeks, how becomingly the orange gown flattered her slender loveliness. Strand, having schooled himself to walk steadily, checked on the threshold. He was elegant in a coat of blue superfine and pearl grey unmentionables. A sapphire gleamed amid the folds of his cravat, and if that cravat was somewhat less than the perfection Green had created, by reason of a nervous finger having been run around beneath his collar several times on the way here, Lisette saw only the worship in the deep blue eyes of the man she loved. She was not conscious of having stood, but suddenly Strand was clasping both her hands. Neither spoke for a moment, each drinking in the adored face opposite. Leaning to him, lips parted for his kiss, Lisette was a little taken aback when he bowed, and instead kissed her fingertips.

"How very kind in you to receive me, ma'am," he said primly. And thought, This time I *shall* do the thing properly! This time, by God, I will woo her with such poise she will fairly *fall* into my arms! Waiting until she had sat down, he seated himself in a nearby chair, his eyes straying to the pendant that sparkled on her bosom.

Her fingers lifted to touch the gem. "Justin, it is so beautiful. Thank you," she said breathlessly.

"I am most pleased it—er—pleases you." He bit his lip in irritation. How clumsy. And he must be smooth and assured. But she looked so unspeakably lovely. . . . He knew he was staring, and blurted, "Have you been well? Er—not lonely, I hope?"

"As a matter of fact," she said with a demure smile, "I *have* been a little lonely. My dear husband, you see . . . was away."

Strand's grip tightened on the arm of his chair. "He had much to do. What I mean is, if you're going to talk of your husband when you receive a caller, ma'am, I must protest."

His eyes danced. Meeting them, Lisette said softly, "There is no one else I had rather speak of."

Again, one thin finger was passed nervously about Strand's

collar. He sprang up and took a turn about the room. Lisette smiled to note that quick imperative stride, and thought, How very dear he is . . . But he was obviously set on wooing her, and she must not spoil his plans. And so she said, "Justin . . ."

He turned to her and corrected with a twinkle, "Mr. Strand.".

"I did not know, Mr. Strand," she said meekly, "that my own husband writ those magnificent verses for me."

He marched up to frown into her face, his eyes a blue blaze. "Well, who in the devil," he demanded, quite forgetting his romantic mission, "*did* you think wrote them?"

"Garvey," she confessed.

"*Garvey!*" He sat beside her. "The deuce! Why should you suspect so revolting a thing?"

"Because I did not recognize your hand, my dear one. You had only ever written me one note, and that was when you were taken ill on the night we were wed. Your writing was atrocious, and I thought it your usual hand. I could only think the poem came from Garvey, and when I mentioned it, he did not deny it."

"That damnable rogue," he murmured and, mesmerized by her beauty, traced the curve of her dewy cheek with one finger.

"Yes," she sighed, swaying towards him, her voice a caress. "Oh, Justin, your poem was so beautiful. If you did but know how I wept over it, believing it to have come from the—wrong gentleman."

He stammered eagerly, "Do you mean it? I'm—I'm so wretched when it comes to—to putting my feelings— Well, I never can seem to say—"

"No. You do not *say*, dearest. Rather, you *do*. All the sweet, dear—" And she drew back, startled, as Strand gasped, "By George!" and sprang up, rushing to open the window that looked onto the rose garden. He glanced out, coughed twice, then proceeded to pour a glass of ratafia and carry it to his bewildered lady.

Lisette accepted the glass, wondering why he did not look at her, but instead scowled at the window.

The sweet notes of a violin arose in the strains of a gypsy love song, soon joined by mandolins and a soft chinking of castanets. Amused and delighted, she thought, In the middle of the afternoon? but said, "Oh, how lovely!"

Strand sat beside her, took the hand she held out and murmured an adoring, "Beloved, will you—"

His words were drowned as the musicians were augmented by a tenor who apparently deemed it vital he should be heard in Brighton. Strand's lips tightened, but persisting, he dropped to one knee beside his love. "Lisette," he said, "you know—"

She cupped a hand about her ear. "What?"

"Lisette!" he roared.

"Yes, dear," she answered, a dimple peeping as the serenade increased in volume.

Strand whipped around to glare at the window and knocked over the glass of wine Lisette had just set down. "Blast and damnation!" swore the ardent lover.

Lisette clapped one hand over her twitching lips, but her mirthful eyes betrayed her.

Strand groaned and clutched his fair locks in frustration. "Dammit all! Why don't they stop?"

Instead, a new note was added to the uproar: The deep, fierce barks of a large dog preparing to protect his property. The tenor's stentorian tones became a shriek. Violin and mandolin were abruptly replaced by voices raised in alarm. Whether from determination or because of the speed of their departure, the castanets could be heard until they, the shouts and the barking faded into the distance.

Strand slanted a woebegone glance at his lady.

Lisette struggled but, overcome, leaned back, dissolving into helpless laughter.

"Wretched girl!" he expostulated. "And that abominable hound! No, how can you laugh so? You must know I shall have to pay those pseudo-serenaders three times the exorbitant price they demanded for that caterwauling, to say nothing of possible doctor bills!" But he was not proof against the ridiculous and, sitting at his wife's feet, succumbed and laughed with her until they both were gasping for breath.

A tambourine sounded outside.

"Oh, no!" moaned Strand.

Brutus jumped in through the window, the considerably tattered instrument between his jaws. "Idiotic creature!" his master declared, standing. Brutus shook his prize enthusiastically. Astonished by the resultant clamour, he hurriedly dropped it, leapt back, then barked fiercely at it.

Strand took up the tambourine, tossed it into the garden, and ruthlessly closed the window on the pursuing dog. Returning to aid Lisette to her feet, he sighed, "You see how it is? I cannot even attempt to be the romantical type. Everything goes wrong."

"Well," she said helpfully, "how had you meant it to go?"

"Why, I would arrive, to find you awaiting me with maidenly blushes and bated breath."

She nodded. "You did."

He lifted her hand and kissed it, and still holding it, stepped closer. "And after some small talk, I would give the signal to the musicians (if you could call 'em that!) and they would play soft, sweet love songs, whilst I dropped to my knees and—er— did the pretty."

Her lashes were lowered at this rather clumsy summation. "And what," she murmured, "would you have said—had everything gone properly?"

He sighed. "All the beautiful and expressive things Leith says to—" He broke off, biting his lip and furious for having mentioned his rival. "God!" he gritted. "What a gudgeon I am!"

"Yes," confirmed Lisette, smiling up at him, her eyes very tender. "A gudgeon indeed to speak such fustian, sir! What other wife has had more beautiful words said to her than you have written to me? What other husband would spend so many patient, caring hours with a troubled boy, as you did with Norman; or be kind to an awkward girl and help her move more graciously into young womanhood, as you did with Judith? No!" She placed soft fingers over his lips as he bent worshipfully towards her. "Let me finish, if you please. I think I know what you have heard, and so I will admit to you that as a young girl I built an altar in my heart to manliness and gallantry. I put a splendid soldier on a pedestal, endowed him with godlike qualities, and childishly fancied myself in love with my impossible creation. Until I grew up and was besieged by a fierce, brusque, demanding, and—altogether adorable gentleman. And then . . ." Her lashes swept down at last, concealing the glow in her great eyes, and a rosy blush swept up from her throat to warm her cheeks. "Then—I really fell in love," she finished shyly. "Totally, and for all time, with my own—"

Strand's control broke. He pulled her into an embrace that was fierce indeed. Lisette was kissed as he had never kissed her before, so that she was dizzied and exhilarated and trembling when he suddenly released her and stepped back. Holding her at arm's length, he scanned her face intensely. "Are you sure, my dearest beloved? Are you perfectly sure you can endure me? I swear I will be as good a husband as I know how."

"And you will never again doubt me or call out any man you suspect of admiring me?"

"Never!"

Caressing his still gaunt cheek, she said tenderly, "And you will try to be more restrained in your activities and not rush about wearing yourself to a shade even when you are not entirely well?"

"I will be a veritable sloth!"

"And should we . . ." she looked away, blushing, "should we be blessed with children, you will be patient with them and not fly into the boughs do they not achieve as much, or as rapidly, as you would have them do?"

The thought of her giving him children brought a dazed look to his eyes. Pullng her close once more, he breathed, "My dear blessing . . . I vow I will do none of those things."

She laughed merrily. "Oh, what a Canterbury tale! You will do them all, and I shall constantly have to watch over and guard you from yourself. And—oh, my very dear, how I shall love that precious task!"

There was nothing for it, of course, but to kiss her again. Having done which, he said briskly, "Hurry and get your cloak. I am taking you on your long-delayed honeymoon! Never argue, wife. Denise knows exactly where we go and has already packed for you. Hurry now!"

Her eyes full of stars, Lisette answered, "Yes, Mr. Strand."

Chapter 20

The afternoon was not particularly pleasant, for the sky was neither blue nor sunlit, the air held a blur of mist and was quite chill. On the box, Mr. Best grunted to the guard, "At least it bean't raining." And the guard, jerking a thumb at the carriage, grinned. "Much they'd notice!"

He was quite correct. Had it been blowing a blizzard, Lisette would have thought it a golden day, and Justin, his love fast cradled in his arms, was in a joyous daze of contentment. He turned her chin with one gentle finger and bent to kiss her yet again, and snuggling her head against his chest, Lisette thought that never had she dreamt to be so blissfully in love.

They had been travelling for some time before she awoke to the fact that she had paid no heed to their route. "Justin," she asked, "where are we going?"

He kissed her ear, making her shiver deliciously. "Wait and see."

She nestled closer. They came to the river and drove along beside it for a long way, the birds swooping and calling over the water, and an occasional gleam of late sunlight drawing sparkles from the ripples. After some while, the river curved to reveal a fair prospect where sweeping meadowland gave way to neatly scythed lawns. Far off, a great old house sprawled, smoke curling from several chimneys, the latticed windows gleaming in the reddening glow of sunset, the whitewashed walls and half-timbering warm and immaculate. Woodland hid the sight, but Lisette sat straighter. "Did you see that lovely old place? It reminded me so of Silverings."

"Foolish little love." Strand smiled. "It *was* Silverings."

"What? But it cannot be! How on earth—"

He chuckled and would only say again, "Wait and see!"

Lisette leaned to the window in a fever of impatience, and they came at last to a familiar curve in the drive, lodge gates, and a small cottage where the gardener and his wife hurried out to wave a welcome.

"It is!" cried Lisette, clapping her hands like a little girl. "Oh, it is!"

The carriage swept along through the park, and the house again came into view. Scanning it eagerly, Lisette said, "Oh, how beautiful it is! Is this where we spend our honeymoon, dearest?"

"No, my blessing. I only wanted to show it off a little, on our way."

She leaned back in his embrace and, her eyes fixed on the rebuilt structure, murmured, "How wonderful that you could get it all finished so quickly. You must have had lots of people working."

"A small army. I gave Connaught the task the very day we returned to the Hall. Please do not be disappointed when we go inside. Save for a few rooms, it is not furnished. I thought we would enjoy to choose the pieces together."

"Yes! I should like that."

Best halted the carriage before the wide, arched doors. Strand jumped out, and Lisette was handed down as though she were fashioned of sheerest crystal. His leathery face wreathed in smiles, Best drove around to the side yard. Lisette did not see that merry look, for she stood with hands clasped, drinking in the restored splendour of Silverings. "How I wish we could live here," she sighed.

"We shall. I am closing the Hall but shall keep it maintained in case Charity might someday wish to dwell there. She has a fondness for the old place."

Her eyes alight, Lisette clung to his arm. "Do you really mean it? Oh, but how splendid! Justin, *must* we leave?"

He laughed. "Would you really give up the delights of London, Paris, and Copenhagen for an almost empty house in the country?"

"I would! For a while, at least. Dearest one, would you mind terribly?"

He said nothing but, bending suddenly, swept her up in his arms and carried her to the steps.

Oliver Green, who had happily watched their coming, opened the door, keeping well out of sight.

On the threshold, Strand paused, looking down at his wife's beauteous and cherished face, his heart in his eyes. "Lisette," he said huskily, "I—I still cannot believe that you love me."

"You will learn to," she asserted. "For I mean to do just as you wrote, most beloved of husbands."

Uncertain, he raised one brow questioningly.

Lisette leaned her cheek against his shoulder and, whispering, for she was not quite sure who had swung open the door, quoted, " 'To with happiness surround you, for as long as I may live.' "

For an enchanted moment Strand was silent, standing there, gazing at this slip of a girl who was his dream, his love, his way of life. Then he bent and kissed her, and was still kissing her as he carried her across the threshold into the true beginning of their marriage that was, most decidedly, past redemption.